"Epic and nuanced. . . . The three pr[...]
the author displays a formidable gr[...]
to a well-crafted story of women fin[...] ...forbidding
odds."

—*Publishers Weekly*

"*Pelican Girls* is a marvelous achievement, an immersive and moving novel, as beautifully written as it is impeccably researched. I haven't been this swept away by a piece of historical fiction since Maggie O'Farrell's *Hamnet*."

—Jess Walter, bestselling author of
Beautiful Ruins and *The Cold Millions*

"A tale of female friendship unlike any I've come across before, Julia Malye's inspired-by-a-true-story *Pelican Girls* is as incredible a feat of research as it is a daring work of fiction."

—*Elle*

"To enter Julia Malye's work is to be completely transported. Every detail in your vision, touch of fabric against your skin, pulse of blood through your veins, is rendered so lush and evocative that reading this novel feels like absorbing a lifetime of experience. The rare page-turner that both entertains and enlightens, *Pelican Girls* is an undeniable achievement of research, storytelling, and human compassion. One of the best historical novels you will ever come across; this book is an absolute gift."

—M. O. Walsh, *New York Times* bestselling author of
My Sunshine Away and *The Big Door Prize*

"Stunning, moving, and remarkable. *Pelican Girls* is more than a novel; it's an act of advocacy for human rights and for historical acknowledgment. Julia Malye has found a rich and compelling voice, unique to those who are experts in navigating between languages and cultures."

—Nguyễn Phan Quế Mai, international bestselling author of
The Mountains Sing and *Dust Child*

"This richly imagined historical saga tells the story of three women, discarded by French society, who have little choice but to make new lives in a country thousands of miles away, married to men they barely know. As their lives intertwine again and again, Malye paints a vivid portrait of displacement and resilience, even as she lays bare the compromises her heroines must make and the ways they become complicit in the inequities of empire."

—Anna North, *New York Times* bestselling author of *Outlawed*

"*Pelican Girls* is a feat of sublime imagination, every page a wonder. Malye has written an unforgettably rich and sensual novel—a triumph."

—Elizabeth McKenzie, author of
The Portable Veblen and *The Dog of the North*

"This book fascinates me. It's moving in every way: a celebration of complicity and love among women and a summary of their difficult lives. It has everything in it: a great story, landscapes, atmosphere, depth, and a finely wrought prose. It makes you feel that you are reading one of those literary classics that make you believe in contemporary fiction again—told with spark and excitement and with the freshness only a young writer can give."

—Pilar Quintana, two-time National Book Award finalist
and author of *The Bitch* and *Abyss*

"Julia Malye's *Pelican Girls* is a richly layered, multicharacter narrative of a long-overlooked period in history. More than that, however, it's an exploration of the varied—and often cruel—ways in which we experience both abandonment and agency. Haunting, heartbreaking, and harrowing, Malye's story is one of survival and perseverance; it is a look into the lives of women who've had everything taken from them but still manage to go on."

—Virginia Reeves, author of
Work Like Any Other and *The Behavior of Love*

"*Pelican Girls* is the kind of book you lose yourself in. It blends the most engaging historical detail with a story so fresh and relatable it was impossible not to feel bound to these women as they journey into their brave new world. I am grateful to Malye for effortlessly introducing me to a piece of history I knew little of and a story which will linger long with me. A beautiful and heart-rending evocation of a haunted, and haunting, moment in history."

—Jan Carson, award-winning author of *The Raptures*

PELICAN GIRLS

PELICAN GIRLS

A NOVEL

JULIA MALYE

HARPER

NEW YORK · LONDON · TORONTO · SYDNEY

HARPER

This book is a work of fiction. References to real people, events, establishments, organizations, or locales are intended only to provide a sense of authenticity, and are used fictitiously. All other characters, and all incidents and dialogue, are drawn from the author's imagination and are not to be construed as real.

A hardcover edition of this book was published in 2024 by Harper, an imprint of HarperCollins Publishers.

PELICAN GIRLS. Copyright © 2024 by Julia Sixtine Marie Malye. All rights reserved. Printed in the United States of America. No part of this book may be used or reproduced in any manner whatsoever without written permission except in the case of brief quotations embodied in critical articles and reviews. For information, address HarperCollins Publishers, 195 Broadway, New York, NY 10007.

HarperCollins books may be purchased for educational, business, or sales promotional use. For information, please email the Special Markets Department at SPsales@harpercollins.com.

FIRST HARPER PAPERBACK EDITION PUBLISHED 2025.

Designed by Elina Cohen
Map by Aurélie Boissière

Library of Congress Cataloging-in-Publication Data

Names: Malye, Julia, author.
Title: Pelican girls : a novel / Julia Sixtine Marie Malye.
Description: First edition. | New York : Harper, 2024. | Identifiers: LCCN 2023017896 (print) | LCCN 2023017897 (ebook) | ISBN
  9780063299757 (hardcover) | ISBN 9780063299771 (ebook)
Subjects: LCSH: Women--Louisiana--New Orleans--Fiction. |
  Deportees--Louisiana--New Orleans--Fiction. |
  Deportees--France--Fiction. | New Orleans (La.)--History--18th
  century--Fiction. | LCGFT: Historical fiction. | Novels.
Classification: LCC PS3613.A5247 P45 2024 (print) | LCC PS3613.A5247 (ebook) | DDC
813/.6--dc23/eng/20230712
LC record available at https://lccn.loc.gov/2023017896
LC ebook record available at https://lccn.loc.gov/2023017897

ISBN 978-0-06-329976-4 (pbk.)

24 25 26 27 28 LBC 5 4 3 2 1

TO MY MOTHER, TO MY FATHER

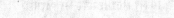

In 1720, a ship called La Baleine *left the French Atlantic coast, carrying* women of childbearing age, raised or jailed at the Parisian hospital La Salpêtrière. Ready to sacrifice anything to avoid further social persecution, these women traveled to La Louisiane at a moment when female settlers were desperately needed in "the Mississippi," as this land was then also known by the French. They reached the colony in 1721. Inspired by their story, this novel is a tribute to all these courageous women who, for too long, have remained in the shadows of American and French history.

PART I

At first they are blinded. It's the New Biloxi sun, uncommonly bright for a January afternoon. Then the women's eyes clear, and the white beach and its motionless crowd appear, tanned and emaciated men standing on tiptoe. In the canoes, the girls hold on to one another. The soles of their shoes have grown so thin that they can feel the rough wood under their feet. When the sailors stop rowing, a few yards from the shore, some women attempt to stand in the wobbling pirogues. The humid air sticks in their throats like wet bread.

For the first time in three months, they can finally see the sand that the water hid from them while they crossed the Atlantic, the bottom of the sea finally showing itself earlier this morning as they disembarked from *La Baleine* and crossed Ship Island's beach—the contorted driftwood abandoned along the waterline, the rats crawling in the dunes and sneaking between the girls' ankles before scampering off again. Some thought that the journey was over, that La Louisiane was nothing more than this tiny island. No one bothered explaining to them that the boats can't drop anchor in New Biloxi, that its water is too shallow. Since they left Paris, the women haven't been told much.

Now they lean over the gunwale, peering into the sea. Rocks, shells, fish: bright and fast, shiny in the corner of your eye. When one of the girls screams, the others, startled, look around and shift in their seats. There is a splash, and the girl tries to reach for the canoe that just capsized. But a nun is already grabbing her by her arm, and two oarsmen right the pirogue, and her serge dress spreads under the surface like black ink, and she tries to stand and seems about to cry but knows that none of the others can help anyway.

So the women do the only thing they can, take one another's hands—and jump.

Marguerite

Marguerite has to make a list. She folds the general attorney's letter, tries to find the right position to lay her bad leg—with the rain of the past few days, pain has swollen from her toes to her thigh, budding all the way up to her fingers. It's the evening hour when the women have been sent to bed, when the sisters have stopped bringing in their daily supply charts, when the artisans have closed their shops. Even the female prisoners locked in the *loges aux folles* have fallen quiet. Marguerite takes her headdress off. She shouldn't be in her office after sunset. By now she should be sitting in her garden, under the blossoming mimosa, with its thick bouquets that remind her of gentlemen's wigs. There, surrounded by daisies and asphodels, even after all these years, she can forget what La Salpêtrière really smells like.

She opens a thin folder. Her hands have become clumsy, shake un-expectedly, and last year's list almost escapes under the desk. She catches it before it reaches her lap. For the past fifteen months, she has been choosing women who would be sent off to the Mississippi. Her first list pleased the general attorney; now Monsieur Joly de Fleury writes that the governor of La Louisiane in person has requested more girls. Mar-guerite brings a candle closer to the paper. For this new list, she isn't sure where to start.

The selection process used to be different. Transferring female prisoners to the colony was her idea: not so long ago, she was free to pick whomever she saw fit. There wasn't enough room anymore at La Salpêtrière, not enough dormitories for those who really needed a shel-ter. Beds were taken by creatures who would never change. It had been a matter of figuring out whom she'd rather get rid of first—poisoners, knife wielders, rebels, or witches. Out of the two hundred and nine girls she selected last year, she has a particularly distinct memory of the conspiracy theorist, the one who had spent her time at the women's prison yelling sinister words at the king. Marceline Janson. Off she goes.

But this year, no one from La Grande Force can be shipped away. M. Joly de Fleury insisted: Governor Bienville does not want any more prisoners. Instead, around ninety fertile, soft-spoken, capable girls. Which means repentant women from La Salpêtrière's Maison de Correction or girls from its orphanage, La Maison Saint-Louis. She immediately pictures twelve-year-old Charlotte Couturière, the red-haired orphan with the beautiful voice, traveling to unknown, barbarous La Louisiane, a land that inspires more fear than wonder in Marguerite. No, not Charlotte. She'd keep the child safe at La Salpêtrière; in a few years, she could become a *sœur officière* here. Marguerite tells herself that she needs stronger women for the Mississippi.

She stirs her feather in the ink. The conspiracy theorist had a sister, much younger, not yet rotten. Marguerite tries to remember the sibling's first name. Antoinette? No, it begins with "E," perhaps. She thinks of her own sister, of the way people always struggled to understand how the strict Superioress of La Salpêtrière and the elegant Marchioness d'Argenson, wife of a retired chief of police and mother of the current one, had grown up in the same house. Under *Passagers de La Baleine*, she writes: *1) Étiennette (ou Antoinette ?) Janson—entre 15 et 17 ans.*

Only eighty-nine to go. Marguerite leans back in her chair, and the pain bubbles all the way up from her feet to her neck. In the pot, the ink remembers the circles her feather drew.

"Madame?"

On the other side of the door, the woman repeats the word plaintively, interrogation the only tone her voice knows. Mademoiselle Bailly is aware she shouldn't be disturbing her after compline, the last prayer of the evening.

"*Qu'y a-t-il*—what is it?"

The wooden door creaks as her new assistant steps in. Mlle Bailly's movements mirror the way she thinks—gracelessly, meticulously, without taking any risks.

"What is it?"

"The supervisor of the *loges aux folles* reported new cases of rat bites."

"Tell me some real news, Mlle Bailly." Marguerite hates the fear she reads in her assistant's eyes. She wishes she'd just solve this rat problem on her own.

"It's the demented woman," Mlle Bailly finally admits. "Émilie Le Néant. Yet another one of her tantrums."

Marguerite brings her bad leg closer to her body. "Can't the guards do anything? What about the sister in charge?"

"They tried. She won't stop."

Of course she won't. A month ago, Marguerite ordered that the girl be kept away from any sacraments. A lost case who would blaspheme at the view of any books, convinced that they were Bibles.

"The other women are starting to become agitated."

Marguerite presses her hands on the desk to stand up. They can't manage without her. Lately the thought comes back more and more often, and she always feels a hint of pride, of relief. Then exhaustion and fear kick in. She shakes her head when Mlle Bailly takes a step toward her.

"Let's hurry, then," Marguerite says.

They can't hurry. Marguerite does her best to cross the Cour Lassay as fast as she can, but they have to stop when they reach the Saint-Louis Church. By now night has fallen, hugging shadows around the guards on duty and a few workers hurrying off to their homes. Marguerite leans against the wall, waiting for the pain to cool down.

"Shall we?"

They cut through the Old Women Building to the Cour Sainte-Claire, where cobblestones catch her walking stick. On their right, only one window is lit in the Workshop for Young Women. La Salpêtrière, her city, stretches on forever tonight. As they walk on to Rue des Gardes, noises pierce through the silence: cries from the dormitories, grunts from the pig pit, insults from the Archers' Building. La Grande Force towers on their left. There is something vicious, foul, about this neighborhood that always gets to Marguerite. If she had overseen the construction of La Salpêtrière, she would have built the women's prison at the far end of the town, where the Kitchens and the Cour des Chèvres currently are. She'd rather have goats at the heart of her hospital than the deranged.

"Superioress," Mlle Elautin calls.

The guards' voices lower as the sister in chief of La Grande Force holds the jail door open. A candle throws a lunar light on her cheeks, but her black bonnet disappears into the dark. The cavy smell of the humid corridor, fresh and nauseating, slides down Marguerite's throat.

"I told Mlle Bailly that it wouldn't be necessary to bother you," the sister in chief says. "It seems like Mlle Bailly isn't yet used to the noises here."

"It doesn't matter now," Marguerite says, and her assistant looks at her like a dog who has just been petted. Upstairs, someone calls for more wine, for Pierre or Jean, then simply for help. "Tell me what happened."

"One of the other prisoners calmed her down," she says.

"Someone entered Le Néant's cell?" Mlle Bailly asks.

Marguerite gives her assistant an annoyed look.

"Of course not. Then you'd have a good reason to call on to our Superioress," the sister in chief says.

"Who calmed her down?" Marguerite asks.

"A woman called Geneviève Menu."

Marguerite is usually good at forgetting about her sister. But Lucie was the one who had this Geneviève Menu arrested and sent to La Grande Force two months ago, warning Marguerite about her former washerwoman's viciousness—Lucie, who never missed an opportunity to remind Marguerite of her ties to powerful men. Before Lucie's son followed his father's path and became the new chief of police, during Lieutenant General de Machault's brief tenure, Marguerite had found it easy to deport women of her own choosing; now the head of the authorities bears once again her sister's last name. That Lucie should come to her mind even once a day is usually enough to irritate her—her walking stick almost hits Mlle Elautin's dress when she raises it toward the prison, La Grande Force.

"*Allons*, show us the way."

As they cross narrow yards, outdoor cells that shrink the sky, Marguerite tries to remember more about Geneviève Menu. Her mind could hold hundreds of names and faces when she started her service here. She still sees Charlotte Couturière's baby eyes, wandering from her to the supervisor of the orphanage, that January night of 1709. But somehow Marguerite simply cannot recall the circumstances of Menu's recent incarceration. They never met, that much she knows. Now all Marguerite can remember is feeling frustrated with her sister, that Lucie should once again dare tell her what to do with her residents. The sister in chief's keys land in her palm, as cold and black as fresh mussels.

"Le Néant is in solitary confinement, all the way in the back." Mlle Elautin hands the candle to Marguerite and a guard helps her pull the door open.

She presses her hand against her nose. It's the week of the month when the dormitories smell like metal and moist skin. Every winter, the drain that runs on the east side of La Salpêtrière flooded when the waters of the nearby Seine raced too fast and too thick; it left the jail soaking in the kind of odor that feels as solid as dried mud or bird droppings—something penetrating that Marguerite knows will stain her dress, sneak under her bonnet. In the dark, she can hear movement inside the cells, masses moving in the straw, a low sob, but none of the screaming that she expected. She stops at the end of the corridor.

At first she doesn't notice anything amiss. The light of her candle crosses the first cell and ripples against the bars of the door's threshold. Then it hits: a knocking, repetitive and restless, insistent. It is a sound Marguerite knows—more than once in La Crèche, she has seen babies banging their heads against their baskets, rocking themselves to sleep with little blows that should have been mothers' strokes. Le Néant too lies motionless, asleep. Her ankles seem thinner where the chains hold them; her naked body is covered with goose bumps and shreds of a worn-out blanket. The noise continues.

When Marguerite raises the candle to the next cell, she finds a kneeling shape, knuckles red as they pound on the wall. The prisoner doesn't stop, not when the light falls at her feet, not even when she turns her head toward the door and lets her washed-out eyes rest on Marguerite, who stares back just long enough to notice the blood vessels that draw an intricate web around the woman's blue irises, to feel the pain reawaken in her own leg. When she walks back to the sister in chief, she can't be sure who turned away first—she or the woman who used to work for her sister.

"Do what's necessary to have the poor creature dressed," Marguerite says when she reaches the door. "And please transfer Menu to La Maison de Correction dormitories."

Mlle Elautin seems about to speak but doesn't. Mlle Bailly timidly offers an arm that Marguerite holds on to all the way up to her quarters. Back at her desk, she adds a second name to *La Baleine*'s passenger list.

• • •

The first time Marguerite stepped into La Salpêtrière, the General Hospital was thirteen years old. She was eighteen. For the last time in her life, she wore a cyan dress, with embroidered silver threads that circled her wrists like handcuffs. Her hair was still the color of a cut-open apple left to breathe on a kitchen table. Marguerite hadn't chosen to become a *sœur officière*, but she was determined not to go home, not to follow her sister into marriage.

The year was 1669. Molière's *Le Tartuffe* was finally allowed to be played. On a warm April afternoon, in front of a mute crowd, Louis XIV kissed the feet of twelve poor people. The day before Marguerite left the capital for La Salpêtrière, Lucie wouldn't stop talking about Paris. She was busy applying a mixture of egg white and white lead on her face, hiding the pox scars that had ravaged her baby skin. She had painted blue veins on her bosoms so that they'd look fairer.

Before their father had decided that she would serve the cause of the young hospital, Marguerite probably wouldn't have paid much attention to any of this. But now that she was La Salpêtrière–bound, she listened with interest to every single story related to the poor. Soon she'd be living among them. She watched Lucie place a patch of dark taffeta on her left cheek and listened as she rambled about the feet kissing. Marguerite pictured black toes and broken nails, the king's fleshy lips. Then Lucie turned to face her. "You shouldn't worry," she said. "Where you are heading, you won't have to kiss anyone. And I doubt there will be that much touching either."

It turned out Lucie was right about the kissing. She was wrong about the rest. Over her fifty-one years at La Salpêtrière, Marguerite has had to hold and pull many scrawny, nailless hands into hers.

She grew up hearing about poor people in Paris. After the La Fronde war, her father would tell her about dispossessed farmers fleeing the countryside, shutting themselves away in *faubourgs* so narrow that air and sun wouldn't make it farther than the chimneys of their run-down houses. He talked about the Chasse-Midi neighborhood, where people would sneak in slaughterhouses to steal animals' remains. In 1642 more than three hundred men were murdered in the streets of Paris; he would repeat the numbers, marveling at them as if counting golden coins. Even after the Cour des Miracles was cleaned out, he'd go on and on about a fake soldier he had heard of, a man who'd unwrap the bandages from his perfectly fine leg after a day spent begging passersby for help. Her father talked about him as if they had met. Then he'd stand up from his love seat and look at the Bièvre, carrying bones and weeping willow leaves to the Seine. It took Marguerite years to understand that her father didn't know a thing about the poor. That they had been nothing more than a topic of discussion with the royal administrators, and ghosts outside his carriage on the way home from Versailles.

Marguerite wasn't his first choice to work at La Salpêtrière. Several years after the king founded the hospital, their father decided to send Lucie. It made sense at the time, even to Marguerite. Lucie was alert and bright; she had a stubbornness that people mistook for patience or determination. She was the kind of person whose oddities were excused in her own name. When she slammed her apartment door in a count's face, there was someone to say, "Oh, this is such a Lucie thing to do." Their father was convinced that, with her ideas and boldness, she'd turn the hospital into a modern institution.

He changed his mind when the future chief of police asked for Lucie's hand. It was a warm winter morning, with an orange sky that melted the snow. He turned to Marguerite, told her once again about the man pretending to be an injured soldier of the Cour des Miracles, said people like him could use the help of a girl like her.

Marguerite isn't sure what kind of girl she is. What she knows is that, at sixty-nine, she is still trying to prove that she's been the obvious first choice all along.

. . .

Marguerite waits for the *sœurs officières* in the dining hall. They'll arrive soon, and they'll be excited to hear about their new mission—the heads of La Maison de Correction and La Maison Saint-Louis will help her with the list. A simple source of inspiration, as Marguerite has been telling herself all morning. She leans close to the window, scans the Cour Saint-Louis for the women's black-and-white uniform, but dinnertime is close and it is impossible to spot anyone in the buzzing crowd. She knows with her eyes closed what lies beyond the Mazarin Building and Saint-Léon Workshop: Saint-Louis Church, followed by a maze of courtyards, tens of dormitories and workshops, more streets that lead to the Kitchens, the Linen Building, and the Infirmary, all of which come to an end at the largest garden of the hospital, Le Marais. And now, right at her feet, subordinated sisters, maids, carters, archers, priests: all packed together between the market booths, by the Porte des Champs, as if La Salpêtrière, her town, were suddenly no bigger than its first yard.

"Madame."

The door bangs shut; the supervisor of La Maison de Correction rises from her bow and takes a seat at the table. Mlle Suivit's cheeks are always flushed—Marguerite can never tell if it's from the cold, the heat, or some mysterious emotion that passes behind her slim eyes.

"I meant to ask about the new transfer. Geneviève Menu. I simply doubt women of her kind are capable of repentance."

Marguerite takes another sip of wine. A few years ago, no one would have questioned her judgment. She'd move prisoners from one dormitory to the next as she fancied. "Are you implying that she doesn't have her place in your maison?"

"I'm afraid I'm not the only one to think so," Mlle Suivit says. "I still think Menu should remain in solitary."

"Then you'll be happy to know that she might not stay in your maison for long."

The supervisor frowns; Marguerite immediately realizes her mistake. She's always tried to keep as much from her staff as she can. When navigating in the dark, they assume that she has reasons of her own for the decisions she makes. There is a knock at the door, then three whispering *sœurs officières* appear, followed by a maid and the smell of flank steak; wine pitchers leave wet, broken circles on the wood. Outside, the church rings for sext, the midday prayer. When Marguerite glances at the supervisor, the woman is staring at her as if she were an eyeless doll, one she used to be fond of.

Back in her quarters, Marguerite isn't surprised to find a letter from Lucie on her desk. She doesn't open the envelope right away. Instead, she goes through the file shelf, muttering the alphabet as she always does when she looks for any letter after D. The document she pulls is white, unlike the papers below, which have turned the brownish color of eggshells. Here is the age of the convict at the time of her arrest (twenty-two), her parents' names (Jacques Menu and Anne Foret), the date of her incarceration (January 12, 1720), the person who requested the *lettre de cachet* (Lucie de Voyer de Paulmy, Marchioness d'Argenson). And, at the bottom of the page, written so small that Marguerite has to lean next to the fireplace to see: abortionist.

Unpleasant, even if she has had to deal with more than one child killer through her career. She knows she should call in the sister in chief of La Grande Force, ask her to bring Menu back to her cell and let her play all the nighttime melodies she wants to Le Néant. Instead, Marguerite finds herself reaching for her sister's letter. She knows what she'll find there. Lucie always made things sound worse than they were. At twelve, she'd call a sour milk pitcher an attempt against her good health. At seventy-one, she'd call a flirtatious maid a murderer.

In her note, Lucie says worse things than that. She wants Menu returned to solitary right away. The paragraphs are dense, full of the usual rhetorical questions and exclamatory claims. Marguerite lingers on the last one—"Pity these children whose mothers are taught the art of barbarous murders!" But Marguerite doesn't feel pity. She feels anger and disappointment, the former toward Lucie for always interfering, the latter toward Geneviève, whose deeds make her so difficult to forgive. She sees the prisoner crouching in her cell, her unwavering blue eyes below the light of the lantern. Outside, wet steps shuffle in the Sisters' Garden. A boy yells that there's Lent fruit for sale.

She won't change her mind. She moves Menu's file from the archives of La Grande Force to the pile reserved for La Maison de Correction. It doesn't matter much to her whether Geneviève is the monster her sister describes. She reaches for a piece of paper; she'll write back to Lucie. She'll explain what her sister should have understood a long time ago—that under Marguerite's guidance, La Salpêtrière can turn an infant killer into a devoted mother.

• • •

Marguerite never questioned the hospital's work. The only time she came close was eleven years ago, in the winter of 1709. That year, when the cold wave hit, neither she nor her staff was prepared. No one in Paris was. Over the first days of January, an icy wind swept through the capital. It turned everything still. In the Bois de Boulogne, trees burst and pieces of frozen bark covered the paths. In two nights, the Seine froze. Soon La Salpêtrière's dormitories were filled with new residents, desperate to escape the city streets. More begged to be let in, in a never-ending flow. No doubt Lucie, in her *hôtel particulier*, was able to heat her rooms when wood had become scarce.

There is one evening of that winter that stays with Marguerite—months of hardships somehow condensed into a single painfully vivid memory. Night had fallen already when she was called to the infants' orphanage. She remembers the cold wind seizing her body so vigorously that it made her head spin; ice made the stairs of La Crèche as slippery as the yards' cobblestones. Marguerite heard the babies' cries, breathed the rotten smell of soiled wool long before she reached the main dormitory. Inside, half of the room was entirely dark. There weren't enough candles anymore; a fire was burning in only one of the two fireplaces. *Sœurs officières*, known as Aunts at La Crèche, fed, cleaned, and soothed children. In their arms, the babies' faces looked ancient, the women's eyes hard. It took Marguerite a long time to find the supervisor.

Once she had, they stepped into the corridor that led to the back stairs. The *sœur officière* seemed so utterly exhausted that Marguerite almost asked her to sit, but there wasn't any chair. Marguerite suggested the babies who didn't have a cradle be sent to sleep with the older orphans of La Maison Saint-Louis, but as she was speaking, they heard a noise. It sounded like a kitten, like a puppy, like something that hurt. It was a baby, no older than six months, lying at the top of the stairs.

When the supervisor didn't move, Marguerite took the child in her arms. Her head seemed huge; she was so skinny that Marguerite felt her shoulder blades roll under her thumb. She turned around just in time to see the supervisor hurry inside without looking back. Something twisted in Marguerite's stomach. The woman couldn't take one more, yet she had to. She looked at the baby—bluish-gray eyes, thin hair that turned red when Marguerite stepped back into the dim light of the dormitory. The girl had been abandoned, then forgotten. There wasn't much Marguerite could do about the people dying in the streets of Paris. But La Salpêtrière was different. In her little city, infants were taken care of, no matter how cold the winter was.

She returned to La Crèche the following day, and the next. It reminded her of being twenty, running from one dormitory to the next. At fifty-eight, she told herself she was going back for all the children and not just for one. She had learned the hard way, as a young *sœur officière*, that there was only so much she could do—that the epileptic woman would have died no matter what, that the pregnant libertine had never been strong enough to give birth. But her institution, her staff, could save people. She could ask for more candles, wood, blankets for the babies, and she did. She could reform the education of orphans, suddenly much more numerous after the winter of 1709, and she would.

She never held the girl in her arms anymore. She knew that, just like any other resident, she could be dead whenever Marguerite visited next. The baby was baptized Charlotte, and Couturière for the piece of embroidery she held in her fist. Beyond that, Marguerite would never learn anything else about where the child had come from. It didn't matter. La Salpêtrière was her future, the only one she and the other residents ever had.

• • •

By the time the supervisors of La Maison Saint-Louis and La Maison de Correction tell Marguerite they have the list of names for her, April has rolled in. The Garden of the Poor sweats day-old rain; a grand Easter mass filled the naves of the Saint-Louis Church with a dazed crowd. The following day, Marguerite walks to the orphanage.

There, the residents are young enough so you can convince yourself they could never turn into the howling bodies locked in the *loges aux folles*. Marguerite tries not to look for Charlotte. She knows the petite redhead won't be among the children. The new *sœur officière* in charge has been warned; Charlotte's name shouldn't be on the list. "They are returning from Sainte-Claire," Mlle Brandicourt now says excitedly, gesturing for a group of girls to join the line. They spend every morning there until terce, and learn how to embroider, needlepoint, and lace. They know the Bible. The brightest can read and write. The new supervisor won't stop speaking, as if Marguerite weren't the one who had designed the children's routine. "Precious skills to bring to our colonies," the young woman adds, nodding as if she's been asked a question.

Forty girls stand in front of them, looking at their feet, at the mattresses they share, at a toddler peering through the dormitory door. Their faces blur in front of Marguerite. The supervisor follows her closely as she walks down the line, as if the residents were a porcelain service Marguerite might break.

Marguerite addresses only one of them, chosen at random. She asks her if she is willing to go to La Louisiane, and although the orphan's voice is a whisper, the proud face of Mlle Brandicourt says everything Marguerite needs to know. She taps the girl's arm. At the last board meeting, the king's general attorney insisted the passengers should be, to some extent, volunteers. If the residents of La Salpêtrière were willing to go, M. Joly de Fleury added, it wouldn't be necessary to use shackles or chains during the journey, like they had with the previous women. No more officers of the watch paid to snatch children and vagrants from the streets. Last month, the Parisians, maddened by the arrests, attacked the bandoliers of the Mississippi— some rumors say several of these policemen were killed by the furious mob.

The vision haunts Marguerite. It meant that the inhabitants had sensed, somehow, what she fears. That the gold hidden in the rivers of La Louisiane is nothing more than the blinding reflection of sun on water; that the land is enormous, inhospitable, its forests full of beasts big enough to swallow you whole.

The *sœur officière* walks her back to the door; Marguerite glances at the orphans. She is doing her duty. Their husbands will protect them. She watches them break their ranks, then stops short. In the middle of the room, Charlotte is running toward one of the candidates selected by the supervisor. Charlotte is frail, even for her age. Her nose cuts abruptly through her cheeks and she looks prettier in profile, but time might prove Marguerite wrong. The girl's face wears the same melancholic, eager, expectant expression, as if she regretted something she hadn't known. She sneaks a strand of red hair back behind her ear, then grabs the blond orphan's hand, wipes her eyes, shakes her head to a question Marguerite can't hear. When she asks the supervisor about Charlotte, the young woman's smile disappears. "She refused to sing this morning," the supervisor says. "She was very upset when I told her she wasn't on the list."

On her way to La Maison de Correction, as she crosses the Cour Mazarine, Marguerite can't shake off the feeling of unease that overcame her in the orphanage. Charlotte has no idea what the Mississippi is like; there, her lovely voice wouldn't serve her for anything. She doesn't know about the soldiers starving in La Louisiane, something Marguerite herself didn't learn until an overheard discussion at the last meeting with the board of La Salpêtrière. She doesn't know much about the colony, but she is certain that Charlotte is safer with her at La Salpêtrière.

When Marguerite steps into the dormitory of La Maison de Correction, the residents stick to their wool bobbins. The *sœur officière* in charge didn't bother lining up her candidates. All of them have sinned already; relatives sent them here in the hope they would change their ways. The wealthiest women have their own rooms, on the other side of the building. The poorest ones live here, in the dormitories. The April sun casts their shadows; when looking at the ground, it's impossible to tell where the girls start, where their spinning wheels end.

"They are almost all here," the supervisor says. She speaks loudly so that Marguerite can hear her above the rolling sound. She starts pointing at a few residents, and some of them raise their heads. As they walk through the main alley, Mlle Suivit explains she has received a request from the family of a woman, one of the rich ones, currently staying in a room of her own.

Marguerite focuses on the cracks of the wooden floor so as not to stumble. When she realizes the supervisor is glancing at her, she asks for the girl's name.

"Béranger," Mlle Suivit answers. "She is called Pétronille Béranger. Her mother wrote to say they cannot afford paying her pension anymore."

Then no more privileges—no more candles, single bed, or wood for her fireplace. "She'll be transferred here, with everyone else," Marguerite says.

The supervisor hesitates. "This might pose a problem," she says. "She is different. Other girls won't understand her."

She glances at Marguerite, waiting. But Marguerite has nothing else to add. She is looking below the window, at the empty seat and motionless wheel. She asks if someone is missing.

"Menu was allowed to take a walk in the garden this morning."

"I'm assuming her behavior was satisfying, then?"

"It was," Mlle Suivit says. She holds her head a bit higher. "Until she missed catechism."

"I'd like to see her."

The wheels keep on spinning, faster, it seems, catching beams of light that flicker on the walls.

"Madame, I'm not too sure—"

"Well, I am."

The woman Marguerite finds in the cell of La Maison de Correction has little in common with the one she last saw crouching in La Grande Force, in March. Her skin is more polished, less gray, and a bit of curly light brown hair fills the bonnet that once fell flat on her shaved head. She seems tall under the small window; light falls on her high cheekbones and into her blue eyes. She considers Marguerite as if anticipating the next move of a large animal.

"Do you know why you have been transferred to La Maison de Correction?"

Geneviève doesn't seem to hear her. Her head is turned toward one of the room's corners, and Marguerite has to lean forward to understand what she is looking at—a handful of slimy rats, their muzzles pushing against the mother's saggy belly. Geneviève is staring at them when she asks: "Does this mean that Lucie d'Argenson is dead?"

Marguerite steps back. It's the first time anybody has omitted Lucie's title as a marchioness; the first time anyone has called her dead. She hears Geneviève say something about Lucie promising that, as long as she is alive, Geneviève would never leave her cell.

"No," Marguerite says. She shifts her weight onto her right leg. "The supervisor is considering sending you back to La Grande Force. If you keep on disappearing like you did today, I'm afraid I will have no choice but to support her decision."

Geneviève studies her, her eyes cold and hard. Then she kneels closer to the rats, holding her arm above them, right through the sunbeam, as if she is about to scoop one up. But she just moves her hands, looking at her fingers' shadow as it tickles the blind babies. Marguerite grabs her walking stick. She'd hoped the woman she was fighting for deserved it.

"In June, a boat will leave for the Mississippi," she says. She can't find the right key, the one the supervisor pointed at. "If you can behave for a few weeks, you might have a chance to be on board."

For a moment, Geneviève softens—the muscles of her neck disappear under her skin, her hand falls back to her sides. As Marguerite leaves the cell, she hears her say: "Aren't you the one deciding?" The tone isn't mean; it reminds Marguerite of the way Charlotte used to ask questions years ago—with a genuine interest, ready to repeat the same sentence until the answer satisfied her. "I wish I were," Marguerite says, her back turned. When she glances back, Geneviève is standing on tiptoe, her head turned toward the tiny window and its small corner of sky.

• • •

Only once does Mlle Suivit ask Marguerite to come back to La Maison de Correction. This time they meet on the other side of the building, where the wealthy residents stay—slightly deranged, temporarily unsatisfying women jailed in golden cells by families and friends. The supervisor wants to speak again about this Pétronille Béranger. "Her mother still pretends to be a grand lady," she is saying, "but from what I heard, she might not be one for long." Mlle Suivit lowers her voice. "The father is a gambler and is squandering the family's fortune." Marguerite follows her up the stairs. She finally recalls what the *sœur officière* said about parents not being able to afford their daughter's pension, about the girl being different. At first the woman Marguerite meets doesn't seem to be. She has narrow shoulders and collarbones like potholes; her eyebrows are dark and thick. But when she turns around, her right cheek is covered with a white birthmark that spreads from her jaw to the corner of her mouth and makes Marguerite want to scrub it clean. Sitting next to her empty fireplace, she leans over the pages of an herbarium.

"What lovely colors," Mlle Suivit says, pointing at the dried petals. "Did you do it yourself, Mlle Béranger?"

The woman looks at the supervisor like someone staring at the flames of a fire or the currents of a river. She turns to Marguerite. "Thank you for coming here." Her voice is steady. Her index finger rests under a delicate flower, purple and yellow. "I'd like to go to La Louisiane," she says.

Then she falls silent. She shifts in her seat and returns to her book.

"As I told you," Mlle Suivit says after closing the bedroom door, "I worried she might not have mingled with the other girls in the dormitories. She would barely speak to anyone when she arrived here, but she has improved." The supervisor smiles at Marguerite. "Maybe it is for the best if she leaves for the Mississippi. Isn't discretion one of the best qualities one could expect from a wife?"

Marguerite isn't sure she'd describe the woman as discreet, and she doubts her husband in La Louisiane will. But she doesn't contradict Mlle Suivit.

"We'll add her to the list," Marguerite says.

For once, Mlle Bailly is nowhere to be seen, and Marguerite makes her way through the Cour Mazarine on her own. The truth is, she barely cares if this Pétronille Béranger embarks on *La Baleine*. She just wants to hand the list to the general attorney. She is tired of being responsible for these women's lives.

. . .

This year, spring falls on Paris so abruptly that it feels suspicious. Rain showers become rare, pushing out of the ground bushes of chives, savory, and chervil. Wigged doctors sweat in the anatomy amphitheater, moss dries between buildings' stones; the price of wheat decreases as the peasants foresee abundance. Between the Kitchens and the Linen Building, washerwomen look at the dry sky and predict a wet summer.

Marguerite has a hard time enjoying the tepid weather, the pain turned soft in her leg. A fortnight ago, Mlle Suivit asked one last time for Geneviève to be sent back to La Grande Force. Some *sœurs officières* complained about how intently other women listened to her. They feared she might have a bad influence on them. Marguerite said Menu would stay where she was; that the staff should keep the residents quiet anyway.

Only three weeks left before she submits her list to the board members. Her letter to Lucie, in which she pleaded Geneviève's case, has gone unanswered. Yet it seems impossible that her sister would surrender so easily. Each time someone knocks at the door, she expects to see Lucie storming into her office, ordering Geneviève to be locked in the *loges aux folles*. But it's always just Mlle Bailly—coming to ask about the quarterly inventory, two young *sous-officières* to be trained, a load of medicine to approve, a newly admitted thirteen-year-old libertine and an adulterous countess. Lately, the assistant has started to take initiative.

Her private garden is the only place where Marguerite manages to forget it all.

She is looking at the honeysuckle, at the white and yellow flowers curtaining the gate, when the wooden handle starts moving. She straightens. Not even Mlle Bailly dares to come here after vespers. Marguerite reaches for her walking stick, but before she has time to grab it, a tiny silhouette, smaller than her assistant, lets herself in. The girl's bonnet is tightly laced under her jaw. It covers half of her forehead, but Marguerite recognizes Charlotte's small nose, her face bathed in freckles.

"What are you doing here?" she asks. Behind Charlotte, the gate is half open. Marguerite doesn't want to imagine what priests coming out of their own garden would think if they spotted a girl in a *tiretaine* dress standing inside the Superioress's. "Hurry, shut the door."

Charlotte does. She obeys again when Marguerite gestures for her to join her on the bench. She sits at the very edge of it. Above them, the early-May sky is a blue so pale it seems white. Charlotte's face doesn't betray any emotion.

"You will miss compline," Marguerite says. When the child doesn't answer, she adds: "I won't ask how you found your way here."

At that, Charlotte smiles. The girl is pleased with herself, happy to know La Salpêtrière as well as she does. It isn't something she should be proud of, but then, Marguerite shouldn't either.

"What do you want?" she asks.

Charlotte looks at her with her wide gray eyes. "Why isn't my name on the list?"

The reasons seem so obvious to Marguerite that she doesn't immediately reply. La Louisiane is a dangerous place, and this list a curse. If Marguerite has to choose residents from La Maison Saint-Louis, it might as well be someone else. You need thick skin to cross an ocean, one neither she nor Charlotte has ever seen, and settle in the colony. She looks at Charlotte, who rocks back and forth, whose hands grip the bench. On her chest, the two timid bumps look out of place. She speaks before Marguerite has a chance to: "Mlle Janson, my friend, was chosen." Charlotte's legs move faster. "When Étiennette leaves, I'll be on my own."

"You won't be. Not at La Salpêtrière."

"I'll be on my own," Charlotte repeats, her voice lower.

Marguerite breathes in deeply. She calls La Salpêtrière her home, her family. She has done so for decades. And now, sitting next to a twelve-year-old orphan, a girl terrified by the prospect of being alone, all she can think about is Lucie and her own solitude. She wishes she could tell Charlotte not to worry, I'm here for you. But then, despite everything Marguerite wanted to believe all these years, it occurs to her she never exactly was—that she never will be, here or elsewhere.

"Please," she hears Charlotte say. Above them, swallows dive deeper in the sky. "Would you rather send a criminal to La Louisiane than me?"

"I beg your pardon?"

"I heard you're protecting a woman from La Grande Force."

Marguerite stares at Charlotte. The child knows nothing except what an indiscreet *sous-officière* said. She doesn't know about Lucie's interference, doesn't know that Geneviève would spend her life caught between La Grande Force and La Maison de Correction if it weren't for the colony—that Geneviève, unlike Charlotte, isn't on her first attempt at surviving.

"What happens to Geneviève Menu is none of your business." Marguerite closes her hand around the knob of her walking stick. The ivory feels cold under her fingers. "You should go now," she says. "The *sœurs officières* will be looking for you."

Charlotte stands up, curtsies rigidly. When she straightens, her eyes are filled with tears. Marguerite watches her cross the garden. Her heart beats hard in her chest. By the time Charlotte has reached the gate, Marguerite says: "Be careful on the way back."

But her voice comes out small, and she can't be sure the girl heard her. Marguerite looks at the wooden gate, pictures Charlotte hurrying down the street, avoiding the artisans walking home and the *sœurs officières* coming out of the dormitories after their last round. Unless accompanied by staff, residents are rarely allowed outside their buildings, and Marguerite has seen more than one drunk apprentice wander through the hospital at dusk. Yet she trusts Charlotte to be careful. She has to. Once Charlotte leaves for La Louisiane, the girl will have to fend for herself.

• • •

On the third Saturday of May, Marguerite is ready to submit the list to the board. Outside the carriage, Mlle Bailly asks if she has all her documents. Marguerite taps the trunk with her foot but doesn't look to see if her gesture is understood—the assistant has become excessively maternal lately. This week, the board of directors meets at the parliament president's home. The seven directors of the hospital, the king's attorney general, the archbishop of Paris, and the chief of police will be there. They will go through the list together; they will approve it. Lucie's son will too.

Marguerite leans her head against the window. The sky is so blue that it looks flat and far; the horses' trot shakes the skin of her neck. There is little around the hospital except the horse market, the windmills perched above the Seine, the Bicêtre Castle and its prison, and beyond, two hamlets known as Ivery and Vitery. It's only when the carriage plunges into the Faubourg Saint-Victor that Marguerite feels like she's reached the city.

Over the years, Paris has come to feel like a larger, less controlled version of La Salpêtrière. Washerwomen walk back from the Seine, carrying with them the harsh smell of the river. Ahead, the Jardin Royal blossoms in front of La Pitié Hospital, and botanists trudge in the mud toward the king's laboratories. The berlin passes by the Saint Augustin canons and their abbey, all the way down to the Place Maubert. It's market day, and the crowd swells around the fountain, around Marguerite's carriage, faces flashing between the curtains, a one-eyed boy swinging a basket full of honey and nut oil, men's shoulders bending under leather ropes. The knot in her chest tightens. For a second, Marguerite imagines that she is already on her way home, where she can be the one to decide when to disperse a crowd, when to let it be.

She opens her eyes as they cross the river. Greenish water appears between the wooden houses, and a woman yells *"Attention"* before she empties a chamber pot out of a window. At the end of the bridge, a toddler crouches between broken eggs, viscous yolk popping between his toes. Then comes Notre-Dame, its towers impossibly high above the island—the cathedral's back full of flying buttresses meeting the main arch like the vertebrae of a monstrous animal. Above her, gargoyles' maws hang open as if trying to swallow some blue sky.

When her carriage enters the yard of Count d'Avaux's house, the men are already there. Outside, their coach drivers lean against the colonnade, the colors of their liveries drawing a curious flag.

"Superioress, what a delight to see you."

Marguerite has always liked the king's general attorney. His sharp features contrast with his unshakable coolness: over the past twenty years, Marguerite has never seen him lose his temper. He also seems completely oblivious to Marguerite's age. He often projects them both into a far-fetched future, making plans as if she should outlive La Salpêtrière and not the other way around.

"Please, have a seat."

Under a François de Troy painting, the men are too absorbed in their conversation to notice Marguerite. She easily spots Lucie's son, Count d'Argenson—as handsome as his father, with the attitude of men used to rule and a heart-shaped mouth that would seem feminine if it weren't for his bulky nose. He is arguing about the Mississippi Company, about shares bought by hundreds at the Banque générale, suggesting the Scotsman appointed by the king as controller general of finances is abusing the stockholders' trust, that M. John Law is leading people to ruin with his paper money. The new chief of police keeps on nodding; Marguerite always admired how indulgent her nephew seems, right before he brings down his interlocutor. This time, she doesn't hear his answer. Their host, the Count d'Avaux, is yelling louder than everyone else, promising that the parliament will fight last week's edict, that there will be no speculation crisis. Nobody listens to him.

"The Louisiane that the controller general sold us doesn't exist," says one of the directors.

"I am afraid it has to. I believe Mlle Pancatelin brought us the list of the girls who will soon join our compatriots."

Marguerite straightens her posture. She'd hoped the men would start discussing wheat prices, that she'd have time to sit by the window and study the orangery. But they all look at her now. Wigs curl into their necks, saggy cheeks rest on tight collars. She hands the list to the general attorney.

"I certainly hope they are better than the depraved creatures we sent last year."

"They can only be."

"At least they are young."

"Who will escort them?"

"Nuns, I believe."

The list is passed around. On the ceiling, Muses hand each other laurel wreaths and violently red apples.

"That should be enough brides to convince these rascals to stay where they are."

"Depending on how many girls survive the journey."

"But I trust Mlle Pancatelin selected only our most robust and virtuous women."

The list has reached Count d'Argenson, Menu's name beating a pulse on the second page. Marguerite lowers her eyes. She wonders how much her nephew knows about Lucie's schemes. As she looks down, she doesn't see the cherubs embroidered in the rug. She sees herself at nine, sitting next to Lucie, listening to their teacher's question: What was the name of the tree under which Saint Louis used to render justice? Marguerite knew the answer, knew that she had only a few seconds before her sister would start spitting seemingly random tree names. But Marguerite couldn't bring herself to speak. She could only stare at the teacher, desperate to be called on, unable to force the words out of her mouth. What Marguerite remembers best is how much she wished she could somehow stay silent and speak, both stay put and flee. Her nephew hands the list to his neighbor. "It looks promising," he says.

When the Cardinal de Noailles repeats his words, Marguerite waits for her muscles to relax, for her cheeks to cool, yet the weight lingers in her corset. The list is added to a pile of papers; it will soon be approved by the regent, a mere formality. On the other side of the table, someone brings up La Salpêtrière's finances. The general attorney promises a sensible donation from the king.

Marguerite hears only vaguely what the men say after that. She is thinking of Lucie coming to find her after the tutoring session. She'd asked more questions about the oak, listening without a word as Marguerite told her about Saint Louis ending arguments against the bark of a tree. And now that the directors discuss next year's budget, that the young chief of police seems to have forgotten everything about her, all Marguerite can think about is how good it felt not to be alone and to hold Lucie's attention, even for a few minutes.

• • •

On the day of the women's departure, heat spreads through Paris like water in a sinking boat. Outside, nothing moves. La Salpêtrière looks like a painting of itself. The market of the Cour Saint-Louis is deserted, but the smells of salt fish, sweat, nutmeg, and alfalfa sneak through tight-shut windows. Marguerite watches from the Management Building doorstep as the servants harness more horses. In June's motionless air, the animals close their eyes on flies. Mlle Bailly said it wasn't reasonable for her to wait here, that it would be cooler in her office. Instead of going to the first floor, Marguerite had the assistant fetch a chair. She needs to bid her farewells.

The girls arrive in a single crowd. Marguerite has never seen them all together. The sisters who surround them must have given them orders, because they cross the yard in silence. But Marguerite notices their quick mutual glances, their whispers floating in the hot breeze. Their shadows stretch on the yards' coal-hot cobblestones. She recognizes the once wealthy woman from La Maison de Correction, the odd one with the stain on her cheek, trailing behind. Then comes Charlotte, walking alongside her friend Étiennette Janson. Marguerite has come to think of them as family, even though she knows they aren't related. She watches as they get into a cart and sit amid the straw, Charlotte whispering something in the blond girl's ear. Marguerite looks away. She hopes she did the right thing. Charlotte was never an obvious first choice.

Then again, Marguerite wasn't one either.

She doesn't have to look for Geneviève; there is only one woman, already leaning against the wooden boards of the cart, who turns around to face the building entrance, squinting. Marguerite doesn't move. From here, she can be whatever Geneviève wants to see—a vague shadow in a dim corridor, a familiar silhouette among fresh stones, an old woman spread over a tiny armchair. Marguerite tries not to think of the moment when the horses will start trotting toward the exit, when she'll have to call Mlle Bailly to help her upstairs. For now, there is time to watch her girls leave, time to linger in the shade, to convince herself that no one else knows La Salpêtrière well enough to decide who gets to leave and who doesn't.

2

Geneviève

Geneviève stands in line with the other girls waiting to receive their clothes before they start their journey. She can't quite grasp how she ended up in the yard of the Faubourg Saint-Victor police station. She takes a step toward the nun and her pile of bundles, toward the carts and their sweating animals. She sneaks a curl behind her ear; after having her head shaved for months at La Grande Force, she is just getting used to her hair again.

They have spent two weeks already in Paris, at the inn on Rue des Boulangers, waiting for chaperones and police officers to make the last arrangements for the journey. In that time, Geneviève thought a lot about the Superioress's decision. At La Salpêtrière, she saw her only three times, the old lady with her clumsy steps and trembling throat, her face lined with pleats, as if her skin were a cloth folded too many times. The Superioress couldn't have known everything about her—only what Madame d'Argenson wrote in her *lettre de cachet*, Lucie d'Argenson who had found out so little and acted like she knew so much. Geneviève wonders if the old woman didn't simply lose her mind. Mistake her for someone else. Use her to fill the passenger list. Only once did it occur to Geneviève that the Superioress might have sent her away out of kindness. That night, she lay awake until dawn. She thought about the months she'd spent alone in Paris after her parents passed away, about the endless weeks at La Grande Force. No one except her friend Amélie had ever acted out of kindness; and Geneviève had failed Amélie too. No. To the Superioress, she was nothing more than a name on a list.

The line moves ahead of her. Women hug their bundles and lift their dresses as they climb onto the carts. Police officers watch from the corners. Geneviève touches the gap between her front teeth with her tongue, like she always does when she is nervous. The pile of canvas bags quickly diminishes in front of Sister Louise, the most cheerful of the three nuns. Then Geneviève feels something weigh on her dress. When she looks at the ground, someone is stepping on it.

"She was here first."

The girl has a doll face that doesn't match the tone of her voice. Sweat dots her forehead like condensation on a pitcher of cold milk. She points at the young red-haired girl standing next to her. "Charlotte was here before you," she says.

A few months ago, Geneviève wouldn't even have responded. She'd have stepped forward and lowered her bonnet to tune out the rude comments. But today she moves to the side. "Well, why don't you go ahead, then?" she tells them.

She watches the two of them as the nun shoves more clothes in a canvas bag. The pretty blonde spits in her hand and rubs a stain on her sleeve. It's her small, freckled friend who grabs a bag for each of them.

"You'll be happy to have a change of clothing when we get there," the nun says. She repeats the same thing when it's Geneviève's turn, and the heap of wool feels rough in her hands, the summer sun weighing her body down, her skin—which doesn't go red like other women's—remembering her youth in Provence. She thanks the nun, crosses the yard toward the carts, looking for a place to sit among the other passengers. Her first week at La Maison de Correction, after months of solitude, she was desperate for friends. Between prayers, she took to chatting in low whispers with the two girls working their spinning wheels next to hers. The third time the supervisor caught her, the woman didn't mince her words: Geneviève was a bad influence, and if she broke the silence rule again, she would return to La Grande Force. Geneviève didn't argue, didn't explain they had merely been talking about the Louvre, the Faubourg Saint-Honoré, their past positions in Paris. She went back to work. She wouldn't risk being sent back to her cell for a few stolen words.

She spots the girl with the birthmark spreading over her right cheek, the one who described the plants of La Hauteur Garden as if she'd spent entire afternoons there. From here, Geneviève can't see if there is room in Pétronille's cart, and by the time she meets the eyes of the freckled girl from the queue, women are already making room for her to join.

Geneviève considers backing up, looking for another spot, but more and more people slide around her. She climbs and sits.

"I didn't mean to be rude," the doll-faced girl says. "But politeness doesn't seem to buy anything around here." Her laugh is coquettish, forgiving. She turns to her young friend, who hugs their two bags against her as if they are dolls. "I told you it's the woman we saw in the garden."

"You said that already."

The pretty girl stares at the freckled one, unfazed. They both look young enough to belong to La Maison Saint-Louis. Yet they aren't glancing suspiciously at Geneviève like the other three orphans did at supper yesterday evening. Then she reminds herself that not every resident from La Maison de Correction is someone to be afraid of—that none of the women sitting in the carts is supposed to know she was once jailed at La Grande Force, where no one ever leaves. It's clear the blond girl doesn't fear her. She turns to Geneviève. "We saw you in the Marais Garden? Once, when you were on your own?"

She is kind enough not to mention the angry *sœurs officières* who had found Geneviève there. It was the day when she'd woken up unable to breathe again, when she'd felt so dizzy at the idea of sitting among a crowd of women that she'd wandered on her own, not far, just to the Marais Garden—sat under a birch tree and watched La Maison Saint-Louis girls play. Then back to a cell, back to the uneven sound of the Superioress's limping steps.

"My name is Étiennette," the pretty girl says. Her eyes are a dark blue that could be mistaken for another color if it weren't for today's sun. "This is Charlotte."

Charlotte gives her a shy smile. She wipes the sweat that runs on the freckles of her nose and squints her eyes under the oily sun; her bonnet, too big, slides on her damp forehead. When Geneviève says her name, the girl's eyes widen.

On the other side of the yard, Sister Gertrude is done counting, screams something to a police officer. Men, out of uniform, run to the gate. Three other women climb into their cart and the wood moans under them.

"What were you doing outside?"

"I was taking some fresh air." Geneviève moves to the back as another girl kneels next to them.

"Listen to her! Fresh air. And I bet it was a wrong dance step that brought you to La Maison de Correction." Étiennette laughs. When Geneviève doesn't correct her, she probes again. "Why were you sent to La Salpêtrière?"

At the inn on Rue des Boulangers over the first few days, Geneviève whispered the same question to a few women. It was a way, like any other, to hear her own voice, if only once a day; she had learned her lesson in the dormitory of La Salpêtrière and rarely said a word in front of the nuns. She leaned close to the girls and listened carefully. One of them had been sent out to the hospital because her father didn't want to see her anymore, another because her stepmother was the one who should have ended up in La Maison de Correction. Pétronille, the girl with the birthmark, started to mutter something, was interrupted by a woman who called her a wealthy hypocrite; it was enough for Geneviève to stop questioning her. She stopped questioning all of them; these conversations left her empty, convinced that maybe she was the only one who truly deserved to rot at La Salpêtrière.

In prison, she would remember the pregnant girls who came to find her, how desperate they were. They couldn't afford to be mothers. Then Madame's voice would whisper, asking who she was to decide a child's fate, calling her names, cursing her. Geneviève's first nights at La Grande Force, leaning against the damp walls of her cell, those words crushed her. Now, on good days, she sometimes manages to ignore them. She remembers she'll soon be far from here: on the other side of the ocean, where Madame will never reach her. But even then her guilt doesn't die entirely. Geneviève isn't quite ready to talk about Amélie, so at the inn on Rue des Boulangers, she remained evasive about her past. Now it strikes her that her silence only left the women hungry for more.

"I met a man," Geneviève says. She pauses. Charlotte lifts an eyebrow. "He was called Félicien. It wasn't all that bad at first."

Étiennette gives a knowing look to her friend, but Charlotte stares between the oxen's ears. It seems to Geneviève that, at La Maison de Correction, the only men these two might have encountered were the carpenters who came to fix shutters and table feet, or the priests, lock-smiths, and fishmongers they spied on from their dormitory windows. Geneviève believes she understands, even if they cannot, how danger-ous this journey might be. Yesterday she overheard a police officer ex-plain to his colleague that, with so many women, a two-week trip to the coast could turn into a month. "A good enough reason to ask for more cartridges," he added. The other man stared at him, visibly at a loss. "Ninety girls wandering in the countryside?" the first man continued. "Don't you think they'll draw attention?" He shoved more tobacco into his pipe. "Wouldn't want to have to answer for the ladies' virtue by the time we reach the Loire," he concluded.

And neither would you want to have to answer for mine today, Geneviève thinks now. Étiennette touches her hand then sits back. "*Ma chère*," she says, "you'll have all the time in the world to tell us about Félicien."

The gate is pushed open. Next to Geneviève, the women fall quiet. There is Paris, right outside the doors, the relentless calls of its street vendors, and the crowd of curious passersby who will sing, clap, and fol-low them, just like they did when the carts left La Salpêtrière. At the time, Geneviève thought that was that; she would never see the city again. But she had been brought here, to the inn on Rue des Boulangers—to another crowded dormitory, to three stone-faced nuns and many more police officers. She had waited long enough to believe that it would last forever. That the journey had been a prank, that she'd be sent back soon to La Maison de Correction, or worse, La Grande Force.

But no: the first carts are already turning on the street; oxen's bones roll under their elastic skin. Paris oscillates with the animals' steps as Geneviève looks around. She was a child when her parents had to aban-don their silk farm after the fire and bring the family all the way from Provence to Paris. The rough piece of silk her mother had given her to play with; the undulating landscape, the never-ending forests and the paths that were lost then found again; the fear that overcame her at night, when she'd watch for the thieves her father talked about. This is all she remembers from the trip. But the memories of her childhood in La Bastide-des-Jourdans are vivid: she can still see the silkworms dragging themselves across mulberry leaves, her siblings being punished for untangling the cocoons before they were ready, her mother leaning over the huge loom. Provence will soon be farther away than ever.

She watches Charlotte looking at Étiennette and Étiennette looking at the street. A toddler perched on a woman's shoulders bangs her fat legs against tired breasts; earthenware makers stop short loading their crates; piles of plates hang between mud and sky. Geneviève closes her eyes on this old world. There is nothing to feel sorry about now. She is leaving too.

• • •

Étiennette was right. They have all the time in the world to chat. Not about La Louisiane, or barely; when a woman mentions the hidden gemstones of the colony, another passenger bursts out laughing. "Nonsense," she says, "people starve there. It seems like their biggest city isn't worth our most pitiable village." Girls shake their heads. Geneviève has heard worse: in the comedy show that was all the rage in Paris before her arrest, actors spoke of ogres in the Mississippi. She refuses to believe any of it. La Louisiane will save her.

Conversations start again, the women talk about themselves: why they arrived at La Salpêtrière, why they wanted to leave, what they will do once they are far from here. They know each other like you know your neighbor across the street, someone familiar but from whom you've never heard more than a *bonjour*. At La Maison de Correction, the girls picked their alliances carefully. You can't afford more than one friendship with stolen whispers. At La Grande Force, Geneviève didn't have even that—only the sound of shifting bodies in the next cells, the punctual howling that made her jump. She swore to herself she'd never be as lonely as she was at La Salpêtrière, or in Paris before she met Amélie. As the carts exit the capital, as they pass the windmills of La Pointe and La Tour, and the Rue de Vaugirard turns into a simple *chemin*, Geneviève joins her voice to the women's.

She doesn't mention Amélie just yet. She says only that Félicien had a sister, and it feels nice to share a bit of her story, to talk about Madame d'Argenson's groom to the two strangers sitting in front of her. In the countryside, there is little to stop the breeze; it blows the grass at calves' feet in the brutal July air, shakes heather and Saint-John's-wort bushes alike, makes the carts smell balsamic and earthly. It feels as wide as an open wound, as overwhelming as a first kiss. After months being locked up, Geneviève rediscovers the freedom she didn't know until it was gone. To Étiennette and Charlotte, she describes where she met Félicien—in the servant quarters of Lucie d'Argenson's *hôtel particulier*—how he once gave her a sunflower because he didn't like roses, or pretended not to.

"Was he handsome?"

Étiennette always finds a new question to keep Geneviève talking. Charlotte doesn't. She hums to herself. Her voice is steady, warm, assured—the kind of voice that makes you wish she were singing louder. Some of the passengers doze, cheeks rubbing against shoulders.

"Yes," Geneviève says. "Of course he was."

Étiennette mentions men, but men who were never hers, and who, Geneviève soon realizes, are only excuses to talk about her sister, Marceline, who was sent last year to the Mississippi. Then Étiennette falls silent, waits to hear more about Félicien. She is such a careful listener that Geneviève finds herself wanting to please her.

Charlotte stops singing, leans forward. "But not as pretty as the cooper's apprentice from the Cour Saint-Louis," she says, looking at Étiennette.

"You only saw him once," her friend replies. "You wouldn't happen to regret La Salpêtrière for the few biscuits he gave you?"

Charlotte doesn't immediately answer. "La Maison Saint-Louis was my home," she finally says.

"She was so young when she arrived," Étiennette explains, turning back to Geneviève, "that she doesn't even remember who brought her there."

Charlotte looks hurt. "That's not true," she says.

Geneviève tightens the string around her canvas bag, tries to find something to say. "You must know La Salpêtrière better than any of us, then," she suggests.

"Of course I do," Charlotte replies. She glances over Geneviève's shoulders. "We're slowing down."

The late-afternoon sky is smoky with pastel colors. Ahead of them, a hamlet stretches on one side of a hill.

"Finally," Étiennette says. "I can't feel my bum anymore."

Another girl says she is hungry, and a few others echo her. By the first team of oxen, Sister Gertrude speaks with a hard-faced farmer. Like everyone else, he stares at the line of carts as if busy counting them; his blond dog inspects the wheels, its tail shaking rapeseed flowers. Étiennette describes the pins and needles that run in her leg and everywhere above, but Geneviève isn't paying attention. It felt easy to talk as long as they were moving. The animals' slow, wide steps paced the conversation—confidences had a beginning and an end.

As the women shuffle toward the barn at the top of the grassy slope, Geneviève feels the familiar unease grow like it did at La Grande Force, when solitude and darkness threatened to make her lose her mind—the unforgiving sky above, its blinding light falling on the bare shoulders of the girls hunched next to her, waiting for their cells to be cleaned. This afternoon, Geneviève felt she was going on an adventure. She had escaped La Salpêtrière. She was moving forward. Now that she is faced again with the reality of an enclosed space, it becomes impossible to ignore the nuns and police officers.

But when they reach the haystacks, Étiennette acts as if no one oversees them. "We should try to stay together. The three of us," she says. She looks around, but the women are already entering the barn, and Charlotte is nowhere to be seen.

"She must be ahead of us," Geneviève says. Étiennette's answer is muted by the women's voices, the discussion of two farm boys leaning against the wooden door. Geneviève hears one of the boys say, "Look at that one! Need some more milk?" and knows whom he means before she spots Pétronille. She thinks she catches a glimpse of Charlotte by a wheelbarrow, but when the girl turns around, she doesn't have any freckles and is at least two years older than Charlotte. Somewhere in the barn, Sister Gertrude asks them to prepare for vespers. Geneviève walks around barrels of grain and women gathering straw, the dust of their dresses rising around them like fleeting insects spiraling in the light. The sunset reaches the back wall, staining the mezzanine, the ladder, and

Charlotte below, sitting in a corner, waving back. When Étiennette calls, she shifts to the right, just enough to let one more person sit.

. . .

Geneviève never would have known Félicien if not for his sister. Amélie was slender but strong, able to carry any laundry load. The tips of her fingers were always icy, bluish in the winter, bright red in the summer. Geneviève would discover years later that it was also true of her toes and nose. They were twelve when they met. Félicien was a year younger, childish-looking, like boys are until they suddenly aren't anymore.

Geneviève's family had passed away the previous year. They died of what never should have hurt them, of the cold and poverty Provence had always protected them from—her mother and siblings during their first winter in Paris, her father six months later. When she met Amélie at Le Petit Marché of Le Marais, Geneviève had been on her own for months—alone in a brutal city she didn't know, its streets filled with mud, rain, and harsh people whose skin remained pale all year long. She was ready to do anything to quit her job at one of the tanneries along the Bièvre and leave the stinking room she was sharing with six children, all younger than she was, all forever carrying the smell of skinned animals with them. When Amélie told her about the washerwoman position opening with Madame d'Argenson, Geneviève could barely believe her luck. For the first time since she left Provence, she had a decision to make. She said yes at once.

It was Amélie who brought her to the washhouse boat where the *lavandières* of the neighborhood worked. On *La Sirène*, Geneviève would sometimes feel Amélie's fingers brushing against hers, as creased and wet as the shifts they rubbed. They beat the dirt out of the clothes and talked, dipped sheets in vats and chatted—stories about themselves and about the capital. Geneviève had her favorite. It was about a desperate mother whose son had just died. How she prayed, put a candle in a bread loaf, the loaf in a basket, the basket on the Seine. How the woman thought it would point to the river spot where her son had drowned, how, instead, it floated to two hay-filled boats and burned the Pont Notre-Dame, pushing ten blazing houses into the water. Amélie had a way of telling the anecdote that made Geneviève giggle; in her mouth, the story wasn't about death and destruction. It said something about human mistakes, unreasonable hopes, and tiny gestures that speak loudly.

Where was Félicien in all of that? Félicien was everywhere. He was in the stables, grooming fragile-legged foals and plump geldings. He was at the kitchen table, Amélie's arms thrown around his neck, a wine pitcher empty in front of him. He was back from Les Halles, where he had spent his few *sous* to buy fruit, apples as polished as baby cheeks. He was handing them to Geneviève and Amélie.

Geneviève always thought he was handsome. Félicien had the same laugh as his sister—a howling sound that seemed too loud until your own laughter covered it. He grew up over one summer, taming his new long arms and legs in a few sunny weeks. That fall, at the street ball on Rue Mouffetard, they didn't join the round dance as they usually did. They had turned into pairs. Amélie and Félicien, Félicien and Geneviève, Geneviève and Amélie—combinations that, try as you might, never amounted to three.

• • •

Pushing southwest, it takes more than ten days to reach the Loire; Geneviève can't remember traveling so slowly when she crossed the country with her family. Peasants stare at them as they ride along the fields; some men touch their hats and wish them *bon voyage,* others whisper words that Geneviève is glad she's too far to hear. She tries not to think about the Faubourg Saint-Victor policeman, the one who said they should ask for more cartridges.

At sunset, the nuns lead them to barns, warehouses where turkeys and chickens tiptoe between makeshift mattresses. Only once do they have to spend the night outside, somewhere near Nemours, the countryside so white with stars that it makes Geneviève gasp when she lies down. She has been sleeping better since they left Paris. Talking to Étiennette helps; after months of isolation, it feels good to finally hand her story to someone else. There is something endearing about the way Étiennette talks and asks about men, ignores the farmers' flatteries—you can tell she's never known actual boys, that she's drawing from her sister's experiences in Paris and Versailles to keep up with Geneviève. Whenever Étiennette mentions Marceline or *La Mutine,* the boat on which she traveled, Charlotte turns quiet, cold. Étiennette ignores her. "It all feels so far now. Don't you think?" she asks Geneviève one day, looking out over the flat land and forest-teethed horizon. Geneviève says yes. She isn't quite lying. Félicien does feel far; Amélie, Provence, other bits of her past never will.

Charlotte doesn't seem to care about Félicien. She barely speaks to Geneviève. When Charlotte talks about La Salpêtrière, she mentions places that Geneviève never heard of—the Apothecary, the Rue de la Lingerie, the Embroidery Workshop, the Superioress's Garden. She lowers her eyes the day Geneviève speaks about one of the seamstresses Madame employed; but when Geneviève asks if she has said something wrong, Charlotte shrugs and doesn't utter another word for the rest of the morning. "A *sœur officière* told her she owes her last name to a seamstress," Étiennette explains that afternoon to Geneviève. When Geneviève asks why, Étiennette shrugs. "Because of an embroidered handkerchief she had when she was brought to La Salpêtrière."

At the inn in Orléans, Geneviève wakes up breathless again, convinced she's heard a scream. Half asleep, she tries to remember who welcomed them that evening, summons the faces of a kind couple and a young man in the lobby, fails to remember other guests. She waits for another sound. But there is nothing—the sad sigh of an ox, Charlotte snoring behind Étiennette's shoulder, and then a quiet moan coming from the other side of the wall, a soft pounding that soothes her back to sleep. The following day, Geneviève hears Charlotte asking Étiennette if she heard anything last night. Étiennette shakes her head. "I slept like a baby," she says.

They leave the city, return to hamlets, fields, and forests. At dawn, farmer women bring in cooking pots, paid for by the nuns. There are never enough bowls or spoons for everyone, and when Geneviève asks for extra plates, she is told to sit and wait. Women huddle against each other, trying to shake away the cold that crept into them in their sleep. Geneviève lets Étiennette eat first. She doesn't feel the early-morning humidity that everyone complains about. At La Grande Force, there were winter days when she'd wake up so stiff she couldn't move, the straw mattress covered with the kind of thick snow that children play with. She tries passing food to Charlotte too, but the girl always waits for Étiennette to be done with her lunch, eyeing her friend as Étiennette presses her lips against the rough edge of the bowl. When Étiennette hands it to her, Charlotte looks away, blushing.

On the day they are to reach the river, Geneviève finds herself alone with Charlotte. It'll soon be time to leave the cowshed; in front of them, Pétronille stares at her meal, resting her chin in her hand. Étiennette has gone squatting outside, where the pile of manure covers the women's odor. Charlotte doesn't pay attention to Geneviève, finishes folding a chemise in two. There is something about her that makes Geneviève uncomfortable, that makes her feel permanently in the wrong place at the wrong time, that makes her lose the control that usually comes to her so naturally. Next to her, Pétronille sips her broth. For once, Geneviève doesn't know what to say; she doesn't share anything with Charlotte but their journey and Étiennette.

She finally breaks the silence. "It seems like we'll never reach the coast."

"You don't mind."

"What do you mean?"

Charlotte doesn't answer, grabs a corset.

"It gives us time to learn to know each other," Geneviève adds, and when she glances at Charlotte, the girl is frowning.

"It gives you time to learn to know Étiennette." Charlotte pauses. "It must feel nice to be out."

A shiver goes down Geneviève's spine. Charlotte ties the string around her bundle. Then another bag lands on the ground, and Étiennette's blond hair swirls in front of them.

"Did anything happen?" She studies them both. "Charlotte, you look awfully cross."

"I am not."

"We were talking about our next stop," Geneviève says.

Charlotte's freckled cheeks blush, an expression so close to hatred that it startles Geneviève. The girl grasps her bundle and stands up.

"Naturally," Charlotte says. "Our next stop."

Geneviève watches Charlotte's skinny arms balance from her sides as she crosses the farmyard. Out of where? she wants to ask. La Salpêtrière, of course. For a brief moment, it occurs to her that Charlotte might know more about her than the other women do, might know about La Grande Force. But that is impossible. How would she? Geneviève focuses on what Charlotte said about Étiennette, and now all she can feel is anger. The girl doesn't know her luck to be with her childhood friend whom no one took away or forced her to leave behind. When she was Charlotte's age, Geneviève struggled to survive in an unknown city that would give her nothing but the solitude of its streets and prisons. She has been on her own too long to travel alone.

"I wouldn't worry too much," Étiennette says, rolling her hair into a bun. "Maybe she's about to start bleeding."

· · ·

At Madame d'Argenson's, when Geneviève missed her period, she didn't say a word to anyone, not even Amélie. It would have meant telling her so much more, and Geneviève didn't want her to know—at least not just yet—what had happened with Félicien, because it had been that one time. It hadn't meant anything, nothing more than the couples having sex in the narrow alleys, the ones they often saw at dusk when they walked home from the river. She couldn't tell her friend what she hadn't understood yet: that being intimate with Félicien had then seemed the closest thing to loving Amélie.

Geneviève decided she was old enough to figure it out herself. She had heard about women who didn't want to have their baby. She had heard that eating absinthe would stimulate her blood. She'd munch the bitter plants in the deserted kitchen at night and wake up tired. In the morning, she'd look for the blood that would keep the other servants' suspicions at bay and find nothing but the salty stains left by her own sweat.

It bought her time, and that was all she could think about. She could see herself growing bigger and then flatter. She could see Madame giving her a look that felt like spit and asking her to leave. She could see Amélie leaning over the vats of the washhouse boat alone. But Geneviève couldn't picture the baby. Only the shadowy, moist

place below her breasts, this pocket she imagined raw red, like under
shut eyelids.

• • •

Geneviève has only ever known two rivers: the Rhône that led her family to Paris, the Seine that took her in. The Loire seems much wider—
much longer too. Over the past fortnight, as the carts followed the river,
Geneviève saw donjons and towers peeking above the forest, castles
perched on hills, as shiny as yolk-covered pastries. Shortly after Tours,
she heard another woman mock Pétronille, pointing at one of the *do-
maines*, saying that they could drop the *châtelaine* home in one of her
castles if she wished. Then the answer, dry and unexpected: "*Tais-toi.*"
The other girl did as she was told. She shut up.

Today even Charlotte seems excited. They would leave the carts in
Paimbœuf, where their boat would be waiting. Right after Nantes, Geneviève overheard Charlotte tell Étiennette about a dog showing teeth,
a little boy giving her a bouquet of daisies. Charlotte doesn't speak to
Geneviève anymore. It was a relief at first—without words, there could
be no confrontation. Étiennette doesn't seem to mind as long as she keeps
them both close. This morning, after the sisters told them about Paimbœuf and the ship, Geneviève heard Charlotte sing. She was watching
her from behind; Étiennette was nowhere around. Charlotte sang loud
and clear, piling up the empty bowls after lunch. Now Geneviève can't
remember the lyrics—only the voice stays, textured and rich. As Geneviève turned around, she found herself thinking of honey, the dark
and powerful kind that her neighbor used to make from sweet chestnut
trees back in Provence.

These past few days, she has grown more and more uneasy—she
can't imagine spending another four weeks like this. She can't help wondering about Charlotte's next move. The insults Madame once whispered
to her at La Grande Force come back. This time it isn't her mistress's
voice Geneviève hears but her own. Don't be silly. Not everything is
about you. Charlotte is only a child.

In the harbor of Paimbœuf, it doesn't take long to get everyone out
of the carts. Around Geneviève, most women are already on their feet

except Pétronille. She tries to catch her attention, but the brown-haired girl doesn't look up, her hands pressed against her sides. A police officer asks her to hurry, and Geneviève does. After weeks on the road, she is eager to stand, stretch, shuffle. She expected to reach the ocean today; she grew tired of hearing Charlotte talk about the *sœur officière* from La Rochelle, who told her about the Atlantic beaches. But now she understands what Sister Gertrude explained this morning to one of the other nuns—that this is only another step of their journey: before heading to La Louisiane, *La Baleine* will take them to another French town where people will repair God knows what on the boat. From the harbor, she can see only the low water of the Loire, its round sand islands sticking out of the river like breasts in a bath.

"Sister Louise says it's that one." Étiennette points.

Geneviève has never seen a boat as big as this one. Its three masts look like Place de la Grève gallows, its folded sails like sunshades, and the beams holding them like the arms of a child trying to keep his balance. Its shallow, pear-shaped draft reminds her of Lucie d'Argenson's panniers. On the deck, small cannons point toward the shore. Men run from the prow to the plumb stern, their movements smooth and silent to the women in the harbor.

The nuns have started counting again. Geneviève feels the hands of the police officers on her shoulders, her back, pushing and pulling, until she finds herself in line behind Charlotte and Étiennette. She can hear a discreet sniffling but doesn't have time to look around because the sound is suddenly covered by a loud bang and she's already turning toward the gangway that just fell between them and the ship.

"I feel dizzy," Charlotte whispers to Étiennette. The first girls are already stumbling forward. The wind shuffles through their dresses, retreating, then surging again. Below them, a sailor screams to be careful.

"It will be fast," Étiennette says, her hand holding Charlotte's.

La Loire is more tumultuous than the Seine, and soon the cobblestones vanish under Geneviève's feet—there is only the wet wood bending under her shoes, step after step, so she can't help but think of the day when Amélie placed her fingers around an egg, asking her to press, harder, swearing that it could never break. Her mother once told her the same of silk.

"Don't look below," she hears someone say from the boat, but it's all Geneviève can look at—the abrupt slope of the hull meeting the moving water. One, two, three more steps and she feels Étiennette pulling her arm, then her shoes meet the faintly moving ground of the deck. When Geneviève turns around, she sees the line of women dangling on the gangway and the houses facing the harbor, immutable. She sees Pétronille drying her tears with her sleeve and would like to ask if she is all right, but someone yells to move on. By the mast, Sister Gertrude stands at the entrance of the hold, watching as the girls go down the ladder and disappear under the open hatch. Charlotte waits next to the nun, her face leaned toward her veils.

"Come," Étiennette says.

"What about Charlotte?"

"Don't worry, she said she'll meet us in a moment."

Pétronille passes. Her face is the sick green of honeydew melons.

"Why?" Geneviève asks.

Étiennette shrugs. "She wants to ask Sister Gertrude something."

Geneviève imagines everything Charlotte could make up about her, everything the nun could tell Charlotte regarding her past. She can't be sure whose version would be worse. She puts her hand on Étiennette's shoulder. "Do you know what it is about?"

"Hurry up, *Mesdemoiselles*, please!"

"I don't have the slightest idea. Come," Étiennette says.

Then she is on the ladder that drops her to the insides of *La Baleine*, its damp between decks, what Geneviève imagines as the belly of a whale. Étiennette stops when she reaches the last step. Geneviève does too. She waits for her eyes to get used to the dark, for the emerald shadows to clear away. When she turns back toward the hatch, she can see Charlotte talking to Sister Gertrude, the two women framed in a square of white sky, looking down at her.

• • •

Geneviève told Amélie about the baby one winter evening by the Seine. The clouds were a fragile pink above them. Geneviève hadn't intended to speak as they gathered their bats and started folding sheets, readying themselves to go home. But on the dock, the sickness overcame her abruptly. When her eyes focused, she saw seaweed moving under the surface, two ducklings, a bonnet caught between cobblestones. Amélie handed her a handkerchief. Geneviève wiped her face, tried to breathe through her mouth to avoid the fishy smell of the river. She was afraid she might vomit again if she had to throw Félicien's name at her friend's face. But Geneviève didn't have to bring him up; Amélie did.

When she got up, her friend was staring at the current, fingers pressed against her jaw, digging into her cheeks, as if trying to contain something violent. "If it had been anyone but my brother," she finally said, "you would have told me earlier." Geneviève shivered in the evening breeze. It wasn't a question, and yet she answered yes. She said she was sorry, that she should have come as soon as she missed her period, then added, no, before that. Amélie nodded. She kicked the dirty handkerchief into the water. "He'd never know how to help you," she said. Then she repeated the same sentence, as if the words brought her comfort. Seagulls called each other by the bridge. "I do."

Two days later, Amélie sent Geneviève to the old woman's house on the Left Bank. Amélie once met a girl who knew a dressmaker who had a sister who went there. If they'd asked around, if it was something you could ask around about, Geneviève was sure they would have discovered other familiar faces—the milk woman's daughter or the housekeeper's cousin, maybe—who stepped into the back rooms of the house on Rue de Buci. Instead, she took an empty basket and crossed the Seine on her own. Amélie had offered to come along, but Geneviève told her they'd draw more attention if they both went. What she didn't say was that she feared she might already have asked too much. She couldn't afford to lose more than the baby she carried.

After she swallowed the herbs she had been given on the Left Bank, minutes of her life disappeared. She forgot them, just like she forgets every evening the very moment when she falls asleep, waking up frightened, baffled at the idea that she can lose track of herself for hours at a time. She knows it doesn't mean that nothing happened. There was a baby and then there wasn't. It's easier like that—no memory, just facts. She was asleep and then she wasn't.

Later, much later, when she would start offering mugwort, rue, and savin to other women, she would take to telling them: "Don't think about it. Soon it'll be as if you woke up from a bad dream. But at least you had a choice to make."

. . .

After spending just one day aboard *La Baleine*, Geneviève doesn't consider the boat big anymore. It looks nothing like *La Sirène*, with its steam so thick she'd forget she worked on the river. The between decks of the ship, which the girls are confined to, feels incredibly small. Just another cell—but at least one that is taking her somewhere else. It is always dark and humid there, the surf forever battering the hull. Geneviève listens to it, her ear so close to the ground that the Loire—then, once they reach the coast, the Atlantic—seems about to swallow her. Those first nights on *La Baleine*, she dreams of water, of a land full of creeks and rotting wood; in these dreams, no one wants to talk to her. She wakes up breathless and the sound of the waves remains, the smell of rot too. "The wet planks will be replaced in Lorient," Sister Gertrude assures them on the third day. She insists that benches and mattresses will be provided for comfort. Geneviève doesn't know what can be done to fix her friendship with Étiennette and Charlotte.

The two of them sit together, away from Geneviève, by one of the portholes no one is allowed to open. On the day *La Baleine* sailed, Geneviève saw Charlotte cup her hands against Étiennette's ears, like children do when they whisper too loudly. Geneviève tries to tell herself that she is being silly, that Charlotte isn't focused on her. Yet she can't help but think about the nuns learning of the abortions, going back on the Superioress's decision, ordering that one of the policemen brings her back to Paris. Geneviève decides to stay by Pétronille, who has been sick since they left Paimbœuf. She holds a bucket under her chin and leans forward to hear her whisper, "Thank you."

The access to the deck remains forbidden to the women as *La Baleine* sails toward Lorient. Sometimes in the darkness Geneviève feels her heart start to race, just like it did at La Grande Force. When her breath shortens, she closes her eyes. She tries to ignore the steps of the sailors that pound above her head, the ghostly sound of the wind against the masts. She pictures herself in La Bastide-des-Jourdans, taking her favorite shortcut home, walking through the lavender fields that you could cross only at sunset, when bees finally left the flowers alone. She stays there as long as she can.

The first time Geneviève sees the ocean, in Lorient, she's reminded of those blue fields. Of the wind blowing through them and the flowers' liquid undulation. From the main deck, she stares at the waves, thick and dark and silver, rolling themselves into the flat line of the horizon. She never knew her eyes could see this far. Facing the Atlantic, she feels giddy, light-headed. It occurs to her that until now, she never truly understood what traveling to La Louisiane meant. Beyond so much water, nothing can matter—she could be free like she once was, in Provence, in Paris. And at this very moment, before they disembark in Brittany, it seems impossible anyone could take that away from her.

• • •

Once the priest and the concessioners arrive, *La Baleine* will be ready to sail, so explains Sister Gertrude. In Lorient, the inn where they will stay for the next few weeks is close to the harbor. But from the single window of the room the nuns chose for Geneviève, Pétronille, Étiennette, and Charlotte, Geneviève can't see the ocean anymore. At supper that first night, Geneviève glances at Étiennette and Charlotte, who sit at the other end of the long wooden table. In the obscurity of *La Baleine*, asking Charlotte about her conversation with Sister Gertrude was impossible. The world had turned too dull and damp already; it felt too similar to La Grande Force. But now that they are back on land, now that they'll be sharing a room, she knows she has to.

When Geneviève walks upstairs after supper, she finds Pétronille lying on the bed they share. The floor is covered with vomit; so is the bottom of Charlotte's dress. Étiennette stands aside, a hand covering her mouth. Charlotte is gently pushing her canvas bag under Pétronille's head. She steps back when Geneviève enters.

"What happened?"

Pétronille gives her a faint smile. Color slowly returns to her cheeks. "It is as if I were still on that boat," she says.

"But you aren't," Geneviève observes.

"I'm going to find something to clean this up," Charlotte says.

Geneviève moves to let her pass, then says, "Wait, I'll come with you." In the corridor, she hurries against the crowd of women returning from the dining hall, to catch up with Charlotte.

"What do you want?" the girl asks.

Geneviève can see only Charlotte's back, her legs heavily hitting the steps. She catches her breath. She waits until they have reached the quieter third floor to speak. "You talked to Sister Gertrude," she says.

Charlotte's eyes fall on the only closet of the corridor. "I did," she replies.

"Why?"

"That is none of your business."

"What she told you about me is."

Charlotte's freckles disappear in the dim light. "You used to be a prisoner at La Grande Force, but I suspected it."

"You suspected it," Geneviève says. At first she thinks Charlotte is bluffing, but the girl holds her gaze. Geneviève's legs go numb. "What else did she say?"

Charlotte kneels by the closet, she won't even turn around to look at her. When Geneviève repeats her question, she barely recognizes her own voice.

"She said . . ." Charlotte stops, clears her throat. "She said she didn't care what we did. That she hasn't chosen us." She pauses. She suddenly seems terribly sad. "The Superioress did. Sister Gertrude is here only to ensure that we reach the colony safe and sound."

For a moment Geneviève is too relieved to speak. What she did in Paris is irrelevant. She'll leave for La Louisiane no matter what. "You said you knew about me," she says. "If you did, why go to Sister Gertrude?"

Charlotte bites her lip. "Because," she answers, "Étiennette wouldn't believe me."

Geneviève looks away. It was all in her head. Charlotte never intended to keep her from going to the Mississippi. She wanted only to keep her away from Étiennette. Geneviève thinks about everything she would have done for Amélie. She doesn't want to understand Charlotte, yet part of her does. She catches herself. Did she, at that age, already know what her relationship with Amélie would turn into? She sees Amélie welcoming her at Madame's, showing her the narrow bedroom that they would share. No, of course she didn't. She hadn't felt anything that day but joy, relief; she finally had somebody to count on.

"Take this," Charlotte says, offering her a rag. "For Pétronille."

Geneviève's hand closes on the cloth, but she doesn't move. She watches Charlotte go down the stairs, buckets hanging from her arms. She isn't quite sure how long she stands there on the landing of the last floor. A heavy summer rain has started to hit the roof, and the inn pulses around her, the water echoing like it did in the between decks of *La Baleine*.

• • •

Amélie kept close to Geneviève after the baby was gone. Her presence filled Geneviève with ease. When Amélie touched her face, she thought of rainbow rims on sunstruck eyelashes, ice-cold linen against feverish temples. She lay next to Geneviève for hours in a row. When Amélie focused, she'd scratch her upper lip, nail facing her teeth, thumb hiding her chin. Scratch right where the triangle of skin between the nose and the mouth turned into lip, then below. The little wound never quite healed, polished and smoothed at best, hard-shelled and blood-crusty at worst. It wasn't something you'd notice, looking at Amélie. But it made every kiss different. As with many other things, Geneviève liked to think that only she knew about it—an insignificant, painless indent whose depth she'd feel with the tip of her tongue.

They met in places where they had never been with Félicien. They met in the attic, surrounded by intrepid mice and furniture that had survived several kings; they met behind the orangery, in the shadows of fruit that shouldn't have been able to grow in this climate. They shared the same bed and thanked their mistress for the tight quarters she forced upon her servants; at night, when fingers ran on rib cages and thighs locked with other thighs, they drew the blankets high above their faces, breathed the unbreathable air that slid between them, and pulled themselves against each other until there wasn't room for anything else.

After, Geneviève would get out of bed and open the window. She'd let the breeze in and watch the colorless dawn. In the street, a neighbor yelled at two children for dropping a jar of milk. Beer barrels left deep round marks in the mud; the locksmith's apprentices hurried behind their master and into his workshop. Life went on, yet the capital felt different. It had nothing to do with the city that killed her family. Amélie had changed Paris for her.

• • •

As August turns into September, Étiennette behaves differently around Geneviève. She wishes she wouldn't care about Étiennette's friendship, but she finds she does. She loses her appetite. In the yard of the inn, she scrubs her greasy curls until they turn chestnut brown again, but no one has set aside a clean bucket for her, and the water she uses is already murky. At night, Étiennette falls asleep after one simple *bonne nuit*. During mass, in the half-built Saint-Louis Church of Lorient, Charlotte keeps her eyes shut, her face raised toward the broken nave. Prayers don't bring Geneviève any comfort. Idiot, stupid, selfish girl, says the voice that haunted her at La Grande Force—of course people would learn what she did in Paris. Geneviève focuses on the wind that blows through the holes of the stained-glass windows, as if their characters were the ones breathing out the sea breeze.

Pétronille hasn't been sick since that first night in Lorient. Yet she barely speaks anymore. Not to Geneviève, not to anyone, and it's the overall silence that Geneviève finds the most painful. Étiennette answers her questions but doesn't ask any. There is no one to wonder with when the boat paint job will be done, when they will finally sail away. Surrounded by so many women, Geneviève feels lonelier than in her Grande Force cell.

One afternoon in mid-September, Geneviève sits on her bed, looking through her bundle. The room is empty—the other women are already downstairs darning their clothes with the needles and wool provided by the local Ursuline nuns. Mending could mean only one thing: they would leave soon.

When the door bursts open, she jumps. But it is neither Étiennette nor Charlotte. Pétronille stands on the threshold, her face pale again, fingers clenched around her bonnet.

"What is it?" Geneviève asks.

Pétronille looks above her shoulder, then back at Geneviève. "I was hoping to find you here," she says. She closes the door behind her. "I've heard what Étiennette says about you."

"Étiennette told you? Not Charlotte?"

Pétronille shakes her head. "Étiennette says you know how to do it." Her voice is matter-of-fact; she could be talking about the flowers of her herbarium, like she once did on *La Baleine*. She lowers her gaze. It takes a second for Geneviève to understand that she isn't staring at her feet but at her belly.

A moment of silence hits. Geneviève no longer hears the maids' songs and the snapping of sheets. All she can think of is the house of the Rue de Buci—the girls with their expectant faces so similar to Pétronille's now. The old woman she'd let peer between her legs, fingers touching her as if peeling a fruit. How the *vieillarde* had motioned her up and shoved into her basket a handful of herbs, herbs that Amélie would crush that evening in a bowl, that Geneviève would later hand to the first shy, teary girl who'd come to her. That day on the Left Bank, Geneviève hadn't been able to help herself. She asked the woman what she should do if it didn't work. Then the shrug, and her answer, that would stay with Geneviève long after the burning was gone, long after she'd changed her sheets for lavender-smelling ones: "Raise your child."

"How long?" she asks.

Pétronille starts. She reaches for her sleeves, pulls threads of fabric, ties them tight around her thumb. "I'm sorry I didn't say anything before."

Geneviève considers the rings under Pétronille's eyes, the brown hair strands falling on her livid, full cheeks. It's been a long time since anybody has asked something from her. "It doesn't matter," she says.

"It happened when we were in Orléans. At the inn."

Geneviève remembers the noises she heard when she woke up that night. She feels strangely relieved. For once, there is something she can do—what she knows how to do best, or almost.

"I'll try," she says. "But I can't promise anything."

Pétronille nods. Geneviève grabs her clothes. She feels dizzy, a bit weak. She is about to open the door when Pétronille calls her name.

"We are lucky to have you here," she says.

Geneviève hears her heart pulsing in her ears. She looks at Pétronille. "Thank you," she answers.

She steps into the corridor, goes down the stairs. Her hands are damp. She feels anxious, but for the first time since she was arrested nine months ago, she knows exactly what she must do, and there is solace in that.

That afternoon in the dining room, Geneviève sits apart from the other women. She mends her petticoats. Once her eyes meet Étiennette's, but Geneviève focuses on the torn fabric. She carefully brings back the broken pieces together, just like her mother taught her for the day when she wouldn't be able to count on anyone but herself.

· · ·

Depraved woman, abortionist. It's more complicated than that, but it isn't something Madame d'Argenson ever gave her a chance to elaborate on. Madame wasn't a liar; she had too little imagination for that. She was never completely wrong nor completely right about Geneviève, didn't know she had done much worse than what these few words, "depraved woman," "abortionist," suggested. If she had known about her relationship with Amélie, or about the dozens of girls Geneviève helped, there would have been a trial, she would have gone to Le Petit Châtelet, she would have been called a prostitute, a *débauchée*. Nobody ever would have found her in the cell of La Grande Force, nor sat her in a cart that would take her to the other side of the world. But Lucie d'Argenson hadn't found out; she'd learn about only the one woman, the baker who had sought Geneviève's help on that cold January day. Geneviève had come to think of the truth as something overwhelming and hidden, a weapon, something that could be used against you. Before their stop in Lorient, she never thought she'd reclaim that part of herself. She never thought it worthy.

· · ·

Talk of travel fills the inn bedrooms again. Over the past few weeks, Geneviève spotted concessioners moving about the harbor, the La Louisiane–bound workers dragging along stubborn cattle, loading barrels of food and water. *La Baleine* lay on its side for days; men brought cables and pulleys, changed rotten planks, scraped the hull. Now the boat has turned as shiny as a waxed wooden floor.

Geneviève knows she doesn't have much time: they are to leave October 1. Before that, she must gather the plants, get the eau-de-vie. Sneak into the inn kitchen. Ask for a maid's help. Pretend to be sick and miss the last mass in the dismantled church. Venture to the market held in the harbor and hope for more than fishmongers.

Her real fear is both Étiennette and Charlotte. Geneviève will need the bedroom, but more than anything, she will need their discretion.

• • •

A few hours before she was arrested, Geneviève ran to find Amélie in the yard where laundry was left to dry. On any other afternoon, they would have sat in the kitchen, asked the cook for some wine or beer. Going to the nearby cabaret was no longer possible: rumors had it that there, women were rounded up by police and taken to a faraway place.

It had been a year since Geneviève had gone to the Rue de Buci house, months that she had been assisting nearby *lavandières*, flower sellers, *dames de compagnie*. Earlier that week, she'd promised Amélie that this girl, the baker, would be the last. It had been a relief for them both. "Good," Amélie had said. "It was only a matter of time before you got caught." So that January afternoon, when the woman Geneviève was supposed to help whispered that she couldn't come in, that her boss knew everything, Geneviève softly shut the door behind her. She wasn't surprised. She thought: If only you'd told this girl no, if only you'd promised Amélie earlier.

The thought was corrosive, dangerous. She needed to remain focused if she wanted to have a chance at seeing Amélie again. Her hands shook so badly that she struggled to open the kitchen door leading to the corridor. She passed by the food pantry, stepped outside; under the winter light, the wet sheets flapped gently. Amélie immediately understood when she saw her. They left the yard together, ran to their bedroom. They had only a few minutes to themselves before they heard Madame d'Argenson storm into the servant quarters.

Today Geneviève still thanks herself for not hesitating, for rushing upstairs with Amélie, for shutting the door as hard as she did. She thanks herself for stealing from Madame what no one could ever take away from her.

She doesn't hesitate with Charlotte and Étiennette either. On their way to church, Geneviève grabs Charlotte's sleeve. Around them, the women are distracted—they look at their feet to avoid stepping into dung or sliding on fish scales; they stare at the sky that they see like this, vast and deep above them, only once a week. Geneviève slows down, gestures for Étiennette and Charlotte to get closer. Inside her chest, her heart is a bird, a butterfly, a starving silkworm. The girls have come to a halt at the corner of the street that leads to the harbor; standing in the salty breeze, they wait for a wine shipment to pass. Geneviève feels her bonnet brush against Étiennette's and Charlotte's. She whispers what she knows and what no one else must learn.

She expected questions, hushed whispers and furrowed eyebrows. But Étiennette remains silent. It is Charlotte, looking grave, who asks: "Did you really think I would tell?"

3

Pétronille

Pétronille would rather have stayed between decks. She prefers the dimness of La Baleine's *belly*, especially now that the boat has started moving, now that she can hear water hitting the hull and sailors running above her head. On the carts, she'd felt tiny, lost among blackberry bushes, stubborn wasps, and trees so big their branches drew alcoves above her; there had been no way to escape the countryside, and when she thought there was—by following the innkeeper's son in Orléans, the young man who'd touched her birthmark and said he'd never seen a woman like her—she had found herself in yet another kind of trap, unable to decide if she had wanted, if she still wanted, his hand to run up her thighs. Here, as long as she doesn't see the sea passing by, Pétronille can convince herself that *La Baleine* isn't much different from La Salpêtrière. That all she'll have to do for the next few weeks is sit still, sleep when the sun retreats, and eat when the food comes. Meals don't nauseate her anymore, thanks to Geneviève. But her belly still feels sore from the cramping, her legs weak, and Pétronille wishes Sister Gertrude hadn't called them to gather at the stern. The nun probably thought she was doing them all a favor, that the women would be thankful to see the continent one last time. Pétronille isn't. She dreads it. No home in France has ever felt quite safe.

On the deck, everything strikes her at once: the violent afternoon light, the screaming of sailors and seabirds, the ocean rolling under the boat like dough under a baker's hands. The ship's three masts tower high above her—one by the hatch from which she just emerged, the others planted into each of the two raised decks. A brusque gust makes Pétronille's eyes water, and she can't be sure whether she tastes sea spray or tears. She climbs the ladder to the stern behind the other girls. She has learned to anticipate the pushes and pulls, the unexpected touching that, not so long ago, gave her chills. She has learned to ignore the nickname the other women gave her—*La Tachée*, the Stained One. Until now, she didn't know she'd ever miss the maid from La Salpêtrière, the one who called her birthmark a curse and hurried out of the bedroom as soon as Pétronille glanced at her. The servant's dread felt better than the women's mockery; at least the maid left her alone. At La Maison de Correction, Pétronille didn't mind the loneliness. Or maybe she did, but only at the beginning, before she settled down in her new routine, got used to the Marais Garden view outside her bedroom. Pétronille had seen the dormitories. She knew where she would have ended up if she hadn't volunteered for this trip, after her mother wrote that she would soon stop paying her pension.

"Étiennette, look!"

Charlotte, *la petite* with whom Pétronille had shared a room in Lorient, who had held her head after Geneviève administered the herbs, points at the mast, at a seagull perched on a nest. Beyond the stern, there is nothing to stop the ocean, none of the forests that used to enclose the fields, the carts, the centipedes that scurried under Pétronille's feet. The October sky is a milky white that hurts the eye. She breathes deeply, just like Paul showed her back at Château-Thierry. She tries to see above the shoulder of Étiennette, who leans on the railing, her arm locked under Charlotte's. If she can focus on the continent, if she can stand long enough to see it melt with the sea, then she will be fine. The girls' comments will be silenced. Pétronille will forget both the wind and the man in Orléans just like she did at the inn, even momentarily, when she'd locked her eyes on the spiderweb above his mattress, how it spun bridges between logs, where nothing seemed to hold it.

"*Mademoiselle, attention.*"

Pétronille registers the man's warning at the very moment she feels the grip tighten around her ankle. She tries to move, but the knot is already too tight. Around her, the women have stepped back. She hears someone say that *La Tachée* is trapped, and the shaking sneaks back into her hands, all the way to her shoulders.

Then the man's voice again, quieter. "If you pull right there, it should come loose."

The sailor is pointing at her leg. He is holding the other end of the rope. When Pétronille remains standing, he doesn't kneel to guide her. He just repeats what he said, in the same tone—encouraging, apologetic, but firm. Pétronille brings herself to the ground. She knows better than to look around at the wall of dresses, at the thick serge curtain surrounding her. She focuses on the rope. The man is right; the knot gives away easily when she pulls, its circle growing bigger and bigger, just like the women's around her, walking away, disinterested, as Pétronille frees her foot and stands up.

"It comes from the mizzen," the man says, turning toward the mast behind him.

His skin is sunburned, his eyes blue. His face isn't particularly pleasant, his nose too sharp for his curved cheeks, a puff of fair hair growing out of the kerchief tied around his forehead. He must be her age—in any case, he doesn't look older than twenty-six. She likes his voice. She likes that he doesn't jostle her, doesn't take without asking. Pétronille hands him the rope, and he thanks her. Then he is gone, taken up by the girls' crowd, and someone has stepped in his place, the woman who helped her in Lorient. Geneviève also has a nice voice, as well as a little gap between her front teeth, and Pétronille doesn't believe what the other women say—that the devil breathes through it. She likes how Geneviève's curls sneak out of her bonnet, how free they fall against her jaw.

"Are you all right?" Geneviève asks.

"I am. Thank you."

Pétronille kept the daffodils Geneviève collected after it was all over. She tied them to the top of her stockings, so soft they barely feel like anything. She suddenly wishes she could raise her dress to make sure they are there.

"Don't turn around," Geneviève says. She frowns. "He is still looking."

Pétronille faces the sea, aware of the sailor's stare on her back, of a curious pressure between her shoulder blades. She tries to focus on the horizon, looking for a crepe-sized layer of land. But all she can see are waves, then water, flat, gray, stretching all the way to the perfectly straight line of the sky. France is gone.

• • •

From her parents' perspective, Pétronille was simpleminded. It wasn't a secret to anyone. At Château-Thierry, her mother would point a long finger at her, and Pétronille would listen to all the visiting ladies in their cakelike dresses murmur "What a pity" and "She's still awfully pretty." They'd treat her as they would a puppy—a tender creature who seemed to understand them but never actually could.

At five, Pétronille barely spoke. Her four siblings, already married, referred to her as *Simplette* in their letters. She had heard adults say she was a remarkable-looking child, with dark hair curtaining green eyes and a white birthmark on her cheek. A friend of her father once admitted that the stain was arresting—it seemed to deepen her face, inviting you to look further, like the vanishing point of a garden pathway. Some said it made her beauty more striking; others shook their head. Pétronille was never ashamed of her birthmark; she had never known her face without it. She was used to the visitors' staring eyes. They always turned around after a few seconds anyway, convinced they had seen everything there was to see.

But Pétronille heard and understood every word they said. The issue was, she couldn't bring herself to answer. The conversations would grow around her, buzz and fuzz, and then she'd start hearing the clinking of silverware, the notes on the harpsichord, the steps of the maids. She'd sit at the supper table, paralyzed, trying to divide the sounds into categories—wind, music, voices. At the end of the meal, as the guests split between the smoking room and the *petit salon*, her mother would kneel next to her, ask how she felt. Pétronille knew what she wanted to hear; she knew it was finally time to go back to her room. She'd always answer, "Fine, thank you."

• • •

Pétronille had no idea the ocean was so big. In Paimbœuf and Lorient, she barely saw it; the nausea was so bad she couldn't even stand looking at the waves that shook the ship, that upset her belly. Now she realizes how much harder it is to travel by sea. In the countryside, at least, there were landmarks. She could tell herself they were moving forward, that they would soon reach the next town, meet the next taciturn peasant. In the hold, all she knows is that the sun sometimes sets and rises.

Over the following week, as the other girls retch and sweat, Pétronille is no longer seasick. She finds that she enjoys feeling *La Baleine*'s undulations ripple through her body; that she can't help connecting them with the sailor's quiet voice, which never quite leaves her. She spotted him a few days ago in the between decks, with his kerchief and short blue jacket, helping a teary ship's boy with a torn sail, showing him how to stitch it. The child's eyes were locked on the needle; the sailor was too absorbed in his explanations to notice her. That night, Pétronille revisited his patient tone, his careful gestures; there was an honesty to him, a gentleness she'd have thought the roughness of life at sea would wear away. She doesn't want to let herself be carried away—she is afraid of misreading people's intentions again, something her mother would often complain about. But she knows men aren't all like the innkeeper's son in Orléans. It was one of the many things she learned by Paul's side in the gardens of Château-Thierry.

The nuns are sick too. They can't give orders as they usually do. It's up to Pétronille, Geneviève, and four other girls to take care of everyone else. The part of the between decks where the women have been assigned has already absorbed the smells of vomit and stagnant water. Daylight and air filter only through the hatch, and Geneviève keeps on talking about the captain's orders—"What harm would it make to open these portholes?"—but Pétronille doesn't complain. She has gotten used to living in semi-obscurity, to avoiding the casks lined up against the walls, to finding her way between the mats. She walks by Geneviève, handing *chopines* of herb-infused water to the other girls, wondering about its recipe, feeding some of it to Étiennette and Charlotte, who spend most of their time sleeping side by side. The nuns said every sick girl should have two sips; Pétronille watches the women's throats move when they swallow, and counts. At night, she listens to the hoarse laughter and snoring of the concessioners piled on the other side of a thin partition, to the prattle and mooing of the cows, chickens, and hogs kept under the after-castle, close to the kitchens.

The between decks is a maze Pétronille can't decipher. She knows that the powder magazine, the one the sailors call *La Sainte-Barbe*, is very close to where she sleeps. She's passed by the pantry a few times, but she has no idea where to locate the helmsman's quarters and the carpenter's workshop she heard the ship's boys talk about. Under the hatch, there is another ladder. The boat's cats climb it on wet paws, disappearing into a yet darker space than the one she's come to inhabit.

Pétronille keeps to what she knows. She empties the bile-filled buckets, wets the rags with seawater, mops lumpy puddles. She doesn't mind. It keeps her busy, it keeps her free to come and go. It gives her time to think of someone who isn't the man from Orléans. The more the sailor's face pops in her mind, the more polished it feels, like a stone rolled by the waves again and again.

• • •

Pétronille's world was never silent. As she grew up, she had her own games and never-answered questions. She'd play for hours with her two hands, fingers galloping against the wall, one palm a lady, the other a gentleman. She wondered about tickling and fruit flies and where they came from. She'd lie down on her bed for hours, staring at the ceiling, feeling her heartbeat in her wrist, in her crotch, in her elbow, trying to track its unexpected journey.

At dawn, she liked to walk down to the kitchens before anyone but the servants were up. If she was lucky, the maids would already be back from the farm, straw sticking out of the baskets they cautiously laid next to the fireplace. Pétronille would lean over the kettle, break an egg, then another. No one told her anything; the kitchen girls had taught her how to poach eggs, they were used to her being lost in her own world. She'd watch the white and the yolk dance in the water, marveled at how they always found each other.

• • •

La Baleine has been sailing for eleven days when Pétronille and the other women are allowed on the deck again. Most of them are still numb, their faces pale. But when Pétronille reaches the top of the ladder and helps Geneviève up, she can't think of the sick girls anymore. At each end of the ship, the forecastle and the quarterdeck break the evenness of the railing, the two raised decks overlooking the upper deck. Out here, the wind dries the sweat, airs her dress, and strokes her face; for a second, Pétronille feels clean. Then there is the ocean, bluer than the last time she saw it, spinning, drawing an infinite dark circle around them, as if *La Baleine* has become the center of a watery world. She wonders if the quiet-voiced man can see her from where he is.

"Let's wander some, shall we?" Geneviève says, and smiles when Pétronille takes her arm.

They climb up the raised deck, cross the forecastle toward the bow. Pétronille keeps her head lowered. The horizon, the water, the emptiness of it all makes her feel jittery. She turns around. There are sailors, dozens of them—going up the masts, handling sails, reeling in ropes. Tanned faces, washed-out pants, and discolored hair. She is afraid he is going to break from the crowd and come to her. She is afraid he isn't here at all.

"We should enjoy it while we can," she hears Geneviève say. "Once the sisters are on their feet again, we'll never be able to come back out here on our own."

Pétronille knows Geneviève is right. Between her fingers, she can feel the threads of her sleeves fraying.

They go down the ladder to the upper deck, pass by the rowing boat, the door leading to the officers' quarters. Under the shrouds, the pilot fiddles with a small disc. He lets it fall on its side and waves at them, clear-cut hand moving against the blue, as if brushing the sky. Then he's back to his instrument, and Pétronille joins Geneviève on the railing. The autumn sun tickles her face.

"*Mesdemoiselles.*"

Pétronille is disappointed when she sees the two men facing them. One wears a cassock, the other a coat too small for his belly. None is a sailor.

"Please let me introduce myself," the big man says, flattening his breeches. His voice is high-pitched, fast, nothing like the one Pétronille expected. "Officer Des Étaux, *La Baleine* surgeon in chief. This is Father Jean Richard." The priest stares at them. The officer adds, "I believe some of your *compagnes* have had a rough time accommodating to sea life?"

Pétronille hears Geneviève say yes, then something about him surely being too busy to help fragile ladies like them. Pétronille isn't sure if the officer catches the irony in Geneviève's voice or how he answers to it. She is staring behind him at the bottom of the mast. Working the cables are three sailors, but only one is smiling at her, the one who helped her with the rope. Her first instinct is to look away quickly, past the surgeon, the priest, and over the sea, then retrace the same path, careful to move her chin as slightly as she can. When she lays eyes on the sailor again, his hands are trying to tell her something. At first his movements are fast and hard to follow, pointing at the sun, drawing an arc in the sky, back and forth, and air-taping the ground, the exact place where he stands. He looks so serious when he starts repeating the same series of gestures that Pétronille lets out a soft laugh, making the surgeon pause and the priest frown.

"I had no idea that the lack of air and light—of primary hygiene measures, should I say—was a laughable matter," Father Jean Richard observes, speaking for the first time.

Geneviève leans closer to the priest. The surgeon squints. "I apologize," she whispers, "my friend can sometimes be confused."

Pétronille knows Geneviève is only trying to protect her, yet she can barely stand the surgeon's and priest's sorry faces—the same expression she saw so many times as a child, when her mother told her guests how slow she was, how she herself had given up trying to understand.

The surgeon clears his throat. "Well, *Mesdemoiselles*." He pronounces every syllable slowly, carefully. "We shall certainly see you again."

Father Jean Richard studies her for another second, then salutes them with a nod.

Pétronille hears Geneviève call her name. She feels weary, irritated now; she wishes Geneviève wouldn't take her arm so hesitantly, that they wouldn't have to walk back to the between decks just yet. As they pass by the sailor kneeling under the mast, Pétronille gives him a quick nod. Tomorrow, same hour, back here.

• • •

Pétronille was thirteen when her father hired a new gardener. Paul was twice Pétronille's age. His hands were always dirty, earth caught in the creases of his palms. He had a small face, with a mouth so close to his nose that she wondered if his tongue could reach his nostrils. She asked; it could.

On the day they first met, Pétronille was walking back to the castle. She had been wandering for an hour, maybe two. She'd go on long walks on her own, bringing back fallen nests, dead insects, and closed buds that she'd pile in her rooms. Her "disappearances" threw her mother into a frenzy. That spring afternoon, she was carrying home a long rose stem. She was thinking of where she'd put it (on top of the dry lavender, behind the dressing table) when she heard a voice. "You know you killed all these flowers," it said. Her fingers almost got caught on the thorns as she turned around. The man was kneeling in the flower bed; he pointed at her stem. Pétronille didn't like strangers, especially when they tried to get close to her. But this one was still sitting when he said, "I'll show you." He cut a peony, his short black nail scratching against the baby-skinned bud. She was the one who moved closer as he kept on peeling, the fragile shell falling around the hunched petals. "See?" he asked. She saw. Yet he didn't ask for her stem. He didn't yell. As she climbed the front steps, Pétronille paused several times to glance over her shoulder; he had already gone back to work.

In the hallway, she scraped one of the roses she had picked. It was the last time she gathered flower buds. The following day, she didn't go on her walk. She sat next to Paul and watched as he trimmed the honeysuckle branches back into shape.

• • •

Pétronille can't return to the deck the following day. Nor the day after, nor on Sunday, when the cook's assistant hands out wine to celebrate the Lord's Day. The weather has changed, swinging the boat from right to left, left to right, waves slapping the hull like a hand on a hot cheek. On the second day, a cow breaks its leg and has to be put down. At night, Pétronille hears the rain fill the tarpaulin that the sailors set above the rowing boat; she hears the provisions and cargo bang against the pieces of wood that hold the ballast in place. She finally understands what the other women are going through—the exhausting nausea, the cramps, the cold sweats. But Pétronille isn't seasick. She is anxious. After their walk, Geneviève told her she'd seen her look at the sailor, that she should be careful, she cannot take any more risks. Geneviève then apologized for the words she'd told the surgeon and the priest. "But you keep to yourself so much, you talk so very little," she concluded, "that sometimes you might want to let your silence speak for you."

Pétronille doesn't want to do that on *La Baleine*. She wants to follow her instinct, which so rarely leads her toward other people. She isn't like her friend, who always carefully ponders every decision, every action. In Lorient, these qualities of Geneviève saved Pétronille. She has grown to trust her, but she doesn't want Geneviève to be right on this matter—if her friend is wrong about her silences, she might as well be wrong about the sailor. On the first day of calm weather, Pétronille pushes the hatch open; ship's boys are coming and going often enough that no one pays attention to her. The deck is crowded, a silver sun flashing in puddles, the shadow of the forecastle stretching over the hatch. For a second Pétronille hesitates. When she came up here with Geneviève, she could at least tell herself that the men's attention was divided. But now that she's reached the stern, she can't help feeling their gaze against her back, so different from the warmth she remembers from the first day. She tries to focus on what she knows. Right below, the girls are dipping cracked lips into small *chopines*. Sister Gertrude walks back and forth, bringing in more rye potage, lining up benches. Geneviève is probably looking for her.

"I wasn't sure you'd understand me."

Pétronille didn't hear him approaching. She can tell he doesn't mean it the way the others do. Her hands are back to her sleeves, pressing against the threads. Now that he stands next to her, she realizes that his nose is slightly bigger than she remembered. But the voice is the same, with the same gestures as last week only faster, until they become as meaningless as a word repeated too often. Pétronille laughs, more openly than she did in front of Officer Des Étaux and Father Jean Richard.

"I am not sure I do anymore," she says.

"I guess it doesn't matter much now," he answers. His hand holds the railing tightly. She is afraid it will move toward hers, but it doesn't. When he speaks again, his voice is hoarse, like someone who has just woken up. He asks for her name and tells her his, Baptiste Dubier.

"Mlle Béranger, where have all of your *compagnes* gone?"

"Nowhere. They are right there." Pétronille points at the deck, and they both look at their feet.

"And you seem to be doing just fine."

"I'm as surprised as you are."

"Is it your first time at sea?"

"Yes. What about you?"

She realizes how stupid her question is only after she's spoken. He smiles.

"Not by any means. But in a sense, you are right. It is the first time I'm traveling to La Louisiane." He pauses. "That much we have in common."

"Where else have you been?" she quickly asks.

"Farthest north and farthest east," he says. "Canada and China."

She remembers her father's atlas, how big and small the world had seemed, reduced to a couple of pages. She can't remember if these two countries rested under her right or left palm. "Was the ship you traveled on bigger than this one?"

He considers the question, then says, "They were a different kind."

"Did they carry women?"

She can't believe she asked. But he is laughing, shaking his head. "Women are bad luck on ships."

And men on earth, she thinks. "Why?"

Words come to her more easily now. He doesn't say anything about her face, doesn't compliment her eyes or hair. He talks about girls angering sea gods and sailors driven mad by mermaids. He tells her about men-of-war vessels, hot tar, and waterproofed hull, describes the translucent wings of flying fish, and promises she'll soon see one. He says that Sainte Barbe is the patroness of artillerymen and asks if she isn't afraid to sleep so close to powder casks. So that explains the name of the powder magazine. But she just shakes her head.

"The place I once lived in," she says, "was called La Salpêtrière because of the saltpeter they used to make."

"Then you must know more about cannon powder than I do."

Looking amused, he does most of the talking, and she likes it better. There is something oddly familiar and comforting in the way Baptiste speaks. His descriptions are meticulous and articulate; they remind Pétronille of the engravings that once hung above her bed, of the afternoons spent in the gardens of Château-Thierry with Paul. She focuses on Baptiste, who now yells something to a man calling from the top of the mizzen, then looks into her eyes and says he must go. She has no idea how long they have been here.

"Will you come back?" he asks.

She wants to say, If I can; she wants to tell him that the sisters might be more vigilant now that they have healed, to explain that if she does, Geneviève might not approve.

"Yes," she says.

• • •

If it weren't for Paul, Pétronille would have kept on killing flowers. She wouldn't have learned about limestone and color-changing hydrangeas, known the difference between silty and clayed soils, or that pine processionary caterpillars can eat dogs' tongues. She never would have grabbed a century-old herbal book in her father's library and read it so many times that she had to press her palm against the spine to keep the pages from flying away. She never would have walked through the French garden and guessed at everything happening under her soles.

Without Paul, she never would have had a friend. She wouldn't have found out how it feels to sit next to someone you know so well that silences don't hurt anymore. She never would have felt the need to speak first, telling him in hastened sentences about the types of plants she discovered in Guy La Brosse's *De la nature, vertu et utilité des plantes*. She'd never have discovered that people are hardly more difficult to read than dehydrated lavender, a blooming bougainvillea, or a vicious twitch-grass patch—that she too could understand them and be understood.

• • •

It does get harder to climb back on the deck. Healthy again, the nuns seem to be everywhere. Leaning mats against the hull, piling up stinky buckets, serving pea soup, cider, and, if the sailors have been lucky, grilled porpoise. After twenty-five days at sea, the girls pinch their nose before they sip the brownish fresh water. Their blankets never dry. Pétronille starts skipping the supper biscuits on the day Charlotte sticks her tongue out and Étiennette discovers maggots moving between *la petite*'s teeth. The following evening, the captain's second tells Geneviève that open fires, including lanterns like the one she holds, are forbidden. Pétronille blows the candle out herself.

She wonders how the others manage. She isn't sure how she would cope if Baptiste weren't here. When she tells him that, he passes his hand behind his neck several times. "I'm sure you would be doing just fine," he says. As he lets his arm fall, she can see goose bumps prickling above his wrist.

She meets him as often as she can. Twice, three times a week at best, any time they have a chance—she emptying chamber pots, he rolling seawater-filled casks in the hull for ballast. Once she spots him near the sailors' quarters, rubbing his feet with brown soap. She quickly turns away, her cheeks warmer than the time she entered without knocking at her mother's dressing room.

As she did with Paul in the gardens of Château-Thierry, Pétronille enjoys listening to Baptiste, learning words she had no idea existed— hawser, capstan, yardarm. He complains about boat captains, explains how hard it is to recruit sailors and how much harder it is to quit. They talk about *mimolette* and harvest mice, peacocks and cacao, scurvy re-opening old wounds. The ship ceases to be a mysterious place. She thinks of it as a three-story house, where she has settled on the second floor, the between decks. Under her feet: the cargo hold filled with crates and barrels, the carpenter stores and the infirmary. Above her head: the upper deck, the two raised decks and their blinding sea, the officers' and captain's quarters—then the sailors', which she likes to picture closer to where she sleeps.

Pétronille doesn't feel threatened or intimidated around him. Baptiste doesn't bring up her birthmark, doesn't reach for it, and, like Geneviève, he wouldn't ever call her *La Tachée*, as most girls whisper behind her.

He does none of the things that the man in Orléans did, the things she told herself she liked and then wished had never happened. She knows that when Baptiste cocks his head to the side, when his auburn hair falls in his eyes, he hears nothing but what she has to say. Paul too was a good listener. But around him, Pétronille never wished her hands were cleaner, her hair free of the lice she finds between her toes. In the rose garden, she never felt the bubbly warmth that fills her throat whenever Baptiste's chin rests right above her shoulder, and he points at an under-water shadow or a thumb-sized frigate, and she takes as long as she can to say, "Yes, I see it."

About a month after leaving Lorient, Pétronille is kneeling in the darkest spot of the between decks when Geneviève joins her. They aren't the only ones crouching, dipping bits of tow into the buckets full of rainwater, rubbing the itchy fabric between their thighs. Charlotte and Étiennette are here, sharing a bucket. The latter says hi to Geneviève, but *la petite*, whom Pétronille once heard sing with a voice that doesn't match her tiny body, ignores her. Geneviève brings her dresses up to her knees. Over the past couple of days, she has stopped asking questions about Baptiste.

"You ignored everything I told you," she says now.

In the dark, all Pétronille can make out is a silhouette. "No. I am listening to you," she answers.

She hears a sigh but can't be sure if it comes from Geneviève or from Étiennette and Charlotte, now walking away, their features flashing in the light of the portholes.

"You would tell me if he hurt you."

Pétronille starts. "He is different," she says. "He never would."

"But you would tell me?"

"Yes."

The rolling of the boat throws rainwater on Pétronille's feet.

"You amaze me," Geneviève says. "You never wonder why the nuns aren't trying to keep you from seeing him, do you?"

Of course the thought occurred to Pétronille. But she told herself that the nuns were busy; that three chaperones were never enough for ninety women; that sea routines had their own rules.

"I think I've understood why," Geneviève says. "Think about it:

wouldn't it be lovely if we could find our husbands now?" She pauses. "Husbands, I mean, who too would one day settle down in La Louisiane."

Pétronille shrugs; she's always hated rhetorical questions.

"Did he ever say anything on this matter?"

Pétronille considers her conversations with Baptiste. He never said anything about marriage, but he did mention sailors spending years at sea, endless contracts that no captain would ever break. She remembers him explaining that he would be traveling for another four years. That day she changed the topic; it was one of the first times they'd met on the deck, it hadn't seemed to apply to her. She feels stupid for thinking so.

"Why would you care?" she asks.

She feels the weight of Geneviève's back when it meets the wood.

"You need to be careful. You know as much as I do that babies have little to do with marriage. I'm not sure I would be able to repeat what I did in Lorient," Geneviève says. Pétronille takes a deep breath. She resents Geneviève for conjuring the man, the inn, the pain. "I am only trying to help," her friend adds.

"But I don't need help," Pétronille whispers.

For a moment all she can hear are pounding steps and the abyssal sound of the ocean. Then Geneviève stands up, knocking a bucket on the ground. Pétronille feels the water slide under her bum, quickly absorbed by her already damp skirts. When Geneviève speaks again, her voice is weary.

"Believe me. You might."

· · ·

At first her parents didn't say anything about her new routine in the garden. They couldn't: Pétronille had never been more talkative since she'd started spending time with Paul. She'd bring back bouquets to her parents, show her herbarium to her father. Little by little, her mother made an effort to keep her inside, trying to get her interested in table etiquette, rouge, and fox fur, in the newly sized corsets she'd just ordered for her. It didn't keep Pétronille from meeting with Paul. But when she'd go home, her mother would always sit her down in the boudoir. A lady shouldn't wander into the wild. A lady shouldn't spend so much time with a gardener. A lady should answer when she is spoken to.

It happened on the last day of July. At the castle, all the shutters were closed, the silk of the love seats hot under the hand, the maids gathered at the washhouse. Outside, it was the kind of afternoon when you can see the moon. Pétronille hadn't planned on meeting with Paul. She wanted to be alone, she wanted to go see if the anemones they had planted around the pond were surviving the heat. They were; the violet flowers leaned above the water and the golden fish chewed on their reflections. Pétronille dipped her feet and let the coolness spread up her calves. Then she flattened her cloak in the shade, lifted her dress up to her ankles so that her legs could dry.

Hours stretched like they do in summer. When she woke up, she tied daisies together, a collar first, soft-looking stems poking through delicate pollen, or maybe even a flower belt, just the right size to fit her waist, and with a few more, a leash for a fragile, docile pet she had yet to own. She finished the daisy chain in the shade, sitting in the woods that spread east of the pond. She was walking back when she spotted Paul kneeling close to the water. He jumped when she let herself fall next to him, and then he asked where she had been, said that he had been waiting to bring her home, and she didn't like the word he used, "bring," as if she were a child or an object, but then a shriek brought everything to a halt.

Her mother stood on the other side of the water, surrounded by two maids and the intendant. All of them stared. It took a moment for Pétronille to realize they were looking at her bare feet, at the cotton dress stopping short above her ankles, at Paul sitting next to her, too close, then abruptly standing up, stepping back. It took a moment for Pétronille to realize they were the ones being screamed at, accused of something she couldn't have fathomed.

• • •

When she goes looking for Baptiste, Pétronille isn't sure what she wants to ask him. She can't help but think about what Geneviève told her. She realizes she had never considered what would happen after *La*

Baleine. Her meetings with him had kept everything else unimportant. She wanted only the present, which was all she could trust.

She is walking toward the pantry when she runs into Sister Gertrude. The nun is so short that she has to raise her head to look at Pétronille. But in the middle of the tiny corridor, she seems huge, ready to punish her.

"There is no need to hurry, Mlle Béranger," she says. "Supper won't be ready for another hour."

Pétronille presses her palm against the wall, as she used to when they first boarded the boat. She is curiously aware of her weight against the wooden floor, of all the water sinking under them all.

"Mlle Menu isn't feeling well. I thought I might go ask for some lemon water," she says.

In the darkness of the corridor, the feeble light rebounds where it can—on the nun's cheekbones, her sea-sprayed forehead, the knuckles of the fingers she points at the ceiling. "Ships are smaller than they seem. They resemble convents that way."

Pétronille waits, motionless.

"There are three of us here," Sister Gertrude continues. "Sister Louise and Sister Bergère were just speaking today of the difficulties of finding some privacy on board, considering how overwhelmingly present the sailors are." The nun crosses her arms. "You should know that I'm not the only one giving orders."

Pétronille doesn't move, then gives her a minute nod.

"If Mlle Menu is feeling sick, you should probably go," the nun says.

"Yes."

Sister Gertrude's face doesn't soften. "We'll see you at supper, then."

Pétronille stares at the nun as she walks to the between decks. The boat is small. But only because Sister Gertrude doesn't know where to look. There are wide spaces no one but Pétronille will ever know— upstairs, on the deck, wherever Baptiste's finger points. Or even here, deep into *La Baleine*, in the food pantry where she finds him kneeling on the ground. He is closing a canvas bag, the kind cooks use to store fava beans. He seems startled when he sees her.

"What are you carrying?" she asks.

He looks down as if he weren't touching it a moment earlier. "They needed help with the supply."

Pétronille lets one of the cooks pass by. At the end of the corridor, the huge brick chimney, piercing the deck, throws a broth-scented smoke over the ocean.

"Did they really?" She is surprised to see him move in front of the bag, hiding it from her, when she comes nearer.

"You'll understand tomorrow," he says.

The thought, insidious, that Geneviève and the nun might be right about Baptiste—that he too might have something to hide, that he might not be the person he pretends to be. "What will I understand to-morrow?"

"Pétronille, please."

Baptiste has never called her anything but *mademoiselle* or Mlle Béranger. Her own name takes her breath away, like the one time she stepped into the pond as a kid, right before the water reached her belly button—except that this time, she is everything but cold. There had been that feeling too, with the innkeeper's son, but today she knows it won't vanish if Baptiste leans toward her.

"You won't tell me, then."

"You're not the only one who can be mysterious."

The only candle throws a glow on his right side—half of his hair turned coppery, a sleeve of his beige shirt the color of beeswax, every-thing else dark.

"You'll enjoy it," he adds. "I know you will."

He throws the bag over his shoulder, and Pétronille takes his hand. She didn't even bother to see if anyone is coming. It is different than in France; she is the one reaching out. In her palm, his fingers feel rough and warm. There is a faint pulse, but she can't tell if it comes from her thumb or his. He brings her closer to him and she gets startled, but not how she used to when she was a child and one of her mother's friends hugged her, when the arms surrounding her felt overwhelming, as if something inside her were about to break loose and she had to get away, then sit far from anyone else, waiting for the buzzing to recede.

It is overwhelming too when Baptiste finds her lips—cool and salty, like the seashell she once tasted with the tip of her tongue, then nothing like it. She doesn't feel the urge to leave, to step back. She lets him run his mouth against her neck, up to her ears, rest his hand flat against her corset right where her breasts meet her rib cage, and she must have been leaning against him because when he pushes back, it takes her a second to find her balance again.

"Coming right away," he is saying, but not to her, and she realizes there must be someone she hasn't heard, very close to them. She pictures Sister Gertrude, both too small and too big, peering into the pantry. She readjusts her dress, tries to breathe more slowly.

"Now are you going to tell me what is happening?" she whispers. He's grabbed the bag already, is ready to step into the corridor.

"Tomorrow is a big day," he says, and she can hear the smile in his voice. "But nobody spoiled the surprise when it was my turn. I swear you won't be disappointed." He pauses. "We'll see each other then."

Pétronille sits on the ground. She doesn't care if she gets caught. Closer to the casks, the smell of vinegar burns her throat. Her heart beats hard and fast. Right now everything seems possible. Baptiste's four-year contract might vanish. He could propose to her tomorrow. As long as she doesn't tell anyone, the clues—tomorrow, the bag, her name, their kisses—are hers to shape.

• • •

Her mother always told her she couldn't stay home because of what had happened with Paul. It didn't matter how many times Pétronille tried to prove her wrong, how many times she repeated that neither she nor Paul had done a thing. So Pétronille stopped trying. The world started to feel far again. She fell back into silence like you'd fall back into a bad habit.

It wasn't before she settled in her La Salpêtrière bedroom that Pétronille understood why she'd had to leave Château-Thierry. It was not because of what her mother thought she had done but because of everything her mother knew she'd never be.

• • •

The following day, the weather is crisp and the sky clear. The only visible clouds bubble far and dark above the horizon. Pétronille is disappointed. She isn't the only one allowed on the deck anymore. For the first time since they left Lorient, all the women have been summoned upstairs. But the orders didn't come from the nuns; it's the captain's second who pulled Sister Gertrude aside. "We'll gather on the deck after sext. Be ready," she said, sighing, when she came back in the between decks.

It's almost one now. Behind Charlotte and Étiennette, Pétronille can see only that they are heading toward the central mast. The atmosphere on the deck has changed—there are fewer sailors, and the only ones she spots wear surprisingly white shirts, as if they have been traveling for a week and not six. Around her, the women speak loudly, looking around for a bit of land, another boat, anything that isn't sea. Pétronille stops next to Charlotte when they reach the crowd gathered around the main mast. From the first row, Geneviève waves to them. Pétronille lets Étiennette answer for them both.

"Do you think they have an announcement to make?" *la petite* asks.

"Maybe," Pétronille says. She isn't interested in guessing why they are here. Baptiste's surprise isn't meant for her; if there is any, it will be something else altogether. She'll have to share. She thinks of their kiss in the pantry, of what he told her yesterday. She was stupid for thinking he'd propose. It hurts to see that he has no idea what she might enjoy—it hurts even more that he might believe he does.

Pétronille jumps when she feels sudden drops of rain. She brings her hand to her bonnet to keep herself dry. But her skin doesn't get wet because the drops roll solid and green, small dry peas that she crushes under her shoes as she moves around to avoid the ones that keep on falling. When they stop, Pétronille looks up.

At the top of the mast, a thin man is leaning over them, an empty canvas bag thrown over his shoulder. It takes Pétronille a few seconds to recognize Baptiste, who is jumping against the shrouds, descending with the slow, calculated movements she'd know anywhere as his. He's dressed up—no kerchief but gaiters up to his knees, tight postilion jacket, a long whip dangling below him, sometimes threatening to tangle his feet so that, for a moment, all Pétronille can think is: Please be careful. The women giggle and throw quick cries when the whip smacks the sky. Charlotte stares, then gladly joins in when some sailors start singing. Étiennette studies Baptiste with an amused smile. "He is quite elegant," she says.

"He is," Pétronille whispers. Now that he has reached the deck, she wishes they could be closer to the mast. She feels angry at herself. If she were still disappointed by the shared surprise, it'd be easy to stay where she is and tell Geneviève later, "I was in the back. I didn't even watch the show." Her friend would stop worrying for Pétronille, explaining, like she did again last night, that Baptiste would never give her what she wanted, that she shouldn't see him anymore. If Pétronille were still disappointed, she wouldn't have to tap on Étiennette's arm as she does now, pushing through the crowd until she reaches the first row and Geneviève steps aside to make room for her. Pétronille expects her to say something—"You shouldn't be here" or "How convenient"—but her friend says only, "I was wondering where you went."

Baptiste has his back turned to them. It doesn't matter to Pétronille. From here, she can see everything he sees—the letter in his hand, the tent set at the bottom of the mast, the captain's second walking toward him. He has become an actor, unreachable, and it makes her want to hold him tight. She feels her cheeks flush when he speaks.

"You've entered our kingdom." The officer takes the letter that Baptiste hands to him. Geneviève whispers that it's both ridiculous and endearing to see how seriously the men take the ceremony. "The Tropic King demands his tribute from all the passengers who have never set foot on this side of the Tropic of Cancer," Baptiste says.

It means her and all of them. The women around Pétronille seem amused but unsure what to expect. Geneviève says, "How silly," and then everyone is pointing behind the tent, at the captain who walks toward the ladder of the quarterdeck, wearing a wig made of tow and wool, his beard falling on the furs he is wrapped in. He is followed by a herd of shipboys, young Tritons surrounding a strangely feminine sailor, his cheeks bare, a corset hugging his flat chest. They parade all the way to the main mast.

Pétronille isn't the first one to receive the baptism of the Tropic King. In the tent, she has time to study the cross, the sailing maps, the drypoints thrown on the makeshift altar. She doesn't laugh like the other girls do as they stare at the captain's costume, even if she knows this is probably the only moment of joy everyone will share at sea. Pétronille doesn't need any festivities to be happy. Her attention is on Baptiste standing next to the exit. There is something unsettling and appeasing about his land-referenced outfit, one that looks and doesn't look like anything she's known in France, as if they had finally disembarked and he would never go back to sea. And for now, this is all she chooses to see—a brisk November afternoon, dry peas falling from the sky, *La Baleine* sailing through a made-up kingdom.

Charlotte

Charlotte sits by the railing, her dress dampened by the wood. She can't see Étiennette anywhere on the main deck, nor the made-up altar by which her friend should be standing, waiting with the other women to be baptized. When the ceremony started, they were together; then the girls rushed toward the tent of the Tropic King, and she lost her in the crowd. Charlotte rubs her wrists together, still wet from the holy water that the captain threw on her hands. A group of sailors passes by, laughing, patting each other's backs, and she presses herself harder against the railing. The men do not even glance at her. She tells herself not to be silly, that it'll be just a moment before Étiennette appears. She buries her hands under her elbows, feels her heart pulse against her palms.

When she followed the girls to the carts, not even six months ago, it was the first time she'd ever left La Salpêtrière; all she knew was La Crèche and La Maison Saint-Louis. Now, after well over a month on *La Baleine*, the sea salt stains stiffen her arms like dried sweat, and lice crawl in the nape of her neck. She hasn't been on her own since the ship left Lorient. Outside, alone, the upper deck seems huge, the ocean that surrounds them ravenous—herself, smaller than ever.

She leans forward when a group of women walks out of the tent, chuckling, their hair and dresses caught in the wind. But Étiennette isn't among them; the only familiar face is Geneviève's. Charlotte sits back. She muffles the tiny part of her that is tempted to wave, because right now Geneviève feels better than no one.

At the beginning of the journey, in the yard of the Parisian police station, when Charlotte first heard Geneviève's name, she felt like she had been slapped. She had remembered at once everything the supervisor of La Maison Saint-Louis had said about the prisoner at La Grande

Force, the abortionist the Superioress was fighting for. On the carts to Paimbœuf, Charlotte struggled to untangle her emotions—the fear and the odd respect she'd intuitively felt, the anger and sadness that soon replaced them. Charlotte couldn't help but notice Étiennette's fascination with Geneviève; she couldn't help but think about the Superioress's list, first choosing a criminal over her. Charlotte wondered what her own mother, the seamstress, this stranger, would have done if she had met a woman like Geneviève.

Her mother had abandoned her at La Salpêtrière. Ultimately, it was a different way not to have her.

"Why aren't you with everyone else?"

Étiennette stands in front of her, her face thinner than when they left, her blond hair so dirty it has turned brown. Charlotte breathes more freely; she stops picking at her nails, which she has started biting again on *La Baleine*. She takes Étiennette's hand, holds on to it, tight, until her friend lets go. "Where were you?" Charlotte asks.

Étiennette glances at the tent. She looks amused, just like she did when she reported the *sœurs officières'* complaints at La Salpêtrière. "This captain makes a poor actor," she says.

"It must be hard with this cold." Charlotte walks close to her friend. By the forecastle, sailors jostle one another in front of their quarters, rolling dice in their hands. They don't look as threatening as they did a moment ago. "The captain was shivering," Charlotte adds.

When she discovered that, for the girls, the ceremony entailed nothing more than kneeling in front of a made-up altar to be baptized, Charlotte was relieved. There would be no sitting over the tub filled with water, no promises made to the crew, no coins echoing on the plank. That was only for the seamen, the few who had never crossed the Tropic of Cancer.

Étiennette snorts. "Captains don't shiver," she says. "It is part of the celebration. He is a Tropic King, and it's November."

"I still like the coach driver best," Charlotte says. The man who jumped down the mast reminded her of the groom who once let her pet the horses in the Stables at La Salpêtrière. "Where did he go?"

"Find *La Tachée* and you'll know." Étiennette turns around to face the hatch. Charlotte doesn't follow her friend's gaze. If she spots *La Tachée*, she'll spot Geneviève too. Ever since Geneviève helped Pétronille in Lorient, the two of them have been inseparable. Thinking about those final days in France makes Charlotte uneasy. In Lorient, she couldn't help but empathize with Pétronille: Charlotte knew all too well what it felt like to risk being left behind. She wouldn't have wished that on anyone, not even Geneviève. Charlotte still hears Sister Gertrude saying that the women's past was none of her business—explaining that her mission was strictly to lead and protect the girls during their journey. The nun didn't care about Geneviève's life in Paris, any more than the Superioress had. On *La Baleine*, Charlotte keeps on trying to be like them; she tries practicing forgiveness just like she was taught by the Aunts, those in charge of the children at La Crèche. She finds it easier when it is just her and Étiennette.

"You know, this ceremony made me think about our journey," her friend is saying. They've come to a stop by the main mast, lining up behind the girls heading back to the between decks. Étiennette points her chin toward the tent that three ship's boys are already taking down. "It's odd, but because it marks the middle of our crossing, somehow it just made me aware that it's going to end."

Charlotte doesn't say anything. She isn't used to Étiennette speaking like this—in her friend's world, the worst never happens. At La Salpêtrière, her lightheartedness was an aura, one that kept her out of trouble: she'd always get away with an evasive answer, a false promise, a witty observation. Now Charlotte half expects her to laugh at herself, but when Étiennette resumes speaking, she looks serious. "I mean that we would one day arrive there."

There: they have agreed that if they don't pronounce its name, La Louisiane doesn't exist.

"Can you imagine if people were already living there," Charlotte says, "and we took their lands and they fought a war, won, and we had to go back?" They are walking down the ladder, and the sky above them shrinks until it disappears entirely. She giggles nervously. "What would we do?"

Étiennette ignores her. "And it occurs to me that this will be my last chance to find out about my sister."

The smell of food settles in Charlotte's throat, bitter. Since the beginning of the journey, Étiennette has barely talked about Marceline, her sister who was deported to the colony a year before them. At the Parisian inn, she questioned a few former residents from La Maison de Correction; most of them knew nothing about Marceline, and the ones who pretended to turned out to be liars. In Paris, Étiennette had stopped investigating her sister's whereabouts altogether; it had given Charlotte a break, a short one. Then Geneviève had stepped into their cart, and everything had changed. Charlotte once again found herself at the periphery of someone else's world, struggling not to fall off the edge.

"So I've come up with a new plan," Étiennette is saying.

"What do you mean?" Charlotte's eyes struggle to adjust to the dimness of the between decks. She makes out long tables, benches, smoking pots.

Étiennette answers, "I talked to Geneviève when we waited to be baptized."

Charlotte bites the inside of her mouth. That's what took her friend so long.

"She said it was impossible that not a single woman here crossed Marceline's path. Someone must have at some point. I was silly to stop investigating."

No, you weren't, Charlotte wants to say, and why can't I be enough for you? She thinks of her mother, of what Étiennette would have said had Charlotte ever tried to find her. She chases the thought; she suddenly fears her friend wouldn't have cared much. Étiennette is already pointing at one table close to the portholes. Girls are squeezing together to make space for Geneviève, and Pétronille holds her skirts, then throws her leg tentatively on the other side of the bench, next to Geneviève. Charlotte has a furious urge to scratch her skull, to gather the lice under her nails and scrape them out.

"Come," Étiennette says.

"There won't be enough room."

Étiennette slides an arm around her shoulders. Even in the between decks, Charlotte can see that her friend's cheeks are flushed—from the wind upstairs, from talking about Marceline. Charlotte feels Étiennette's fingers dig into her skin where the sleeve is held together by only two threads.

"Trust me. I'll get us our seat."

• • •

At home, at La Salpêtrière, there were four thousand people. None of them were related to Charlotte. At La Crèche, she often played around with her made-up family, attributing her features to one imagined member or the other. Sometimes she gave her gray eyes to her *papa* or her freckles to her *maman*. Occasionally she pictured a long series of flat-chested aunts and cousins, who, just like her, resembled children until they gave birth to their own. Charlotte enjoyed this game. It was like having a baby, guessing whose cheeks or ears it would inherit, but the other way around.

On the rare occasion when the Superioress came to visit the orphan-age, Charlotte paid close attention to the woman's features, searching her face for freckles. She'd tell herself the hair that escaped the old wom-an's headdress once was red. She waited, her heart fluttering in her chest, for the Superioress to look at her, which she always did. If Charlotte was very lucky, the director would smile and pat her shoulder—touch her cheek, even. When the other girls told Charlotte she was the Superior-ess's favorite, Charlotte didn't say anything. Not just her favorite, she wanted to answer them, I am her secret daughter. The idea ceased to comfort her once Charlotte realized it was pushing the other girls away, making her lonelier than any of the orphans at La Maison Saint-Louis. At five, she stopped believing the Superioress was family. A real mother would have told the other residents the truth; she would have saved Charlotte, brought her home with her.

Things changed when Étiennette arrived. Étiennette talked to Char-lotte when no one else would; she didn't care about the Superioress or what the other orphans thought. She had been loved by her sister—Marceline, ten years older and daring, vibrant, a woman who was said to have smuggled salt all over France, fallen in love at Versailles, done ev-erything for Étiennette after their parents' death. Étiennette didn't crave the *sœurs officières'* attention like the other girls did. At the orphanage, she seemed to need only Charlotte's company.

Last April, when the sister in charge gathered the candidates for La Louisiane, Charlotte sat in the corridor and peered into the dormitory. She held her breath when the Superioress asked one of the residents if she was willing to go to the Mississippi. Charlotte couldn't hear the answer. Her own throat felt tiny, narrow, a funnel. She pulled her knees closer to her chin and closed her eyes. It used to be her, chosen among many.

• • •

On *La Baleine,* Charlotte and Étiennette have a game. Étiennette came up with it the first time they were allowed on the deck, when she dug her nail between two wooden boards, retrieving a perfectly round pink seashell. She held it right under Charlotte's eyes so that, for a second, the periwinkle was entirely blurry and silver, then covered with bright dots as the shell came into focus. Étiennette placed it against her lobe and it became the first item of what Charlotte later called their *"trousseau de mer."* Over the past month, their sea trousseau has filled with everything but dresses and linen. Dried seaweed, half of a washed-out sea star, two oil-stained flasks, six small strings, a tobacco pouch made from a bird's throat; a corner of a torn-up sail that Charlotte once wrapped around her head, calling herself a pirate, until she remembered everything *La Tachée* told her about the British bandits after gold dust—the ships they burned, their vessels haunted by the devil, the sailors they hanged on deserted islands. She quickly untied the turban.

She prefers this game to the ones Étiennette invented at La Salpêtrière. Some of them were fun; others, less so. One winter morning when Charlotte was eight years old, she found herself crossing the Cour Lassay, holding a copper pan stolen from the Kitchens. Étiennette had dared her to tie it to the tail of the orange cat, the one that always slept on the windowsill of the blacksmith's shop. Étiennette had a way of pitching her dark blue eyes into yours, a look that reminded Charlotte of a needle piercing a clean linen cloth, a look that had convinced more than one *sœur officière* to let them have an extra slice of bread or play outside for just a few more minutes. Charlotte still feels her hands closing on the coarse hair when she tightened the string around the patchy tail. The cat barely meowed when she gave the knot a last pull. It stared at her with its glassy green eyes. When it tried to get up, its joints let out a cracking sound, like shoes on gravel. Charlotte watched it all: the pan pulling the tail, the cat's claws ripping the stones, the animal crashing onto the anvil under the window.

It never occurred to her that she could have said no to Étiennette and walked away.

. . .

It's been a week since the Tropic of Cancer ceremony. In the between decks, women whisper and doze, their snoring reminding Charlotte of purring cats. Some of them lean on the door of *La Sainte-Barbe*. A month ago, when *La Tachée* told them what was inside of the small room, Étiennette giggled. "Girls and gunpowder," she said. "Of course, you'd want to keep all the dangers together." Charlotte has always preferred sitting next to the portholes anyway. At least there is light here—oblique, faint, but light, now falling on Charlotte's latest find, a blue-gray feather. Étiennette is tying strings around it, placing it around her neck. "Do you mind?" she asks.

Charlotte shakes her head. The feather feels dead and dry in her hand. She has been gloomy ever since the ceremony. Twice Étiennette went to kneel next to Geneviève before bedtime. She suggested Charlotte come with her the first time; the second, she promised it would only take her a moment. Both times Étiennette returned with a secret smile that left Charlotte envious, frustrated. She doesn't want to feel threatened by Geneviève.

Charlotte suddenly hears yelling. She drops the makeshift necklace, listens as Étiennette kneels to pick up the feather. The man on deck isn't screaming from pain but repeating the same word—one word that she first mistakes for *tare*, flaw, flaw, and then understands as *terre*, land, land, land.

Upstairs, the deck is full. The concessioners gather on the raised deck at the prow, behind the captain and his officers. Charlotte follows the other women, tries to stand on tiptoe, but trips before she has a chance to glance above the crowd. She is about to tell Étiennette that she can't see anything, but when she turns around, her friend is all the way in the back, not far from the hatch. Charlotte calls, but Étiennette doesn't hear her. When she tries to wave, to head back, the crowd pushes her toward the sea.

"*Regardez*, right there!"

Charlotte stops struggling to look around. At first the strip of land seems out of place—its color, beige and hazy, unusual. She has grown used to shades of blue, forgotten how assertive and comforting warmer tones can be.

Women move toward the ladder of the forecastle, and Charlotte lets herself be carried left and right, right and left, up to the raised deck, until her hands land on the railing. When the women start disembarking, Étiennette will be able to join her. They'll walk down to the beach together. But when she turns around, she meets Geneviève's pale eyes instead, catches sight of the gap between her front teeth when Geneviève speaks her name.

"Charlotte. I haven't seen you in quite a while."

Charlotte stares ahead of her. The colors blur, like they do when you hold them too tight between your eyelashes. The feeling of unease she had grown used to, in the carts, resurfaces. Around Geneviève, she forever feels like she'll come second, like she might be let down at any moment. She has to stay on guard. "There are people on the beach," Charlotte says. She can't imagine stepping out of *La Baleine* with Geneviève.

"I'm not sure we've reached our destination yet. Don't you think the sisters would have warned us?"

"I don't see why."

"I'm afraid first impressions matter."

Geneviève shows her dirty gown, and Charlotte glances above her shoulder. On the upper deck, down the ladder, the mast cuts the crowd in two. Close to the railing, Étiennette is chatting with *La Tachée*.

"I meant to tell you," Geneviève says, following Charlotte's gaze, "Pétronille is very grateful for your discretion in Lorient." She pauses. "I am too."

"What are they talking about?"

"What do you mean?"

Geneviève looks at Charlotte's finger, pointed at *La Tachée* and Étiennette, still absorbed in conversation. She seems confused. "Oh, I just thought Pétronille might know something about Étiennette's sister. Pétronille was at La Salpêtrière for much longer than I was."

Charlotte wishes that she didn't want to cry so badly, that she'd been the one to suggest that Étiennette go talk to *La Tachée*, that no one knew anything about Marceline anyway. She turns away from Geneviève and faces the land—white beaches, bushy hills, and grain-sized figures. She wishes they have finally arrived, that she will soon leave this boat. Then she remembers what it means to disembark, and everything she'll lose when they do.

• • •

By the time Étiennette arrived at La Maison Saint-Louis, Charlotte didn't think of the Superioress as her secret mother anymore. Instead, she spoke of the piece of embroidery after which she had been named. To avoid explaining where the handkerchief was—lost, mistaken for something it wasn't, years ago—she told Étiennette about a dream she had. Charlotte called it a memory, though: the more she talked about it, the truer it felt.

In the dream, she is very young. The scene is silent; the weather, unbearably cold. Two women stand in the room. One wears the color-less dresses that Charlotte would later recognize as the clothing of the Aunts. The other has a bright yellow hat, a small bonnet with blue threads drawing complex shapes. In Charlotte's dream, the woman doesn't have a face. She doesn't have a voice either, although she must have sung to Charlotte, for some lullabies have a way to break her heart as no other songs do. The woman has only a distinct, overbearing smell that Charlotte breathes in when she is lifted up and pressed under the hat, deep in the woman's warm neck. Freshly made butter, week-old milk, wet flowers. And with the smell comes the feeling—something that says, You're safe, I'm here.

Years later, lying on the mattress they shared at La Maison Saint-

Louis, Étiennette brought Charlotte close to her. Charlotte's bed had been empty for a week then; the girl with whom she used to share it was gone. No one had told her where Catherine went, but Charlotte liked to imagine that a woman visited the dormitory one evening or early morning, when they were all sound asleep, and recognized Catherine for who she really was—a daughter, a sister, a niece; family bonds that were foreign to the children of La Maison Saint-Louis—and took her away, far from La Salpêtrière. Catherine had slept close to Charlotte only in the winter, when it was so cold they'd wake up with their teeth chattering, their jaws stiff. But the night was summery when Étiennette held her.

Charlotte was five, Étiennette nine. There was a warm neck to fall asleep against, butter at supper, or maybe flowers had been cut that day—tulips or mimosa, the ones she once smelled in the arms of a woman wearing an embroidered bonnet. Whatever it was, Charlotte wouldn't let anyone else drift away.

. . .

Geneviève had been right about the island—Sister Gertrude said they would stay in Saint-Domingue only a couple of days. As *La Baleine* gets closer to the shore, Charlotte can make out screaming, mooing, crying. She discovers how the land sounds once the water has stopped lapping against the boat's sides—then, once the wind retreats and the heat falls upon them, how it feels. It takes Charlotte a while to find her way through the crowd, to cross the upper deck and spot Étiennette on the aftercastle, sitting against the railing. She isn't sure where Geneviève disappeared to. She feels silly for reacting so strongly to her. In the tentative shade of the mast, Étiennette uses her bonnet to wipe the sweat from her temples.

Charlotte crouches next to her friend. She knows that by refusing to help, she's only getting further away from her, but now that she sees Étiennette's cross face, she isn't sure how to start.

"What happened?" she asks.

"Nothing."

Charlotte expected Étiennette to start rambling about what *La Tachée* told her as soon as she sat down. Étiennette never spared any details about Marceline, seemingly unaware of how painful every new line of her sister's story was to Charlotte. Now Charlotte discovers that it feels worse to be excluded, incapable of changing anyone's fate, let alone her own.

"What did she say?" Charlotte asks.

Étiennette looks sad, furious, or maybe disgusted. Charlotte can't tell, and it scares her.

"I told you already. She said nothing because she knew nothing, so nothing happened."

Étiennette sticks her face between the wood panels of the railing. When Charlotte imitates her, she feels paint flakes tickle her cheeks. Ahead of them, there are small huts, cocoons of dead leaves hanging on sharp-looking trees.

"I think you should ask Sister Gertrude," Charlotte says.

The sun beats against her head. She can feel Étiennette's knuckles brush against hers. "If someone can tell you anything, it has to be her," Charlotte continues. She turns as much as she can, meets Étiennette's eyes, which look alert again. "She knew about Geneviève. She knows about all of us."

"You're right." Étiennette laughs. "I don't know how I didn't think of that before," she says.

"It just occurred to me."

Étiennette pushes her chin farther so that she can almost fully face Charlotte through the rails. "Thank you," she says.

Charlotte leans farther too.

"Can you imagine if we were stuck like this?" Étiennette asks.

"A fish could get us."

"Or a giant bird." Étiennette smirks. "Not if I look at them like that."

Charlotte laughs. For a moment she stops wondering whether she should have suggested this. She sticks out her tongue. "Then we would have to stay here forever," she says.

"I'd find a way to set us free. Then we'd go see Sister Gertrude."

Charlotte tries to nod, but the wooden panels brush splinters against her cheeks.

· · ·

La Salpêtrière taught Charlotte how to embroider and sing. In the Sainte-Claire workshop, she worked on her canvas until her neck and arms hurt. She hoped her hands would remember better than her mind who her mother was. They never did. In embroidery class, Charlotte was clumsy, her ring finger never where it should be, her needle always falling off.

Things were different at mass. The other girls turned around to stare when she joined the chorus; the Aunts marveled at what they called a "lovely mezzo." Charlotte didn't know who was to thank for her voice. But when she sang, she didn't think of anything, of anyone. She came to think it was hers only.

Étiennette was neither a talented singer nor a good embroiderer. When she arrived at La Maison Saint-Louis, it was Charlotte who showed her how to cross-stitch, no matter how poorly. It was Charlotte who warned her not to wander too far from the orphanage. Not because it was forbidden—she herself had walked a few times all the way to the Kitchens, where the young cook would sometimes give her extra gruel. But when Charlotte crossed the yards of the hospital, she carefully chose her way. There were places at La Salpêtrière that were best avoided.

She told Étiennette she wouldn't like the *loges aux folles*, but that morning, her friend came to a stop only when they arrived under the walls of the Epileptic Women's Building. Heads shaved, female prisoners were huddled against each other; one woman had a white gash on her face, a line that bleached patches of her eyebrows as it stretched from her forehead to her chin. She was the one who called out to Étiennette, who made her reach for Charlotte.

But Charlotte stood too far to grab Étiennette's hand. She leaned against the Sainte-Laure Building and focused on the maids who threw fresh straw in the huts. She knew when not to look, and now Étiennette would too.

• • •

Étiennette says she'd stay downstairs, but Charlotte decides she'd still go on the deck with *La Tachée*, whom, she realizes, she'd rather call Pétronille. They have reached what is called the Sea of the Western

Indies, or what Pétronille's sailor refers to as the Caribbean Sea. Over the past couple of weeks, the water has turned so blue that it doesn't seem as deep as the Atlantic; you can see under the surface, the lean shapes that flutter and disappear, their name lingering on the tip of your tongue. Shark. When Charlotte asked Étiennette if they should maybe rename their *trousseau de mer*, her friend rolled her head on her stretched arms. Recently, she has been distracted but kind. "Whichever name you prefer," she said. "You choose."

For once Charlotte is eager to follow someone else. Around Pétronille, she doesn't feel vulnerable or threatened. Pétronille never tried to take her place; she knows how to navigate the boat better than any of the other girls. Her self-assured step is endearing. "Careful," she says when they go up the ladder and Charlotte's foot slides on bird droppings. "Here." She tightens her grip on the ramp, and Charlotte follows. "It's easier."

Charlotte knows their excursion is only an excuse to find Pétronille's sailor, but it's such a relief to reach the upper deck, the sky and sea, its stretches of white sand that come crumbling to the surface. Today the warm wind leaves her hair alone. Pétronille gave her a pin to tie it up before they climbed on deck. When Charlotte returns downstairs, she'll add it to the *trousseau de mer*.

There is another boat close to them, just like in Saint-Domingue. Charlotte glances at the merchants, who are bringing casks of wine and vegetables aboard; they appear no different from the ones who sold them supplies on the island. Looking at them from the forecastle, two girls giggle. Charlotte recognizes Thérèse from the blue flowers she sewed on her bonnet. She doesn't know the name of Thérèse's friend, but she remembers Étiennette whispering that the woman had been given an orange just because she was losing some hair. Later that day, Charlotte saw what Étiennette hadn't—the girl's hurt gum, blood drawing thick triangles between her teeth. She shuddered. Before they stopped by Saint-Domingue, two other women had showed similar wounds. They haven't been brought back from the infirmary; the nuns will say only that the surgeon is doing everything he can for them.

On the raised deck, Thérèse's friend seems to be doing better. Charlotte has never talked to either of them. But she can tell the two girls are as relieved as she is to be outside. Recently, women have been able to go up more often—after more than two months at sea, it has become harder for the nuns to stop them from strolling for a few minutes.

She points at an islet, smaller than *La Baleine*. "Do you think people live there?" she asks.

Pétronille shakes her head. "An archipelago's waters are not deep enough to disembark," she answers, and Charlotte wishes she too knew a sailor who could explain everything she doesn't understand about their journey. Pétronille stares at the sea. "Doesn't this island's shape remind you of the Granary?" she asks. "You know, this stretch of sand, doesn't it look just like the south wing of the building?"

Charlotte laughs and realizes that at La Salpêtrière, she and Pétronille lived only two buildings apart. Yet if not for their decision to leave, they would never have met.

"No, it's more like a square, similar to L'Ange-Gardien," she says. "What about that one?"

A rope falls to the ground. A tall man crosses the deck, walking toward the group of merchants. The sun bounces off his silver watch, and the blinding light forces Charlotte to look away. Pétronille spots the Sainte-Thérèse Building, then says no, it really has the shape of a palm tree, with its roots digging into the bottom of the ocean, and Charlotte can't help but wonder what would happen if the roots broke, how the islands would start floating, drifting away. She turns around, unsettled by the image. She pictures herself alone, separated from the other girls, and the idea fills her with dread.

"What about that one?"

The captain keeps on talking to the man with the silver watch. His voice is low, insistent. The other merchants suddenly seem to be everywhere on the deck, but Charlotte doesn't pay attention to them. She has caught sight of Étiennette, standing at the top of the hatch, deep in conversation with Sister Gertrude. The sun blurs their features, flattens their expressions. Charlotte freezes, staring intently as if she could read their lips, but is shocked out of it when a sound pierces the air. The moment lingers: ivory horses gallop on the pistol's handle.

Before it raises again, Charlotte has time to look at the armed man, whom she hadn't spotted before. His nose is arched, and he wears beads in his beard. To his right, the merchant with the silver watch presses his gun against the captain's chest.

There are more men of his kind, spread evenly between the masts, up on the forecastle and quarterdeck, in what appear to be strategic positions—blocking the entrance to the sailors' quarters, one man in front of each of *La Baleine*'s small cannons.

Before sea and sky start spiraling around her, a thought flashes in Charlotte's mind. She hears Pétronille telling her what Baptiste said about pirates and their blindfolds: how they use them to keep one of their eyes always used to darkness, to walking into the black depth of a ship's hold and taking what they want.

Charlotte feels for her friend's hand. But her fingers close on a wrist that is already sliding away, and she bumps into a sailor whose ear is bloody, flapping, gone, her own face falling against the deck, prickled by splinters. A spent bullet rolls ahead of her, under the rowing boat, out of sight. She follows it, crawling on the floor as quickly as she can, steps echoing in her hands. Someone screams to stay put, and she resists the urge to lift her head and make sure that nothing, no one, is coming for her. She throws herself forward, under the rowing boat's shadow, then its hull, her head hitting the wood, the keel scratching her dress as if to tear it open. She finds a spot between the cradle's boards. Everything smells like lichen, whiskey, wet wood. From here, she can see calves and feet, faces even, if she presses her cheek hard enough against the ground. She knows it means that if someone were to kneel, they could spot her. Her thighs feel warm, glued together. She tries steadying her breath, situating herself. She pictures the upper deck from above: the forecastle and sailors' quarters to her left, the quarterdeck and the stern to her right. In between, by the main mast, the hatch. Then, parallel to the railing, the rowing boat. Herself, lying underneath.

She sees clearly what she should have done: climb inside the boat, untie the knots of the tarpaulin, and zip up the sky above her. She jumps at the sound of another gunshot, so close this time that she brings her hands to her ears, winces at a sharp pain in one of her fingers. The nail is cut in half and her knuckle feels liquid, hot. Then the smell of gunpowder is sneaking under the hull and Charlotte is pushing herself farther away from the open deck, as close as she can to the railing. Her good hand stumbles upon something metallic and wet. Not Pétronille's pin, as she first thinks, but the bullet that led her to this poor shelter. When she grabs it, she can't be sure whose blood stains it—hers or a sailor's.

• • •

On the upper deck, the firing stops and silence falls. Charlotte's breath feels deafening under the rowing boat. She is painfully aware of the sounds of everything that runs, flutters, beats inside of her body. Blood, spit, and heart: how much she wants to shut them down, how much she wants to keep them going. She tries thinking of a song, something sooth- ing and familiar, but can't come up with anything. Even inside her head, song means sound, which now means death. Her broken nail meets a puddle of water and the salt bites the wound—and that too seems like it should make a noise. The pin Pétronille gave her has fallen from her hair and pinches her chest. She hears approaching steps. She makes herself as tiny as she can, like the babies did at La Maison Saint-Louis when they slept on their side, their hands curled like pincers. Charlotte thinks of Étiennette, who must be safe, who, she hopes, went down the ladder in time.

The shadows recede. The steps fade away. Charlotte counts until one hundred, staring at the sun on the deck, afraid it'll turn dark again if she stops, cheats, goes straight from *cinquante-quatre* to *soixante*. Then, cau- tiously, moving only her head, she leans her cheek against the floor. She guesses blue skies. Under the main mast, men whom she recognizes as *La Baleine* sailors are being pushed by the pirates toward the forecastle, to their quarters. One of the bandits teases a ship's boy with the point of his sword. She hears them rushing past the rowing boat, their cries muf- fled as they walk into their dormitory. A sailor trips, swears, a blow lands on someone. The door of the crew's quarters lets out a banging noise and she turns on her stomach, looking toward the rowing boat's bow, in time to see one of the pirates locking it. She realizes: Without the sailors to fight back, we are lost.

Then a man's legs appear. He stands so close that Charlotte finds her- self staring into the eyes of a whale splashing water, the tattoo caught between ankle bone and leather shoes. Her hands are so sweaty that they feel slimy. He speaks in a language she doesn't understand. He sounds enthusiastic. Then his feet vanish, replaced, farther away, by the bottom of dresses that Charlotte knows all too well. She remembers Thérèse and her friend laughing on the raised deck, how far away they'd strolled from the open hatch.

As the women start to scream, her eyes close shut. She tries moving her tongue, but it feels swollen, too big for her mouth. Her teeth taste like blood. There are more steps, more yelling, and Charlotte wants nothing more than to make them stop. She resists the urge to dig her fingers into her ears. She needs to listen as carefully as she can; if she does, she'll recognize Étiennette's voice. Her shriek when a maid let a kettle fall in the Kitchens and two drops of boiling oil scarred her wrist. Or her gasp, months ago, the morning she woke up to a farm dog licking the sweat on her calves.

Charlotte doesn't know when it will come to an end. She counts to three hundred once the last man is done. When the girls stop crying, she isn't sure if their silence feels better or worse. A few steps away, something rolls on the deck. The pirate with the tattoo asks a question in his odd language. The captain of La Baleine answers non, then something else. There is a loud thud and he too falls silent.

She opens her eyes only because she knows what will happen next, what is already happening: boots, ten pairs at least, all heading toward the hatch. Her last hope vanishes that Étiennette, Pétronille, and Geneviève might remain safe. This time it wouldn't be two women but ninety, this community of girls whose company she'll one day come to miss. Their screams would rise under her, as if they came from her own chest. She imagines being next. She lays her palm on the floor and feels Pétronille's pin under her hand.

Charlotte raises her head toward the sailors' quarters. The door is locked, but the two men who were guarding it abandoned their post, probably assuming there would be more to gain if they reached the between decks first. Charlotte knows she doesn't have much time. Her heart pounds everywhere at once. She is terrified at the idea of what she must do. She sees herself last May, sneaking in the narrow alley that led to the Superioress's Garden, her hand closing on the gate handle. Back then Charlotte couldn't remember ever feeling so afraid—afraid of not being heard, of failing to convince the director to add her name to the list. Yet none of that happened; now here she is. She crawls toward the rowing boat's bow.

Only a few steps separate her from the door of the sailors' quarters. The sun feels abrasive, ready to melt her to the ground, but when she glances at the deck, she sees only backs. The men—pirates mostly, but a few officers from *La Baleine* too, tied and wounded, closely watched—are all looking toward the between decks. At the sight of the bodies behind the mast, their shirts drenched in blood, Charlotte feels nauseated. She catches herself; two bandits are already pulling the hatch knobs.

She plunges forward. She pictures herself as one of the fish she saw with Étiennette in Lorient Harbor—agile, gone before you knew it. In her closed fist, the pin digs into her palm. Then she is in the shadow of the forecastle, facing the door.

She expects screaming, arms pulling her back, reaching for her dress like they did with Thérèse's and her friend's. Nothing happens. The lock feels cold and hard under her hand. Her fingers shake so much that she has to give it three tries before she manages to push the pin under the doorknob. She presses harder, feels something resisting and loosening, resisting again.

Then there is a heavy thud—the hatch of the women's quarters opening, a sound she is used to greeting with relief when, after days of bad weather, light is finally released into the between decks. She turns around, immediately hating herself for doing so, for wasting time, for becoming part of the frozen painting that the deck has turned into because, under the open hatch, at the top of the ladder, is Sister Gertrude holding a pistol pointed at the men.

At first Charlotte thinks that someone is crying. But as the clamor grows, she understands that the pirates, staring at the armed nun, are laughing—frantic, incredulous, irrepressible laughs. Laughs that say: Woman, did you ever believe you'd be a threat to us? Charlotte pushes harder against the lock. She hears Sister Gertrude's cry.

There is a ticking sound. She almost falls in when the door props open. On the other side, a sailor, two sailors, many more in the dormitory, stare at her. The whites of their eyes flash pale in the dark; one of them has a scar that runs under his chin. Then she is pulled inside, struck against the wall, as the men rush out onto the deck. A ship's boy leads her to a bunk, and she runs her tongue on her lips, tastes tears and mucus. He tells her to wait here, considers the pin in her palm. "*Merci,*" he quickly says before running back to the door. On the upper deck, there are firing sounds, yelling, the unstoppable unwrapping of sails. The water behind it all sneaks into every silence.

She is left alone between mattresses, chamber pots, and greasy clothes. She blows her nose into a shirt that reeks so strongly of tobacco that it makes her sneeze. She curls up in a corner. She tells herself that she is crouching in yet another dorm, at La Salpêtrière, watching from the threshold, ready to whisper to herself, Let's go, the road is clear.

• • •

The between decks hisses with whispering. Although the pirates are gone, the air remains thick with fear—an acrid smell that leeches into Charlotte's throat when Sister Gertrude helps her down the ladder. Étiennette is the one who runs to her. At first Charlotte isn't sure if her friend means to slap her or hug her. Then she asks, "Are you all right?" in a tiny, urgent voice. When Charlotte doesn't answer, Étiennette puts an arm around her shoulders, gently, and leads them next to one of the farthest portholes. She seems about to say something, then closes her mouth and starts massaging Charlotte's hand instead.

"I could bring our mat here," she offers.

Charlotte stares at the dusk in the sea. Her knuckles are getting sore from the rubbing, but she doesn't ask her friend to stop.

"You could."

And so they lie next to each other, listening to the water. Étiennette points at Charlotte's wounded nail.

"Pétronille might know how to help with this."

"Where is she? How is she?"

"Over there, by *La Sainte-Barbe*. She made it back right before Sister Bergère shut the hatch."

Charlotte feels again her hand closing on air, Pétronille gone, the panic rising in her chest. She tries to inhale deeply. Pétronille is safe; so is she. She forces her head up, looks where Étiennette is looking. There is Pétronille and, behind her, Thérèse and her friend. They are huddled together on a mattress, taking the blankets, the food handed to them. Thérèse's flowery bonnet is gone. Charlotte lowers her gaze.

"What happened?" Étiennette says.

Charlotte remains silent. She can't go back. "Did you learn anything?" she asks.

"What do you mean?"

"I saw you talking to Sister Gertrude. Before they arrived." Charlotte rests her cheek against her arm. For once it's a relief to talk about Marceline. Étiennette shakes her head as if to say no or it doesn't matter. Both. She seems immensely sad when she says: "Even if I knew anything about your sister, how would this matter now?"

It takes Charlotte a second to understand that her friend is quoting the nun's words. Étiennette's lips shiver. There is something hollow about her face which wasn't there before. Charlotte reaches for her hand and gives it a soft squeeze. "I'm sorry," she says. She means it. The nun's answer doesn't bring the relief she expected. It tells her: Everything you left behind is forever gone. Charlotte knew that already.

Somewhere underneath her, the cats scream at each other. She moves her fingers and finds them equally numb, her body weighing heavily against the mattress—with a bit more pressure, she feels she could almost join the cats in the cargo hold. She opens her eyes when Étiennette says, "Sister Gertrude says we owe you."

"What?" she asks. Pride stings her. At La Salpêtrière, this feeling had been forbidden, a sin. "She had a pistol."

"That wouldn't have changed anything. Without you . . ." Étiennette's voice trails off, shy all of a sudden, and Charlotte doesn't identify with the girl who stepped out of the safety of the rowing boat, who opened the door of the sailors' quarters.

"Where did Sister Gertrude find the gun?" she asks.

"I heard that one of the police officers gave it to her before we boarded. But Pétronille swears she saw her walk into the armory shortly after we stopped in Saint-Domingue." She shrugs. "I'm not sure."

"And she stood on her own at the top of the hatch?"

"Yes."

"She is courageous."

"So are you."

Charlotte lies on her side, listening to the water. She closes her eyes. Relief leaves her weak, stunned. *Courageuse*. She repeats the word to herself. It soothes her. *Courageuse, courageuse*. Somehow it feels wrong too. She wonders what Étiennette would have done up there, and whether you can be courageous when you don't have a choice. Now that she thinks about it, she sees that she did have one—wait for them to find her like they found Thérèse and her friend, or jump and give it a try.

Even if it isn't courage, it is something that kept her alive. She hadn't needed anyone to tell her what to do. Charlotte thinks about the Superioress; she wishes she could tell her she made the right decision—then hopes that somehow the woman knows it already. She listens to her own breath, a splash in the water, then Geneviève's voice, asking how she is doing. A smell of boiled vegetables spreads in the between decks. Behind her, hidden in the hold, a mouse scratches the wood. "*Oui*," she says. "*Tout va bien*."

She doesn't know if they hear her. She feels herself sink and drift, a solitary water-lily island, like each of the girls will become once they reach La Louisiane.

PART II

Terre, terre! The women hear the word above the wood cracking, the crew yelling, and the water rushing. This time there is no mistaking it for any other. Some girls want to scream along. They fear land might disappear if the sailor stops calling, and it feels wrong that a continent could seem so fragile. So small too, a mere layer of sand floating on the surface. The women stare in disbelief: they traveled all this way to disembark on a desert island.

The wind is charged with water, and they momentarily breathe in the sea instead of air. As soon as their feet meet the ground, the whole world starts spinning around them, and they hold on to each other, hands clasped on their dresses—at least their gowns aren't wet yet; at least they don't have to jump into the water, as they soon will. For now they are trying to regain their balance. They squint as the furious gales batter their faces, glance at the shrubs folded by the storms, the crabs crawling in the tide pools. What they ignore, what only the sand knows, is that they aren't the first French girls to disembark here: a year ago, after months of travel, two groups of prisoners from La Salpêtrière were abandoned on Ship Island, with not enough food and clothing, left to fend for themselves before they were finally taken to the mainland. Their steps have long since been erased, and yet some of the girls of *La Baleine* shudder—this place is no less haunted than their Parisian dormitories.

Then they spot a party of gaunt men and, behind them, narrow boats. The nuns don't bother telling the women the journey isn't quite over. Soon those sailors, those canoes, will bring them to the continent.

It takes hours of navigation before the women catch a first glimpse of their new home. When they do, they fall silent. La Louisiane doesn't look like much from the pirogues. Still and flat, like everything that is far—movement wiped out by the distance, trees as blurry as a child's drawing. They stare as if studying the face of a stranger. They imagined this moment so many times that it feels almost wrong to live it. What is there to look forward to, now that they've crossed the Atlantic?

Geneviève

Geneviève crouches by the creek with the other girls. She lowers her bucket of laundry into the stream, gasps when her hands meet the freezing water, full of plants and insects whose names she ignores, like so many things she sees and hears in La Louisiane. The opaque dawn resembles the one she woke up to yesterday, and the day before, and every morning of the past month and a half she has spent in the colony—feeling the wind sneak between the disjointed logs of the warehouse's ceiling, listening to swamp rodents sprint through the grass. She grew used to the noises. She had to.

On this side of the Atlantic, she hates how foreign everything feels: the feathered trees, the red mud, the soil as soft as mold. She's craving simple, familiar pleasures. A thick soup on a humid day, the first tepid sunbeams hitting the bushes, and, as the icy current numbs her skin and mind, the relative warmth of the straw mattress she shares with Pétronille. Then her first bucket is full, her fingers pruney, and her mind clears. This morning is different. Half an hour ago, when they were awakened for mass, Pétronille kicked the rough linen sheets off with an energy that Geneviève hasn't seen from her in weeks. Today is her friend's last chance to see Baptiste.

Geneviève lifts the second bucket and reaches for her yoke. The sound of the stream, which runs where the damp yard meets the pine forest, seems to be coming from everywhere at once. Behind her, the windowless warehouse rises. At this hour, light barely sneaks through the door, illuminating the first of the forty-five straw mattresses that fill the room where the nuns locked them in since their arrival in La Louisiane. Because of last night's bad weather, the logs swelled with water, and the smell of rain will linger in the warehouse for days. Just a moment ago, Pétronille was gathering dirty clothes, clumsy with anxiety. Geneviève knows there is no time to lose. Soon all of them will be married, like Étiennette was in early February, a month ago—soon they will all have to follow their husbands to New Biloxi, where people keep on dying.

Tomorrow Geneviève will become Pierre Durand's wife, and once she does, she won't be able to help Pétronille anymore. Geneviève's Canadian suitor has come to see her twice. She wasn't expecting him to propose, but he did, with words that struck her as strange, almost comical. The nuns gave their approval at once. But since then Pétronille and her obsession with Baptiste, and then the disease, have kept Geneviève's mind off M. Durand.

Nearby is the hut that was built when the first women fell sick. The illness is different from the one that claimed two girls on *La Baleine*. It turns your face and eyes yellow. It makes you vomit black bile. It locks your knees and back and bakes sunlight into poison. In New Biloxi, so many people passed away last month, weddings had to be postponed. The women waited at the warehouse. Priests were too busy anointing the dying.

Geneviève waits for the water to balance itself on her shoulders. Laundry day was her idea. Laundry is Paris and Paris is Amélie. When she grabbed the washing bat this morning, Geneviève almost saw *La Sirène*, heard the washerwomen calling one another. If she'd turned her head, she could have seen the Seine, running high. The stream of the backyard is as cold as the river, but Amélie isn't here to tell her to shove her hand in her own dress, between her breast and arm, where the skin is tender and warm.

By the warehouse door, Geneviève spots Pétronille heading toward the cauldrons. The hope that Baptiste might be in New Biloxi, waiting with *La Baleine*'s crew for the ship to return to Lorient, is the only thing that has stirred life in Pétronille since they arrived here—the belief that her lover isn't irremediably gone, that, even if they couldn't get married, they would meet again. Two weeks ago, when Pétronille overheard the nuns saying that *La Baleine* sailors were lodging less than a league away, that they weren't out of reach, Geneviève wanted to believe her friend.

She knows what it feels like to say goodbye to someone you love; she never wants to find herself walking down Madame's staircase in Paris after having to leave Amélie. Now, as the yoke pulls her head down and ahead, as water splashes from the buckets, she realizes Pétronille's hope to be reunited with Baptiste belongs to her too—a sign that maybe La Louisiane, despite all the marrying and the locking up, might offer them more than France ever did.

Geneviève avoids an anthill teeming with red insects, moves toward Charlotte's cauldron. Since Étiennette was the first bride to get married, Charlotte's sadness has softened her. Rumors had it that Étiennette's husband was to take his bride to another settlement, farther north, by the Yazoo River. It seemed like Charlotte might never see Étiennette again, no more than Étiennette would ever find her sister, Marceline, in these vast lands of the colony.

In the cauldron, the shifts spiral like big white fish. What remains of the clothes that were packed in their bundles dips, floats, and drips in the rosy dawn. Geneviève empties the buckets in the boiling water. Charlotte glances at her briefly. The flames drown her freckles in an orangey glow. She stirs the stained clothes without looking at them. The plan that they have concocted for Pétronille is so simple it feels infallible: Baptiste, warned by a note given to him in New Biloxi last week by the doctor's assistant, is to meet her by the main gate of the warehouse while Geneviève distracts the nuns with Charlotte's help.

Beyond the moving bonnets, Geneviève can see Pétronille bringing more clothes outside. She is swaying from the weight of the gowns; her dark hair turns violet under the first sunlight. She is thinner; you don't need to know her to notice she is anxious. Geneviève takes the pile of soiled shifts from her. "It is time," she says. She tries to keep her voice steady. "You should go now."

Pétronille's eyes and forehead shine. She buries her trembling hands in her elbows.

"Is everything all right?" Geneviève asks.

Pétronille starts. She glances toward the alley that leads to the front yard. There, wild honeysuckle swallows the meager wooden posts meant to separate the warehouse's garden from the woods—a ridiculous attempt: the vegetation is so thick that bushes are already reconquering land.

"Yes," she says. She clasps her hands together. "I'm fine."

Then, before Geneviève has time to say anything, Pétronille turns around, trudges forward, her clogs sinking in the damp weeds. She isn't carrying anything anymore, and yet her steps are uncertain. Geneviève wishes her friend could wait for her nerves to calm down. But there is no time for that. Geneviève needs to do her part or the nuns will stop Pétronille. By the creek, Sister Gertrude watches over the girls kneeling by the water; Sister Louise stands close to the taut rope that will welcome the clean gowns.

This is it. Geneviève lets the first shift hover over the cauldron, and her fingers touch Charlotte's. They look at each other. Then Geneviève lowers her hand, brings it closer to the burning wood. Blood comes back rushing into her fingers. She drops the shift, the fabric touches the flames, collapses among them, except that it brings down another petticoat, then a corset, the clothes missing the copper one by one and sliding into the fire. Genevieve lunges forward to stop it from spreading, but the flames, bigger than she ever wanted them, are blowing down the line, larger and larger, toward a brunette standing a few feet away. The fire reaches her, licking around her arms, and she screams even louder than Jeanne and Thérèse on *La Baleine,* then runs in the opposite direction. Suddenly girls are hurrying to her with buckets of water, clothes dropped on the grass.

Charlotte watches motionless, her eyes wide. Her fingers clench the stirring stick. "What did—" she starts.

Geneviève cuts her off. "Everything is fine," she says, but her own voice shakes. The flames are already turning into smoke, receding. Women surround the burned girl, making it impossible to see how hurt she is. Before long, one of the nuns might go fetch the doctor in town, and if they do, they'll stumble upon Pétronille and Baptiste at the gate. The sun rises, pink and yellow. Geneviève runs through the grass, crosses the garden, follows the wall of honeysuckle.

When she reaches the end of the alley, the front yard is empty. She rushes to the fence, presses her hand against the main gate, shakes it. Locked. She tastes bile in her throat. She registers a white spot in the corner of her left eye, kneels by the wheelbarrow. There, in a nettle patch, is Pétronille's bonnet.

Her friend is lying on the ground, hidden by haystacks. The sun sneaks between the cedars' branches, smashing long shadows on the moist grass, on Pétronille. A huge beetle crawls up her wrist; flies are caught in her muddy hair. She breathes deeply, like a soundly sleeping child, like she meant to come rest here all along. When Geneviève touches her forehead, her palm comes back hot and damp.

Before running to the nuns, Geneviève glances beyond the main gate. The road, wet from last night's rain, stretches between the trees. Birds and squirrels have left fresh prints in the mud. Geneviève's eyes reach the sharp bend where the path disappears into the cypress woods. There are no footsteps in the dirt, no sign of a cart. Baptiste was never here.

• • •

The evening of the incident, when Geneviève and Charlotte are allowed back in the dormitory, Pétronille has already been taken to the sick girls' hut. Sister Bergère was firm: Mlle Béranger needed rest. In the dormitory, no one cares about her. The women only talk about the brunette, whose dress had been too wet from the kneeling by the creek to catch on fire. Her burns aren't severe. Still, Geneviève and Charlotte would be punished for their carelessness, their clumsiness. They fasted, repeated the assigned Ave Maria, but the nuns broke their solitary confinement after only a few hours. Not out of kindness. Fire or not, Geneviève and Charlotte are brides. There is no need to tell their two suitors about the incident. They will still be married tomorrow.

Geneviève's last night in the windowless warehouse is pitch-black, just like *La Baleine*'s hold used to be after sunset. On the ship, sitting by the portholes, she'd watch the moon turn into this enormous pale glow—a lighthouse, announcing a port that didn't exist. Then it'd disappear, return the sea and the sky to darkness. In the between decks, Geneviève struggled with the panic that rose in her chest.

Tonight she is calm, alert. She waits until she doesn't hear the guard's steps anymore. She pats her dress to make sure the dried peas are there.

She collected them from a canvas bag this afternoon, packed them in a piece of fabric—dirty, yellow, manly, something she imagined could lie at the bottom of Baptiste's pocket, a reminder of the day they crossed the Tropic of Cancer.

Now Geneviève wonders what the nuns will do with the dried peas once they find them between Pétronille's fingers. Throw them away? Cook them? Or will they be too busy trying to make Pétronille's fever recede to pay attention to anything else? But Geneviève won't leave her friend without giving her something to hold on to—won't leave her unarmed to face her losses when she comes back to herself.

She walks past the door in the backyard, where the smell of urine pierces the air. Sometimes it feels like the walls of La Grande Force followed her over the ocean; like they could catch her here as they did in Paris. The chamber pots are lined up next to the alley, as far as possible from the sky-opened room where the nuns lead the men, every afternoon except Sunday, since mid-January.

There is a shadow squatting, and Geneviève recognizes Charlotte before she rises. She can't quite reconcile this child with the bravery shown on *La Baleine*. Her fearlessness gives Geneviève hope, makes her wonder what each of the women is capable of in La Louisiane. Yet she also sees the price of Charlotte's courage. On the day *La Baleine* reached Ship Island, Charlotte stubbornly sat on her mat, surrounded by what was left of her "*trousseau de mer.*" She had been forbidden to take anything from the boat, but Sister Gertrude eventually gave in. "The pin," the nun said, sighing. "Nothing else."

Tomorrow, on the first day of March, Geneviève will walk with her to the church. Charlotte keeps forgetting the name of her future husband.

Charlotte turns toward the sick hut, where Geneviève is headed. "Don't go there," she says.

Geneviève considers reminding her that if it were Étiennette ill, she wouldn't think twice about it. But Étiennette has been gone for weeks, and Geneviève doesn't want to shake Charlotte's mood. The girl has been less sour recently, even agreeing when Sister Gertrude asked her to lead the women's singing at vespers, which surprised Geneviève.

Since the pirate attack, she hasn't heard Charlotte sing once. This morning their hands touched when Geneviève brought the shifts close to the flames—and for a second Geneviève caught a glance that Charlotte had often given to Étiennette.

"You know I will," Geneviève says now, her eyes on the hut.

Charlotte's steps recede and Geneviève's anxiety comes galloping back. Beyond the grass, the shack isn't the dark spot it usually is: it seems wrong that the bedridden girls would have let a candle burn. She stops, listens for Sister Gertrude's voice, resumes her walk when she hears nothing but frogs.

Inside, the hut is full of flies and mosquitoes, the smells of disease and ointments even stronger after the night air. It erases all the laundry drama, the past week's hopes, makes them seem petty, irrelevant. It seems impossible that just a few weeks ago she and Pétronille stood on Ship Island, waiting their turn in the canoes. Impossible that Pétronille was ever strong enough to wave at Baptiste, even resist Sister Gertrude when the nun grabbed her hand and dragged her to the pirogues that would take them to the continent. Geneviève still sees her friend sitting next to her on the canoe, ignoring the men who had paddled the two and a half leagues from New Biloxi to get an early look at them. The water was so close that she felt sure they would fall in; Pétronille stared ahead of her, silent. When they had to jump from the pirogues, she didn't scream like some of the other women. She let herself slide in the sea, as if she didn't care whether her feet met the ground.

Now, even if she wanted to, her friend can do nothing but sleep, half-open lips parting her birthmark like a wound, hands above the cover. And really, it's the hands that make Geneviève's jaw clench, the veins drawing blue lines underneath the skin. Pétronille was never afraid of the illness. She never spoke about it, as if she thought it could happen only to others. Geneviève finds herself wondering whether she could have noticed signs of the disease earlier if they hadn't been so obsessed with Baptiste.

A few days ago, Geneviève heard Sister Bergère say Governor Bienville was desperate. Disease and famine were killing the best workers, highly paid in tobacco, the price of their tools sometimes covered by the

Company, to come practice their precious trades in the colony. Without them, La Louisiane would slowly decay. Without the women, it wouldn't survive the span of a generation.

On the other half of the mattress, the candlelight worsens the yellowish complexion of the second woman's face. So far, they have lost very few girls: only four since the fever first struck the warehouse five weeks ago. The doctor saved one—which makes Geneviève believe Pétronille will, can, be cured.

"Pétronille," Geneviève whispers.

Her friend opens her eyes. She seems at a loss for a second, then smiles faintly. "Is Baptiste here yet?"

"Not yet," Geneviève says. On Pétronille's hand, a fly brushes its many eyes with its front legs, like a cat cleaning itself. "You'll have to tell me all about it."

"Tomorrow?"

"Whenever I see you again."

Outside, there are footsteps on the grass. Of course, somebody was here. The sick women didn't light the candle themselves.

"Listen," Geneviève quickly says, "once you're out of here, look for Madame Durand."

Pétronille does not repeat Geneviève's new name. She has closed her eyes. Geneviève buries the wrapped peas by her friend's side, wedges them in place under the linen. She jumps when the palmetto fronds hit the ground.

"You should be in bed." The purple pockets under Sister Gertrude's eyes look like wine stains. She stands in the doorframe as still as she did on *La Baleine* when Geneviève saw her tiny fingers clench around the pistol. Geneviève feels bad for her. The nun has gone through enough.

"I wanted to say my farewells to Mlle Béranger," Geneviève says.

"You wouldn't want to disturb her now. It is time for her *pommade* and then for her to rest."

Sister Gertrude's tone is matter-of-fact, her quiet voice made for tired children and pregnant women. Geneviève stands up. Before leaving, she waves goodbye; from the bed, Pétronille stares at her with the same stunned expression as that late afternoon at the inn in Lorient when Geneviève told her that it was over, that there wouldn't be any baby, that she would be able to leave France with them all. Pétronille shook her head, and Geneviève knew what she thought—that she couldn't believe it, that for a moment she'd thought the pain would last forever.

"No," Geneviève had said, "it won't."

• • •

Her first week in La Louisiane, Geneviève made a promise to herself. She decided there were things that hurt too much to be looked back on. Her house in New Biloxi would be something small but neat, with the ocean out of the window and curtains to frame the view. She'd be able to guess the weather from her bed without even opening the curtains. In her home, there wouldn't be any frogs jumping from behind mattresses, like on her first night at the warehouse. She'd line up marmalade jars in the food pantry, with evenly colored fruits that, like everything valuable, revealed themselves only when you leaned close. She wouldn't ask for anybody's permission before throwing away a rusty plate. She would put a piece of calabash under the house's gable so that nightingales could nest—she'd make sure the wild cats wouldn't get to them. In France, Geneviève never owned anything but what Amélie gave her, and the few memories she had at the family silk farm in Provence. La Louisiane would be big enough to have a couple of rooms to herself.

Today she is up early. The nuns are more lenient on wedding days; the girls always get excited. Because the rest of the women won't attend the ceremony, the last couple of hours with the brides matter the most. Everyone helps with the preparations—everyone but Thérèse and Jeanne, who stay together, rarely talk to anyone else. Geneviève barely knew them before they were stranded on deck during the attack. She had talked to Jeanne once, after she learned the woman had worked for two years at one of La Salpêtrière's silk workshops. For a moment Geneviève imagined that Jeanne came from La Bastide-des-Jourdans, that they'd known each other as children in Provence. At the end of yet another broth meal, Geneviève asked where Jeanne had learned to weave silk, and if there were silkworms to be found somewhere between La Grande Force and the Sainte-Claire dormitory. To the first question Jeanne said, "In Paris," and to the second, she said no, there weren't any.

Jeanne wouldn't answer Geneviève's questions after the attack. Geneviève's urge to help was constantly shaken by another certainty—that none of what she could do would ever be enough. Still, she asked the two women whether they were cold, hungry, thirsty. In a transparent voice, Jeanne's friend answered for them both. *Merci*, but we don't need another blanket. Yes, the bleeding stopped. It hurts like nothing ever has.

In the warehouse dormitory, Geneviève waves to them. Thérèse doesn't see her, but Jeanne nods back. Once, during their first week in La Louisiane, Pétronille told Geneviève that the two girls scared her. "Nonsense," Geneviève said. Her hand tightened around the last lace of Pétronille's stays. "How unkind of you. They need our help." But she knew what her friend meant. Passing by Thérèse and Jeanne, Geneviève sometimes felt similarly—chilled, vulnerable, hurt. She'd think Pétronille's thought. It could have been me that day on the deck.

Now she might never hear Pétronille's voice again.

Geneviève has an hour left at the warehouse. In the backyard, she tries not to look toward the hut, the guard watching it, and Pétronille inside. She picks a couple of magnolia flowers to scent the clothes in her bundle. Once in Paris, Amélie brought her a small silk shawl, sprayed with perfume, that she had taken from Madame's boudoir. It was early afternoon; it would need to be back by the time their mistress came home. They had it for an hour, and for an hour, Geneviève pictured herself in Provence, in the dim room where the silk was stored. She let Amélie spread the shawl all over her throat, until Geneviève felt the fabric slide on her nipples, so light and soft she could tell it wasn't there anymore only when Amélie's lips replaced it.

"Did you say goodbye to her?" she hears Charlotte ask.

Petals stick under Charlotte's soles. *La petite* is afraid to leave the warehouse, but she will never admit it. If Étiennette had been around, she might have told her; Geneviève isn't sure. On *La Baleine*, there was something in the way Charlotte behaved around her childhood friend—alert, too thoughtful, rarely annoyed—that reminded Geneviève of herself with Amélie. "I did," she tells her.

"I thought you'd been sent to solitary confinement again."

"Why would that be?"

"I heard Sister Gertrude walk back shortly after you did last night."

"And you think she'd have me punished for that?"

Charlotte cocks her head. "So you did run into Sister Gertrude."

"She wouldn't want me to smell like onions on my wedding day. On our wedding day."

"I guess not." Charlotte's voice is a whisper, and Geneviève regrets bringing their husbands into the conversation—but Charlotte, hero or not, sometimes looks so naive that it feels tempting to push her just a bit off balance, the way she did on their way to Lorient.

She points at the flowers gathered at Geneviève's feet. "What do you do with them?"

"You take them apart," Geneviève says. Pétronille would have hated seeing them do that, but she isn't here. Geneviève shows Charlotte how to pluck the petals, how to spread them equally among the clothes and rub the canvas until it warms your hands. Tie it close with a rope, lift it with care. Don't open it before it's time.

• • •

Sometimes Geneviève wants to take the easy path and blame it all on the nuns. They are the ones who took them to this miserable settlement, who treated them like cargo no different from sugar, tobacco, and coffee. Their concerns were only for marriage vows, foreign men, and unborn babies.

Then there are the other days when Geneviève can't help but see Sister Gertrude for what she really is—one of the three unfortunate women held responsible for the safety of ninety girls. She saw the nun's first move after the pirate attack. As soon as the crew had the ship back under control, she went upstairs to fetch Thérèse and Jeanne, who had gathered what was left of their clothes and pressed them against their bare legs, bare stomachs, bare faces. One of the pirates' blows had opened the nun's eyebrow arch, and the blood had dried in a clear stream on either side of her nose. Sister Gertrude was about to walk down to the between decks with the two girls when the second officer whispered something to her. From downstairs, Geneviève saw the nun's face change as he spoke.

Geneviève knows that the women aren't the only ones who can be punished. Shortly after arriving in New Biloxi, Sister Gertrude was summoned by the governor. When she was brought back, Geneviève couldn't help but recognize herself in the contrite, guilty expression that froze the nun's face into a mask. It took her a few days to untangle what was true from what wasn't. Sister Gertrude was blamed for letting the girls wander on the deck: true. Bienville believed she had tried to save everyone from an even more somber outcome: false. She would be made to pay a hundred *livres* fine: false. She would be sent to France earlier, as soon as *La Baleine* was ready to sail back: true. She would forever carry with her the memory of what she probably found that day on the deck—naked women, flying fish landing on blood-drenched wood, Charlotte standing by the door of the sailors' quarters, covering her eyes. True, true, and true.

• • •

Geneviève leans against the pew. Behind her are Charlotte and the other girl who will be getting married today, the blond one who keeps on anxiously rummaging through her bundle. Geneviève carries with her everything she could take from the warehouse. She would never come back here. But she would see Pétronille again. She has to believe that.

The priest, the one who traveled on *La Baleine*, readjusts his cassock. The chapel is like the rest of the town: it barely looks like one. A few benches, a makeshift altar, and behind, a violent representation of Christ—a beige, scarlet contorted figure lost in a wooden frame. Father Jean Richard seems much more at ease here than on the boat where Geneviève met him. That was one of the first times women were allowed on deck—back when the nuns' reticence to let them wander seemed silly. Now that Pétronille is sick, it strikes Geneviève that she should have let her friend gesture at Baptiste all she wanted, that the priest's and surgeon's opinions didn't matter. She wishes she had kept the two men busy chatting and let Pétronille drift away from them.

"*Mesdemoiselles.*"

Sister Gertrude has found her way between two benches. In the daylight, the rings under her eyes grow purple. "You will walk separately to the altar, where your husband will meet you," she starts. "When you exit, do remember to take your bundle. You wouldn't want to find your-self with only one pair of stockings."

As usual, the nun speaks very fast. Then she stands there and gives each of them a glance—worried or relieved, it's hard to tell. Behind them, the doors open.

Pierre Durand is the shortest of the three men walking into the church. Even during the visits at the warehouse, he seemed half present, as if he'd been dragged there against his will; he didn't speak as loudly as the other suitors did. He has broad shoulders, thick lips, and pale hair that must turn red in the summer. Geneviève was never afraid of him. She knew all along that leaving La Salpêtrière had a price.

Later, she will barely remember the ceremony. Unlike Étiennette, she had never dreamed of flowers, dowries, and banns. In Paris, she'd never imagined she'd get married. But she'd thought that a wedding would take more than a couple of sentences and nods, promises and prayers—candle flames leaning under the priest's breath and her own distant voice repeating *oui*. There is the odor of sweat and incense, then something raw rising from the fur of her husband's coat, something that instantaneously brings her back to the tanneries by the Bièvre. Freshly shaved skin grazing against her cheek, a rough hand holding hers as she turns around to see Charlotte moving forward. In Geneviève's canvas bag, the magnolia flowers already smell like an abandoned bouquet. Her husband opens the door. Geneviève follows him outside, the town as for-eign and unknown as the man by her side.

• • •

New Biloxi is a miserable village: most houses look like simple huts, so Geneviève calls herself lucky. Hers is built from split cypress logs, its interstices plugged with Spanish moss. There is no ocean out of the win-dow but a backyard full of overgrown grass, with chickens leaving deli-cate footprints around an overturned canoe. The house has even been whitewashed inside and out, so its two rooms are bright, not like the dusk the warehouse was plunged into. The kitchen has different sets of pans, kettles, knives. In the bedroom, the mattress disappears under heavy white-haired and brown-fuzzed blankets that look like sleeping dogs.

Pierre has never been to France. He comes from much farther north, from New France, where, Geneviève learns, all kinds of marmots and enormous rats live, the same ones that lie on her bed. He laughs when she asks him what it is like up there. "People are much stronger in Québec City. They weren't born in satin like in France." She wants to answer that he was born among furs that probably cost much more than the worn sheets she remembers from Provence, that the silk was never for her. Instead, she smiles.

Geneviève smiles a lot during these first days—for her husband but also for herself: she wants to believe she could be happy here. Her situation could be worse. She knows many girls are less fortunate: married to French convicts, accused of robbery or worse, dirt-poor settlers who don't have enough to feed themselves, let alone a wife and children. Geneviève can't help but feel for these men. She knows what poverty did to her family—and how little you can do to fight against it. In France, she too is considered a criminal.

When Pierre is gone, she moves the scarce furniture around to dust the floors, takes care of the mosquitoes and the chubby orange spiders that give her chills. The back door opens onto the woods and the animals who, to Geneviève, exist only through their howls, the sounds of their paws and claws. Even from afar, the forest is suffocating. Geneviève doesn't want to imagine what might emerge from it. She clings to the hoarse meowing of the cats—broken creatures who would have lived much longer if they had stayed in the holds of the ships that led them to the colony.

At night, her husband sometimes says something nice about the red-marbled petals she gathers—his silhouette behind the desk, the marrow-bone broth she's prepared for supper growing cold beside him. In bed, the furs come back to life as Pierre brings her close to him. Right after the wedding ceremony, he wouldn't kiss her; when he finally did, his teeth bumped against hers and he moved away, embarrassed. The first few nights together, Geneviève couldn't help but associate his clumsy, pushy haste with the violence of this continent, the oily darkness of its forests, the crushing loneliness of the few hundred men gathered by its rivers.

Over the last two weeks, his gestures have grown less awkward, more confident; he finds her lips more softly now. Geneviève makes it easy for Pierre—she spreads her legs open, rests her hands on his stocky back, guides him in. He comes so quietly that she has to pay attention to his breath, to the weight of his body against hers, to know when she can move away. Then he retreats to the other side of the bed, abandoning her to La Louisiane's loud, wild nights. As she dozes off, Geneviève thinks of Pétronille behind the palmetto fronds, of how far she would go to see her again.

• • •

News from the warehouse reaches Geneviève three weeks after her wedding. In the main room, her husband discusses with his business partner and a boat guide the situation of the hundreds of people hoping for transportation to reach their concessions, the parcels of land they came to exploit. On *La Baleine*, there had been workers too, headed for Pascagoula, to the estate of a wealthy landowner, Madame Chaumont. Concession men keep arriving on every European ship. They disembark in the clear sand of New Biloxi, wander through the bayous' sharp reeds, linger around the pine trees. They can't work; they wait.

Geneviève recognizes the boat guide, the man who always seems about to laugh—he is Charlotte's husband. His light eyes remind Geneviève of Amélie's compliments about her own. She hopes Charlotte didn't make any fuss the first night. She remembers when *la petite* had her first period shortly after they settled in the Mississippi—the horrendous cramps that shook her. She hopes Charlotte didn't suffer as much during her wedding night. She feels sorry she didn't tell her to lie still and breathe deep. But then no one had said anything to Geneviève either, in Paris.

She throws the chicken intestines in a bucket with a splash. In the main room, the men speak loudly. Dozens of French men stuck in New Biloxi, not enough food here for everybody, people stuffing themselves with oysters so as not to starve. There is a need for pirogues, fast, to bring the workers where they are needed. Not only for white men: *Le Duc de Maine* and *L'Africain* have recently arrived with some of the first enslaved Africans, deported from somewhere called Ouidah. More than five hundred men, women, and children stuck here too, doomed to die after surviving an impossible journey. The only dark-skinned people Geneviève ever saw were the ones she glanced at when *La Baleine* stopped for supply in Saint-Domingue.

"You should thank us," one of the men says, and Geneviève recognizes the voice of her husband's business partner, the *coureur des bois*, these independent trappers whose blood-ridden hands drag furs out of the colony's forests. "You'd still be eating raw food if we hadn't brought you to her."

"I needed time."

"If you still need some, I'd be happy to replace you."

"No need to. There are plenty of brides."

"Until they run out." Someone spits. "I bet they'll all be married before the end of the spring."

"Unless that *mal de Siam* gets them first."

"It's deadly. Another girl just passed away."

Geneviève's hand clutches the knife and she stares at the headless chicken.

"I wouldn't worry about your wife," the business partner says. "She looks as healthy as one of our ladies."

And then again, barely audible, her husband: "But she'll never be a Canadian woman."

Geneviève wipes the blood off the blade. She feels like everybody can hear her heart pounding in her neck. She thinks of what she always thinks of when she is about to cry: rats, snow, and howls, the cell that used to be her home. But it doesn't work. The feeling clings to her, persistent, weakening—she is on her own if Pétronille has died. She fought against that same loneliness once in Paris, when she was eleven, trapped in the foul stench of the tanneries. Back then, the capital seemed as far from her childhood home as La Louisiane now does from Paris. It feels impossible to stay if Pétronille is gone—impossible that Geneviève would lose her only true friend, be left alone after Lorient, the ocean, the waiting.

That night, after she has laid the fur above her husband's naked back, she lets her fingers wander on his neck. Pierre's face rests under her breasts. From here Geneviève can see blond hair and the skin of his head, taut like the belly of a pregnant woman. She takes a deep breath.

"I was hoping to go visit Mme Charpillon tomorrow," she says. It feels odd to call Charlotte *madame*.

At first Pierre doesn't answer. She feels his knee move against her thigh. He pulls on the sheet to cover them both. When he blows out the candle, her lips meet his mustache.

"Do as you wish," he says. In the dark, his hand finds hers. "But be back before sunset."

• • •

Charlotte will know more about Pétronille. Geneviève could have arranged to meet her at the market, with its half-empty crates and hard negotiations, but Pierre said M. Charpillon didn't let his wife go out on her own—that he was afraid something might happen to her. Apparently, Pierre doesn't share those fears.

Geneviève hurries up the muddy road that barely deserves to be called a street, mosquitoes dancing around her. It's one of the first times she has walked anywhere on her own since she was led to La Grande Force. It's elating; scary too. In Paris, she never glanced over her shoulder like she now feels prompted to. There were parts of the city she knew so well that, by the time she reached Madame's gate, she wouldn't remember passing the apothecary on Rue du Faubourg Saint-Antoine, the blind statues of the *hôtel particulier* at the northern end of the Rue du Temple, the booths full of monkfish, runny Brie, and brown eggs of Les Halles. She'd get where she was headed as surely as there'd be piles of soiled laundry waiting for her the following morning. Here, she can never be sure. Boys herding their precious cattle turn around and let their eyes linger on her. A flight of frigate birds heads toward the sea, their red throats setting the midday sky ablaze.

Charlotte's house isn't as big as hers, nor as well built. Even the doorknob seems fragile, as if, after Geneviève, there will be no more letting people in and out. She knows Charlotte's husband, as a simple boat guide, was only visiting her home for the help he could bring to

Pierre—M. Charpillon's social standing wouldn't have given him any other good reason to be there. At the entrance, Charlotte stops short. She has lost weight. She wears a gray dress that makes her look serious, older; yet her gestures, as she presses her cheek against the edge of the door, are true to her age.

"Who is it?"

Charlotte's lips haven't moved. The voice comes from behind, and Geneviève instantly recognizes Étiennette's.

Charlotte lets go of the door, and it almost closes on Geneviève's foot. "Well, come on in," she says.

In the narrow corridor, Geneviève wonders if she could backpedal, offer to come back later. She thought Étiennette was supposed to follow her husband to Fort Saint-Pierre, by the Yazoo River. Still, she knows exactly how excited Charlotte must have felt when she learned that her friend hadn't left New Biloxi. Then Geneviève had shown up at the door, stealing that moment from her.

She tries looking at it the other way: since Étiennette has been living in New Biloxi for a few months, she might have heard something about the warehouse. On the doorstep of the main room, Étiennette plants two loud kisses on her cheeks.

"This day is decidedly full of surprises," she says, sitting back on her chair. Her fuller face and her new gown make Geneviève wonder whom she is married to. She assumes Étiennette brought the small pitcher and the loaf of bread; the blue kerchief that covers them doesn't belong to Charlotte's desolate home. "First my husband ceases to be a bore and finally allows me to come visit. Second, you knock at the door."

"I thought you'd left months ago."

Étiennette leans forward. "And I did. But only the warehouse. He didn't take me as far as he said he would. Nowhere near Yazoo, only a couple of streets up." She laughs. "Men are liars. I knew Charlotte wouldn't know any better, but I thought that you'd see more clearly into M. Feuger's game."

"It crossed my mind," Charlotte says, apologetic. "I simply didn't want to get my hopes up."

Étiennette rests her hand on her waist. Charlotte freezes, the jar in her hand hanging high above the corn bread she is serving to her friend. "But it turns out you sometimes should." She lets go of Charlotte. Thick syrup gushes over the slices of bread, and Geneviève recognizes the maple tree sap that Pierre loves so much. "Did this horrendous disease hit you as badly as it hit us in town?"

Geneviève glances at Charlotte, who is handing her a plate too. She takes it, surprised; she didn't expect her unannounced visit to be forgiven so soon. "That's why I came here," she tells Charlotte. "To inquire whether you'd heard anything."

"I haven't."

"I have," Étiennette says, playing with her kerchief. Her self-assurance unsettles Geneviève. "My husband's associate is looking for a wife," Étiennette adds.

"*Alors?*"

"Well, another girl died."

Geneviève leans back; the smell of the syrup is nauseating. "Do you know who?"

"Pétronille fell sick shortly before we left," Charlotte explains, darkening her own slice of bread. She explains that Geneviève managed to visit the hut the night before they left but that they know nothing else. "Do you?" she asks Étiennette.

"He didn't say anything about a birthmark," she answers.

Geneviève gets a serviette to wipe the sweat off her face. Étiennette explains that she wished she could have attended the funeral, but M. Feuger doesn't allow her to go anywhere. There is a Native maid who does all the shopping and cooking.

"What a luxury," Charlotte says. "We don't have that sort of money here."

"A luxury?" Étiennette starts giggling. There is something about her laugh that makes Geneviève uncomfortable. "*Ma chère*, you haven't lived here for long. You'll learn quickly. On that note," she says, turning to Geneviève, "I'm surprised your husband lets you walk around like that after what happened."

Geneviève feels the muscles of her shoulders tense again. She doesn't like the pity she guesses in Étiennette's eyes. She doesn't like how little this girl sitting across from her resembles her friend from *La Baleine*. "What do you mean?" Geneviève asks.

"M. Feuger told me about the other woman. The first wife your husband brought all the way from Canada."

Geneviève shakes her dress, and crumbs spread on the floor. "I should be on my way."

Étiennette ignores her. "She died a few weeks ago. You know, the same disease."

"Étiennette," Charlotte says.

"What? I thought she'd like to know. Look at her, she does. Your husband, Charlotte, he's well known for visiting houses by the beach where—"

This time it's Geneviève who cuts her off. She asks about the boat situation, how come there aren't enough of them, and where is it everyone is so eager to send the concessioners to. Charlotte is staring at her feet. The flush from her cheeks slowly recedes. They listen to Étiennette babble about Fort Rosalie, the plantations that are being built there, endless tobacco fields, horses, even. "Have you ever ridden a horse?" she asks.

They both shake their head. Of course not, they've never ridden a horse. Geneviève finds Étiennette tiring. She stands up and reaches for her cap. "You seem rather excited about Fort Rosalie. Are you certain your husband lied when he said you'd settle somewhere else?" she asks.

For the first time, Étiennette appears caught off guard. She lowers her eyes. She starts fidgeting with her nose, and Geneviève finally recognizes the girl with whom she shared a cart from Paris to Lorient. When Étiennette speaks, her voice is uncertain. "Of course," she says, "otherwise why wouldn't we be on the road already?"

Charlotte is looking at Geneviève, who shrugs. "Men might be liars, but they have their own secrets," she answers.

"I would have heard about it," Étiennette says. "He would never give up his position as a storehouse guard and . . ."

Charlotte reaches for Étiennette's hand. "You would have heard something about it," she says.

Étiennette doesn't answer but cups her knuckles under her palm. She glances outside, toward the roof of the Company's single warehouse, the bad weather rising from the sea. "Our neighbor's baby has been teething for weeks, and it wakes me every night. I saw men fighting for food on the beach last winter, and again last Sunday." She looks at them. "These two months, in this town, on my own, have felt like ages. And all of you living together."

Charlotte strokes Étiennette's hand. Geneviève waves a fly away from the maple syrup. She straightens her cap, pulls the strings until it hurts. She tries smiling at Étiennette. "But then without you, how could we have learned the truth about New Biloxi?"

· · ·

The night of Geneviève's visit to Charlotte's, a warm wind sneaks in between the houses, carrying a smell of stagnant water, cow dung, and dying flowers. In the bedroom, Geneviève ties her hair back in a chignon. Two images keep coming back to her: Pétronille sleeping again with the other women, blue veins retreating; her husband's first wife, lying below her feet, cuddled in the mud. Her own fragile alliance with Charlotte, Étiennette's attitude, she'll save for later. She reminds herself that the dead girl Étiennette mentioned had no birthmark; yet whenever the image crosses her mind, Geneviève sees Pétronille among magnolia roots, buried in some mass grave.

"*Tabarnaque!*"

Pierre, water all over his breeches, swears again in the backyard. Geneviève steps outside. He is emptying another bucket on the pirogue.

"Would you care for some help?" she calls.

Her husband's few hairs are so blond in the last sunbeams that they blend with the skin of his head. "Yes, please."

She makes her way between the chickens, cooing softly to themselves. Pierre kneels by the canoe, studying its hull. "We'll need more water."

"What is this for?"

"The cypress logs. If you don't sometimes soak the pirogue when it's beached, the wood doesn't swell, cracks might appear. It's dangerous."

Geneviève suddenly worries that it's her turn: that tonight—men are all liars—her husband is going to tell her about another long trip, up the St. Louis River this time. Then she will never learn if Pétronille is well or not. "We are not leaving, are we?"

"No. I'm selling it to a fellow I met today. If they wait for the officials to provide them the boats they need, they won't reach Fort Rosalie before the next year." He hands her the last bucket. "It needs to be spread evenly. Here. The benches are still dry. *Encore un peu*. Just like that."

The bucket is heavy but not more than the ones she used to carry on the washhouse boat or the ones she pulled from the stream of the warehouse. The opaque water drops to the bottom of the embarkation and vanishes, drunk by the wood.

"You saw Mme Charpillon today."

"Another friend was there too." Geneviève grabs the empty bucket. "She told me one of our *compagnes* died at the warehouse."

A purple light has fallen on the backyard, blurring everything—chickens turned to shadows, Pierre's face into an outline. His shoulders fall. When he speaks, his voice surprises her: "That is why I don't want you near that place. That disease spreads faster than—" He looks around, points at the water sinking into the boat. "You cannot take any risks. Is that understood?"

Geneviève isn't sure how to read his tone. Her dress moves against her legs. "Yes," she answers.

He nods, fingers clenched on the bucket handles. Then he puts a hand on her shoulder and says: "I'll go fetch more water."

Geneviève lets him help her. She doesn't tell him she can manage on her own.

· · ·

The sticky heat marks the end of May. The pirogue disappears from the yard and the chickens mourn it, retracing its shape in the overturned earth. In about two weeks, a few embarkations should finally arrive to transport workers and a couple of families to the concessions.

Geneviève stays inside as much as she can, to avoid the white sun and the damp air. She gets up before dawn to kneel by the cow Pierre bought with the pirogue money; she trades some of its milk for chestnut-smelling potatoes that make, she is told, wonderful marmalade. Pierre has become more considerate these past few weeks. Geneviève isn't sure

what it is, but sometimes, at night, they stay in the sitting room long after the hard cider is gone, once the *potage* leaves stains of braised salted
meat on their plates. Geneviève can't bring herself to ask him to take her
to Pétronille, not just yet. She proceeds carefully with Pierre, not because
she fears his reaction but because she's learned that he rarely goes back
on his decisions.

It never occurs to her that she could compare her husband to Amélie.
She listens to his stories about Island of Montreal, the endless woods that
surround the icy water, how he once saw a frozen boat, its passengers
sitting still, blue faces and rigid postures, as immobile as the trees. When
Pierre is reminiscing, he often looks up, as if watching the scene unfold
somewhere above them. His parents, true people of the North born in
Québec City, his older sister, Laure, who might soon be settling in the
Illinois Country. Geneviève is thankful he never speaks about the other
girl, the first bride from Canada.

Rather, Pierre talks about the Iroquois. He almost never pronounces
the word "Indian." If Geneviève says it, he asks her which tribe she
means, and she good-heartedly admits that she has no idea. He smiles,
picks up his story where he left off, describes these women who don't
hesitate to cut the thumbs of settlers and *coureurs des bois*—and Geneviève can't help but wonder if that is simply the price to pay for wandering too deep into the woods of Canada.

"Or at least that's what people say," concludes Pierre, using a dying
candle to light another one. "No one really speaks about the Iroquois
themselves, their experience."

At Charlotte's, Étiennette mentioned only the Natives' cruelty, the
priests bound on pieces of bark, their skin covered with black maple sap
and hungry insects. She sounded excited. Geneviève could tell she wasn't
thinking of murdered tribes and tortured settlers; Étiennette talked as
if these were fairy tales, as made up as Cinderella and Bluebeard. To
Geneviève, although the stories felt far from her life in New Biloxi, they
seemed nonetheless too real—a warning, almost, something deeply true
and troubling.

"Tell me about France," Pierre says. He helps himself to more cider. "I doubt anyone has heard of Iroquois there."

She is aware he wouldn't like to listen to most of what she did in

Paris, be it in the tanneries or at Madame's, so she carefully chooses her stories, revives memories so old they feel foreign. Provence is hazy; she starts with her family's arrival in Paris in the winter of 1709. She tells him about the freezing wind, the chilblains, the bursting glass, the impossible burying while so many were dying. When she explains how the Seine turned solid, Pierre nods knowingly. Churches became dormitories, poor and sick people begging for a shelter at the Hôtel-Dieu. "My father brought me there in time," she says. She is thankful to Pierre for not asking about her mother or her siblings.

"What did he do?" he asks.

"What he could," Geneviève says.

"What about you?"

She sticks to 1709, August this time—the frosted crops and lack of food, more and more soldiers sent to die for a certain Spanish throne. The Seine was overflowing, had become impracticable. Yet her father was smiling for the first time in months: the king had just ordered the opening of public workshops for people like them. Hard, leveling work for a few *sous*, but the promise was enough to send her father on his way right after sunrise, when the center of Paris was a blur of old stones and new light. Geneviève was eleven. She remembers how their landlady grabbed her hand as soon as they heard about the riot, how quickly they reached the angry crowd, where many, many more people than expected by the government had gathered, all looking for a job and not enough soil, tools, and wages for everyone, the woman's nails digging in her forearms—and how, at that very moment, Geneviève understood it was bad, because the landlady, a stranger, was holding her tight. "After that, it went fast," she says. "The police prefecture and the royal officers turned against us and started firing."

Pierre sips his cider. He looks pensive, and for a moment, Geneviève regrets letting herself get carried away. She stands up and piles the bowls.

"If more embarkations don't reach us soon," he finally says, "there won't be enough military to keep the concessioners in order."

Geneviève leans against the doorframe. "Boats will come," she says. "This famine can't be worse than the one my first year in Paris."

Pierre seems about to answer, as if, for a minute, he might have been ready to hear out her arguments. Then he shakes his head and walks to their bedroom. Geneviève hears the bed squeak under his weight. As she scrubs the darkened kettle, she wonders how many stories it'll take before she finds the strength to ask about Pétronille—before she accepts there might be an end to that story too.

• • •

The day after the Pentecost, in June, Pierre comes into the kitchen. Geneviève is coughing above the fire, waving a pan around her. She's found that if she spreads smoke in the morning and at night, the mosquitoes keep away. She can feel drops of sweat getting caught in her stays. It isn't nine yet, but the heat already pushes against the closed window and door.

"Leave all of this for now. M. Charpillon and his wife are waiting for us." Pierre rubs one of his fingers against his own nail. "The boats arrived. I thought you might want to watch them depart."

Geneviève hasn't seen Charlotte since that visit in late April. She hasn't been back to the beach where she disembarked in January, when Pétronille had turned mute, when the wind and the men whispered in the dunes.

"I'll be with you in a minute."

When Geneviève steps outside the house, her husband and M. Charpillon are speaking in agitated whispers. John Law's disgrace is all Pierre can talk about—news just came from France that the controller general of finances, ruined, fled the country. She tries not to think what his downfall means for the colony, of who will be supporting this land if its main advocate abandoned it. Behind Pierre, watching a magpie butcher a peach, is Charlotte. She seems both disgusted and fascinated by the bird. Under her freckles, her skin is livid. The magpie digs around the pit of the fruit, flies away when Geneviève joins them. The men, deep in their conversation, head down the street.

"I wasn't sure you'd come," Charlotte says. She seems neither happy nor discontent to walk together. Geneviève asks her how she is doing. She shrugs. "Nauseated," she answers.

She is as skinny as ever. Under her crossed arms, her belly is still flat.

They pass by a house that smells like mulberry vinegar. In the yard, chin resting on his scratched knees, a little boy spreads ash on half-cut potatoes. "Enough, *bon Dieu*! They'll never dry," a thin voice screams. The child pauses, then empties his bundle in one angry move.

"It'll get better," Geneviève says.

"Of course you'd know."

Geneviève had hoped she'd find the Charlotte from the warehouse, but that friend is gone. She wonders how much of Étiennette Charlotte saw over the spring. From what she can tell, a lot. She feels acutely aware of her own loneliness these past few weeks, and she resents Charlotte for it—for being less alone, for not reaching out, for always being the one to choose the terms of their relationship.

"What did I do to you?" Geneviève says. She has meant to ask for a long time, and it comes out before she can stop herself.

Charlotte looks stunned, then alarmed. She shakes her head. "Nothing," she replies.

Courageous enough to brave pirates and too much of a coward to answer a simple question. Geneviève walks faster. At the corner of the street, three men burn reeds. Charlotte jumps when the flames reach the green plants and they let out a pistol sound. "Did you ever hear about Pétronille?" Charlotte asks.

For a second, Geneviève considers lying. She died months ago, I saw them burying her into the mass grave behind the dunes. Charlotte too would lose a friend. The pain would be split in half.

"No," she says.

They turn right and see men trading overripe melons for rancid bread, workers exhausted by the heat and the monthslong wait, dozing in the shade—maybe dreaming of the blue corn, lead mines, and wild oxen they were promised. Under Geneviève's soles, the dry mud crumbles like old dough. She feels Charlotte's hand on her arm.

"Listen," Charlotte says, "I heard that Sister Gertrude sailed back to France last month. That there are only four brides left in the warehouse. That the governor said if they had brought twice as many of us, they all would have found husbands. That *La Baleine* sailed back to La Rochelle with furs, and something else I forgot the name of." Charlotte pauses. "Here. That's all I know. I'm sorry about Pétronille."

Around them, a few girls appear, their stays loosened, hair barely covering their shoulders, just like in Paris. "Drink lemon juice on an empty stomach," Geneviève says. She steps aside to avoid spit. Scrawny men eye the women from the other side of the street, pointing as if they have a choice to make. Under a tree, two boys barely older than Charlotte argue vehemently. In New Biloxi, you're always fighting for something— a slice of bread, a shaded spot, a bit of comfort. "It'll help with the nausea in the first weeks."

"I'll try," Charlotte says.

Geneviève is thankful to Charlotte for meeting her halfway, yet tired of trying to navigate her many different angles. "Good," she says.

"*Mesdames!*"

M. Charpillon gestures for them to hurry up. Geneviève can already see the crowd gathered on the beach and, beyond, the pirogues dangling like ducks. People screaming to please move and hurry, the odors of clams and sweat, a veiled sky reflected in the calm sea. The scene is familiar, oddly reversed. Looking at the men dragging trunks in the sand, at the boats sinking deeper as another traveler steps in them, Geneviève sees herself six months ago, pushing through the water behind Pétronille, trying to stick together in the crowd.

Pierre leans over her shoulder. "Let's see if we can reach the dunes," he says.

Geneviève hears M. Charpillon explain to Charlotte that four families are leaving for Fort Rosalie, plus thirty concessioners. Turtle eggs crack under her shoes. Geneviève hasn't been around that many people for a long time, probably not since the warehouse. She longs to be surrounded again by the same women she once wished would disappear—at least they were familiar, all heading to the same place. Her feet slip into the sand, and she holds on tight to Pierre's hand. She catches bits of conversation, breathes in the smell of flannels and garlic, lemongrass and unwashed hair, and feels the too many arms and legs that graze against her dress.

"Look," Charlotte suddenly says.

At first all Geneviève can see are silhouettes. The sun strikes behind the canoes and makes it impossible to tell things apart. Then shapes and colors appear—a toothy snake painted on the side of a pirogue, a writing desk, a child weaving seaweed around a dog's neck. More people wait to board the boats there, and Geneviève stands on tiptoe to see their faces better.

One of them, a woman, timidly enters the water—Pétronille, as silent and focused as she was on the gangway that bridged Lorient to *La Baleine*, when Geneviève felt her friend's fingers press against her shoulders and then, together, they climbed on board for this land they would soon have to call home.

Pétronille

This journey has no end. That's what Pétronille used to tell herself, more than two months ago, when she sat in the pirogue that carried her upstream on the St. Louis River, her feet cramped from being still for so long, her hands grasping her knees, not because she wanted to but because there was no room and nothing else to hold on to. She envied the concessioners who could paddle: at least they had an oar to anchor them and steer through the troubled water. They could feel the resistance of the current. They could push against something. Pétronille couldn't. She had been brought here and instructed to sit still, first by her husband, then by other men.

They were taking her to Fort Rosalie, a settlement which, as M. Ducros seemed to enjoy explaining to her, bore two names: either Fort Rosalie, after the second wife of the Count de Pontchartrain, or Natchez, after the Natives living there. On the second day of travel, her husband befriended an engineer who was returning to Fort Rosalie, a man who told him stories of little dogs playing with cougars, of being locked in the New Biloxi jail by the second-in-command, of importing Vauban fortification into this new land. Pétronille soon grew tired of M. Cléry's incessant talking. Were it Baptiste on *La Baleine*, she could have listened forever. She could have asked him again what an *ancre* of eau-de-vie was, although what stayed with her wasn't the liquor recipient's special design but how Baptiste brought it to her lips right after the pirate attack, saying that it would restore some of her courage. Pétronille couldn't help but think how wrong her mother had been about the gardener, Paul, how ignorant it was to consider him capable of the kind of violence inflicted on the girls on *La Baleine*.

Courage was still needed on the pirogue that took her to Fort

Rosalie, when the winds shifted against them and they had to come to a halt in the region the concessioners called Le Petit Désert; courage when they settled for the night ashore past Baton Rouge, when the men gathered the weapons in a pile and kept watch over them. She fell asleep imagining everyone and everything they could be guarding them from. Tigers, crocodiles, Native warriors, British soldiers. She lay under the forever-wet linen, her husband muttering in his sleep. She felt the disease, which had devoured her body for days and then lingered for weeks, still winding in her veins. Come get me, she'd tell herself.

That changed on the evening the bear attacked them. They had traveled almost six leagues since dawn, and the men were happy, hoping they would keep up the steady pace all the way to Natchez, beating the fast current. They sang to Neptune, their voices buoyant and angry. Night was falling. M. Ducros chatted with M. Cléry; Pétronille noticed the bear before they did. It was swimming ahead of them, moving the water as if it were a thick cloak. From afar, its head looked compact and hairy. Then she remembered the one she saw at a village show near Paris, the gigantic beast that rose on his paws, unmindful of the chain that cut through his fur. It was missing so many fangs that the inside of its mouth looked pitch black.

What followed still petrifies Pétronille. She heard the commandant of their boat order the concessioners to paddle faster. Not toward the riverbank, where they should have been landing already, but toward the animal. It was moving toward land, its head bouncing above the water, not paying attention to the men straining to reach it. From the bow, the officer shot. The sound of the pistol sounded both brutal and incomprehensible. Blood started to run from the bear's ear, and then the animal was swimming toward them, their boat, its muscles readable under the water.

Pétronille wasn't sure whether she screamed or if the cry came from someone else's throat: the claws of the bear ripped against the hull, its front paws took hold of the bow, the men folded themselves under their seats. Pétronille felt the grip of her husband's hand, M. Cléry pushing her aside. She felt the dangerous dangling of the pirogue when the bear leveled itself on board, and she scrambled under the seat, a smell of wet fur and moist earth infiltrating the wood, her breath cut short by the curious angle her body formed, waiting for pain she couldn't imagine and something in her rebelling against it. The one thought that kept on looping in Pétronille's mind, a lullaby that hypnotized her as she lay under the seats of the boat: How stupid must one be to fire on a bear?

The animal walked over them. It dislocated a man's shoulder blade, barely missed another's head. Then it jumped back where it had come from.

Today, as Pétronille lies in bed, this is one of the memories she clings to, the question she asks herself when she doubts she'll be able to get through another day in Fort Rosalie. If a bear were threatening to crush your head now, what would you be praying for? For nothing. Or for the beast to be fast. For her baby to be safe. But back then, on the water, she wasn't pregnant yet. She can't quite imagine that she'll be a mother in a few months.

The door slams open. The maid used to knock when they arrived in Natchez. Renée used to do a lot of things: readjust her pillows, move the clock with the carved roses to dust the table, ask about Pétronille's journey to La Louisiane, whether she too had been brought to the fortress of Saint-Martin-de-Ré with other volunteers. Renée liked to brag about the conditions she negotiated with the recruiter of the Company—the servant could never remember whether it was the Company of La Louisiane, of the Indies, or of Occident—a one-way trip that included one hundred *livres'* worth of tobacco per year, medicines included. She often referred to her contract, which she called her "document." She liked to remind Pétronille that it exempted her from plowing fields, as if anyone ever suggested she should.

"How is Madame feeling today?"

Renée's blond hair is messy, her eyes intent. She piles the dishes on the tray, and the noise lasts longer than her gesture. She always asks after Pétronille's health when she's about to leave, says nothing when she comes in.

"Well, thank you," Pétronille says. She knows what she looks like: pale, gaunt, tired despite all this rest. But answering is important. It will echo in the kitchens; it will be reported to her husband. Renée nods and leaves. Pétronille leans back onto the pillows. There is a hole in one of them, and feathers come flying out. A breeze, as light as ever, is blowing through the bedroom.

The pregnancy is as good an excuse as any to stay in bed. She can feel herself grow inward, like she used to in Château-Thierry before Paul was hired, during her first months at La Salpêtrière, or at the beginning of the journey before she met Geneviève. She finds some comfort in going back to what she knows, no matter how crushed she feels. There is something familiar about the deep silence of her room, the buzzing of her own mind, the solitude that protects her from hopes and disillusions.

She was married in May, as soon as Sister Gertrude judged her strong enough to stand through the ceremony. On her wedding day, Sister Bergère pinched her cheeks so hard that Pétronille thought she'd draw blood. The nuns had overestimated her: her legs kept on shaking in front of Father Jean Richard. Her husband seemed to value her weakness as a sign of a fine descent, a delicate nature one should take care of—a nobility suggested by her origins and hard to find in this land. After the ceremony, in the house that was supposed to be her home, he'd often look at her and say, "Where would you little princess be, if it weren't for me?" She shrugged. With another man, a bit like you, a bit unlike you, who would have taken me to Mobile or to the settlement near the delta, the one they call New Orleans that was ruined by a storm last year. It didn't matter where. Pétronille would never again see Baptiste, Geneviève, Charlotte, or any of the other girls. It was as if she'd fully vanished from the world—be it old or new.

In New Biloxi, M. Ducros would tell her not to worry, that they would be moving to Natchez soon, I promise—to a place so big you'll get lost. She hated the idea. She felt disoriented enough without her friends. Last May, she wanted to see Geneviève and Charlotte so badly. But she didn't know where to start looking for them: some mornings, she'd find herself too weak to dress, and she'd go back to bed. On good days, she'd be disappointed with herself. She'd realize that she would soon lose her friends, if she hadn't already, and her breath would shorten. She'd remember Geneviève's voice or Charlotte's laugh and wonder how long they would stick in her memory. Sounds always go first.

On bad days, she didn't feel anything.

She was happier when she was sick. In the hut by the warehouse, she had felt like she spent days, weeks, with Baptiste. The harsher her fevers, the more frequent his visits. He'd appear by her bed, his fingers fiddling with the dry peas she found by her side. He'd empty the buckets she couldn't remember filling, and sometimes, when he dried her forehead or searched under her eyelids for things she couldn't fathom, he'd be accompanied by a brown-skinned woman. She came in with arms full of plants, and once Pétronille asked Baptiste if he could ask her for the name of the root she was chewing on, but he only shook his head. Kneeling at his feet, the woman rummaged through her basket. "Doctor, I don't have enough," she said, and Pétronille wanted to tell her she was mistaken, that Baptiste was a sailor and not a surgeon, but her tongue was too heavy for words.

In the evening, Baptiste came back alone, always. He'd sit by her mattress and tell her about the rumors of corruption he'd heard in New Biloxi, how Governor Bienville threw soldiers in jail for months or failed to provide subordinate officers with clothes and food. He'd lean closer, ask if she remembered the time when a ship's boy threw a bucket of water so hard it wet her dress. The time he had her sip lemon juice to protect her from scurvy. "Yes," she said, "of course." She remembered everything.

The memories feel better than the reality. Baptiste was no more with her in the sick girls' hut than he had been in the front yard. Her fevers were to blame for his imaginary visits; the dried peas had been left by Geneviève or Charlotte. As for their missed rendezvous, Pétronille could only speculate about what obstacles had kept him from coming to her. She pictured him stuck at the sailors' barracks, unable to leave. Trying but getting caught. Taking a wrong turn and missing the warehouse. There seemed to be too many ways to explain his absence. Baptiste had sailed back to France already, died, or injured himself; he'd never learned the date of their meeting because the doctor's assistant hadn't delivered her response. Pétronille had no way of knowing the truth. At the time, her worst fear was never finding out why he hadn't met her. She was terrified that, without another explanation, she'd have to face the one reason she couldn't bear—that he didn't come because he'd stopped loving her.

She reminds herself it is all behind her. Now that she is so far away from the sea that she knows she'll never see him again, she manages to find a few pleasant moments in Natchez. Very early in the morning when the bedroom—fully furnished, if not by her—seems to glow, before the mosquitoes come back and after she hears the enslaved Africans leave for the neighbor's tobacco fields. Around noon, when the sun pours like egg yolk and a fat stroke of light falls from the head of her bed to her pillows. When supper is over, and the evening closes upon her, and she knows she will be left alone for hours.

The sun is setting. Tomorrow, at the same hour, she won't be free to stay in her room. They have been invited to the engineer's. M. Cléry disappeared for weeks, stuck in Pascagoula, and now he's back. His wife, a dressmaker, will be there, and Pétronille can't help but picture her similar to her husband, as if they were siblings. Talkative and self-absorbed. The truth is, she doesn't know. Apart from the maid, Pétronille—herself once surrounded by ninety girls and three nuns—hasn't talked to a single woman in months.

· · ·

The last few weeks on *La Baleine* had been agonizing. Pétronille couldn't see beyond them at the time. She couldn't imagine what would happen to her once they dropped anchor, the idea of being alone as unthinkable as land breaking between sea and sky. The pirate attack had given her a glimpse of a future without Baptiste—as she sat in the between decks listening to the fighting, terrified, she pictured him wounded, dead, forced to join the pirates' ranks. She wondered if he would be able to save Charlotte, whose hand had escaped hers, for whom she had pleaded to go back on deck before Sister Gertrude shook her head and said, "It is pointless, my dear."

Both Charlotte and Baptiste were returned to her. Pétronille couldn't quite believe her luck, and it quickly turned out she had been right not to. Baptiste could not marry her, could not stay with her when they landed. The officers of *La Baleine* didn't care how bravely he'd fought back the bandits: defending the ship was his duty, nothing more. After the attack, discipline would be enforced more strictly—the crew needed to be ready in the event of another assault, and the girls would stay under strict watch. Baptiste's contract bound him to the captain for another four long years. For the rest of the trip, he was told not to go near her, to stick to his tasks. He had to obey his orders.

After that, part of Pétronille had wished for these last few weeks to go by faster. There were too many last times. The last time she'd be able to meet Baptiste in the cellar. The last time he'd stroke her nose with his thumb, the calloused finger meeting her salt-beaten skin. The last time he'd rest his palm against her lower back and she'd feel him between her legs. Flesh, touch, were anchors amid all the displacements. Last times started to feel like first times: both were unique, irretrievable.

· · ·

On the porch, waiting for the carriage, the sun beats hard against her skin. The afternoon comes to an end, but the summer light is voracious, unforgiving. She wishes she could send herself somewhere else, jump into her own future, just like she did as a child. She'd focus on one single image, and it'd take her out of the present and right where she needed to be—in bed, stretching to find a cool spot between the sheets; in the garden, moving the earth to grow strawberries from a cutting; at her dressing table, adding dried tulips to her herbarium, handling the petals carefully so that they don't break.

"I was looking for you," she hears her husband say, "but you are here."

She looks at M. Ducros. He often states the obvious, which makes conversations easier—there are only so many ways you can answer him. He is wearing the blue cloak that is so tight it makes her cringe in the heat even more, and he keeps on passing his hand through his flat dark hair. As always, he seems vaguely annoyed, although he never says why. Anxious, almost, tonight. He glances at his pocket watch one last time before giving her his arm.

"Are you happy to see M. Cléry again?" he asks as he helps her climb into the carriage.

"He is your friend," she answers.

"He was your traveling companion as well."

Pétronille thinks back to the day the bear hauled itself on the boat, how M. Cléry selfishly pushed her against the hull—so hard that, for a terrible moment, she thought she wouldn't be able to hide. "He certainly was," she answers.

A tobacco field flashes between the orange trees. M. Ducros could hardly conceal his disappointment when they laid eyes on Fort Rosalie: the blossoming tobacco industry he had described was almost nonexistent. As they settled, Pétronille had to agree with him on one point—she could get lost here. Natchez was big, the kind of vastness that betrayed a void, a lack of construction, overwhelming nature. M. Ducros had pointed toward chunks of forest and insisted the trees would be felled and tobacco farmed. He's been doing just that on their land.

Pirogues took so long to reach New Biloxi that their home was built already by the time they finally arrived in Fort Rosalie. In their first days, her husband showed her the purple bushes that denote the end of their property. "In the opposite direction," he said, "is the Grand Village of the Natchez," and Pétronille hadn't known how to picture a Native village. She still doesn't know how. Nor does she know what the slaves' quarters look like at her own home. Only that they are empty for now: buying enslaved Africans is one of her husband's obsessions—the key, according to him, to start his flourishing business. Pétronille remembers the enslaved woman she saw on her second day here; the woman was coming back from the fields of their neighbor's plantation, walking very slowly, holding her child with both hands, her feet so torn and bloody that Pétronille rushed to M. Ducros. "That isn't a topic suited for ladies," he said. She never saw the woman again.

The idea that one could own other people leaves Pétronille incredulous. She used to see dirt-poor peasants working the fields around Château-Thierry, families crushed by the king's taxes—but if they had taxes to pay, that meant they were earning money. There isn't anything of the sort here. *Livres* go from one purse to the next but only once: no wages are ever paid. After seeing the wounded woman, she hopes her husband's dream will never come true.

On top of a hill, the fort looms over the St. Louis River, but from the road, the water remains hidden: it's as if the fort of palings is hanging over a blur of trees and grass. There are more fields, some worked by

French laborers, others by enslaved people, probably from the Sainte-Catherine Concession; a garden with tomatoes so big they seem closer than they are; a boy following cows, mimicking with his hands the movement of their tails. Pétronille has been to the trading post only once, her second week here. As they pass, she sees that the man who was then smoking his pipe is still there, puffing away at nothing.

As always when she goes out for the weekly promenade that pleases her husband, Pétronille isn't sure whether she'd rather be sitting in the carriage or back in her bed. The only order she wishes she could give the coach driver would be to bring her back to New Biloxi, to her friends.

The engineer's wife would be the kind of person who'd dare do that. On the doorstep, Madame Cléry waves them in, as if they were children.

"I hope you didn't come to see my husband," she says as she leads them to a narrow porch in the back of the house, "he's off somewhere. Drawing or fishing, you'll be able to tell by the state of his clothes." She gestures toward two chairs. "At least there is brandy. I think you enjoyed it, M. Ducros, the last time you came to see M. Cléry. We'll be able to entertain ourselves without him."

The glass feels tepid in Pétronille's hand. She isn't used to conversing anymore, wishes it could be Geneviève sitting in front of her instead of this woman she doesn't even know. There seems to not be enough time between what she might need to be saying—that's enough brandy, thank you—and the thoughts that cross her mind—a rabbit just leaped through the grass in big jumps. Mme Cléry looks nothing like her husband. Petite, assertive. Almost no chin.

"With that kind of idea," M. Ducros says, "M. Cléry's long absence mustn't have weighed too terribly on you."

Mme Cléry turns to him. "Not at all," she replies. She smiles indulgently at Pétronille.

"You shouldn't have waited for me," a voice calls from across the lawn.

"I assure you we did not, darling," Mme Cléry says. There is no answer, but the silhouette stretches, and Pétronille watches her husband glance at Mme Cléry, then walk down the steps to meet their host, close enough that Pétronille can make out the man.

"So, fishing or drawing?"

Pétronille let her eyes wander from Mme Cléry to the engineer. His clothes are muddy. He isn't carrying anything that could help her guess. "I'm not sure," she admits.

Mme Cléry starts laughing. "Right answer," she says. "He always returns so dirty I can never tell either. Maybe he's doing something else entirely out there," she adds, her tone secretive and inviting, although Pétronille isn't certain what she's implying. "I'm very glad you were able to come this time."

Pétronille declined two other invitations before the engineer left town, but Mme Cléry's voice carries no resentment.

"So am I," she replies.

"When we first arrived here, eight months ago," Mme Cléry says, "I only ever saw the commandant's wife. Such a dull creature. Only cruelty animated her. She was a very predictable woman." She helps herself to more brandy, leans back in her chair. "But one becomes used to solitude. Even if solitude means something quite different in this land, don't you think?"

Pétronille feels a pinch in her chest. "It does," she answers.

The men are back. They rest against the railing, talking. The liquor acquires a new transparency in the sun, and the reflection of the light against the glass ricochets into Pétronille's eyes, blinding her.

"I was extremely disappointed when I discovered this village," Mme Cléry is saying. Pétronille nods. No one has ever talked to her about Fort Rosalie like that. "This controller of finance is a terrible liar, don't you think? The only gold that can be found on this continent is more than a hundred leagues north from the mouth of the Arkansas River, buried in a pond. A pond, of all places. He couldn't have made that up."

"But he didn't," says M. Cléry. He sits by his wife. M. Ducros doesn't move. "There is even a process by which you can collect the metal from the bottom of the river. A very elaborate method." He nods to himself but doesn't say more.

Mme Cléry turns to Pétronille as if the others don't deserve to hear her. "First," she says, "you use one yard square of limbourg cloth to make a net. Then you attach to it a stone, but not too heavy, about a pound and a half." She explains that it should be dropped where the water is quite shallow and left there for twenty-four hours, then retrieved, and the cloth left to dry. The net should be stroked with the finger, firmly but not too much so. "This way, you can gather one eggshell of powdered gold."

"That's it, that's it," M. Cléry says. He turns back to M. Ducros. A breeze shuffles the grass all the way to their feet.

"The Arkansas River," Pétronille says, "isn't that close to where the *mer de l'ouest* is supposed to be?" It was one of her favorite tales from Baptiste, who, as soon as he learned she'd be settling in the Mississippi, told her about the mythical inland sea that was supposed to be found in this country.

"Who knows?" Mme Cléry says, her tone genuine. "It could be anywhere, couldn't it?"

They keep on talking about the possibility of a water passage west from La Louisiane. Sometimes M. Ducros glances toward them, but for once she doesn't feel the need to be alert to his mood. Cantaloupe is brought to the table; the sun sets. For the first time in months, Natchez feels tangible to Pétronille. It exists in relationship to other geographical features, features that were described by Baptiste long before she ever set foot on Ship Island, features that are known by people other than him—like this woman, a stranger but one who seems to share with Pétronille things she thought were hers only. It makes her feel grounded again—events and people linked together, drawing a map that feels, if not immediately understandable, at least coherent.

When it's time to go inside and eat, her husband leans toward her. "Are you having a pleasant evening?" he asks. She says yes, thank you, and can't remember when she last answered him honestly.

• • •

In the mirror over the dressing table, Renée looks stricken. Pétronille rarely asks for her help to get dressed and yet now she closes the maid's fingers around the brush. Mme Cléry is coming at a quarter past ten to accompany her to Natchez's only tailor. "In a month or two, this dress will be too tight, and you'll need a looser corset," she told Pétronille yesterday, pointing at her belly. Pétronille agreed. Maybe she wouldn't spend the rest of her pregnancy in a nightgown after all.

"No need to look so alarmed," Pétronille tells Renée. "Something simple will do." She never thought she would use her mother's commanding voice, or that it would ever come in handy. While Renée brushes her hair, Pétronille looks into her own eyes. For the first time in months, she is curious to know what she looks like, what is forever gone, and what can still change.

She has seen a lot of Mme Cléry these past two weeks—she is to call her Marie now. Marie and her husband have been in Natchez less than a year, but Marie's stories make the landscape sharper. They fill groves and fields and people with meaning, just like Paul helped Pétronille see the gardens of Château-Thierry, just like Baptiste helped her understand what it meant to be at sea. Now when Pétronille passes by Fort Rosalie, she sees beyond its high palings. Six years ago, the hill was only a hill. Then French militaries refused to smoke the peace calumet and broke their alliance with the Natchez. Four French men were killed in response, and finally, a vengeance was led by the lieutenant whose name Pétronille recognized from her days in New Biloxi, Governor Bienville. As part of the peace treaty, Natives were forced to provide the lumber needed for the construction. Pétronille wonders what obligations were imposed on the Frenchmen. She guesses none.

Before her visit at Pétronille's last Saturday, Marie barely mentioned her life in France. And even then she kept her voice low as she talked about the journey in shackles, wearing nothing but a shift in the freezing hold of a boat called *La Mutine*. She said she and the other women were barely fed, that there were dozens of men on the ship and they didn't even bother untying the chains before attacking them; she says so many girls died at sea that she thought she would never make it to La Louisiane alive. On Ship Island, her doubts remained: they were abandoned there, either forgotten or ignored by the authorities, without any food or clothing. Marie is one of the few survivors.

Pétronille considered mentioning the pirate attack; but on *La Baleine*, the bandits hadn't managed to walk into the hold. Mostly, she wondered what Marie and these girls had done to travel in such horrendous conditions. When she finally dared asking, Marie let out a bitter laugh. "I walked into a fancy shop of the Rue Saint-Honoré, and I was accused of stealing a ribbon. Shot with gold and silver, according to the owner of the store." She looked away, and when her eyes found Pétronille's again, her expression had changed; she seemed furious. "None of this would have happened," she explained, "if it weren't for this evil director of La Salpêtrière. There were terrible roundups in Paris that year, she set up women. I guess the police needed to find settlers so badly that the officers were ready to do anything to bring us here." Marie shook her head. Hers wasn't the worst story: she had heard of a cook deported because she had come home late after going dancing; of a maid accused of seducing a master who had raped her; of a baker jailed because her brothers had accused her of "dirtying their reputation."

Pétronille was silent for a moment. She couldn't have known any of these girls—she had been taken directly from Château-Thierry to La Salpêtrière. Yet she found herself thinking of Étiennette's questions on the boat, how desperately Charlotte's friend had been looking for her sister last fall. She struggled to remember the sibling's name, then asked: "Have you ever heard of a woman called Marceline Janson?"

At that, Marie's face dropped. "Yes. She died. On the boat, shortly after we left Le Havre."

After that, Pétronille never brought back the topic of Marie's years in Paris, and neither did Marie. The only time her friend alluded to their conversation, it was to talk about M. Cléry and his wild dreams for La Louisiane. Her husband despised the other engineers, who'd stay for only a few months at a landlady's in Mobile. He wanted to settle for good, to build the cities of this new land; he had arrived a bachelor right around the same time Marie landed in New Biloxi. "It turned out to be easier than I thought," she said, "to be exactly what he wished me to be. A girl from Montereau who came to Paris to become a dressmaker, and who decided, just like him, that she'd be luckier in the Mississippi." She smiled sadly. "He believed it all, and I almost managed to convince myself too. But there is barely any fabric here and hardly anyone to dress."

In the carriage that waits in front of Pétronille's house, Marie wears the kind of gown Pétronille thought was reserved for young girls. When they enter the tailor's shop, the man's eyebrows rise. Marie barely pays attention to him, starts opening the trunks. Looking at her, Pétronille can't help but think of the made-up ribbon that led her friend here, wondering what would happen if they were to be accused of theft now. But there is no other faraway place to be sent to; they are already on the edge of the world.

"We might as well reinvent the fashion here," Marie observes. "By the time Parisian trends reach us, they will be obsolete."

The tailor shakes his head, looking bewildered; his mustache seems to move independently from his lips. He leads Pétronille to the back shop for measurements. Beyond the curtain, she can hear Marie sorting fabrics, describing a piece of blue linen. "For your dress? What do you think?"

"Lovely," Pétronille says. The tailor's helper rounds a tape measure around her biceps. Pétronille moves her arm. Quick, she thinks. She is glad the woman went for her belly first. She's started to hate being touched there.

"I'm afraid that we wouldn't have enough of that linen for a gown," the tailor's assistant comments from somewhere below, "but we might have something similar in brown."

"Did you hear her, Marie?" Pétronille says. She drops her arm, and the assistant shouts another number to the tailor. In the shop, the main door slams, and Marie says *bonjour* to someone. Her greeting goes unanswered. Soon the opening and closing of the trunks stops. "Marie?" Pétronille calls again.

The wind brings in whiffs of strawberries and manure. The curtain moves faintly, beyond Pétronille's reach. She hears Marie again, whispering to the new customer. The man speaks so low that at first Pétronille can't make out what he is saying. Then his voice comes into focus, materializing around a single word, because she knows exactly how it sounds in her husband's mouth—"*Femme*," becoming one single syllable when he refers to her as his wife in front of Renée or with guests. Her husband is right here, in the shop, and yet he won't come to her.

"I apologize, Madame," the tailor's helper says, "could you please—"

Pétronille steps to the side, and the tape measure falls from her shoulder to her hips. Her throat feels dry. "M. Ducros?" she calls.

The door shuts. Marie's face appears, the curtain cutting under her chin so that her head seems to float. She looks like someone who has just stopped laughing. "What did you just say?"

"I was calling for my husband. I thought he was here."

"M. Ducros at the tailor's?" Marie asks. The idea doesn't seem unthinkable to Pétronille—before going out for supper, he'd often take more time than she did to get dressed—but Marie makes it sound this way.

"I thought I heard him," she says, uncertain now.

Marie tries patting her shoulder without letting go of the curtain, but she's too far and her hand lands in the air. "How understandable," she answers. "M. Mézières also speaks with his nose." Pétronille never noticed her husband spoke with anything but his mouth. The tailor's assistant brings her back her petticoats. "But I doubt you know him," Marie adds, "you were bedridden when he joined the garrison."

On their way back, Pétronille considers asking her husband whether he went to the tailor. By sunset, she's changed her mind. She imagines the curtain thicker, the shop noisier, her friend nothing but genuine.

• • •

The nausea is gone. There is a hardness to her belly, something that makes her want to both touch and avoid it. Her skin has turned surprisingly malleable. She wonders about her mind—whether, just like her body, it could expand, shrink, her thoughts transforming with this changing tide so that she is fit to spend her life in Natchez.

Back in Lorient, she was acutely aware of the child growing inside her. Today she has to tame her body. To pat her own belly like you'd touch a sheepish dog or a ripe melon, wondering what lies behind the eyes, the outer rind.

Her husband has mostly left her alone since they learned about her pregnancy. But a week after her visit to the tailor, she hears a knock on the door. She doesn't know what time it is, only that insects are humming, that they will be for a few more days until hurricane season hits. In La Louisiane, even storms bear another name—one that promises a fury Pétronille hopes she'll never live to see.

"Come in," she says, not loud enough to be heard. The door closes behind M. Ducros. She knows he's still angry about the letter he recently received from M. de Laguehay, whom he met in Clairac four years ago. The directors' assistant had come to recruit men to work the lands owned by the Company—back when John Law, the disgraced controller general of finances of France, was better known for creating the Banque générale and driving investment in the uncharted lands of La Louisiane than for provoking the greatest financial disaster of the beginning of this century. M. Ducros used to refer to M. de Laguehay as his friend, then his partner, then only by his last name. Now he's "an imbecile."

Or at least that's what M. Ducros called him this afternoon when Marie asked why he looked so frustrated. Pétronille knows he wouldn't have told her. Yet he explained to Marie that the Company owes him half a year's service, that M. Guenot, the man running the Sainte-Catherine Concession, should be more mindful of how he treats Natives, that more boats are needed to export tobacco and pelts to France. Marie laughed. "Are you sure you deserve it?" she asked. "Why waste time discussing an idiot's choices? Quit complaining and arrange for the boats to be built." M. Ducros almost seems to appreciate her teasing remarks. They give him a choice: challenge her back or surrender.

Now he sits at the end of the bed, his back turned to Pétronille. This is unexpected. She is used to him warning her of his visits, lifting the sheets in one sudden move as if it has to be done quickly to be painless. Their first night together was rough, worse than the one she spent with the man in Orléans: back then she hadn't known what it was like to be touched when you were in love. The morning after their wedding night, in their New Biloxi house, Pétronille could still feel M. Ducros inside of her. Not only inside—on her arms, chest, shoulders, everywhere his hands had laid. She couldn't get rid of him, thought she'd never be alone, clean, again.

She tried to compromise because she had to. Still, the pain was suffocating; it filled her whole, cramped her belly, left her with a buzzing headache. He tried learning her ways. There were places he never touched again—Baptiste's favorite spots, although M. Ducros would never understand why he could kiss her on the jaw and not on the cheek. What Pétronille and Baptiste used to do together couldn't be associated with him, couldn't turn into this. And yet it did. She resented him for that.

After they arrived in Natchez, she'd come back to Baptiste on her own. She'd touch herself in the middle of the afternoon when the sun was warm and her belly so full it made her feel drowsy, half gone. She'd move her hand to other places, the ones that were forbidden to her husband. The inside of her wrist, the fallout of her breasts, the tip of her nipple. Then one day after dinner, M. Ducros came into her bedroom without knocking, interrupting her. When he reached between her legs, he looked surprised. It hurt less that day. After that, he would often ask her whether she was tired at dessert, and she knew that if she said no, she had to get herself ready. She hated him for putting himself between her and Baptiste, her memories. Yet it was a solution to a problem. She found other moments to herself.

"What is it?" she asks now.

He doesn't initiate anything. "Nothing," he answers.

"Are you certain?"

"Yes."

She envies how frankly he inhabits his emotions—unequivocally, uncompromisingly, as if they are so overwhelmingly right that no other contradictory feeling could coexist. She sometimes finds his stubbornness moving. But she is tired. She brings his hand to her thigh, flying it over her stomach. This part of her body too is now forbidden to him.

"Here," she says, feeling bits of flesh rounding under the pressure of his fingers.

That night is both similar and different from the others. Pétronille has never had sex pregnant. Part of her wants to protect herself from him, as she did during their wedding night; part of her knows it is impossible. M. Ducros moves in a hurry, more so than usually. He cups her neck in his hand, a spot she never had to protect because he never laid his hand there. He is careful about her belly; he has her come to her knees.

He stays for the night, which he has done only twice before. Pétronille realizes she got used to sleeping right in the middle of the bed, and by morning, she finds him curled at the edge of the mattress, about to fall.

• • •

Pétronille's memory holds almost nothing of that February morning when the women were doing laundry, the day she was to reunite with

Baptiste. Bloody shifts, butter-yellow petticoats, stockings hard from sweat. A weakness in her arms, her forehead burning, shivers running down her spine. Charlotte looking at her from the other side of a steaming cauldron, holding the washing bat tight. Geneviève taking the pile of clothes from her and saying she should go now. Pétronille's own answer, then the wet grass sticking under her soles, the mud clasping her feet as if to keep her from moving forward.

Only one image clears up. She's left the lawn and screaming girls behind her, reached the end of the alley. She is in the front yard of the warehouse, where Baptiste should be meeting her. As the yard's items fly past her eyes—empty rags, harnesses, a wheelbarrow—the place widens. Big enough to hold all of *La Baleine*'s crew, but not Baptiste, no one but her as she stumbles toward the gate—and how could she ever think that she'd be able to hoist herself above palings as high as these? The wood is rough and wet under her fingers. She leans against the fence, and the world thins to fit into a crack, this road built by the men and then left to the women, the birds of La Louisiane. Today, on the path that brought her all the way here, there is nothing but a fat pelican shaking its empty pouch in the humid breeze.

• • •

October 1. Marie stands on the threshold of her home, arms crossed against her chest. Her white dress glows orange in the early fall sun. She repeats that the Native girl, the one supposed to bring the remedy recommended by the neighbor's maid, should arrive soon. Pétronille told her friend that the knot in her lower back was gone, but Marie kept on insisting, and Pétronille finally gave in. She didn't have the words to explain that the pain she feels today is different.

"Here she is!" Marie says.

Pétronille stands and watches as a round, brown-skinned girl approaches. Her lips are thin, her cheeks full, her steps hesitant; she looks even younger than Charlotte. She wears a skirt made of a fabric that Pétronille has never seen, and holds an earthenware jar. Her chest is naked, her expression as smooth as the water of a lake.

"Come, come," Marie calls.

At the sound of her voice, the girl freezes. The wind plays with the feather that tops her dark hair. When Marie starts walking toward her, she steps back.

"Wait," Pétronille tells her friend.

The girl glances at Pétronille, then bends over, leaves the remedy on the ground, never taking her eyes off them. On her left shoulder, a small sun carved in her skin follows the movement of her arm. She straightens up, scratches her nose. Then she turns back, disappears under the trees' hairy branches that fall above the path, as if the road didn't exist, as if it didn't need to be there at all.

"Her name is endless," says Marie. "Oodoo'wah something. It seems like everyone in Fort Rosalie has heard of her aunt Tattooed Arm. Anyway. The maid said this would help," she adds, pointing at the jar.

Pétronille stares at the woods. The forest is as impenetrable as ever: she couldn't pinpoint the exact spot where the girl just vanished. The ointment Marie brings inside is the only sign she was ever here. Marie leaves it on the table, picks up the pregnancy gown she has been working on for Pétronille. Pétronille leans over the green mixture in which a fly struggles; it doesn't smell like anything she knows. She has heard of Natives' remedies, which seem more sophisticated than the French ones, and the fevers cured with four pipes of tobacco followed by a salad, curdled milk, two bottles of Bordeaux, and two drams of eau-de-vie. Pétronille pushes the bowl away. The plants will do nothing against the crunching pain she woke up to this morning, a woozy feeling up in her chest, the way she imagines her belly will feel when the baby starts kicking.

A year ago to the day, she was standing with Geneviève on *La Baleine*'s deck, watching France fade away. Her foot trapped by a rope, she was listening to and looking at Baptiste for the first time and not finding him very handsome. Geneviève by her side, Baptiste guiding her with his voice. These facts seem impossible.

"Are you well? Is it that damn disease bothering you again?"

"What disease?"

"The fever you suffered from in New Biloxi."

"Oh," Pétronille says, "no." The fever, just like Baptiste, has been consigned to a set period of time. One she considers past and gone; the other will haunt her forever.

"So what is it?"

If her friend hadn't insisted, Pétronille wouldn't have brought up Baptiste. Yet she can't help but think of Marie the first time she came to her home, how she confided in her the details of her arrestation in Paris, the horrific crossing of the Atlantic. Marie hadn't hesitated to trust her with her story.

"It is a man I used to know," she said. "Today is the day I met him. Last year."

Marie flicks a crumb off her sleeve. She seems tense. "What was his name?" she asks.

"Baptiste Dubier."

"Where did you meet him?"

"On the boat that brought me here."

"And you loved him very much."

Pétronille isn't sure whether it is a statement or a question. Saying Baptiste's name out loud gives credibility to her sadness. It gives it power too. She hasn't cried in front of anyone but Geneviève since she left France.

"Now, now," Marie says. She doesn't motion toward Pétronille to comfort her. "Love isn't something to cry over, isn't it? It is to be celebrated. And I know exactly how." Her voice gains in intensity. "We should go horseback riding." When Pétronille doesn't reply, she adds: "You were taught how to in Château-Thierry, weren't you?"

"I was." She remembers the first time she rode on a horse. She was twelve. She held on to the reins so tight her palms bled. The following summer, she rode almost every day through the estate on her own. That sense of freedom is hard to remember, as if it belonged to someone else. "But isn't it dangerous here? Especially the two of us on our own?"

"We wouldn't be venturing far." Marie shifts on her chair. She looks delighted. "We could go from your house to mine. Didn't you say you wanted to see more of this place?"

"I did."

"In a few weeks, you surely won't be able to anymore. You're barely showing for now."

There is an urgency in Marie's tone that makes the offer easy to accept. Pétronille could be raising other issues, and her friend would have the answer, like whenever Pétronille asks about the enslaved Africans, the crops, the Natchez people. Slaves shouldn't be forced to work on Sundays, yet they are. Look at all those mulberry trees: if only someone tried to raise silkworms here, they would make a fortune in La Louisiane. Natives celebrate the new year in March and divide the year in thirteen moons; the Grigra, Jenzenaque, and White Apple villages are pro-British and shouldn't be approached. Through Marie, Fort Rosalie is becoming decipherable, reachable.

Pétronille glances out of the window. An insect lingers on the glass. The light is golden, unbelievable for so early in the afternoon.

"When shall we go?" she asks.

• • •

At supper that night, she is nervous. Her husband seems upset again. She watches him help himself to more ale, stir his broth until it cools. Thin clouds roll in the sky outside the window, and the room glows pink with the last sunbeams of day. M. Ducros has barely said a word all evening. Pétronille knows it is irrational, but she worries that her husband might somehow sense or know about her excursion with Marie, set for the day after tomorrow.

"What is it?" she tries.

He pushes back a half-eaten slice of bread, then rubs his temples with his knuckles. "My letter," he tells her.

She breathes more freely. "What are you talking about?"

"My response to this idiot from the Company."

It takes her a few seconds to remember who he's referring to. Then it comes back: M. de Laguehay, who owes M. Ducros money. Her husband hasn't mentioned him since receiving his letter a few weeks ago.

"What about it?" she asks.

"We won't receive his payment any time soon," he says. "My response didn't leave as it should have today. It'll be months before it reaches France."

"It always is." She means to be reassuring. She suddenly wants her words to carry as much weight as Marie's. But M. Ducros doesn't seem to hear her.

"The only comfort," he says, "is that *La Baleine* should soon reach La Rochelle."

She opens her mouth, closes it. She understands nothing about this sentence—neither how it is related to her husband's mail and financial concerns, nor why *La Baleine* would take so long to reach La Rochelle when it sailed in February. The name of the boat echoes in her mind like that of a loved one. Her husband pats her hand. "My bills to the Company," he explains. "I managed to have *La Baleine*'s captain take them aboard last May."

Pétronille tries to keep her face neutral, but her hands are shaking. "Last May?" she asks. "Didn't she sail last winter?"

"The sailors' quarters emptied in February," he corrects her, forgetting to even question what she based her assumptions upon. "But the ship itself didn't leave until mid-May." Images of herself last spring flash in Pétronille's mind—weakened, bedridden, recovering. Then come new ones: *La Baleine*, still in La Louisiane; Baptiste, not yet out of reach, somewhere outside the windows of her bedroom. "But you're right," her husband continues, "it would have been better if she had sailed earlier. M. de Laguehay wouldn't have written this nonsense after receiving my bill."

"Where did the crew go last winter?" she asks.

"I didn't know you cared so much about this boat business," he says, reaching for the ale pitcher. She stares at him. "To Ship Island for a few weeks," he tells her. "Doing repairs on *La Baleine*, arming her for the return journey."

Pétronille doesn't reply. She hears herself say that she's tired, then forces her legs to stand up and carry her upstairs. Her thighs sweat, her stomach cramps. In her bedroom, she sits on the edge of the bed. For a moment, she is afraid she'll be sick. She stares at the windowsill, as if the two obsessive thoughts that fill her mind were carved there. When she moved to New Biloxi, Baptiste was still in the colony. In February, he had missed their rendezvous only because he was away, working on Ship Island.

That night, a new thought strikes her, one that she couldn't have fathomed hours ago. It doesn't matter when *La Baleine* sailed; Baptiste's absence had nothing to do with his feelings for her. She sees herself waving at him for the last time and wonders how it took her so long to understand what now seems obvious—that their relationship had ended long before, on the early-January morning when the ship first dropped anchor in La Louisiane and she was herded down the gangway with the other girls. Now that she knows his love for her may never cease, it becomes possible to accept what she has known all along—that she was meant to stay here and he wasn't.

Pétronille thinks of Geneviève and Charlotte. Outside, the night fills with sounds. She sees her friends deciding with her where to meet Baptiste, distracting the nuns during laundry—feeding her hope to keep her alive. Moonlight filters through the curtains. Pétronille is surprised to feel the tightness in her chest loosening.

• • •

The horses are M. Cléry's, the itinerary Marie's: they will ride from the Clérys' to the Ducroses', then back. Meet up for lunch, then go. They will have all morning to explore and will be back at Marie's in time for dinner, and their husbands won't notice a thing. Stuffed between two meals, the excursion seems more casual, something they could repeat. If they were men; if they didn't live in barely charted territory. Pétronille tries not to think about that. Her husband looked calmer today; he'd found another boat for his letter. When she told him she would be calling on Marie, he shrugged, looking distracted. "I'm about to go to the Bernège brothers' anyway," he said. "They finally have silkworms to sell me." Pétronille nodded. One word from Marie about the abundance of mulberry trees, and her husband ridiculously thinks he is ready to produce silk. But his eagerness to follow her friend's advice doesn't bother Pétronille like it would have two days ago.

Like every morning, M. Cléry would be locked into his office, working on a map of the settlement for the Company of the Indies. Marie shook her head. "I always find paint stains everywhere when he comes out of there," she explained.

When Pétronille asked what Marie would say to the lads, she looked startled. "To get the horses ready. What else should I be telling them?" Pétronille shrugs. Until now, besides the maid and the cook, she has never given orders to anyone at her home. The thought of not having to justify herself is exhilarating.

She doesn't tell Marie what she discovered about Baptiste the day before yesterday; she doesn't want to hear that what she thinks of as truth might be only supposition. Pétronille knows this is the closest she'll ever come to closure—La Louisiane will never give her more.

Outside, clouds float lazily around. The Clérys' alley feels entirely new, the distance between her house and the stables infinite. Marie is wearing a navy blue waistcoat that falls midthigh and petticoats the same color. "Thanks to you, I'm finally getting to use the riding habit I made," Marie says, and Pétronille can't help but ponder the "thanks to you." She hasn't initiated this excursion, doesn't feel responsible for what they are about to do. Yet Marie's words touch her. It has been a long time since something has been done thanks to her.

Two lads stand up at their approach—both are the neighbor's sons, a plowman from the southwest of France. One of them holds the double bridles of a hazel mare who is chewing on her snaffle. In the other stall, a robust horse vehemently scratches its nose against a pole. Pétronille knows there are many things she should be afraid of, but at that moment, all she fears is not remembering how to ride.

"Nonsense," Marie tells her, pressing her right hand on the shoulder of the younger-looking boy to hop on the mare. "Some things never leave you."

Pétronille knows this is true as soon as she places her foot on the intertwined fingers of the lad and lifts herself onto the saddle. The horse—the sturdier one—moves to and fro to balance this new weight. His movements, the throwing of her knee over the pommel, the way she is adjusting her petticoats, everything feels so strangely familiar and remote that she isn't sure where she is anymore. She gathers the reins in one hand, steers toward Marie. The muscles of the horse roll under her thigh; she has never seen the countryside from this high, never felt as at peace in Natchez. She's been sleeping well these past two nights. For the first time in months, she feels refreshed. She strokes her own belly. Everything will be fine. She is simply taking her baby on a ride.

They head toward the cypress forest that lies between Fort Rosalie and Sainte-Catherine Creek, leaving the house behind them. The flowers they pass by are enormous, almost aggressive-looking; Paul wouldn't have known anything about them, and neither does Pétronille. Perhaps one of them is the plant that relieves back pain. The one with the white corolla could help ease fevers. Who knows what the tiny purple ones might do. She spurs her horse forward. The pommel massages her bent leg.

Soon there is nothing to be heard but birds. One sings over the others, its cries resembling those of an angry cat. Branches trickle under the passenger pigeons that M. Ducros swears he can kill by tens with a single gunshot. She and Marie agreed not to follow the road that swirls between the farms, the one they take with the carriage. They'd be too easy to spot. Instead, they start on the forest trail that M. Cléry regularly uses as a shortcut to pay visits to M. Ducros. On the map he showed Marie a week ago, the path is colored a light pink; it goes straight, she said to Pétronille. Then she drew a straight line in the air, as if crossing herself.

The path bends a first time. A second. Pétronille tells herself that if it curves again, she'll ask Marie if they are on the right road; but as the trail becomes more sinuous, she finds that hearing her friend acknowledge they might be lost scares her. Marie knows what she is doing, Pétronille repeats to herself. Soon, she can't see the houses anymore. The woods are dense, like an overly decorated room. In places, the path disappears entirely under reeds that break under the horses' hooves. Then it clears again.

"We should soon hear the creek," Marie says. Her voice is cheerful. Pétronille can't see her face.

And they do hear water. It slides soft and persistent under the chirping, whooshing, cracking of the forest. Then come other sounds. The playful screams of a child, of many children—the language unknown but the sounds unmistakable. Another bend and the trees become scarcer, and then they see them, six or seven Native girls and boys, knee- or waist-high in the creek, their splashing and swimming stirring sunlight in the water. On the opposite bank, an old man sits on a rock. His eyes are right on them, as if he heard their horses coming from a long way.

Fear bludgeons Pétronille's throat. She feels her horse move under her. Marie's whip rises above the mare's rear, then freezes.

Beyond the man is a hilly village, parts of it hidden by berry bushes. Two mounds towering above huts, a central plaza. Women grinding corn, some of their backs and breasts covered with drawings. A girl spreading what looks like bear oil on a child's arms. His lean body glows in the sun as if wet. Boys, barely twelve, aiming with their bows at a hand-size haystack stuck on the top of a high post. One of them giggles when his arrow cuts through the hay. But the sound of the bows and laughter are covered by the splashing water—the children have glanced at the old man and resumed their games. His eyes meet Pétronille's. It doesn't last: the whip never froze, it smacked the mare's hips twice already, and now they are galloping along the creek, past the children, and as the wind and branches fly past, all Pétronille is taking with her is the man's incredulous look—their sight maybe even more bewildering, threatening to him.

When they come to a halt, the horses aren't ready to stop. Their hooves trample on the fallen reddish leaves, slide in the mud. Marie is out of breath. Her little hat has fallen, and her hair reaches her shoulders. Pétronille has never seen her like that.

"That was the Grand Village," she almost shouts.

"I thought you said they were our allies."

"Yes," Marie answers, but she is shaking her head. "We weren't supposed to come all the way here. We must have gone east somehow."

"You don't know where we are."

Marie ignores her. "Do you think they'll follow us?" she asks.

Pétronille thinks of the children pausing, then jumping in the river again. What do they do next? "I don't know," she says.

Above them, the sun shines so brightly that it seems impossible they could be lost. Pétronille's head hurts. Marie points her whip upstream. "If we follow the creek, we'll reach Sainte-Catherine Concession."

Then what? Pétronille doesn't want to ask. Galloping wasn't liberating. She feels fragile. She wants to tell the baby she is sorry, then feels silly for wishing so. She needs to bring her, him, home. Marie starts trotting; Pétronille calls out for her to slow down. Her friend turns, rolls her eyes, but holds the mare back. They progress slowly along the water.

Sometimes Pétronille thinks she can hear steps trailing behind, children playing in the river. But it's only a deer, a fox, a magpie. The world feels enormous.

When they reach the first tobacco fields, Marie gives out a little cry. She starts trotting on the trail that runs on the edge of the plantation, calling out. Pétronille follows at some distance. The concession is the second biggest in Fort Rosalie after Terre Blanche, even she knows that. Between the huge leaves, enslaved men and women stare at her, then return to work. She tries not to look at their hands, the broken nails, the sweat that runs in skin folds. A baby rests in a half-filled basket in the shade of the plants, his closed fists to his nose, scratching it with a determination that strikes Pétronille. A man wearing a dirty shift says something that is lost on her.

She pushes her horse forward. What else is there to do? she asks herself in horror, even if she knows the answer already.

Marie is riding between the woods and the fields. When Pétronille catches up with her, the horses nod their muzzles at each other, as if they know something no one else does. From here, the plantation's main house disappears behind a mulberry grove. Wind sweeps through the tobacco leaves in abrupt bursts, plowing one section of crops after another. An enslaved woman stands firm, holds still, until the gusts are gone.

When Pétronille lifts her eyes from her face, though, she sees beyond her a group of Native men. They are much farther, coming out of another forest clearing. Only their backs are visible from the trail. Their silhouettes tiny and yet recognizable, the sun meeting their bare skin, the curve of their feathers and bows a curious prolongation of their hair, hands.

This time it's Pétronille who jerks her bridle, slams her whip, heads back to the woods—hoping there will be no one to watch them, catch them, bring them back to the places they didn't choose.

• • •

What they learn when they reach the main road and run into the soldiers who were sent to search for them, after the stable boys alerted M. Cléry, is that danger isn't where you think it is. It isn't by a creek where children bathe. It is on the plantation of a white man hated so dearly by the Natives that their chief, the Great Sun of the Natchez people, sends only his poorer men to talk to him, unwilling to reduce his most esteemed warriors to such a degrading task. The danger is in being seen with or considered an ally of the man running the Sainte-Catherine plantation, M. Guenot. Pétronille heard this name once or twice before. He was her husband's favorite example, when M. Ducros criticized the Frenchmen who treated Natives like dirt, calling them "feathered slaves" and mocking their peace calumet. Around noon today, Pétronille and Marie were riding on the edge of his plantation.

Pétronille's house is closer, and so they are taken there. When her husband meets them, M. Ducros is shaking. The fury in his voice reminds Pétronille of a boiling day last summer when she sat on the porch and watched hills and fields tremble in the heat. M. Ducros shouts louder at Marie than he does at her, and for a brief moment, it is a relief.

Now that her friend has gone home, Pétronille sits by her bed, grabs a brush, gathers her stained clothes. Dirt clings to her like something dear. She feels muscles in her legs that make her think she barely knows herself. She doesn't call Renée but scrubs the mud herself. She wants it all gone. She feels the weight of all the things she doesn't know, all the secrets that this land holds, buried in its forests, bursting outside of her bedroom. This morning, for the time she was outside, she felt she understood it all. It was so obvious then. All she saw were people trying to make a life, people trying to protect theirs, and people longing for the one they had been forced to leave.

She reasons to herself. It can't be that simple; even a child, her child, could understand that.

Then there is the other secret. Closer, more intimate, and yet no less unfathomable. After she and Marie were given broth, after she went to fetch cider in the kitchen, she kept on expecting to hear horses, M. Cléry coming for Marie, but everything remained silent. The early-afternoon sun sent short shadows through the small window. And when Pétronille did hear a carriage, it wasn't the Clérys' but theirs that she saw parked in the alley.

She watched her husband, walking ahead of Marie, gesturing for her to follow. M. Ducros would be giving her friend a ride back, yet she hadn't even said goodbye. Pétronille considered calling her, then thought better of it and rushed to the door. She stopped short on the threshold. She watched her friend in her husband's arms, his fingers white and her waistcoat creased, half hidden by the branches of a massive pecan tree. At first Marie kept her face buried in his shoulder. Then she raised her head, eyes searching the house, staring at the open door, at Pétronille. None of them moved.

There was no whip now to send them galloping toward a future they both ignored.

$$\bullet \; \bullet \; \bullet$$

The following morning, Renée announces Mme Cléry's visit from the top of the stairs. Pétronille's body goes stiff. She slept so deep last night that she woke up groggy, a bit sick. She isn't sure if she is ready to hear any explanation. She felt so close to Marie yesterday, like she once had to Geneviève and Charlotte. Then she found Marie nestled against her husband. The two feelings seem irreconcilable: her deep connection with Marie and her friend's betrayal.

Marie wears the yellow dress she had on the day they met. She stands by the armchair where she usually sits. "I came here to apologize," she says.

At least she is true to herself: she doesn't lack courage. "Have a seat," Pétronille says, and Marie lowers herself on the armchair cautiously, as if Pétronille might change her mind.

"I suppose you do not care to know how it all started?" Marie asks.

Pétronille sees herself spending the summer in her room; her husband somewhere, anywhere, as long as he isn't in her bed; M. Cléry gone on an endless trip to Pascagoula. She realizes she knows already.

Outside, the carpenters who might build her husband's silk farm measure the field, yelling at each other.

"I'm deeply sorry," says Marie.

"He looked more worried for you than he did for his own child yesterday." That's what hurts Pétronille most. Almost: what hurts her most is her friend's disloyalty, not his. "Please don't deny it."

"I am not." Marie pauses, then continues, "I love him dearly, you know."

In another world, in a world where she is married to Baptiste, that sentence sweeps away everything, confines Marie to a phase of Pétronille's life. Not in this one. In this one, it puts Pétronille back at the main door, staring beyond the pecan tree at the two of them. This time she doesn't see her husband and her friend. She sees a lovers' embrace—recognizes the way in which Baptiste, who never stopped loving her, used to pull her in close, her breasts pushed against his chest, her nails playing again and again with the rough hair at the nape of his neck.

"I know you do," Pétronille says.

"I'm not asking for your forgiveness." Marie's palm strokes the buckskin of her gloves, her wedding present, the fabric changing color and texture as she brushes it one way and then the other. "I was hoping I would find you dull when I met you," she adds. "It would have made things easier."

"You don't think I'm dull? Animated only by cruelty, and unbearably predictable?"

Marie shakes her head. "Predictable? I wouldn't have expected you to join me on a horse ride."

"I would have expected the offer."

"So I am the dull one after all."

"No," Pétronille says, "the cruel one."

She lies back against the cushions, rests her hand on her belly. Inside of her, everything is quiet. What will remain of it all in a few months, once the baby is here? A bedtime story. She'll hold her child so close and say: Picture two women. The month is October. They are riding along a creek where children swim, some barely older than you. Bathing like you would, if only the women understood the creatures that live underwater, which they never will. Yet that day, the children keep playing, the women riding, unharmed.

Charlotte

Charlotte wishes she could scream, but she'd wake up the baby. Either she's dressed too warmly for April or it's too hot in the bedroom. Her back dampens; her corset gathers sweat. From her stool by the window, she catches a glimpse of Étiennette and her son, wrapped in linen on the bed. M. Feuger just went back to his business, excusing himself too loudly after squinting at his new child. Hugo looks nothing like his brother, who was born big and loud. He sleeps a condescending sleep amid the girls' excited chatter. All three of them—Marthe and the twins, Léonie and Sophie—had been on *La Baleine* and recently arrived with their husbands in New Orleans. Charlotte knows she should be marveling at the newborn with them, enumerating his body parts, from his tiny hands to his tiny nose and nails. Her own baby's arms and feet should have been tiny too. Her baby should have screamed, fussed, and farted like Hugo did before he fell into this unfathomable sleep. But she never saw her child, never knew whether she should refer to it as him or her. It was a clot of blood when it came out of her. Nothing about the clot was tiny.

That was a year and a half ago. She was living in New Biloxi then, in the small house by the bayou that her husband had built. Louis was working on the river when it happened; she had to mourn the death of their child alone. And she isn't sure if she is entitled to call it a death— can someone who never lived die? The priest was adamant. A runt would not be baptized.

"Charlotte," Léonie says. She is only two years older than Charlotte, and yet at almost seventeen, she carries herself in a way that makes her look much older. Her twin sister sits by Étiennette, petting a dog, explaining that swaddling newborns is barbaric. Children should be free to move their limbs.

"We'll talk again when your son is clubfooted," Étiennette says in a very loud whisper.

Léonie turns to Charlotte. "How are you feeling?" she asks.

"Slightly dizzy." Charlotte motions her hand toward the window. Outside the shoemaker's workshop, a boy bumps into a young woman, who trips and falls into the drainage ditch that runs in every street of New Orleans. The moat is filled with last night's rain.

"We barely had a chance to chat this afternoon," Léonie says.

The shoemaker comes out and examines a pair of clogs under the timid sun. The girl in the ditch is gone. Charlotte turns to Léonie. "I just needed some fresh air."

In Étiennette's arms, Hugo starts screaming and Léonie rushes toward him. His cries fill Charlotte's ears, travel through her chest. She doesn't know what they did with her baby. She remembers seeing a woman carry it out of the room. She remembers moving her legs through something viscous, trying to lower her shift to cover herself, bringing back a hand so bloody it turned black. Her memories stop there.

When she woke up, Étiennette was there for her, both a blessing and a curse: her friend was six months pregnant when Charlotte lost her child. For the first time in her life, Charlotte was shocked to feel that she would rather have been visited by Geneviève, who once made babies disappear. But Geneviève was already gone by that first fall in La Louisiane, having followed her Canadian husband to the Illinois Country—even farther north than where Pétronille had gone almost two years ago. Over the next weeks, Étiennette talked to Charlotte about everything but the miscarriage—a horrid word that Charlotte couldn't quite associate with what had happened to her. She'd lost her baby. That, she could relate to: the event, the indescribable pain that came along with it. That phrase created space for a child, allowed it to live and die. The term "miscarrying" was different; it made her responsible for failing to carry her son, her daughter, as she should have.

Charlotte has been trying to become pregnant for a year, enough time for Étiennette to give birth to this second boy. When her first child was born, it took Charlotte three weeks to go see him. Aurélien was painful to think of, to look at. He was kicking, brutally alive. So last Sunday, when Charlotte learned her friend had gone into labor, she promised herself she would do better this time.

"You're right to sit over here." Marthe drags a chair toward Charlotte, and part of the carpet comes with it. She is a lanky girl whose last name Charlotte knows is now Valade, but they've never talked. She saw her on *La Baleine* and a few times at Étiennette's in New Biloxi. Then not anymore until they both settled in New Orleans three months ago. "We should give her some air," Marthe adds.

"Yes," Charlotte answers. "But it's hard to stay away from a child as lovely as hers."

Marthe's face brightens. "Just what I was about to say." Then she starts fidgeting with her ring. She keeps on glancing at Charlotte, like some of the other women did after the pirate attack—like an object of curiosity, as if Marthe is trying to convince herself that this child-girl really had the courage to do what she did on the ship. Charlotte sometimes wonders the same of herself.

"Isn't your husband a boat guide?" Marthe finally says.

"He is." Charlotte knows that M. Valade is a trader, that he's a lot wealthier than they are. But she isn't supposed to know. She forces herself to ask.

"I couldn't say what he trades for my life, only that he's just been asked back in Natchez," Marthe says. "He is gone a lot. But you must know what it feels like to long for your man's return."

"I do," Charlotte says, and most of the time, she genuinely does.

"You must fear for his safety. These rivers are treacherous."

"No more dangerous than Indians trading with you one day and turning against you the next."

Marthe's eyes widen. She lowers her voice. "Have you heard of the Natchez war?"

"Why, yes. Everyone has."

Marthe seems impressed. Her eyes remind Charlotte of cows'— bulging and interrogative. Charlotte tries to be kinder. "A friend of mine lives there," she explains, "and I was worried about her."

"What's her name? Did she travel with us?"

"Mlle Béranger—Pétronille," Charlotte says, but Marthe shakes her head. "The girl with the white stain on her cheek," Charlotte reluctantly adds.

"Oh, of course. Such a strange creature. Is she safe?" Marthe asks, looking distracted.

"She is." Last fall, the war had been short—a relief to Charlotte. She knew that if it had lasted longer, Louis would have had to fight. Fort Rosalie's garrison counted no more than eighteen men under one captain, all gathered behind a rotting palisade—why maintain the posts if the relationship with the Natives was peaceful and had been for years?

Everything changed last October, more than a year after Charlotte saw Pétronille leave New Biloxi. Louis told her that the trouble all started when a French sergeant named La Fontaine threw a fit because a Natchez man failed to bring the corn he'd promised as part of a trade they'd made. Sergeant La Fontaine was barely reprimanded for the killings that ensued. "The Natchez were furious," Louis said.

Charlotte's fear for him and Pétronille grew as the violence escalated. In late October, the manager of the Sainte-Catherine Concession was wounded at the collarbone. M. Guenot was known for mistreating the Natchez allies, and he barely escaped the five shots that were directed at him. The Natchez warriors were far from done with him: the men from the White Apple Village fired on his concession for an entire week—and Charlotte couldn't help wondering how close Pétronille lived to Guenot's plantation, whether she could hear the sounds of battle or watch the Natives gather and aim from the hill.

"The war could have been a lot worse," Louis insisted. Charlotte agreed: the events happened so fast, reported by one exhausted envoy after the other, that there was almost no time to recover from the last news before the next arrived, rippling from Fort Rosalie to New Orleans, all the way to Charlotte's home in New Biloxi. By the end of October 1722, Tattooed Snake, the Natchez war chief of the Grand Village, was already seeking an agreement between the French and the Natchez of the belligerent villages. Peace was restored three days later. Louis said the Natchez delegation even came to New Orleans, bringing their calumet to Governor Bienville. But the words meant nothing to Charlotte. They did to Louis, who obsessively listed the peace offerings that were given to the Natchez people. Horn-handled knives, awls, vermilion, ells of limbourg.

But Charlotte couldn't care for these gifts. She pictured Pétronille, lost in her own world, cuddling her baby boy in her house in Natchez, whispering to him that they were safe now. Even Pétronille has become a mother.

"I should say goodbye," Marthe says, gesturing toward Étiennette. "Are you staying?"

The spring light sneaks between the curtains. Outside, cows parade down the street, their tails whipping the wheels of a cart.

"I guess not," Charlotte says.

She feels Étiennette's eyes fall on her as soon as she stands up. The twins call their dogs, and the animals go off running in the corridor, their claws clinking against the wooden floor. Léonie mouths a final *au revoir*, and Étiennette waves at her from the bed. In Paris, at the warehouse, her friend barely cared about the girls' pasts, whether they came from families of street sellers or master tailors. On *La Baleine*, they were all equal. But once the women were married, Étiennette started paying attention to the husbands' positions. The unlucky ones, those who were married off to starving farmers, suspected criminals, or destitute cadets, were never invited to her home. That, in itself, had been disturbing. The men changed the way they saw themselves, each other—what the women wanted and hoped for, what they felt they deserved.

Étiennette stopped looking for her sister a few months after marrying M. Feuger. Charlotte remembers the day her friend asked him, during the spring of their first year in New Biloxi, whether he could find out anything about Marceline. M. Feuger argued that the search was pointless, but he finally went to the administration building. He came back empty-handed. He told Étiennette what he had learned: that the wedding certificates of recent years had been destroyed by a storm, unless it was a fire, the intendant repeated only what he had heard, he was in Paris at the time. In any case, they were gone, and without these records, what other way could there be to track down a woman in La Louisiane? Charlotte stared at her feet, wondering whether this was true—if they were all really only one document away from vanishing.

After that afternoon, Marceline was never brought up again. Charlotte hopes Étiennette came to understand that even having the marriage certificates wouldn't have mattered much—that given how vast, how dangerous, La Louisiane was, they'd all better stick to the people who are still here, whom they know best. Sometimes Charlotte can't help but wonder if Étiennette would be her friend had they not met so long ago. Then she feels bad for thinking this: when the food becomes so scarce that only "friends" of the governor can enter the warehouses, Étiennette always brings something back for her.

Charlotte sits on the edge of the bed. The newborn wriggles inside his linen swaddle, then gives up.

"Here you are," Étiennette simply says.

Charlotte makes a point of staying after Marthe is gone and the wet nurse has carried the child away. Only then, when it's just the two of them, does she really recognize Étiennette. The way her friend passes her hand over her face in one clean stroke when she is tired, as if skin against skin could sweep the fatigue away. Sometimes Charlotte sees her own palm passing over Étiennette's forehead, following her nose, brushing her lips. Her cheeks burn, and she tries to focus instead on a locket, a candlestick, a closed chest. She has been punished enough for her thoughts—her womb an unwelcoming place, cold and threatening, a narrow hole babies drown in.

"I saw you speaking to Marthe," her friend comments, lifting herself up on a pillow.

"She is quite interesting."

Étiennette laughs. "You can't lie to me."

"Fine," Charlotte says, "she is who she is."

"I knew you'd find her remedies appealing."

"What do you mean?"

Étiennette frowns. "She didn't bother you with her secret recipes? Tell you the very, very long story of how she finally succeeded in having her child?" She rolls her eyes. "What on earth did you talk about then?"

"Pétronille and the war—never mind. She didn't say a word about any of this."

"Well, given the situation," Étiennette says, "I thought the topic would come up quite naturally."

Charlotte leans back in her chair. Her belly shames her. She knows how the other women see her—a broken vessel, a broken wife. "You're the only one I tell about these things," she answers, and her voice comes out too quiet.

"Well, maybe you should mention it to others," Étiennette says, "because they might be better able to help."

Could Geneviève have helped? She knew more about babies than any of the other girls who traveled on *La Baleine*, though her knowledge had served the wrong purpose. And now Geneviève is too far, long gone.

"Fine."

The small bell of Saint-Louis Church starts ringing, muffled by the wood panels. The building on the Place d'Armes doesn't deserve its name: for now, masses, baptism and wedding ceremonies are celebrated in a mere storehouse. Charlotte has no idea what time it is. "I should go," she says.

Étiennette nods. She scratches her nose, looks at her. "I'm glad you came," she says, and pats Charlotte's hand. It takes all of Charlotte's will to move hers away.

• • •

She can't always resist. There are nights when it's impossible not to see herself lying in the warehouse, a bit over two years ago, her face so close to Étiennette's neck that she could feel her friend's baby hairs shiver against her mouth. It was cold during those first weeks in La Louisiane, and when nightmares full of howling women and distorted pirates woke her up, she told herself there was nothing wrong with seeking warmth where she could find it. She'd shared a bed with Étiennette for years at La Salpêtrière. But it wasn't before that night in the warehouse that she understood there were many kinds of warmth. She remembers the exact date, January 16, because it was the day she woke up with blood encrusted under her nails for the first time, cramps ruining her lower belly and back, and had to go splash water between her thighs while a girl called out, "*La petite* is finally one of us."

That January night, she had been half asleep. Today she isn't sure whether that's true, but back then that's how it felt: everything slow, dark, possible. There was straw under her head, a wool blanket itching her calf, Étiennette's legs, then her mouth, grazing against the nape of her neck, lingering there for a moment. The vulnerability of it all—perfect and disastrous. There was no doubt Étiennette had woken up—you can't say no so clearly in your sleep.

In New Orleans, Charlotte still feels her chest swing when she sees Étiennette. Her friend's body changed over the past couple of years: it became rounder, more assertive, as if she could take on more than before. She probably does—otherwise how could she deal with her boys, their constant need for food, attention, love? She gives them so much. Pie slices that end up smashed under Aurélien's feet, alert glances from the other side of a room, kisses so voracious they leave his hair messy.

Charlotte gives to her husband but sparingly, when Louis happens to be home. She feels stuck in time, back in the warehouse, the moment when Étiennette shifts to her side and whispers no. The affection she feels for her husband is nothing in comparison with what she knows herself to be capable of. She would love her baby so much. A guiltless kind of love, one she can't imagine.

• • •

Louis should have been back the week Étiennette gave birth. Charlotte is used to the delays, the silence, the uncertainty, but it's the first time Louis has been gone for so long: he left almost a month ago. This time he isn't working on L'Anglois, a river south of New Orleans, but somewhere north of it—beyond Lake Pontchartrain, gone with a soldier patrol in need of directions. When she asked how he could guide people somewhere he had never been, Louis laughed. "Believe me, I can read a current or a wind better than any of these men," he said.

She knows he feels happier on the rivers. Louis comes from Oléron Island, off the coast of La Rochelle. His first memories are of the ocean, of being three on his uncle's fishing boat—of a gigantic bass hitting him so hard with its tail that he nearly lost consciousness. "Point is, I was no stronger than a fish at the time," he told her once, shortly after she lost their child. "And I can see you think the same of me," he added, glancing at her. She smiled: he constantly needed reassurance. She told him he was as strong as she could hope him to be. He didn't seem convinced but stroked her cheek. She was thankful for his stories, which often ended like jokes. Jokes were what she needed at the time. Even now.

They moved into their new house three months ago, in January. Looking at New Orleans right after their arrival, she found it hard to believe that a storm had ravaged the town barely four months earlier—destroying the church, rectory, and settlers' huts, the overflowing Saint-Jean Bayou threatening to drown all the powder, which was saved at the very last minute. In New Biloxi, the wind and water had taken everything with them; Charlotte had been relieved to leave this devastation behind her. In New Orleans, people tried their best to talk offhandedly about the September 1722 hurricane. It raged for hours, but the death toll was relatively low. The huts weren't meant to last, they didn't fit the alignment of the town: they should have been torn apart and rebuilt anyway.

Charlotte's experience in New Biloxi was different. Homes had been shattered, the town entirely flooded; she could still see bodies floating down these new streams, hear the cries of people who had lost everything. She knew that girls from *La Baleine* had perished in the storm; she was relieved that Pétronille and Geneviève hadn't had to live through it. Despite what everyone said in the capital, Charlotte could feel the hurricane's impact on the colony. West of New Orleans, the rich coast that M. Feuger calls the "garden of the capital" was inundated, its crops destroyed; even the German farmers, the settlers harvesting this fertile region of the colony, struggled to keep the prices down. Eggs and peas became expensive—smoked beef, a luxury. Shortly after their arrival in New Orleans, Louis hastily built palisades around their land, as per the governor's order. They could barely afford the timber that would supposedly shield them from the next storm. But they couldn't have paid the administration's penalty either.

The few arpents they were allotted lay at the northern edge of New Orleans. The property lines were cleaner on paper. Charlotte doesn't know if the cypress woods that border her garden belong to them, and she doubts anyone knows. They live where the town recedes and gives way to the forest. They were lucky: when they arrived, part of the land had already been cleared by the employees of the Company. Louis had to finish their work if he wanted the plot to be theirs, and Charlotte helped him as best she could. She weeded, gathered fallen reeds, pulled creepers and roots out of the damp soil. She got bitten by a wildcat, saved two baby birds when Louis wasn't looking. New Orleans broke her lower back, blew blisters under the skin of her hands. Yet, for the first time in two years, the woods of La Louisiane showed a wounded face. The forest resisted, but the opaque green wall that used to taunt her in New Biloxi gradually receded. Neighbors came to help fell the trees and canebrakes they would need to build their house—the same carpenters, roofers, and masons who had survived a hurricane and restored a city in a few months. The dirt road where Charlotte lives has recently been named Rue de Bourbon.

The river runs on the opposite side of the town, but its acrid scent penetrates her home: it is this delta that convinced officials the capital of La Louisiane should be moved to New Orleans. Passengers, goods, and animals would no longer have to stop at Ship Island and be loaded into pirogues to continue their journey. The boats could land thirty-two leagues south, then follow the St. Louis River upstream directly to the city, the other forts. The river would become the watery avenue the royal administration had dreamed of. When the decision was made, Louis didn't hide his disappointment. New Orleans was nothing more than a bog, flooded half of the year. He said these wigged men knew nothing about the difficult stretch at the mouth of the St. Louis River, where vicious sandbars forced exhausted crews to unload and reload their ships just to enter the river. "Still better than Mobile," he'd conclude. But New Biloxi, where they had already settled, wouldn't become the urban center of this swampland.

Charlotte barely remembers anything from the journey west. She was too relieved that Étiennette's husband had decided to move to New Orleans as well. Many had, after the terrible storm hit the coast. On the longboats and pirogues that brought them here, Charlotte recognized more than one face from *La Baleine*. It was cold then. Most women held babies to their breasts.

A week after her visit to Étiennette, Charlotte decides to inquire about Louis at the intendant's house. Nightmares have been clouding her sleep lately; nightmares as vivid as the ones that haunted her after the pirate attack—the rowing boat gone, the deck as big and flat as the sea, the men coming for her. Now, the violence of the dreams that shake her awake is quieter. In them, Louis is gone, and with him her hopes for a child. Étiennette has disappeared; so have Pétronille and Geneviève. Charlotte is alone.

She puts on her finest dress to go to the intendant's. The right sleeve's lace is torn, but she hides it under her coat. She doubts she will be received—the only women she has seen enter the administrative building on the Place d'Armes were accompanied by men. But Louis is away for the good of the colony. He's guiding soldiers to the northern outposts, helping secure the fragile French settlements. She can only hope an exception will be made for her.

The day is unusually cold for late April, jasmine shrubs already in bloom, brightening up the gray and brown streets that have only recently received names. Charlotte turns on the corner of Rue d'Orléans. A child sells worn knives and shining handles, blows on his hands to keep them warm. Charlotte is lowering the hood of her cloak when someone calls her name.

"Madame Charpillon," the female voice repeats. The woman who is walking toward Charlotte is also wrapped in a coat, but the linen seems newer. It takes Charlotte a second to recognize Marthe's round cheeks, her benevolent smile. "I thought it was you," she says, resting her hand indecisively on Charlotte's arm. "Are you heading to Étiennette's?"

"Not today," Charlotte says. She went to see Étiennette yesterday, and her friend asked her again whether she'd talked to Marthe. Étiennette seemed disappointed, almost angry, when Charlotte said she hadn't, as if Charlotte was guilty of not looking for help where she could find it. "I'm going to the intendant's," she tells Marthe.

Marthe follows her down Rue d'Orléans. German workers unload tools and wooden planks in front of a plot still full of weeds and reeds. By the parapet, brown water slides in the moat. Flood season started last month, and Charlotte knows she'll have to wear damp clothes until the end of June.

"What for?"

"To inquire about my husband," Charlotte says. She doesn't want this woman's pity, doesn't want to hear her ask questions she has no answers to. "Étiennette insists I talk to you about children."

Marthe's face drops. "Did something happen to her sons?"

"No." Charlotte lowers her voice. "I meant about having children." She expects a cascade of questions. But Marthe remains silent. She looks pensive. "I have been trying for over a year now," Charlotte says.

A wigmaker opens the door of his workshop so brutally they almost run into it. Marthe repeats her question. "What happened to you before?" she says.

Except for Étiennette, Charlotte has never told anyone about the miscarriage. If Geneviève were there, she would have known what to do—like on the day they watched Pétronille climb into a pirogue and she recommended drinking lemon juice to beat the nausea. Yet Geneviève's mission had never been to save babies.

Marthe's remedies are elaborate. They involve staghorn and cow dung, hair and honey; the instructions are whispered in Charlotte's ear. Make a belt of goat hair, soak it in asses' milk, and wear it to bed with your husband. Drink honey water before going to sleep, then wait for a sting by your belly button—if you feel it, there's a child inside you. Watch for your belly's shape: a bigger roundness on the right side announces a boy, on the left a girl. "It all comes from my stepmother," Marthe explains, "who wouldn't give any children to my father."

"Did she ever?"

"Yes," Marthe answers, looking suddenly sad, "and we all regretted it."

They stop on the Place d'Armes between the jail and the rebuilt guardhouse. Three men come out of the soldiers' temporary barracks carrying drums and powder horns. Inside, someone calls for a sergeant, then for the captain of the Swiss regiment.

Marthe raises her voice to be heard. "I'll provide you with the necessary ingredients," she says. Charlotte promises to try. What does she have to lose? There is something appealing about Marthe's instructions—their specificity a guarantee of success. That is, if Louis ever comes home.

She crosses the square, passes by a tiny donkey led by a boy barely taller than it, women selling unripe fruits, and a priest sneezing in the cold, entering the pavilion that serves as a church. From here, she can see the river that takes Louis, that brings him back. Louis always tells her the same story about the harbor, one he heard from his crew members and that still amuses him: how last October, *La Loire* and *Les Deux Frères* saluted New Orleans with a salvo of guns, and how the young capital, too weak and ill-supplied, was barely able to answer the ships' honors with a single shot. Charlotte looks away from the water, hurries up. The doors of the warehouses are open, barrels of rice and peas being unloaded; a carter yells to her to get out of his way, although she never was in it.

She has no difficulty entering the intendant's house, but there, no one can tell her any more than what she already knows. Louis left, along with the other men, for the Pascagoula River. They should have been back eight days ago. Shouldn't a young lady like her be at home with her children?

• • •

Only once in New Biloxi did Charlotte attempt to talk to Étiennette about the January night at the warehouse. She could afford to at the beginning of fall 1721. She was pregnant, she felt protected; the child was a token. With him, with her, there would be no more secrets in the dark, no more lips searching skin. There would be two friends, two mothers. That September morning at Étiennette's in New Biloxi, she was looking for closure. For a word that said her friend forgave her. But something fell on the ground, a maid came knocking, her friend's unborn baby started kicking. Étiennette was distracted. She asked Charlotte to repeat what she had just said. "Nothing," Charlotte answered.

She hadn't said anything.

Her body punishes her every month for these thoughts. The pain that comes with her period is unspeakable—a blade that probes, kneads, and stirs the insides of her lower belly. It turns her into a puppet, has her move to her side, her back, every position as untenable as the others. It climbs to her mind and erases her thoughts, builds into a nausea that sends her kneeling above a bucket: if only she could get something out of her body, she would feel better. She spits bile and crawls back to bed. She's learned she will have to get used to the pain.

It seems impossible she should suffer that much for nothing.

• • •

Louis comes home two weeks after Charlotte's visit to the intendant, a week after her period ended. It's early May by then, and rain falls on the city, hard and persistent, flooding the streets. When Louis arrives, Charlotte is trying to get rid of the neighbor—Pinet, a French gunsmith who was sent away, for reasons she doesn't know, from the Company's colony in Senegambia. "The escapees," Pinet whispers. He always stands too close to her, his breath smelling like candle wax and vinegar. "They were here again yesterday. Are you hurt? Did you hear them?" She says no— she always tells him no, even when noises wake her up at night. Formerly enslaved Natives who escaped the French do roam through the forest, killing cattle and robbing settlers. But she refuses to let this man's terror gain her. Once you've given in to fear, it won't leave you; *La Baleine* taught her that much. Pinet's African wife stares at them from her doorstep. And beyond her, walking the dirt road, is Louis. Charlotte waves at him, runs past their neighbor and into the street.

She stops short a few feet from him. These first few seconds, each time he comes back, Louis turns into the stranger he once was. He grins. She comes nearer.

"Was he bothering you with his nonsense again?" he asks. He gestures toward Pinet retreating, hands readjusting his breeches.

"I'll start worrying about him the day he stops," Charlotte answers.

The door of the Pinets' house closes. Louis is sweaty, bringing in the smell of egret and silt that sometimes takes days to leave his clothes. It fills Charlotte's nostrils when she presses her cheek to his chest. Louis has become Louis again.

"I'm sorry you were worried," he says.

"Not that much." She holds him tighter.

"Is that so? I can barely breathe." He laughs.

She lets go of him. He looks like someone who spent weeks traveling—linen in need of repair, beard of a clean shave, cheeks of a good meal. His eyes seem lighter against the dirt of his face. He has a bad cut on the elbow but nothing that won't heal. Two years ago, he came back from his first trip staggering with fever, his skin burned, his arms and shoulders covered with blisters. That summer, Charlotte feared for his life. Louis didn't seem too concerned; he'd study his wounded hands and joke about snakes shedding their skin.

He follows her inside the house and drops his boots by the bedroom door, although she keeps on telling him to leave them out of the way. She takes them out to dry.

"I'm not to blame," Louis says, "this evil lake is. We should have returned three weeks ago." He sits on the chair by the fireplace, massages his feet. "You'd think you're back on the Atlantic over there," he says. He shakes his head disapprovingly, as if talking about a naughty child rather than water. He explains that, on the way back, they were about to reach mainland when they met winds so strong they had to reverse their course and land on Round Island. They were stuck there for two weeks, eating oysters, raccoons, and once or twice, wild pigs. "But we would have called ourselves lucky even without them," Louis says. "We found a creek on our second day there. Without that, you would have had good reason to worry."

"I didn't need to know that to fear for you."

He smiles at her, drops his foot. His hands are dirty, but she sits on his lap, lets him bury his face in her neck. When they met, she felt both anxious and curious—Louis was the very first man she had ever known. She'd heard horrible tales about becoming a wife. Nightmarish wedding nights, told in whispers and broken sentences. Hers hurt—of course it did. But not more than what she had been warned, than what she had feared after the pirate attack. What no one told her was the nights that would follow could be painless, almost enjoyable. At least when Louis isn't drunk or in a hurry.

He isn't perfect, but there are many ways in which he could be a lot worse.

The house seems bigger when he's home. In the morning, she finds him fixing his net, cross-legged by the fireplace. When he travels, Charlotte eats her meals directly from the kettle and spends most of her time in the garden, fighting against the bushes that threaten to claim back what was once theirs. Sometimes she sings songs from her years at La Salpêtrière—nursery rhymes she learned from the Aunts, ballads she heard on *La Baleine*. They made her feel less lonely—maybe, out there, someone is listening to her.

She never wanders in the unfurnished back room where Louis likes to read. It had been one of the most surprising things about him after they married—to discover that a man like him, who seemed more at ease on the water than on land, could appreciate leafing through Challe's novel or some essays when he came back from the rivers. He owed his reading skills to the uncle who raised him, a gentle, lonely man who knew as much about poetry as he did about winds and tides. But in the narrow room that faces the forest, Charlotte no longer sees the books, only the crib in which Louis stores his hooks and baits. He was the one who insisted they bring the cradle with them from New Biloxi. He told Charlotte they would have many children in New Orleans, that the babies were just waiting for them to settle for good. That she shouldn't worry, she was not even fifteen, she had all the time in the world.

He is right; time is all she has.

Other days she feels she has none. Louis soon tells her he is about to leave again, south from New Orleans this time, to the new fort of La Balize. He has been chosen to replace a sick coast pilot, and he'll be steering the incoming ships across the dangerous bar that marks the entrance of the St. Louis River. She knows the forest becomes so dense a few leagues in that it becomes impossible to sail and that ships have to be winched—it sometimes takes six weeks to reach the capital. But when she asks how long he'll be gone, Louis shrugs. "Depends on the fellow's health," he says. They have had only a handful of nights together. She tries not to resent him for being gone so much. If he weren't, there would be no home, nothing to wear or eat—she could starve to death, just like the child of their neighbors in New Biloxi. Part of her thinks he is too kind a man to stay. She knows you need good reasons to be blessed.

Still, during these two weeks with Louis, she gives Marthe's remedy a chance. Marthe doesn't bring her a goat-haired belt but a mixture for Charlotte to bury under their mattress. It stinks, though less than she would have thought. She has no idea where the powder of staghorn comes from; the cow dung, she can easily guess.

Louis leaves. Charlotte does what she does best. She waits, her heart hollow.

She goes back to Étiennette. At her friend's, time translates differently, it feels more tangible. Hugo is almost a month and a half old and already sleeping through the night—a wonder. Aurélien laughed for the first time last winter, on the way to New Orleans, at a man who fell from a pirogue before being fished out by a barge-maker. Now, at the end of May, he stumbles from Charlotte to Étiennette, staring at his mother as if only her attention is keeping him on his feet. Maybe: as soon as Étiennette glances away, he falls on his rear. Charlotte helps him up. She hates the child; she loves him. The horrible pains should have hit her at the beginning of the week. They didn't. She is four days late.

Then a week. Two. It rains so hard the city might disappear under the silty reeds and the thick moss, turn into the swamp it only recently was. The feverish feeling that overcomes Charlotte each time bayous and rivers rise, each time they threaten to carry away the docks, storage sheds, rice paddies, as if her entire world could drown—that fear is gone. The rumors that Bienville forbade a begging crowd from boarding *Le Dromadaire*, *La Loire*, and *Les Deux Frères* to escape the colony and return to France become easy to ignore. Her belief that she might be pregnant is an anchor; the town, sturdy enough to resist another spring. She sits outside, the sun shining again, drying up the barns, her house, bringing back Louis. In front of him, Charlotte can't keep her mouth shut. She hasn't told anyone, not even Étiennette or Marthe, but the day before he is set to leave again, she blurts it out.

"See," he says, "I told you everything would be fine," and she wants so badly to believe him.

No one expected summer to be this humid. Street vendors foresee more flooding, farmers worry for their crops, but Charlotte is too far removed from their concerns. She wipes the puddles by her fireplace, hangs the sheets to dry, goes to Étiennette's. The thought that she might not be quite on her own when she visits, that there might be someone else always with her, gives her strength. It makes her Étiennette's equal— a mother soon, not a girl anymore.

One stormy day in June, she follows Étiennette's maid to the garden of the Rue de Chartres house. The sky is darkening, the air heavy; hornets buzz loudly above the strawberry plants' white flowers. With Hugo napping beside her, Étiennette is stitching in the shade of a plum tree. Charlotte sits next to her, their armrests touching.

Étiennette resumes her work. She starts chatting about the party she's hoping to have here mid-August—a party that might not have deserved the name in France, but that also would be unthinkable if

M. Feuger didn't manage the storehouses' stock. She pauses. "Are you listening?"

"You were wondering whether to invite the surgeon."

"I was asking if you could sing. Never mind. What is it?"

"I've never sung a cappella."

"There would be musicians. Forget about that for now. Did anything happen?"

"No."

Hugo starts fussing. His feet push against his mother's breasts as if they were dough, sheets, air. Étiennette readjusts the cord that sinks into the fat of the baby's neck.

"What is that?" Charlotte asks.

Étiennette fidgets with the necklace, retrieves what looks like a small rock. "A foal's tooth." She shrugs. "According to Marthe, it'll keep teething pains away."

"How long is he supposed to wear it?"

"Would you happen to take Marthe's remedies seriously?"

"I probably should."

Étiennette lets go of the tooth. She squints at Charlotte. "Why haven't you said anything?"

"I don't know," Charlotte answers. She does: her hopes of being pregnant become real if she speaks them out loud.

"I wasn't sure for Hugo until I felt him kick," Étiennette notes. "You don't seem sick."

"I haven't had my period."

Étiennette's face softens. She suddenly looks like the girl Charlotte welcomed at La Salpêtrière, to whom she whispered which Aunt to fear, which one to trust. "Then spare yourself," Étiennette says. "Quit walking so much. I'll come to you next time." She corrects herself. "Or send a carriage to fetch you."

Charlotte nods. She lets Étiennette pat her petticoats. The usual warmth rises under her friend's hand, persistent and familiar. She looks beyond Étiennette's fingers, at her own belly. She swears it's grown bigger.

• • •

The other women have never been as kind and considerate with Charlotte as they are that summer. It was different during her first pregnancy; the last girls had just been married, others were learning their husbands' ways. They were shier, less zealous, than they would one day become. It took time and a new capital to re-create the solidarity born on *La Baleine*.

In June and July, some girls even come to visit her at her place. They bring flowers, pictures of Sainte Marguerite, and whisper prayers to the Virgin that Charlotte never heard. Someone suggests she takes up a musical instrument, maybe the harp or the flute, as if those could be easily found here. In any case, she should sing more. They say it starts now, long before you'll meet your baby. What matters is what you lay your eyes upon. Surround yourself with beauty, and avoid any disturbing sights.

Charlotte does as she is told. By mid-July, the construction of the Hôtel-Dieu is finally completed. Louis comes home saying that hundreds of people rushed to the hospital, when its sick ward counts only eighty beds. He seems worried; he heard a master wheelwright and a joiner talk about desertion. Charlotte reassures him: things will get better, they'll stay, they have no choice. The baby will be here soon.

When Louis leaves again, the third week of July, saying goodbye doesn't hurt Charlotte as much as it usually does: he will be gone for a month, but she won't be alone. The girls will keep her company.

One afternoon, as Marthe kneels to grab a spoon that Charlotte dropped, Étiennette laughs. "That's what I hated most when I was carrying a child," she says, "how everyone treated me as if I were myself one." But Charlotte doesn't mind being helped or cared for. And she doesn't feel like a child at all. There is power in this state, to shape the life growing within her.

The women don't talk as much about her belly as they talk about her eyes—"My eyes?" Charlotte says, amused, the first time they mention them. The women are imperturbable. Yes, they say, images becoming vibrations, feelings, sliding all the way to your baby. Charlotte has no control over her belly, but she can choose what she wants to see. At night, she tosses and turns on the mattress, which feels too big without Louis. Are thoughts images? Can you unsee what you dream of? Étiennette moving in the straw, her head lowering, leveling, nose grazing at Charlotte's chin, lips retreating into a smile, a tiny hole between the teeth, eyes turning bluer, brighter—June blue, almost transparent. And when the woman in her dream speaks, when she asks, "Are you asleep?" it is Geneviève's voice Charlotte hears.

When she wakes, she is breathing fast. It's dawn. Her heart beats hard, her crotch feels wet. She fights back tears, lies motionless until sunrise. Then she gets up, washes herself, breaks kindle, spreads butter on the fragile crumbs of stale bread. When there is enough light, Charlotte looks around her. She shakes the dream away, and it is already easier to ignore Geneviève's face. She focuses on the women again—what matters is what you lay your eyes upon. She chooses carefully. A freckled egg, raindrops caught in a spiderweb. She walks to the backyard. Bees reflected in the eye of a cat. Leaves flickering white and green like waving hands.

No more dreams. Charlotte wonders what her mother saw when she was pregnant with her, but all she can picture is a yellow bonnet. She tries not to think of this woman's despair, of the atrocious winter that froze Paris that year. Bearing a child is the only experience she will ever share with the woman who brought her to life, then to La Salpêtrière. Her mother will remain a question mark—but Charlotte will know everything of her baby.

• • •

On her way to Étiennette's for dinner, Charlotte thought she felt cramps, tight and relentless. She did her best to ignore them, blamed the roads' bumps and the horses' brutal halts for her pain. On Rue de Bourbon and Rue de Chartres, the carriage jumped, its wheels falling into ruts filled with water. Another storm was brewing, and the horses were sweating under the July heat.

As soon as she joins the other women—Étiennette, Marthe, the twins—fat needles start poking her lower belly, nails scraping invisible skin. The smell of meat nauseates her, makes her never want to eat again.

"What is it?" Étiennette asks when Charlotte pushes her plate away.

"I'm feeling unwell," she whispers.

"She is very pale," Léonie says.

"She should lie down."

"Help me bring her to my bedroom."

Charlotte feels herself being lifted, carried through a door, then another one. She keeps her eyes shut: the world and the pain are impossible to handle simultaneously. Her head collapses in the mattress, then someone pushes a pillow under her neck.

"You should eat, ladies," Étiennette's voice says. "I'll meet you in just a moment."

Marthe replies something Charlotte can't make out, but Étiennette hushes her and shoos her away. The door closes behind her. The pain grows: it's a shadow against a wall, of something approaching fast, always getting nearer. It makes her mind blank, her brain hum. But today a single thought, a horrific one, sneaks through it all.

These cramps aren't exceptional: she has been here many times.

Étiennette brings a wet cloth to her forehead. She doesn't speak. Once, at the warehouse, Charlotte told her that when the pain kicked in, she shouldn't be touched or spoken to. Étiennette remembers this rule.

The bleeding starts an hour later. Étiennette sits by her side, looking at her. She smiles and nods, but Charlotte doesn't know what to do with either. The sheet under her legs is damp. She doesn't look.

She must have dozed off because when she wakes up, a bluish light falls on the pelisse lying on the bedroom bench. She needs a few seconds to find her bearings, and when she does, she wishes it had taken her longer. The sharpness in her belly is gone. It feels stiff now, a belt of pain embracing her lower back. Étiennette, Marthe, the twins are scattered in the room, murmuring.

"Poor thing."

"Two miscarriages, who would have—"

"She is awake."

Charlotte presses on her palms to sit. The linen under her crotch moves with her. She sees blood, clots, so dark they seem flat, without volume. They are tiny, so much smaller than the ones she saw when she really lost a child.

"Don't look," Marthe warns her.

"Let her be," Étiennette says flatly.

Charlotte does look. She recognizes what she sees, and it isn't a baby, not even the beginning of one. Menstrual blood, nothing more, fat and thick like she is used to. She doesn't tell the other women what she and Étiennette understand. That her body lied to her. That she is used to the spasms, the pain, the nausea. That it happens every month, whereas a child comes once in a blue moon.

· · ·

Charlotte bleeds for an entire week. Étiennette tries, without much conviction, to tell her it is more than her period. But when Charlotte finds her shift clean on the eighth morning, she knows her friend is wrong. Charlotte is too tired to lie to herself. Her womb is dead. Some mornings, powerlessness and sadness could choke her.

The week her period ends, she goes out only once. She has heard that a shipment might soon arrive from the German coast, although there hasn't been a single delivery in weeks. Fresh vegetables have become scarce: the rare farmers who still have something to offer are sold out long before they reach the market, so Charlotte goes straight to the levee by the St. Louis River. She is far from being the only one waiting for the pirogue, but it feels like the shallots and leeks she manages to buy could feed her for weeks.

At mass, her mind wanders—by the time the service ends, she can't remember a word the priest said. Outside, the crowd is bigger than it usually is. Reptilian-eyed egrets stand watch. Charlotte feels fear and excitement in the air, smells sweat and urine. She moves toward the guardhouse and stops as soon as she spots the wooden stage.

A boy is being led where everyone can see him. He is her age, maybe a couple years older, but smaller, so skinny he seems to hover in his own shift. The skin of his face is a violent red—burned by the sun or by early-morning eau-de-vie. He stands in front of the crowd, but his eyes don't register any movement. Charlotte has never seen anyone so still in the face of danger. A week ago, she would have immediately left the main square, avoided the violence that would soon unfold there. Marthe once told her about a pregnant lady she knew in Paris who gave birth to a malformed girl after witnessing an execution. But Charlotte was never a lady. Nor is she carrying a child.

She listens to the official read the man's charges: the boy was rotten fruit in France already, he was sent here for theft in La Rochelle; no one should be surprised he would now steal and kill a landowner's cow. He would serve three years as a convict and be lashed for three days.

Charlotte's legs shake, but she stays as long as she can stand it. She watches the punishment until it becomes hers, until the prisoner is taken away, folded in two, his back a bloody mess. The wounds remind her of wet, viscous seaweed. They'll heal, but the scars are there to stay.

She doesn't go out after that day. The pain has waned, but she'd rather not see anyone. At sunset, the smell of the delta fills the house—fishy, raw, invasive. She sometimes hears Baguette, the city's official drummer, play music next door. When it isn't raining, Charlotte retreats to the garden, behind the damp palisades. She sings, but never for long. Her voice seems buried in her own throat. She stays outside until the first stars rise. A red moon glows white and clean once it reaches the top of the trees, pushing forward on the path it was always meant to follow.

She wishes Louis could be here. He is the only one with whom she could share her disappointment. Not Étiennette, absorbed by her children and her parties; not Pétronille, lost in some forest—certainly not Geneviève, who, in Paris, taught girls' bodies how to do what Charlotte's does to perfection.

Four days after the bleeding stops, there is a knock at the door. It can't be Louis—he isn't to return before the third week of August. Water is boiling; peas shelled. Charlotte doesn't bother washing her hands before stepping into the corridor.

Marthe is looking at something in the grass. For a split second, the door could still be shut. Charlotte motions for her to enter.

"I meant to come earlier," Marthe says behind her, "but Étiennette told me you'd rather be alone."

"She's right." Charlotte leans over the kettle and drops the peas. The boiling water instantly quiets down. "What do you want?" she asks.

"To see how you were," Marthe says. She sits on a stool. "I also gave some thought about what happened to you."

"But you don't even know what happened to me."

Marthe looks surprised. She shakes her head. "I thought of something else you could try."

Charlotte leans toward the fire. She can't take it today. No more tales of an unborn baby being a girl if salt melts on a nipple, or of mixing wine with hare testicles to have a boy.

"Maybe your husband is to blame," Marthe says.

Charlotte almost drops the kettle. "No," she says. Louis was kind, he was gone, he could make love to her more often. She is the issue; her one and only pregnancy, a brief miracle she could not even hold on to. With another woman, Louis already would have been blessed with two, three children.

"How can you be so certain?" Marthe asks.

Charlotte shrugs. Over the past year and a half, she's experienced this deficiency of hers so intimately that she has come to feel protective of it. It defines who she is. An incompetent wife, a girl unable to fulfill the mission she was sent on—even the Superioress had been wrong and never should have listened to her.

Now here is Marthe, suggesting that Charlotte could still become a mother, that she is not the one responsible.

"How would I know for sure?" Charlotte can't help but ask.

Marthe stands up from her stool, pauses like she did in April when she tried remembering the last ingredient of one of her recipes. But she shakes her head, gives Charlotte a sorry smile.

"I'm afraid you can already guess how."

• • •

Étiennette's party will take place two days after Assumption Day. It's the first time she invites that many people to her house. The festivities seem out of place in a land where food is too often scarce. But not for M. Feuger. The endless rains of the past months have destroyed part of the crops: at the market yesterday, Charlotte could barely believe the prices she heard. She bought what she could, tried not to think about next winter. She swore to herself Louis would have everything he needed.

She's relieved he won't be at Étiennette's and is ashamed for feeling so. If Étiennette lends her a dress, it will be easier to hide what her husband does for a living, how little he brings back home. There will be other men at the party. She thinks of M. Feuger's associates, the ones she sometimes saw at Étiennette's. She heard them talk about nuns, about prostitutes. Comment on the tallest twin's waist. She wonders if the men ever talk about her. As much as she tries, she can't ignore Marthe's advice.

She attends the Assumption mass on August 15. Pews have been moved to make room for the busy crowd: the packed church should reassure the Capuchin fathers, who Louis said were desperate about the settlers' lack of faith. Soon Charlotte won't be worth much more than they are. She prays fervently that day. Not for her feelings toward Étiennette, not for her lost child, but for the crime she might soon be guilty of. It seems improbable the Virgin would forgive adultery. Still, she asks.

The day of the party, the overcast skies make her head ring. She gets ready with Étiennette, borrows a silvered-lace gown she fears she'll ruin. Her friend hands her rouge, combs, a brooch, pushes an engraved case toward her. "Take a *mouche*."

The taffeta patches are called "flies" because the dark dots look like insects, but Charlotte knows the fake beauty marks are a lot more elaborate than their name might suggest. They speak their own language, a language she and Étiennette ignored at La Salpêtrière, when the girls made fortune *mouches* out of scraps of *tiretaine*. A patch in the middle of the cheek, like the one Étiennette wears, means she is gallant. One on the lips signals a coquette. Charlotte picks a *mouche*, stares at herself, the freckles she has hardly concealed under white powder. She sticks the patch on her temple, then quickly turns her head away from Étiennette. A *mouche* by the eye signals a passionate nature.

A maid helps them with their hair. Downstairs, the last pieces of furniture are being moved so there is room to dance; New Orleans's only *pâtissier* fulminates against the midges. The musicians tune their instruments. Charlotte is to sing tonight, though she hopes Étiennette might have forgotten. A voice yells at a servant to hurry; outside, the doors of a carriage slam. Étiennette quickly moves away from the window. She looks anxious and excited. "They are already here," she says.

"They" are the royal lieutenant and his wife, both equally short and taciturn. But others soon follow. Marthe, to whom Charlotte stays close, but also her husband and five more traders, agents of the Company with their wives, officials working for the governor, a captain, a handful of lonely officers. Their conversations muffle the music of the ensemble. Flies softly land on meat; strawberries are smashed under heels. The room smells like wig powder—lavender, orange—sweat and liquor. The panniers of the women's dresses are so large that they almost send a table tumbling down; one of the guests hid a tiny dog behind the whale-bones of her hoops, and the animal cries until the girl sets it free. M. Feuger barely moves from a corner of the dining room, hiding behind two Canadian fellows. Étiennette is everywhere. Showing off the children to cooing ladies, sending the wet nurse away, offering more wine to a red-cheeked couple, tapping Charlotte's shoulder.

"What is this?" Étiennette whispers, looking not into Charlotte's eyes but right at her temple.

The taffeta patch burns by her eyelashes. Charlotte glances at Marthe, who glances at the dog whining at their feet.

"Isn't it the charming mezzo I once heard?" a man asks from behind.

The officer towers over them all. A friend of M. Feuger, whom Charlotte saw twice in New Biloxi, at Étiennette's. She lets him kiss her hand. Her throat is gluey, she feels her friend's gaze on her. She opens her mouth, but nothing comes out.

"You're right to save your voice," the man adds, then winks at her. "They are waiting for you."

She realizes the music has stopped. At least one violinist is looking at her.

"Take it off," Étiennette whispers to her ear.

But it's too late to remove the *mouche*. The crowd thins, opening a passage to the little stage. The musicians move their instruments to make room for her. Faces blur. In the corner of her eye, Charlotte can see the dark shape of the patch. They can all see it. She thinks of Louis somewhere on the water, fighting bad winds. She thinks of all the things he doesn't know.

"You said you wished to sing 'Je tâche en vain de faire résistance,' didn't you?" the harpsichordist asks. He is twisted on his seat.

"Yes," she manages to answer. "By M. Bacilly."

The silence falls, but never perfectly. Charlotte looks at her short nails, the flowers embroidered on this dress that isn't hers. The cello goes first, then the violins join in. She waits for the second measure. She starts so low it seems impossible she'll be able to reach the correct octave. She stands, her eyes turned to the ceiling, beyond the guests. She wants her voice to distract them all from the *mouche* on her temple. She wants to make herself forget about the message written on her own skin.

For the length of a song, it works. Onstage, all she can feel is air rising from her lungs and belly, a belly that might not be fit for children but doesn't fail her singing—the air reaching her throat and mouth, vibrations turning into sound into words into music, falling from her lips to land on the instruments' chords, then fading, her chest empty, reaching for air to start all over again.

The guests start clapping before she is done. The music dies down after her, the instruments like people tiptoeing out of a room. Charlotte thanks the musicians. Someone requests another song, but she shakes her head. She doesn't want to stay exposed onstage.

She hurries through the crowd, eyes down. Cake debris, smoking pipes, powder giving way under the heat. Her own hair is rigid with sweat, her forehead wet. When she pats her temple, the *mouche* has disappeared. She walks faster toward the double doors. The air clears with every step.

When she reaches the garden, it is all night, figs, and stars. Charlotte stops under the jasmine, inadvertently crushes a snail under her shoe. She can finally breathe.

"You did well."

The moonlight strikes Étiennette's back, Charlotte's face. Charlotte plants her finger where the patch used to be. "I took it off," she says.

"The heat took it off. Or the music. Whichever." Étiennette shoos away a mosquito. "What matters is why you put it on in the first place."

"You wouldn't understand."

"That you'd want to betray your husband? No, maybe you're right. I wouldn't." Étiennette glances back at the half-opened door, at the silhouettes among the candles. Inside, a woman giggles so hard she starts coughing. "I'd rather be pitied than blamed."

"But what if I weren't to be pitied? What if it weren't about me?"

"Is that another of Marthe's brilliant ideas?"

Charlotte feels exhausted. She wants to go home. They take a few more steps on the lawn, on fallen fruits.

"I'm only trying to protect you," Étiennette says. "I know you're a lot stronger than this." She passes her arm around Charlotte's shoulders like she used to when they were girls, then lets out a little laugh, as if amused by what she is about to say. "Otherwise, you'd still be acting nonsense like you did at the warehouse. Remember what you did one of our first nights there?"

The punch doesn't spare any part of Charlotte's body. She stares at Étiennette's face, looking for someone she might recognize there, something that might erase the gap her friend just opened between them. But Étiennette is smiling, a stranger. Charlotte's eyes land on a flower bed, teeming with lightning bugs. Up until now, the only thing left from that January night was Étiennette's answer: if it hadn't been spoken so clearly, Charlotte could have believed she'd dreamed the whole thing. But she definitely didn't dream the sensations—the pulse in her crotch, the blood in her cheeks, the weakness in her legs—that filled her each time she visited Étiennette in New Biloxi and New Orleans. And yet, to her friend, none of that exists. Charlotte's feelings belong to the past, to a deranged mind.

If only you knew how much you mean to me, you'd know that I am a lot weaker, Charlotte thinks. But she can't lose every battle; she needs to believe she will one day win. She turns to her friend. Étiennette is still smiling. The moonlight carves curious shadows onto her face.

"No," Charlotte says, "I don't remember."

8

THE ILLINOIS COUNTRY
MAY 1726

Geneviève

Geneviève's daughter keeps talking on the path to the cemetery of Prairie du Rocher, asking out loud who these men are carrying her father, and if it wouldn't be too dark for him under the oak wood. Since Pierre died three days ago, Geneviève's mind too has been buzzing with questions— angrier ones that have little to do with the funeral and a lot more with its aftermath. She envies Mélanie's simple sadness, the odd objects it latches on to. Her daughter is obsessed with the kind of tree that was used to make her father's coffin. The day it was brought to their home—back when Geneviève still thought of the house as theirs: the clerk hadn't come yet to tell her that Pierre had left it to Mélanie alone—the little girl was so upset about her father being put into a box that Geneviève came up with a story. A story in which the coffin would turn again into an oak after being buried, an invisible tree that would sprout from the ground and serve as a ladder to the heavens.

Now Geneviève regrets it. Oak forests are everywhere in the Illinois Country. On their way from the church to the cemetery, Mélanie wouldn't stop pointing at their sturdy branches, begging Geneviève to help her climb. No, Geneviève kept saying. She didn't remind the girl that her father was still—and would stay—in the wooden box; she didn't try to make a more pious story in which Pierre wouldn't need the help of a tree to rise to heaven. Mélanie will be four next month. Geneviève wonders how long her story will hold. Never long enough, she guesses.

Watching through her veil, she does her best to avoid roots and holes. The light is dimmed by the fabric, her daughter's round face a grimmer shade, the sunny May morning flattened gray—the color everyone would want a widow's world to be. Mélanie rustles in her arms, and Geneviève knows exactly to whom her daughter is waving: her sister-in-law and her husband, their five children. After the ceremony, Laure rested a motherly hand on Geneviève's shoulder, fidgeted with the veil that she and her husband paid for along with all the other mourning attire. Geneviève's dower isn't even enough to provide her with these sad dresses. It's maddening to her, satisfying to Laure, who, at thirty-four, enjoys treating Geneviève as if she were her senior by twenty years and not six. Laure does have more experience in some respects. Born and raised in Canada, she knows a lot more about the Illinois Country than Geneviève. She is as familiar as Pierre used to be with the thick forests, the horrific winters that spread south of Lake Michigan, all the way to the junction between the Kaskaskia River and the St. Louis River, where Fort de Chartres and Prairie du Rocher were built, the place they chose to call home.

On the other hand, Laure has never crossed an ocean, never traveled on the damp bayous of the southern part of the continent, never seen a mulberry tree nor smelled lavender scent in Provence. All Laure will ever know are these rich prairies, where wheat grows like weeds, where she convinced Pierre to join her almost exactly five years ago today, Geneviève's first summer in La Louisiane. Her dear brother coming to live right by her—a victory Laure was still proud of. On the church doorstep, Laure stopped tugging at Geneviève's veil. "Isn't it too short?" she asked, and Geneviève shook her head, turned away, stepped into the sunlight.

She finally stops by a grove. Only a few graves remain here—most without a tombstone, rusty crosses that took on odd angles under the winters' blows. The priest is there already.

"See, a proper burial would never have been possible in the south," Laure says, to her right.

Geneviève doesn't turn to her sister-in-law. She stares at the hole in the earth, releases Mélanie to stand on the ground. Laure spent the past few years reminding her of the advantages that the north offered. No more corn bread here. No hurricanes, only blue skies and wheat flour— a soil dry enough that skeletons do not rise up with the next flood.

"Also not here, in the winter," Geneviève says.

"I'm glad to see that your wits remain despite the circumstances."

Geneviève hasn't cried once since Pierre fell sick. The last time she wanted to was the day he came back from his visit to the Illinois people, his eye sore, his hand a mess. You couldn't tell he'd be dead in a week; that the infection would sneak from his thumb to his forearm, from his shoulder to his chest—that the window of time when he could have been operated on would close before they knew it. That May evening, when Pierre returned late from the prairies and told her about the lacrosse game he had played with the Native men, Geneviève didn't hold back her reproaches. Despite what he might think, Pierre wasn't like the Illinois warriors, never would be; one day or another, he'd get injured. She was tired of him disappearing for days.

That night, there was still time to disagree, argue, and reconcile. The wound hadn't become infected, she wasn't trying to protect him yet.

Pierre was surprisingly sensitive to pain, even more so when it was someone else's—the ingrown nail that bugged Geneviève for days last spring, the neighbor's broken arm. But nothing that happened among the Natives could bother him. Since their very first day here, he'd been fascinated by the Illinois, by their warriors. He had learned the language and was familiar with many of their customs, which made him famous in Prairie du Rocher. At first as a trader—then, as he grew less and less interested in money and business, as a guide and an interpreter. But this year, ever since the Illinois had come back from their winter sojourn at the end of March, Pierre spent most of his time with them: before he hurt himself, he had meant to follow the men on a five-week hunt. He seemed always to find an excuse to go back to the summer villages and avoid home. Geneviève had only one place to be. Each of her husband's excursions reminded her of her own limitations, of this freedom she'd never know even after crossing an ocean.

The men lower Pierre's coffin into the open earth. The priest, a bald man who moves in ample gestures, prays so quietly no one can hear him. An imperfect silence sets in; birds can't refrain from singing. Geneviève rests one of her hands on Mélanie's light brown hair, then removes it. She forces herself to look at the hole in the ground. She had to stare at Pierre for hours after his death, and yet she can't link his distorted face to the scene unfolding in front of her. Her mind is numb. She watches the men, sweaty now, step away from the hole; she follows the priest's motions, hears the loud sobbing of Laure and her family. Things are exactly what they are, empty of meaning. The coffin, a box disappearing under handfuls of dirt. The small crowd, friends and relatives gathered on a bright spring morning. Herself, a woman standing on a patch of grass.

Pierre can't be here. He is somewhere else, gone to the prairies and the buffaloes and the strawberry fields.

After the funeral, Geneviève brings Mélanie home, gives her a rag to blow her nose, puts the kettle on the fire to soothe her with something hot. She adds maple syrup to the milk and says, "Careful, wait before you drink," and watches as Mélanie insists and burns the tip of her tongue, giving an apologetic smile. While she empties the bowl, her pale blue eyes don't leave Geneviève, as if she fears her mother too might disappear. Then Mélanie is in bed, Geneviève in the parlor, and nothing is what it seems anymore. It's the armchair in which she used to listen for the hooves of his old mare, the cracked plate he unexplainably favored, the arrow he built that Mélanie kept on trying to play with. Every inch of the house has its own way of stinging. Geneviève leans back in her chair, closes her eyes. Pierre will never again slide his fingers through the curls of her hair, nor point to the little gap between her front teeth and swear he'd recognize that smile among thousands. He'll never again lead Mélanie outside so she can say good night to the moon. Geneviève understands none of these facts.

She tries remembering what Pierre once told her about Illinois funerals. She imagines kettles, blankets, and hatchets passing from hand to hand, grieving family members and relatives exchanging presents. Naked warriors reproducing war tableaux for a dead chief, scalping invisible enemies. Women crying in their cabins, whether they had loved their husbands or not.

. . .

It took Geneviève time to get used to the Illinois Country. Her first summer in La Louisiane, in 1721, she watched Pétronille leave as if it could happen only to others, as if her own journey had ended the minute she married Pierre and he brought her to his New Biloxi home. That morning on the beach, when she stood by Charlotte, Geneviève was so relieved to see Pétronille alive that it hadn't occurred to her then that her friend's departure would be yet another kind of loss.

A month after Pétronille left New Biloxi, Pierre made arrangements for their own trip. From July to the brisk September day of their leaving, he talked every day about his sister and her husband, who had settled in La Louisiane from Canada. It had been odd enough to discover that Pierre had a sister—that Pierre could, would, see her again. In Geneviève's world, siblings, mothers, fathers didn't belong in the Mississippi. You came alone to the colony. Your family started here.

But Pierre's sister, Laure, lived close enough to be reached. Pierre kept on talking about the Illinois Country as a place far more welcoming than New Biloxi or Mobile, where you could be granted lands that were more profitable than swamps, where the heat would be more bearable than here, and the cold not as implacable as in Québec City—a place run and ruled by a Canadian man, M. Dugué de Boisbriand, governor of the Illinois Country. Unlike M. Law, he held his promises: gold, topaz rock, and lead mines would be found in the north, not in the south.

The trust Geneviève had in Pierre faded. She heard in his tales the rumors of La Salpêtrière, the chatter about an extraordinary land that would give you everything you wanted and more. At first she tried to convince herself that leaving for the Illinois Country would be an escape. But these first eight months in New Biloxi had already confirmed what she hoped she had been wrong about. You didn't reinvent yourself with a new continent. You only adapted, working with who you already were, with whoever happened to be around you.

So when the time came to climb into a pirogue, she did the only thing she could. She would adapt once more.

• • •

Her first nights without Pierre, Geneviève can't sleep. Mélanie breathes deeply against her, spread in the middle of the mattress. Geneviève knows she should be missing the way Pierre's body weighed on the bed—how, on good mornings, she enjoyed waking up next to him. But it's resentment that keeps her awake, not sadness. Part of her understands why Pierre decided to bequeath the house to Mélanie. What if Geneviève remarried and gave it to her new children? Still: she'd never thought he would leave her so destitute, with a dower barely able to support her for a few weeks, caught up in the contradictory obligations of a widow.

A widow. By the end of the customary mourning period, she will be a year short of thirty years old. A year and six weeks wearing dark dresses; three meals a day for two people. One winter in Illinois. She sees herself again in Paris, her own father knocking at a church door, his finger joints eaten by the cold, begging to let them in when they had nowhere else to go. Poverty had killed her family already. She wouldn't let it have her or her daughter.

When Geneviève arrived in the Illinois Country, nothing indicated money would ever be an issue. Pierre was a good listener; he never spoke more words than needed, and Natives appreciated him for that. He had a solid house built, used cedarwood for the roof, asked Canadian neighbors to help her with the garden, brought back from the Illinois settlements recipes to bake corn and dry pumpkins so thoroughly they lasted for an entire year. Introduced her to his family, which, if Laure hadn't been who she is, would have been a blessing. Geneviève knew what Laure thought of her: she was a stranger, a French woman whose past was mysterious and therefore suspicious. An unpleasant surprise brought back from the south when Pierre was mourning his first Canadian wife—and who but Laure cared if he had remarried so soon? Widowers, unlike widows, were tied by no obligations. But Geneviève would never be anything like Pierre's first wife, whom Laure had known her whole life in Québec City, welcomed into her family long before her brother married her.

Geneviève was never family to Laure. Even less so now that Pierre is gone and his property Mélanie's.

Mélanie is unaware of it all. She has just woken up; she lies flat on the pillow, drawing figures with some of her fallen hair. The room is already bright, the sun high. Geneviève feels exhausted.

She hasn't been up for an hour and Laure already knocks at her door, flanked by her two noisier children—a boy and a girl who, at seven and eight, seem to have no age difference. They always sing religious songs when they walk on the trails of Prairie du Rocher, and today is no exception. In the garden, Laure unpacks the biscuits she brought. To her, Geneviève's pantry is forever empty.

"Do you want some, darling?" Laure calls out to Mélanie.

"She just ate," Geneviève says.

Her sister-in-law ignores her. She fills Mélanie's palms with sweets. "How is she?" Laure asks, looking at Mélanie as if she were deaf.

Geneviève wipes the crumbs off her daughter's dress. "How are you?" she asks Mélanie.

The child looks at them both as if the correct answer were written on her mother's or aunt's face. "I miss *Papa*."

"Why, of course she does," Laure says. She lifts Mélanie on her lap. Geneviève hates how she touches what doesn't belong to her. "She would be so much happier with siblings."

That is another of Laure's favorite topics—her superiority as a mother of five. A few months after Mélanie was born, she started questioning Geneviève about a second child. "Still nothing?" she'd say, rolling her eyes. It became worse when she stopped asking. The questions turned into suspicious looks—surely something was wrong with this marriage, with this woman. Pierre was forever Laure's younger brother, never to blame for anything.

As for Geneviève, she couldn't explain to herself this absence of children. Twice she'd had her doubts—a missed period, a week of nausea, but nothing that stuck. She had been surprised enough when she found herself pregnant with Mélanie. After what her body went through in Paris, when Amélie helped her with weeds and kisses, she'd feared there would be no more babies. The abortion—and the assistance she brought to other girls at Madame's, to Pétronille in Lorient—are among the few secrets she managed to keep from her sister-in-law. But either way, she remained the same old threat.

"I was afraid you would be too devastated to take care of her," Laure observes. She releases Mélanie, then starts listing widows who drove themselves mad. A woman of Trois-Rivières who cried from dinner to supper and started mocking her confessor. A girl in Québec City who locked her husband's heart in a credence, knelt every day for seven hours in front of it. "But it seems there isn't much to fear for you on that side," Laure concludes.

"Would you rather have me mock our priest and sit still for hours?"

Laure shakes her head. She makes a quick gesture with her chin toward Mélanie. "That wouldn't help you feed her."

"Working will," Geneviève says.

"While you're mourning?"

"If I can't eat, I don't see how I'll mourn."

Laure seems temporarily contrite. She stands up, calls her children. Michel is trying to pinch a bee on a tulip while his sister draws his attention to an ant's nest. Mélanie watches them, mesmerized. Laure kneels by her. "While your *maman* is gone, would you like to come play with your cousins?"

Mélanie glances at Geneviève, her blue eyes wide. "Are you gone?"

"I'm not," she says, tensed. "Come over here."

She lifts Mélanie. Laure is already pushing the gate open. "Well, in any case, if you change your mind," she says. "Five or six children, who would know the difference?"

In the south, everything would be different. She could ask Étiennette or even Charlotte to watch over Mélanie. She knows that many people left New Biloxi for New Orleans when it became the capital four years ago. At times she pictures Charlotte and Étiennette in this settlement she barely saw when she started her journey north with Pierre—its miserable huts swallowed by the mud, the sows lying in the middle of these roads that didn't deserve to be called streets. But she's heard that New Orleans has been rebuilt since then, that it is a real city now, and so she likes to imagine herself there too, arriving with Mélanie on a magical boat—the two of them living in a house by the delta.

Then she looks around her: the trail that leads to the Old Wind Mill, the road to Cahokia, Fort de Chartres barely hidden by beech trees, its bastions quickly deteriorating under the recurrent flooding of the St. Louis River. She can dream as much as she wants. She'll die here, just like her husband.

• • •

Widows are expected to cry, but not too much. They shouldn't seem happy, although there is a lot to rejoice about: they are free from the sins of the flesh, ready to belong to Christ only. They should not speak too much, nor—God forbid—use their experience pleasing their husband to seduce other men. Those who don't remarry, these saints, will become a model of modesty, compassion, and selflessness for their peers.

Geneviève nods to the priest in the confessional, to the neighbor's wife passing by, to the butcher's sister who drops off a plate of pork chops, two weeks after Pierre's funeral. They all mean well. But Geneviève knows that people's kindness fades over time. That in another fortnight, the gifts will become scarcer—no more plucked chickens, heads of lettuce, earth-spotted eggs. Words of advice will keep coming, but they never fed anyone.

She has sold the mare already, and if it comes to that, she knows she could do the same with the arrows, the pelts, the buffalo wool. But she'd rather save those for the winter. For now she'll find a job, any kind. The idea of working makes her feel—and she can't explain it better than this to herself—at the heart of her own life. It brings back Provence, Paris, Amélie kneeling among the washerwomen, the city turned upside down on the river. It tells her that the girl who could work twelve hours a day isn't entirely gone.

When she starts asking around for a position, people give her embarrassed, aggravated looks. The baker needs an apprentice but is looking for someone half her age. Hands could be used at the dyer, but the owner only shakes his head. "I wouldn't allow a fine woman like you to dirty her hands in cow skin."

She tells him she did it in Paris already, she mentions the tanneries by the Bièvre, but the man finally announces that the skins of La Louisiane have nothing to do with the ones she handled in France. She understands: a young widow is supposed to stay at home. She should be praying, caring for the poor, educating her children to be good Christians.

The answer is brought by Laure, and Geneviève hates her dearly for that. A month into Geneviève's search, Laure's husband delivers a large order of brand-new barrels to the home of M. de Monreuil, the governor of Prairie du Rocher. Laure's husband heard from the cook that a kitchen helper was needed and, why, immediately thought of her. Or at least that's what Laure tells her. "You remember what I said about taking care of Mélanie," she adds before leaving.

Geneviève brings Mélanie to work. It seems fine in the beginning.

The kitchens are the largest she has ever seen, especially here in the Mississippi; the fireplace of the main room is big enough that she could stand in its hearth. There is no risk the child will be in anyone's way. The pantry counts so many shelves that Geneviève fears she'll never be able to navigate the place, to find her way between the marmalades, preserves, and dried herbs. She hasn't seen this level of abundance since her days at Madame's. The smell of food is aggressive—at first it opens her appetite, then it kills it. It seems to have worked its way on the head cook, an extraordinarily thin and hasty woman who rarely speaks in more than three words. "Quiet and obedient?" she asks the first time she sees Mélanie. "Yes," Geneviève answers, and the cook nods, then points toward a bench by the main gate. Over the next few weeks, this is where Geneviève often finds Mélanie asleep, curled either under or on the bench, after spending hours playing in the farm courtyards with the other domestics' children.

So when Laure comes by and Mélanie starts listing her new friends' names, Geneviève can't help but smile at her sister-in-law's blank face. A dozen children to play with should be worth a few siblings. When Laure asks if it isn't dangerous to let them run free, Geneviève tells her they are never alone in the courtyard. Laure shakes her head. "This is meant to end badly."

In her sister-in-law's world, most things are.

Geneviève never sees the governor, nor his wife. Bowls of turnip broth and plates of buffalo meat leave the kitchen shiny, come back scattered, never quite empty, as if a fussy animal had found its way in the dining room and tasted it all. She hides the leftovers, brings them home. The job reminds her of washing clothes at Madame's: linen turning dirty, clean, then dirty again, satisfaction always short-lived.

The other women ask little about her. They don't question her experience. At first they glance at her dark dress; one of them asks for her husband's name, then shakes her head, leaving Geneviève unsure whether she had never heard of him or that it was a shame he had died. "Was he the man who spoke the Illinois language?" another girl says, and when Geneviève nods, the frail woman adds that her own husband used to talk about him a lot. In which way, she doesn't specify. She resumes her work, corrects Geneviève's hand on the knife so that she doesn't hurt herself. The woman glances at Mélanie playing with dough figurines on the bench by the door and brings her finely cut thyme to give them eyes, noses, mouths.

As June comes to an end, the head cook announces that Canadians will arrive soon, guests of great influence, friends of the governor of the Illinois Country—of another even more important man, M. Dugué de Boisbriand himself, now governor of La Louisiane. Bachelors, the worst kind of visitors to entertain. There will be feasts, and hunt outings, and dances, which means, for you, only work: come in early, pluck another duck, open more pots of bear oil, bring the best wine out of the cellar. "Rumor has it they will be here next week, much earlier than expected," the head cook says, then adds: "Damn Lake Michigan's winds."

Damn Lake Michigan's winds, Geneviève keeps on telling herself over the next few days. Her shoulders and arms hurt as much as they used to on the washhouse boat in Paris. The smell of food never leaves her hair, her dresses, her skin. When she lets herself fall on the bench, fatigue settles in a knot in her lower back. Mélanie is sitting beside her, then playing, as she waits to go home.

At the end of the week of preparations, Geneviève finds the bench by the door empty. Dusk is descending over the village, has been for hours, and her hands hurt from all the afternoon's kneading. She doesn't worry at first: the children regularly follow a young kitchen helper to bring the chickens back into their coop for the night. But when she reaches the tiny wooden hut, the helper is alone, working the rusty locks of the coop. The chickens coo gently inside.

"Aren't the children with you?" Geneviève can't help but ask.

The woman shrugs. "They preferred the water over the birds today."

The evening air gets caught in Geneviève's throat. As soon as the weather turned hot, the children started accompanying the laundresses to the Kaskaskia River. Geneviève told Mélanie it was the only place where she wasn't allowed to go. She knew that the laundresses wouldn't care to look after the little ones when they worked. The oldest girl in the group—Rosie, a twelve-year-old who would join the kitchen team next month—was to bring Mélanie straight to her in the event of an excursion. The day isn't even that warm for late June; no one came by today.

Geneviève hurries toward the river. She crosses the plum grove, un-ripe fruits rolling under her feet, trees a dirty blue around her. She calls herself irresponsible, an idiot, resurrects a vicious inner voice she hasn't heard since she left Paris. Why didn't she just tell Mélanie to stay inside the kitchen? Because she is a child, because I'm a widow, because I'm her mother. She should have left her under Laure's watch. And barely see her, and let her sister-in-law replace her. She was afraid she'd lose Mélanie. She knows the thought is irrational, knows it's better to have her daughter in good hands than running wild.

She bumps into the laundresses right before she reaches the water. They walk in file, their baskets occupying the width of the path.

"Have you seen my girl?" Geneviève asks. She gives a description of Mélanie that even she can barely comprehend.

"The one with the wavy hair?" a young woman says.

Geneviève clears a curl from her own face. She nods. There are a few children among the women, most of whom Geneviève recognizes as the sons and daughters of the laundresses. Neither Mélanie nor Rosie is among them.

"She was here just a moment ago," says a girl carrying a load twice her size. "I was playing with her. We said we were about to head back, and she went to wash her hands."

Mélanie's uncommon repulsion for dirt, sand, silt, anything that could stick to her skin. How meticulously she'd scrub her palms clean— the image hits Geneviève with a disturbing acuity. She pictures Mélanie kneeling by the river, the water striders sliding on the surface as if it were a mirror, as if sinking were impossible.

"Where is Rosie?" she asks.

"She was sick today."

These women, blocking the trail when all Geneviève wants is to run. She pushes past them.

"Wait, we'll come with you," someone says in her back.

"I thought the little girl was following us."

"I swear she was walking right behind me."

The laundresses' voices are astonishingly loud. They'll point to the place where they sat, Geneviève wouldn't know it by herself, she should be careful not to slide, be very careful with mud. They are saying all these words, and yet none of them makes sense. Geneviève walks faster then stops, grabs a branch to steady herself: the river looks calm, almost inviting, but she knows about its dangerous currents, how violently they crash into the St. Louis River. In the sand, you can still guess the shapes of the women's palms, knees, and baskets. The riverbank thins on her right, in the direction the laundresses point toward. Trees lean over the water, boughs shaping a dark corridor of floating wood, intricate bushes, and sinuous roots—and at the very end, before the next bend, a small silhouette, so tangled in the reeds and briars that it could be nothing more than a fat bird, nesting.

Mélanie calls out before Geneviève does. She has the hiccups, and her words come out broken.

"Do not move," Geneviève calls. "I'll be right there."

But unlike her daughter, she is too tall to sneak through the branches. She can barely make her way past the first bush, her face and hands meeting thorns too thick to break. Her clogs slip in the silt, leaves batter her face. She turns around as best as she can.

"I'll try," someone offers above her.

The girl, the one who swore Mélanie was following them, kneels by her. Her crooked tooth flashes when she smiles. She whispers her name, Margot.

"Be careful," Geneviève calls when all she meant to say is thank you. But the girl is gone, the tunnel of twigs and reeds spitting angry sounds at her passage. Geneviève retreats with the other women, gathered in an interested pack on the sandy beach.

"Thank God this isn't the St. Louis," one of them says.

"There would be no one to rescue."

"The poor child. She must be so scared."

Please quit talking, Geneviève thinks. Her eyes hurt from staring at the hole in the branches, the shrubs, sky, and river different shades of dark now. The little voice in her head grows stronger—it says murderer, it says shame, it says all the ugly words Madame once spat at her, the words that were locked with her in the cell of La Grande Force, the ones she thought she'd left behind in La Maison de Correction, at Lorient Harbor. And yet here they are, on another shore, where there is no one to save her.

"I think I see them."

Geneviève's feet sink, a small fish swims against her ankle, leaves get caught under her bonnet. The tunnel is more somber than it was just minutes ago; inside, movement and forms are erased. Then a lighter shape, the laundress's baby-blue dress piercing through it all, leading a tinier silhouette on firm land. Something gives way in Geneviève's chest. She pulls a branch to help Margot get through. Mélanie is right behind her, the foliage grazing her hair. She stares at the ground.

"Come over here," Geneviève says.

"She was so entangled I had to cut her skirt," Margot says, her own petticoats a mess of silt and mud. "She regrets very much what she did."

Widows are expected to cry, but not too much. What does anyone have to say about mothers, about single women?

"Come here," Geneviève repeats, trying to steady her voice.

Mélanie crawls in to her. Geneviève carries her back on the beach. Her body feels smaller, warmer. It fits perfectly in her arms. Geneviève hears herself breathe mechanical phrases, phrases that, in another world, mean exactly what they are supposed to. It will be fine, I'm here now, I'll never let you down again. Mélanie doesn't say anything. Her wet fingers grab Geneviève's bonnet, cup her ear. She blows flakes of mud against her lobe when she speaks.

"Don't worry, *Maman*," she whispers. "I was trying to reach the oak trees. There, look—do you see them?"

. . .

Rumors travel fast in a household as serviced as the governor's. They fly from mouth to mouth above dirty clothes, hover above the river's imperturbable whisper, mingle with the cows' weary mooing in the stables. They are brought back to the kitchen with feathered eggs, blown over fire smoke, then passed along corridors with tea and cookies and left in another room, for anyone to pick. The rumors are excited whispers, knowing looks, worried remarks. They are never quite what they are. Geneviève knew the child was missing. She was too busy with a lover: the barber, the farrier, the one-armed lad.

One thing is for sure: if her husband were alive, he wouldn't want his daughter to live with such a depraved creature, a weakened mother, a French woman who, some say, was once jailed in Paris for her crimes.

Laure wastes no time. She is at Geneviève's the morning after the incident.

"I'm so very sorry," Laure keeps on repeating, shaking her head. "But you know our dear Mélanie deserves so much better. What would Pierre say if he were here?" She pauses, as if listening to her brother's answer. When she resumes speaking, her voice is matter-of-fact. "There are different ways we can handle this situation, some more pleasant than others. No need to involve men in this, don't you think?"

By "men," Laure means her husband; the governor's officials; the clerk who, at Pierre's death, interpreted his last will and let Geneviève know she could live in their house but that the place belongs only to her four-year-old child. She stares at her sister-in-law, whose dark dress is more severe than hers, her smile an elaborate mix of pity and victory.

Anger burns Geneviève's throat. "Leave," is all she manages to answer.

Laure shakes her head once more, stands up. Before she reaches the door, she blows a kiss goodbye to Mélanie.

• • •

Geneviève, the day she saw Amélie for the last time: the inside of her, gutted. Raw, unattended, like something left under a boiling sun or placed under a sharpened knife. Otherwise, how could you explain the pain that overcame her long before the crying, a fresh wound that wouldn't leave her alone until she numbed herself with tears?

She can never be like that anymore. Not because there will never be another Amélie but because she's responsible for Mélanie now. Mélanie who holds her hair up in front of imaginary mirrors, who kicks so much in her sleep that she gives herself bruises, who has a way of holding you that'd make you think she's bigger. Mélanie who looks in your eyes a beat too long, making sure you're paying attention, before she buries her hand in yours and shows you her latest game. Geneviève used to have friends, used to belong to a community of women. All of that disappeared as soon as she left the south. Mélanie is the only thing La Louisiane gave her after that, and now it wants to take her back. Sometimes, when Geneviève is about to fall asleep, she sees the two of them from far, far above. She sees an ocean as small as a pond, rivers like veins swirling through infinite land, forests growing nearer and nearer so fast you can count houses and deer one by one, hear a church bell and, if you lean closer, the shy song of a bright yellow bird. Then it seems possible that the pond could be crossed, the river followed, all the way to what she knows best.

. . .

You can't keep a little girl still any more than you can keep mouths shut. Dough figurines crumble too fast. A mother's attention never lasts long enough. Rules serve their purpose only temporarily: don't touch the bread, stay away from the fire, quit bothering the bakers. Kitchens are dangerous places. They aren't meant for children. A week after the incident, two days after the Canadian guests have arrived, the head cook rests her bony hand on Geneviève's shoulder. "I hired you," she says, "not her." Her fingers leave a flour stain on the black of Geneviève's dark dress. "One of Monsieur's friends asked for a glass of cognac. Bring it to him."

Cognac, rabbit stew, cold veal cutlets. Over the next few days, Geneviève brings many things to the two Canadian guests. Work doubles. It feels like a test—perform your duties and keep your job, or go home with your child. She burns her last chances with the other women. "Only this time," they say when she swears she'll be back in five minutes, three, then just one. And when she doesn't have the strength to ask, she scrubs Mélanie's cheeks clean and tells her to follow, not to make a noise, and to stay behind while *Maman* knocks at the door of some gentlemen. Once she comes out of the *petit salon* to see that one of the guests, a blond man with a fine nose and girlish lips, observes Mélanie. But he doesn't say anything, only smiles at her, then at Geneviève, and shuts his door.

She should have a plan, but for once she doesn't. Laure hasn't reappeared with her ghastly suggestions, but it is only a matter of time. Financial worries slide into the background. If Mélanie is taken away from her, Geneviève knows no money will bring her back. The house will turn into a cell, outside of which she'll hear the angry whisperings of the town, casting her into someone she thought she would never be, just like in Paris. When Geneviève lets the head cook know that she won't be back tomorrow, the woman crosses her insect-like fingers. "That is probably for the best," she says.

It is the kindest thing Geneviève has heard in weeks.

The following day, she wakes up to loud pounding at her door. Mélanie is already awake, studying her big toe. Geneviève feels her bottom lip shake. She smiles at her daughter, then reaches for her stays, laces it halfway through, grabs her petticoats.

"Get dressed," she says. "And wait for me here."

"Can I choose what I want to wear today?"

Geneviève glances at her daughter's two skirts, both black. "Yes," she answers. She resists the urge to take Mélanie against her, to hold her so tightly she'll protest. But she knows that the letting go would be more distressing than the embrace. A day like any other, then, whatever awaits outside that door. She pushes her long hair under her bonnet, adjusts the collar of her dark dress so that it shows nothing but her neck, and walks outside the bedroom. She feels terribly weary.

Three men stand in front of her house. The clerk isn't among them; Laure is nowhere to be seen. Only one face looks vaguely familiar to Geneviève.

"Madame, please receive our sincere condolences, as well as our apologies for calling on you unannounced," the tallest one says. He squints at Geneviève as if she isn't standing right in front of him. His thick eyelashes shadow his eyes. "We know you are in a difficult position to welcome visitors, but we were hoping you would make an exception. M. Melet and M. Beaulieu"—he glances at each of the men standing by him—"are visiting us for a few days and were very intrigued by the treasures your husband brought back from the local tribes."

Only then, when the man he presented as M. Melet smiles, does Geneviève recognize him as one of the Canadians staying at the governor's, the guest who saw Mélanie waiting for her in the corridor. She moves to the side.

"Please come in," she says. "But you might be disappointed by these so-called treasures."

They mutter thank-yous and follow her inside. The relief she felt when she found out who they were—strangers, nothing more—has vanished. No man has stepped inside her house for the past three months, and their presence feels both invasive and from another time—a time when she wasn't alone here, when no one was trying to steal from her the little she had left. She sees the power in these men, both how little they would care to help and yet everything they could do for her. She shows them into the sitting room, where she stored most of the artifacts Pierre brought back from the Illinois villages. He'd sometimes take with him goods that other settlers would give him, and later, he'd look for anything in the house to trade with the Natives—powder, eau-de-vie, wool. She begged him to stop the day she caught him sorting through her corsets. Today the trunk reminds her of nothing but his absence.

M. Beaulieu and the man with the heavy eyelashes lean over the pile of objects. The third guest, M. Melet, doesn't pay any attention to the stuffed kingfisher, the colorful quiver, the headdress topped with the horns of an ox. He stares at Mélanie, leaning against the doorframe, sucking her thumb pensively.

"Isn't she the little girl I once saw at the governor's?" M. Melet asks.

Geneviève doesn't have time to answer. Mélanie runs through the room, pointing at the bow M. Beaulieu holds, the one she used to covet for her own games. She stops short at his feet. "It is very fragile," she tells him. "You shouldn't hold it this way."

"Forgive her," Geneviève says, reaching for the child's hands, but Mélanie buries them under her armpits.

"How so?" M. Beaulieu asks.

Mélanie turns to him, surprised to be heard. "Well," she starts cautiously, and in that moment, she looks so much like Pierre that Geneviève feels her legs soften. "It is very sharp, you might cut yourself."

The two other men are listening to her now. M. Beaulieu points at a gourd. "What about this? What should we know about it?"

"This," Mélanie says, "is a *chichicoya*." She explains that the inside is filled with glass beads, talks about sickness and songs. When she shakes it, the man is startled. She hands it reluctantly to M. Beaulieu. What would Geneviève tell them if she had their attention? Please intervene. Talk to the clerk. Make them see that I am not who they think I am.

"She has a lot to say." M. Melet's hand rests on the back of her chair.

"Sometimes too much," Geneviève answers, her voice dried out.

"Your husband must have been a very knowledgeable man. I used to think that M. Dugué de Boisbriand was the only person who could speak the Illinois language. I'll ask if he knew Monsieur . . ."

"Durand," Geneviève completes. She doubts the current governor of La Louisiane will remember Pierre. Her husband and the founder of Fort de Chartres met once, and only by chance, the day M. Dugué de Boisbriand came to see the few Illinois girls whom the Jesuit father swore he had converted to Christianity. When M. Dugué left for New Orleans to replace M. Bienville, two years after Geneviève and Pierre had settled in Prairie du Rocher, Geneviève asked her husband how long he gave the new governor before he too was called back to Paris. "How about you try and trust him?" Pierre replied. She did try; it wasn't her fault if she felt one defeat after another. And yet sometimes bets were all she had.

"Are you on your way to New Orleans?" she asks.

M. Melet looks at her. His shoulders are square, his eyes a light shade of brown that, in the right light, could be considered green. His hand drops from the back of her chair. "The Illinois Country is so very similar to Canada that it is quite disappointing," he says. "I thought this land would be warmer, dryer. Your impressions were probably different when you arrived from New Biloxi."

Geneviève tries to flatten her expression. She never mentioned anything about Lower Louisiana. She suddenly feels extraordinarily vulnerable, alone in that room with these men.

"I might not know Canada," she forces herself to reply, "but I share your views on this place."

M. Melet is about to answer when the man with the dense eyelashes interrupts them. "We've bothered you too much already," he says, looking suddenly alarmed. Mélanie is running after him, babbling about buffalo manitou and strangled bucks. This time Geneviève recognizes her explanations for what they are—a story she made up. The men never would have guessed. She brings Mélanie close to her.

"Not at all," she says.

"I believe these gentlemen have had their share of exoticism."

M. Beaulieu nods, but M. Melet keeps on staring at the gourd Mélanie placed on the only armchair of the room.

"Not quite. With your permission, I might return with M. Soulant, who would be very much interested by everything your home has to offer."

The two other men exchange glances. "Of course," Geneviève hastens to say.

They leave. She watches them go away, picturing herself walking behind them, a trunk in her hand, Mélanie in the other. All she wants from this place is to leave it.

• • •

When M. Melet comes back two days later, he is alone. He wears hunting clothes, quite filthy; he seems less impressive that way, a simple visitor passing by her house on his way somewhere else. He looks in the trunk, asks for the price of an otter fur, drops it back in even though she knows the price she offered is too low. He refuses to drink or eat anything. He explains that he has been summoned by one of his compatriots, the governor of La Louisiane himself, that M. Dugué de Boisbriand is offering him a position as one of his counselors. "If a man born and raised in Québec City can survive the heat, then so can I." He laughs when no one else does, and shows dimples she wouldn't have suspected. He doesn't hint at her past like he did the previous day. He only asks her about the south. "The continent is difficult to reach, but if the day is clear, you can see dolphins," Geneviève hears herself explain, when all she wants to say is how hard it was to miss Pétronille's departure by so little or to never know the name of Charlotte's baby—Charlotte, who was nothing more than a terrified pregnant thirteen-year-old girl the last time they met. This man, standing here in her sitting room, is going where she last saw them. The facts seem incompatible, almost magical. "I'll leave you alone," he finally says. He looks at her hands, grabs his whip. He doesn't say whether he will come back.

• • •

Laure shows up dressed for the occasion: her wool gown is pitch-dark, thick, hooded, a nightmare given this kind of summer day. She wears her drops of sweat like tears, washes them away with a gray handkerchief. She takes forever to explain what she's come to say. She met with the clerk, the bald one with his sunstruck skull, does Geneviève remember? A very pragmatic man, extremely thorough, who agreed with her before she was done speaking—long, long before she had laid out the situation in front of him. It was quite obvious that Mélanie should live with them. Of course, mothers were always favored as guardians. Careful mothers, that is. A child's needs should come first always, didn't she think? Geneviève would be welcome to visit them—why, Laure wasn't a monster. And the man could be trusted. He would take all the necessary measures, including the transfer of Mélanie's inheritance. Geneviève would keep her dower, at least for the coming year, but Laure promised Pierre she would take care of her niece: promises to the dead shouldn't be broken.

You're right, Geneviève thinks. They shouldn't be broken.

The following day, she doesn't wait to see if M. Melet will return. She takes Mélanie and goes back to where she used to work, the farmyard and kitchens remarkably unchanged, women looking at her beyond their overflowing cauldrons, the wet sound of meat being sliced, then the potage smell fading in the corridor, the thick carpet muffling her steps, Mélanie tripping over it as Geneviève hopes she won't run into anyone but this man she barely knows and is about to ask so much from—her breath tepid against her lips in the darkness of this velvet corridor, looking at three doors, trying to remember from which room she once saw him walk out. She has no idea what she would say to the other gentlemen if she encountered them.

"Wrong one."

A fourth door is cracked open behind her. M. Melet's shadow cuts through the sunbeam that licks at the carpet. He is smaller than in her memory. "Do come in."

She takes Mélanie's hand too firmly, the shaking of her own fingers caged into her daughter's palm. She barely takes note of what surrounds her—a salon full of light and shadows, the smell of sun on silk. She can't see beyond this moment.

"I wish to accompany you to New Orleans," she says.

He looks at her, seemingly more amused than surprised. "Accompany me? And you would join me as my—"

"I can cook, I can wash," she says. "I can do anything."

He is playing with a little watch, catching light, sending it elsewhere. "My wife doesn't cook or wash."

"Your wife?"

"You said you could do anything, didn't you?"

Mélanie tugs at her dress, but the gesture comes from an infinite distance. Geneviève holds perfectly still. She sees the Superioress leaning on her cane at La Maison de Correction, bringing her another offer she didn't expect. Baby rats sleeping at her feet, all the things the old woman knew about her, all the things she ignored. A boat sailing far, where none of it would matter. Her future becoming her past, blurring into ocean, land, and river, images irremediably leading to the woman she has become. "What would people say?" she asks.

"Probably nothing worse than what they are saying now."

She is thankful for his honesty. "And why would you want to marry an irresponsible mother? An intrepid widow?" She was never sure why Mlle Pancatelin chose to save her.

"Precisely for these reasons."

"That can't be true."

"But if I were to tell you I've always been curious about French women, would you believe me?"

"No," she says.

He laughs and glances around him as if just realizing where they are. In a room, at the governor's, an attentive child between them. There is a silence. A door slams in the distance. "Should I take that as a yes?" he asks.

When she answers M. Melet, Geneviève looks beyond him, through the open window, toward all the things she can't see.

. . .

He warns her the journey will be long, even if they are going downstream. He talks about several hundred leagues, a three-to-four-week trip, but that can't be right. Geneviève remembers it took her and Pierre months to travel to Prairie du Rocher; she also knows that the waters are unpredictable, that there might be storms, harsh winds, whirlpools, beavers, bears, and broken hulls. Geneviève doesn't care. For the first time in her life, she is going where she wants to. She won't be buried inland forever. The water could take her anywhere. It'll take her to the place where she first settled, it'll bring her daughter to the delta. Geneviève doesn't allow herself to think that Charlotte and Étiennette could still be there. But even if the two of them are gone, there will be—there has to be—at least one other woman she once knew from *La Baleine*. Someone who could remember Paris, La Salpêtrière, Lorient, and the way it felt to watch it all disappear, forever, from the damp deck of a *flûte* named after a whale.

She never thought Lower Louisiane would one day feel like home. She hopes that by the time she arrives there, her widowhood will be nothing more than a rumor—a crack in the woods, a splash in the water, a noise that vanished in an instant.

She finds out M. Melet's Christian name is also Pierre. The coincidence is uncanny. She carefully pronounces the two syllables of his last name, makes a point of calling him Monsieur, and wonders whether she'll ever be able to think of him otherwise once they are married.

She has months to decide. They won't marry before they reach New Orleans, and even there they will wait, enough time to make sure that Geneviève's first husband isn't the father of her potential child if she's pregnant. She knows she isn't, but there is no need to stir people's attention, neither here nor there.

She barely sees M. Melet as she prepares for the trip. She doesn't know what he told his travel companion about her. When she asks, he lays his hand on hers. "You shouldn't worry about that," he says. He's never touched her before: the stroke travels all the way to her elbow. His fingers are as cold as his signet ring—she never noticed his nails were that sharp.

Mélanie asks few questions about him. She cares little about the man, only about the journey. She wants to know what people look like in the south, and if she'll be as cold as she was here in the winter. She asks about the size of spiders and the color of the sky. Geneviève describes ocher soil, green water corridors, trees whose foliage looks a bit like her daughter's long, wavy hair. Her own enthusiasm surprises her. The Louisiane she's offering to Mélanie is devoid of mosquitoes and famines, full of fruits, silkworms too; the heat is only slightly more humid than what she remembers from her own childhood in Provence. By now she understands that the fantastic tales Pierre and the girls used to tell in New Biloxi and on *La Baleine* were as much for themselves as for her.

A maid comes to help her pack—a woman whom Geneviève, thankfully, doesn't remember seeing at the governor's. M. Melet told her to take everything Pierre traded with the Illinois. The trunk is carried away before her own, and it feels wrong. Though it is huge, she keeps it light. She never had the chance to bring much with her. Nothing but the dress she wore when she was sent away from Madame's, and barely more when she left La Salpêtrière. She ends up shoving stockings, petticoats, and shifts in the old bundle that was once handed to her in a Parisian police station.

The day before their departure, she goes to visit Laure. The idea is rather unpleasant, but Geneviève does it for Pierre, for herself, maybe even for her sister-in-law. She couldn't leave without seeing her again. Farewells matter: they might be the only power Geneviève has ever had. She can still feel Amélie's suddenly frail shoulders in her arms, the deep conviction that seized her right then: as soon as one of us lets go, there is no way back. She can still see Mlle Pancatelin's eyes meeting hers the day carts gathered in the Cour Saint-Louis—the Superioress sitting motionless in the shade, the chair disappearing under her dress, her cane resting between her feet like a third leg. Now Geneviève wishes she had gone to her. She isn't sure what she would have said. She just knew it was a luxury to be aware that she was seeing the old director, this place, for the last time. She wouldn't spoil that, not even with Laure.

Out in the yard, Mélanie plays with three of her five cousins. A cat follows the ball's clumsy arcs. From the parlor, the children's mouths let out nothing more than muffled cries. Laure gives her a nod when she enters. She has turned very quiet since she learned about Geneviève's journey.

"I won't stay long," Geneviève says.

"Not with a boat leaving on Sunday."

"Which is tomorrow."

"Tomorrow," Laure repeats.

Geneviève leans toward her. "I wanted to tell you that you could use Pierre's house until Mélanie returns," she says.

Laure turns toward the window. The children's hands, with the distance, seem to touch her face. "We both know she will not," she says softly. She pauses. "You never believed me when I said I was acting in her best interest, did you?"

"I didn't, no."

Laure nods. "Do you think this man will be good to her?"

Geneviève won't know before she is gone already.

"I will be there," she answers. She expects her sister-in-law to laugh at her, but she looks solemn.

"Pierre wouldn't have wanted any of this," she says. Then she opens the door and, without another look at Geneviève, leaves the room, reappearing outside as if on a stage, interrupting the children's games and the cat's show. The window frames the scene perfectly. Laure kneeling on the ground and Mélanie running to her, the boys staring at their mother and cousin, the ball rolling away from them and in between the cat's paws. Mélanie's and Laure's faces disappear in the dark fabric of a dress, the chubby arm of a child. A quiet sob reaches Geneviève, the beginning of one of her nephews' religious songs, or perhaps something else entirely.

· · ·

The river: gray, blue, and brown, and more often than not, a shade that doesn't bear a name. It is movement more than color—the water shaken by unseen forces, straining under them. The pirogues are a lot bigger than the ones used for Geneviève's first trip: there is room for her legs, room for Mélanie to lie beside her like she used to on the bench in the kitchens. But now Mélanie is never alone. At night, the Canadian men rowing their boat entertain them with their adventures in Canada—explain how dangerous rapids are, what a *portage* is, and how they sometimes have to carry canoes and baggage for days when rivers become impracticable. Their stories aren't always meant for a child. Geneviève calls out for them to stop on their fourth evening, when she catches one of them showing

Mélanie his four-toed foot, describing how the big toe froze against an ice-covered rock and had to be amputated. Geneviève has never seen men as big and robust as these *voyageurs*—who, when they help her on board, make her feel like she weighs no more than Mélanie. And yet, when she shushes them, they fall into an embarrassed silence.

She and Mélanie share their pirogue with these men, a deaf cook, a fifteen-year-old boy, three trunks, and a smelly dog who always seems on the verge of falling overboard. M. Melet is on another boat, which Geneviève understands. She travels as a widow, not as a bride. What confuses her is the man's inconsistency. Some evenings she is sitting on the riverbank with the curious, smiling stranger she met the day he showed up at her door. Others he is so distant she wonders if he even remembers the promises he made to her.

Two weeks into the trip, after a halt at an outpost in Chickasaw Country, she hears from the *voyageurs* that the governor of La Louisiane, M. Dugué de Boisbriand, will likely face the same charges as his predecessor, accused of deteriorating the colony. That he might even be called back to France, just like M. Bienville was. "A Canadian man at the head of the whole of La Louisiane," one of the men says, "it didn't last for long." Thick fingers play with the logs. A gigantic flame erupts, then recedes: the *voyageurs* never burn themselves. "I bet these are only rumors," Geneviève suggests. The men shrug, shake their heads. She feels uncomfortable. M. Melet was to sit on the governor's council in New Orleans—but what happens if M. Dugué de Boisbriand is gone by the time they reach the delta? She doesn't want to try and guess what this decision would mean for him, for her and Mélanie.

The following evening, M. Melet shows her a map. She doesn't sit too close to him; she can feel M. Beaulieu's gaze on them. She leans over the tired paper. There is a compass in the middle of the ocean, a sun caught in a circle, its beams dying as they touch the continent. Little mountains, not unlike waves, frozen here and there on land, the St. Louis River the only obvious road cutting through it all. Thicker strokes of ink around Lake Orleans and Lake Superior—lakes battling for a name, bearing two instead of one, Lake Dolphin being also Lake Illinois and Michigami. Names Geneviève never heard for places she'll never know—Turtle Island, Shawnee Country, New Mexico, and New Spain—as if adding the word "new" in front of a place's name is enough to lay claim to a land. Then one she instantly recognizes when M. Melet reads it—Natchez, caught between the Tunica River and the Houma Villages. Her nail covers it entirely when she points at it.

"Will we stop here?"

"Where?"

She moves her finger away. Her heart beats hard in her chest. She asked Pierre the same question five years ago, and the answer was no. They got supplies in Yazoo instead.

"Likely so." M. Melet shrugs.

Geneviève doesn't ask about Pétronille until the day they arrive in Natchez. She doesn't want to get her hopes up. She has learned her friend's married name only thanks to Pierre, who, in New Biloxi, had heard of M. Ducros and his plantation in Fort Rosalie. Geneviève might not know anything else about Pétronille, but she can already hear what her friend would say: "If he lets us meet, take it as a sign of a kind heart. If he doesn't, fear for the future." Pétronille, who read messages in flowers, who dreamed big anything small.

The sun is still high when they reach Fort Rosalie—the day overcast, the hills silver, the light sharp. The fort towers over the river, its shadows absorbed by the forest. For once the landing is easy; the pirogues slide onto the sand as if it were butter. The settlement unveils itself cautiously. A manured shack at the end of the trail, a farm, then two. Many more, forest giving way to pigs, sheep, and fields, people working them, French peasants or enslaved Africans. In the carriages that the governor sent to fetch them, Geneviève barely glances at the landscape. It is pointless to try and guess which house might belong to Pétronille. On her lap, Mélanie snores irregularly. Geneviève stares at M. Melet—his jaw tensed, small wrinkles running on his forehead. It isn't a good day, but it is the only one she has.

"A friend of mine," she starts, then stops. The words are kindle to her cheeks. "Madame Ducros. She lives here. I was hoping to see her."

He looks outside the window, frowns, leans forward as if he's recognized someone. Then he turns to her. His face is blank. In that moment, he is the perfect stranger he always was. "Do as you wish," he answers, unfazed.

She opens her mouth, but nothing comes out. She isn't relieved. She feels invisible, like something that could be forgotten, erased. "Thank you," she manages to say.

She is still trying to shake the feeling away, an hour later, when she hops on another carriage—with only Mélanie this time, a soldier sitting by the coach driver. M. Melet disappeared as soon as they entered the residence of Fort Rosalie's governor. He said she would be taken to Mme Ducros, that he had important business to conduct—probably to verify the rumors about M. Dugué de Boisbriand being accused of corruption, to make sure he has a job waiting for him in New Orleans, although he didn't say a word about any of this. "I hope the reunion with your friend will be pleasant," he added. He seemed genuine then, a flash of kindness. How much weight last words can carry. She clings to this single sentence like a rope.

Then she is on her way to Pétronille's. The carriage leaves the main road. Mulberry trees are everywhere, just like in Provence. Oranges too, like the ones she used to eat in New Biloxi, their sweet juice biting her gums. Under her, the carriage dangles like the pirogues did the last time she saw Pétronille on the beach, five years ago.

The horses stop. The house is big, well built. This is Geneviève's first thought, one she could have had for her own daughter: her friend has a sturdy roof above her head; she is being taken care of. Vine grows around the windows. Below, flowers Geneviève never knew existed explode in rich, wild colors—a bouquet of shades so different it's hard to think of them individually. The porch is deserted except for a robin that flies away at their advance. Mélanie retreats behind her dress.

"*Maman*," she whispers. She points at the window. "Look."

At first Geneviève doesn't recognize Pétronille—the reflection of the yard hitting the window and melting with the inside of the house, branches and sky across her friend's face, Pétronille's hand on her mouth, her birthmark barely visible, her eyes as stunned as if she has seen a ghost. Then she is standing in front of Geneviève. The same dark hair, her eyes less green than in Geneviève's memory, the slight frown of her eyebrow, mulling over a question no one but she had asked.

"I mistook you for Marie," Pétronille says.

Geneviève doesn't know whom she is talking about. She resists an urge to take her in her arms: her old friend wouldn't appreciate that. But Pétronille holds her delicately, as if an abrupt gesture could shatter it all. Her embrace is barely stronger than when they last met, in the sick girls' hut, when Geneviève told her to look for Mme Durand once she'd left the warehouse. Mme Durand. In a few months, that woman wouldn't exist anymore—she'd carry another name, would have become impossible to track. Geneviève made it here on time.

Pétronille takes a step back. "How did you arrive?" she asks.

Geneviève looks around her. Suddenly she can't explain it to herself either.

"We are traveling with big men," Mélanie intervenes. "And M. Melet."

Pétronille stares at her, incredulous. "Who is that?" she asks, and for a moment Geneviève isn't sure whom she means—her daughter or the man Mélanie just mentioned.

"I don't know," Mélanie answers.

Pétronille starts laughing, too hard for such a small sentence; Mélanie smiles, proud of her joke that wasn't one. Pétronille turns to Geneviève. "But you do know who he is, don't you?" she asks.

Geneviève gives her a faint smile. The feeling she had in the carriage rises in her belly again—something invasive, whole and hard, that threatens to swallow everything else. She hangs to this moment: Pétronille, the orange scent, the silver light. Mélanie kneeling on the porch, looking at a lizard sneaking between the wooden boards.

"Let me go get Émile," Pétronille says, then clarifies: "My son. The baby, Hélène, is asleep."

Geneviève follows her friend inside the house. This is where Pétronille has been all these years, where her children are growing up. She can't believe that she is seeing, stepping into, her friend's home. The furniture is elaborate, its wood polished. On the table, there is a bouquet of dried flowers, pink and white. An armchair faces the fireplace. When Geneviève spots the shawl lying on the backrest, her heart pounds fast against her chest. Its silk catches the sunlight in a way she immediately recognizes, a way she hasn't seen in far too long. In the next room, she hears a child fussing. When Geneviève touches the perfectly smooth shawl, she thinks of Provence, of baby hair, pebbles shined by river currents, the skin on the inside of a woman's thighs.

"You would have enjoyed M. Ducros's whim when he decided he'd produce his own silk," she hears Pétronille say. Her friend is standing behind her, holding a dark-haired boy, no older than three or four.

Geneviève gently waves at him, then points at the shawl: "Did your husband make this?"

"Absolutely not. He bought it for me." Pétronille smiles. "He didn't have the patience or the dexterity to reel the silk from the cocoons. He said it was a woman's or a child's work."

Geneviève sees her mother's careful hands, her meticulous gestures when she handled the worms, their cocoons. Of course it's a woman's work, she thinks.

●   ●   ●

You can't summarize five years in an hour—can't describe the little joys, the moments of despair, the bursts of anger that led them here. They pick and choose, sometimes more cautiously than others. They talk about their husbands—of cheating, dying, and forgiving. They talk about children, but not that much: Mélanie and Émile play right on the porch, and their games tell enough about each of them—Mélanie, resolute and inventive; Émile, dreamy yet uncompromising. "It's a good thing he is such a quiet boy," Pétronille says. She tells Geneviève how young he was when the skirmishes of October 1722 started, how she was cradling the then six-month-old baby on this very same porch the day Natchez warriors passed by her house. How afraid she was the baby would start howling and draw the men's attention to them. But they marched on, ignoring her. The warriors from the White Apple Village were after someone else that October day. Pétronille heard them firing at M. Guenot's plantation for an entire week. She prayed she and her family would be spared, and the praying did save her, but not other settlers, whose houses and farmsteads were soon burned to the ground.

"But that war was uneventful in comparison with the one that came after, the following fall," Pétronille says.

"How many wars were there?" Geneviève asks. She doesn't want to sound alarmed, doesn't want to break her friend's disconcerting indifference.

Pétronille shrugs. "Things have been quieter for almost three years now." She pauses. "I'm not even sure how the last war started." She goes on explaining how, in the fall of 1723, some Natchez people killed cattle that turned out to be on the property of some settlers. Or maybe that happened later, when boats had already filled with soldiers from New Orleans, joined by Tunica warriors, then by Native missionaries from the allied Natchez towns. She says soldiers burned huts and granaries in the Grigra and Jenzenaque villages, but she doesn't mention the battles. She hurries toward resolution: Tattooed Snake asked for peace and brought the heads of unruly warriors to Governor Bienville. To Geneviève, the scene is impossible to visualize—in Pierre's world, there had never been any conflict with the Natives, let alone a war erupting. All she sees when she hears her friend's accounts are drummers beating a rat-a-tat like she once heard Illinois men do near Prairie du Rocher, and the white armbands her friend describes, worn by allied warriors to signal their alliance with the French.

"Émile slept through it all," Pétronille concludes. But her tone is uncertain. She speaks mechanically, without looking at Geneviève, goes on talking about the wife of a sergeant who was captured, led to a ravine, where she fought the Natives with a lard slicer she had hidden in the sleeve of her nightgown, and killed one before being scalped. Pétronille starts laughing bitterly at the horror of her own story.

"I have learned a lot since then," she says. "Exactly a year before the first war, I was horseback riding with a friend on the property of M. Guenot, the plantation manager who caused it all."

"Horseback riding?" Geneviève asks, bewildered. The image of the sergeant's wife, fighting back when she could, is still with her.

"Such a foolish idea," Pétronille admits. "I don't regret it, you know."

They fall silent. A red dragonfly hovers in the middle of the porch. That is the difference between them. Pétronille doesn't regret a thing she did. Not here in Natchez, not on *La Baleine* with Baptiste, not at the warehouse when she was ready to do anything to see him again.

"What will happen to you now?" Pétronille asks.

"I don't know," Geneviève says. She expected her breath to fasten, her temples to burn, the anguish to rise like it so often has since Pierre died. Nothing happens. A breeze dries the sweat on her collarbone, blows Pétronille's dress against hers. Her future is unknowable but not unreachable, and that's what she focuses on. She is kneading it right now, not with water and flour but with words and actions, and it is taking shape, a path stretching from everything she's done and turned away from. So far, this is where it led her—to her best friend, with her daughter, to a place she thought she'd never reach.

Her past, she knows it already; it will always be here, swallowing her if she lets it. She rests against the back of her chair, watches Mélanie take away a rag from Émile, Pétronille not moving an inch by her side, letting them solve what is for them alone to solve. And beyond them, the soldier smoking his pipe on a rock, the coach driver already dragging back the recalcitrant horses. The carriage door ajar, the future open for her to enter.

PART III

The women have children. Some of them would rather have remained girls, spouses, but even they were aware it was unlikely. They knew that one day their bellies would swell, that they wouldn't be quite alone anymore in La Louisiane. The children are called Mélanie, Hugo, Émile—their names don't matter: just like the women's, they will be forgotten. The children were born in the Mississippi. By now they are old enough to ask questions. They always were; it only took their mothers time to figure out what they were asking. There was a time, not so long ago, when their mothers had the same questions. They too were new to the colony—they couldn't have known the name of the local canoes, whether this flying creature was a huge insect or a miniature bird, or why the sun set so early here.

It took the women years to understand what surrounded them. They want to spare their children the confusion, the faux pas, the delusions—the bitter feeling that this land doesn't want them any more than Paris and their home-towns did.

So they say hastily: A pirogue. A hummingbird. The sun is a mystery to us all, honey.

The children have other questions, ones that the women are shier to answer. If you didn't grow up here, then where did you? Where is Paris? Does it still exist? Will we go one day?

No, the women say. They brush away the memories of their own mother, of the half-broken stool they used to sit on by their parents' bed, of the fireplace that sometimes smoked so badly they tasted ash on their lips, of all the places they'll never see again. The women stroke the children's heads, the perfect skin of their cheeks. They kneel by them, point at the garden, the hills, the forests, the pelicans gathered by the water. They hope their voices won't break, and yet at times they do.

Look, they say. Our life is here.

As if to answer them, the birds fly away, their wet wings flapping in the evening air. The children sit on the women's laps—they watch the pelicans hover, circle above the green river.

9

NEW ORLEANS
NOVEMBER 1727

Charlotte

On Rue de Bourbon, carriages rattle and shake through the morning air. This winter is the most humid of the seven Charlotte has spent in La Louisiane, with water threatening to sneak through the door, a voice she needs to warm up before singing, and pages bent in the few remaining books piled in her sitting room. She has never been very interested in reading. She associates it with listening to the chosen girls of La Maison Saint-Louis, who were made to decipher the Bible out loud. Charlotte wasn't one of them: she belonged to the church's choir, not to the classroom. At La Salpêtrière, the Aunts and Mlle Pancatelin had quickly decided her talent lay solely in her voice. Today she can only guess what the director of La Salpêtrière would say of her decision to join the Ursuline convent.

Before shutting the door to her house, Charlotte takes a final glance at the empty room, at the trunk where she used to store Louis's few books. Three months after he died, she finally decided not to sell them. It took her weeks to get used to the idea that she would never find him kneeling in the back room of their home, flipping pages he had read too many times to count. That he was gone for good and, with him, her hopes of ever becoming a mother.

Not that she hadn't buried this idea already, or at least tried to, as she settled in New Orleans. She never believed herself pregnant since that summer four years ago. Charlotte stopped trying to figure out whose fault it was, never followed through on Marthe's silly ideas. She saw what pregnancies could do—bring life but also death. Last February, Étiennette's fifth boy had almost killed her.

Charlotte was home that winter morning when one of Étiennette's maids came in crying, explaining that the doctor was trying to save her mistress, when, only seconds ago, Charlotte didn't know there was anyone to rescue, was only getting ready to rehearse with the choir at Saint-Louis Church. Étiennette had given birth to her previous babies so smoothly and uneventfully that the servant's news was hard to believe. Charlotte sat in front of the maid, who must have been talking because her lips wouldn't keep still. But Charlotte couldn't understand a word she said. Couldn't breathe. The emptiness that built up in her chest made her hollow. She had never felt that way before, never would again, not even six months later when a sailor from Louis's crew came to announce their boat had been ravaged by a storm. What she felt on the day Étiennette almost died, she regretted not feeling at Louis's funeral.

Now that she is on her way to the convent, it is pointless to think of Étiennette, whose husband made enough money to finally leave this cursed coast and buy land up north. Étiennette said she had given up trying to understand him. New Orleans finally had started resembling the city they had dreamed of; a popular song even sang the beauty of the capital, comparing it to that of Paris. "Pure propaganda," M. Feuger would answer, set on leaving.

At the end of last summer, Charlotte paid her friend one last visit before she left for Canada. Étiennette talked about huge trees and forests tangled like spiderweb. She held her very tight, and Charlotte buried her face in her neck, let herself be squeezed. She didn't bother hiding her feelings that day. They would never see each other again.

The Ursuline sisters will keep Charlotte on the right path. She believes in these women, whose presence in the Mississippi is a miracle. A few months ago, the governor and general superior were convinced they had perished; their boat had left Lorient on February 23, and in May, no one knew where *La Gironde* was. The ship had finally reached La Balize with a two-month delay, at the end of July. The nuns weren't deterred by their awful journey. Charlotte has heard they are not letting anyone, not even the governor, tell them what to do; that they're fending for themselves, intent on achieving their mission—spread God's faith and educate the girls of La Louisiane. Charlotte longs to be part of this community of sisters, this family of brave women, one she sometimes imagines as a much kinder, freer version of La Salpêtrière. A place that no one but she will have chosen for herself.

"Charlotte!"

She turns around. Sitting in a small berlin, M. Valade looks at her. He's the last person she wants to run into—Marthe's husband, who, although kind, can't understand why a nineteen-year-old widow wouldn't choose to remarry. But the voice calling her is female, and Charlotte barely has time to scan the interior of the carriage when its door opens on a pile of blankets, a red nose, Marthe.

"This cold!" Marthe calls. "Surely you'll join us. Come on, *montez*!"

Charlotte hesitates. The summer when Marthe tried to help her have children feels like another lifetime ago. The last time they saw each other was for what Étiennette called "a ladies' musical hour" a year back. That fall afternoon of 1726, singing was quickly abandoned for rumors. One of the twins said that the new governor would arrive in January with his wife, and asked whether anyone knew the man's name or reputation—if he'd be any better than M. Dugué de Boisbriand and M. Bienville, both summoned back to Paris after being accused of mismanaging the colony. "Who cares," Étiennette said. She stared at them, seemingly savoring the more interesting news she was about to deliver. Did they remember Geneviève Menu, from *La Baleine*? The women looked at each other. Charlotte shivered at the name, unsure if she felt too cold or too hot. Well, Étiennette continued, Geneviève is back from the Illinois Country, about to get married to a counselor working for the new governor's administration.

Charlotte went to open the window for some brisk air, but there wasn't enough of it. Flashes of the dreams that kept on troubling her resurfaced; she was terrified that now Geneviève would only appear more often in her sleep—assured, determined, beautiful. Charlotte couldn't bring herself to sing that afternoon.

"I don't wish to be a burden," Charlotte says, glancing at Marthe's carriage, at the muddy street.

"*Alors*, where should we take you?"

Charlotte can tell Marthe is trying too hard—a sad attempt to bring back a long-gone friendship. M. Valade fidgets with something she can't see from the parapet; the horses breathe heavily in the cold air. Charlotte clears her throat as she climbs in the carriage with her small trunk.

"The Ursulines' house." At that, M. Valade glances at her, then goes back to studying his monocle. "But you might let go of me when you reach—"

"*N'importe quoi*—rubbish!" Marthe leans toward the window to tell the coach driver. "None of us would want to let you walk in this cold. Isn't that true, Jean?"

"What I'm really wondering is why you'd decide to visit such a dull place."

His wife throws him a dark look. "One must look for company where one can find it. Dear, you must have been so lonely since—"

"Just like you are whenever M. Valade travels to Fort Rosalie," Charlotte says. Marthe seems cross. Charlotte turns to M. Valade. "I thought you were still up there."

"I came back last week," he says.

"How was it?"

"Greener, hotter, than here. Everything that wheat and humans need. I was able to negotiate ten bear-oil barrels thanks to M. Ducros." He pauses. "He and his wife have a second child now. A girl."

M. Valade always mentions Pétronille in passing, as if to tease Charlotte. Then, as soon as she questions him further, he feints surprise and blurts, "How would I know?" Today she won't ask him anything. She pictures Pétronille and her son—who must be five, by now?—her baby girl. The thought of other women and their children still hurts, but less than that of Étiennette traveling to Canada's buzzing forests. Charlotte never left the south. She can't even picture the place where her friend will spend the rest of her life. She tries not to think of Geneviève's unexpected return—tries not to hope that Étiennette too might one day come back. She massages the back of her neck. The Ursulines will help rid her of these thoughts.

"I'm glad to hear that Mme Ducros is happy," she says.

The streets fully bustle as they get closer to the water. Women pile hops and fava beans on crates. Girls sell nuts and winter squash. Wheat, the last shipment of the year, should soon arrive from the northern concessions—some vegetables, even, from the coast, harvested by German farmers.

"I'm not sure what M. Charpillon would think of you visiting these nuns," M. Valade says.

Charlotte's throat dries up. "I guess we'll never know," she answers. She turns to the window. The carriage is touring the Place d'Armes, passing by Saint-Louis Church, by far the most ambitious building of the city—past the intendant's house and its council chambers, where the important decisions are being made, where men like Geneviève's husband go to work every day.

By the river, the horses trot faster. Enslaved African men are busy restoring the huge levee, as wide as a street, that lies between the quay and the harbor—the one meant to protect the city from flooding. Behind it, boys dig the moat that runs along the riverfront, supposed to attract the floodwater. Charlotte has heard of the slaves rebelling on the ships that traveled from Senegambia to La Balize; she remembers seeing Frenchmen pointing at half-naked girls in the harbor, and how she shuddered when she saw their expressions. She isn't sure what Bienville's Code Noir, passed three years ago, did for the enslaved Africans. Louis despised it. He said the legal text didn't keep overseers from having slaves work on Sundays, from inflicting harsh treatments upon them. He witnessed more than one horrific sanction during his journeys.

"These streets are unspeakably dirty," Marthe mumbles.

No one answers her. The carriage turns on the quay bordering the river, following the water. It passes by the brickworks, the Hôtel-Dieu. Thicker groves appear between the scarce buildings. More enslaved African men work in the woods, cutting the underbrush, knocking down trees. Louis had explained this was Governor de Périer's idea to let the air flow to the city and its windmill. In this foreign part of town, his absence is suddenly overwhelming. Charlotte shifts on her seat and accidentally hits Marthe's foot.

"The runaways," Marthe says, undistracted. She looks at the stretch of thick forest they are passing by. "Don't you fear them?"

Charlotte thinks of her house by the woods, of the many times she was alone there. "No," she answers.

"There will be fewer and fewer of them," M. Valade says.

"How so?" she asks.

"Governor de Périer toughened the measures. Masters will be punished if their slaves escape," he says. "At least that's what I heard in Fort Rosalie. Natchez warriors told me they were asked to catch and bring back runaways or they'd be considered our enemies." He mutters something about needing less than that to be our enemies.

"How do you mean?" Charlotte asks, but Marthe cuts her off.

"Is that it?" she says.

Charlotte glances outside. The big two-story house marks the end of the town, where the pine forest presses close to the garden fences. M. Valade is looking straight at the convent. Charlotte pushes the blankets off her lap.

"Take care, Mme Charpillon," he says.

His tone is so gentle that Charlotte almost trips on the pelts when she steps out of the carriage. She doesn't look back. She hurries through the crisp air, trunk in hand, and knocks at the door.

• • •

Last spring, Charlotte was visiting Étiennette when a storm descended on the city. The clouds turned purple, transitioned to a yellow black, a sick color that drained all the light from the sky. Lightning printed blinding silver trees above the roofs. When the rain started, the drops were fat, generous, filling the ditches so quickly that the parapets disappeared. The streets turned into thick, dark streams.

"You'll stay over," Étiennette decided. "We'll sleep together, just like we used to."

Charlotte's chest burned. She tried breathing more steadily. She wasn't such a bad liar in the end. Étiennette didn't seem to believe or notice any of Charlotte's feelings for her, any more than she had after her party four years ago, when she referred offhandedly to one of the most crucial moments of Charlotte's life. Her sins weren't affecting anyone but herself.

That night she stayed awake. She was terrified she might move in her sleep. She held the edge of the mattress with her right hand; she crossed her legs and pressed her thighs hard against each other so that the warmth she felt there wasn't unnatural, only muscles contracting, her own skin rubbing against itself. She didn't want to close her eyes because she knew exactly what she would see. So she stared at the ceiling, examined the way the corners folded into walls. She listened to the rain, crashing so hard against the tiles that, after a while, the sound felt more like spark than water.

. . .

There are eleven Ursuline nuns in the convent, and nine boarding students from the Old Continent—Charlotte is the tenth. Four more women, enslaved African and Native girls who will stay until they become good Christians. Then numerous day students from diverse origins, girls joining the permanent residents at seven in the morning for mass and staying until suppertime, around five. All these numbers are recited by Mother Tranchepain, a woman in her fifties in an office the size of a pantry, her desk covered with letters. A round painting of the Passion of the Christ hangs above the Superioress like a dark halo.

"The Company rented this house for us," she says. "We won't stay here for long. The royal engineer and Father de Beaubois are in charge of building our convent, but our mission couldn't wait for such trivial matters. When did you arrive in this country?"

Charlotte counts and answers. It's cold in the attic, but only she seems to notice.

"My dear, you must know how needed we are here. None of those people in Paris can quite grasp it, but this settlement will never prosper among the impious. And if the mothers cannot raise decent Christians, then vice will continue to crawl like vermin in these bayous."

Charlotte feels uneasy. She'd had the idea that she would spit Étiennette's name as soon as she'd sat down in the Superioress's office. If the Mother Superior asks her one question—why did you come to us?—she'll tell her the truth. She'll confess, she might even heal. But the nun doesn't ask anything. She is too concerned with the resilience of the Ursuline settlement, insulted, as she explains, that Governor de Périer would want the nuns to become *filles de charité* at the hospital while their true mission is to educate and raise girls in God's faith.

"At least here, we can do as we please. You'll see for yourself. The few indigenous students have a lot to learn and probably as much to forget. But I expect you, a virtuous woman, to help them find the right path. Our sisters are here to teach them, to teach you. But your influence is equally important. They should all soon know their letters and prayers and be ready to receive the baptism of the Holy Spirit by Nativity Day."

"I will do as best as I can," Charlotte answers. Her fingers turn white, bloodless, but she doesn't know if it's her nerves or the cold. The Mother Superior assumes she can read; Charlotte doesn't want to disappoint just yet. Books have always intimidated her, and she never questioned whether she would be able to decipher them.

There is a knock on the door. A girl with a face eaten by smallpox scars steps in.

"Well, Sister Marie-Madeleine will be pleased to show you our humble house. I shall see you at dinner."

Charlotte thanks Mother Tranchepain and follows the other woman to the staircase. Before the door closes, she sees the Mother Superior looking through the window. On the other side of the thin fabric that stretches over its frame, the endless forest turns blue when it touches the sky.

"We are all delighted to welcome you here, Madame."

Among the black veils and the ravaged skin, two joyful eyes stare at Charlotte. A bell rings in the distance, its sound echoing like pebbles on water. Sister Marie-Madeleine won't stop talking. She speaks of the royal engineer and his grand plans for their convent, of girls living five or ten leagues away from the capital who have never even heard of God. She assures Charlotte that they all want to become nuns, then lowers her voice to add, "Our Reverend Father de Beaubois would rather see them turn into Christian mothers. Our deepest desire, of course. You'll meet him soon. He kindly gives us mass."

Charlotte nods. She has seen the Jesuit priest quite often at the Saint-Louis Church, but to Sister Marie-Madeleine, the outside world seems to have vanished. I too will forget it, Charlotte thinks.

"Where are the other sisters?" she asks. She hasn't seen anybody except the Mother Superior and the nun who led her upstairs. On the empty first floor, closed doors face a frozen vegetable garden and a huge yard with tall grass.

"Oh, we're all kept quite busy here. Some of us are teaching right now, others meditate. Sister Françoise is thawing the chickens' water and, well, here is Sister Cécile." Through the window, Charlotte glances at a silhouette, ax in hand, slamming logs in two. Cutting wood, something Étiennette did without hesitating at the warehouse. Charlotte wishes she could start at once, that she could keep her mind busy instead of touring the silent house.

"I hear you enjoy singing," Sister Marie-Madeleine ventures.

Charlotte nods. "Would you mind if I sat in one of the classrooms?"

The nun considers Charlotte's black cloak. "Let's first find you something suitable to wear."

Charlotte draws her cloak closer. She wonders what they'll do with her widow clothes—whom she'll be left to think of when she dresses. She wants to ask if they can keep the gown for her but doesn't. The nun says they would be short of everything if it weren't for the governor's help; there might be one remaining dress. She'll write up an order to the warehouse for an extra pair of clogs. Then she looks at Charlotte. "I imagine yours can do for now," she adds. "This way, please."

At the end of the corridor, they enter a vast room with long tables, four wooden chandeliers, an empty red copper basin. They cross the refectory. Before Sister Marie-Madeleine opens the door, she looks around and says: "The *sauvages* and Negresses study the catechism in a different classroom."

Inside, there are about fifteen women, shifting on their seats when Charlotte steps in. Feathers and inkpots in front of them, shaky letters on rough paper. In the back, the nun doesn't come to a halt. She keeps on reading from her prayer book, her voice like the patient scream of a cuckoo. Charlotte scans the girls, most of them already turning back to their teacher. Then she notices that one of them stares at her, not paying attention to the story of sacrifice and a bloody billy goat. It takes Charlotte a second to recognize Geneviève. Something sinks into her chest. She fears her legs will give way beneath her. When the nun points at a nearby table, it takes Charlotte all her might to move. She acts like she didn't see Geneviève.

• • •

The ten boarding students get up in the dark. Here, hours bear the name of prayers, and matins is first, shaking everyone awake in the middle of the night—then come lauds at sunrise, prime, terce, sext at midday, none, vespers, and compline before bed. Matins again. Sleepy women reaching for their dresses, the sounds of someone blowing her nose, clearing her throat. Charlotte helps the two little girls shivering from the cold, the orphans brought to the Ursulines when they were left to the frosty mud of New Orleans. She was utterly relieved to learn that Geneviève is only a day student. When Charlotte saw her in the classroom, she felt a short burst of joy erased by a confusing mix of anger, fear, and embarrassment. The emotions are too raw to be untangled: all Charlotte knows is that the convent isn't the fresh start she was hoping for. She will have to see Geneviève every day from terce to vespers—at mass, in the refectory, in class for most lessons, everywhere but in the dormitory.

She doesn't understand what Geneviève is doing here. Since when did she ever care for God and His rules?

Since Geneviève came back from up north, Charlotte has caught sight of her in New Orleans only once, on the day she married her second husband, a man called Melet. December 5, 1726, almost exactly a year ago. Charlotte wasn't invited to the ceremony—a boat guider's wife would have had nothing to do at the wedding of a governor's official. But last year, it had been impossible to ignore their marriage. It shook the entire city.

Geneviève and M. Melet arrived in New Orleans just in time to see a governor replaced by another—M. Dugué de Boisbriand by M. de Périer. Geneviève's fiancé was from Trois-Rivières, in Canada. He wasn't an aristocrat, far from that. But as Charlotte learned from Louis, he was the kind of man who knew how to move through empty lands, incoming administrations, and young cities—how to make alliances with less influential but more stable council members rather than betting it all on the most powerful men, who would one day fall. As she witnessed from her bedroom window, he always wore a blue-feathered hat that announced a face older than the one it concealed.

As for Geneviève, she was never seen outside.

Charlotte heard the other rumors at the market by the Saint-Jean Bayou—he was too good for her, Geneviève's first husband hadn't been dead a year yet, and who knows what might have happened up north.

But the Illinois Country was far. What story could travel so many leagues unaltered? The fishmongers, the farmers' wives, the washerwomen could sense that. Soon the marriage festivities had all their attention.

The feathers on the groom's hat were red on the day of the wedding last December. A sharp wind split them like wild grass as the open carriage crossed the Place d'Armes. Geneviève would have to be wedded under a wooden roof again: the construction of the new church had started months ago, but there wasn't enough timber, more bricks should have been manufactured, and it seemed like years would go by before a steeple stood there. When the bride and groom's carriage stopped, Charlotte recognized Geneviève instantly. She sat next to her husband, upright, the ermine of her coat far from the back of the seat. She didn't seem to need its support. Her hand disappeared under her husband's, and even from the street corner where Charlotte stood, their embrace looked like a compromise—his fingers, too arched, barely covering her closed fist.

• • •

Lauds: Charlotte follows the other students to the chapel, a simple room that could be nothing more than a dormitory, an infirmary, a hall, if it weren't for the few benches lined up in neat rows. Sister Marie-Madeleine, looking strangely awake, nods at each one of them as they take their places on the pews. The little scars around her mouth move when she smiles. The Mother Superior stands next to the altar and gestures toward the back of the room. The enslaved African and Native girls have stepped in, but there are none of the unfriendly whispers Charlotte expected— she remembers how snappy Étiennette turned whenever her Native maid was around. Here, the women mingle with everyone else, the silence troubled only by their feet against the hems of their dresses. There is a brief sniffling and Charlotte notices that one of them, a Native girl younger than she is, rubs her wet eyes. Charlotte looks away, helpless.

"Very Blessed Virgin and most honored Mother of God, Queen of heaven and earth . . ."

Thick accents knead the oration and prayers. In the chapel, Charlotte forgets where she is. There were accents when she was at La Salpêtrière, sharp intonations from southern France edging the end of words,

Breton's slow rhythms washing over sentences. Here, the sound of the town doesn't even reach the convent—there is no screaming, banging, neighing, or weeping under the windows. Instead, the female chorus rises in the bright chapel as the peach-colored glow of the early morning turns yellow. The Superioress recites a hymn to Sainte Ursule, and Charlotte bows her head. When the women start singing an unfamiliar song, she accompanies them wordlessly, letting the other voices guide her, the vibrations of her own chest merging with everyone else's. She hasn't felt this calm since she stood on *La Baleine*'s deck in Lorient, Étiennette close to her and France moving farther and farther away. Rather than thinking of the weight of her arm against her friend's, Charlotte focuses on the relief she felt when the horizon turned flat, as if the continent had fallen on the other side of a round cliff. No more *sœurs officières*, only the ocean.

Then somebody taps on her shoulder, and her cooled muscles jump against the touch. Beside her, Geneviève whispers, "*Bonjour*," and Charlotte realizes that the other women are finding their way out, that the crying Native girl is gone, and that Mother Tranchepain is gathering her prayer books. Soon Charlotte will be left alone with Geneviève in the chapel.

"My husband is heading to Mobile today and had me come earlier," Geneviève says. She lowers her voice. "Unless he lied and it is part of his strategy to make me a pious wife. But I kept wondering what you were doing here. Did M. Charpillon abandon you to the nuns for the nights?"

"He passed at the beginning of the fall," Charlotte mutters. She is stuck between the two benches. She forgot how blue Geneviève's eyes were.

"I'm sorry," Geneviève says, her tone softer. "Still, wouldn't you be happier outside of this place?"

"*Mesdames, s'il vous plaît.*"

Sister Marie-Madeleine is showing them the door. Charlotte brushes against Geneviève as she hurries toward the exit. She sees herself years ago, pregnant, walking to the New Biloxi beach with Louis, Geneviève, and her Canadian husband, wanting as badly then as she does now to avoid Geneviève. It was the day Pétronille left for Fort Rosalie. But what Charlotte remembers best is the way through town, trotting behind the men and next to Geneviève—the faint admiration, the brutal relief too, when Geneviève finally confronted her: "What did I do to you?" In Charlotte's head right then, as blatant as pinched skin: you tried to take Étiennette away from me, then everything the thought implied—that back then, already, there had been more than a friendship to steal. Today more thoughts come to Charlotte's mind: you killed babies in Paris when I will never have my own; now you are taking away from me the last refuge I hoped I'd find in La Louisiane.

• • •

The first class runs between prime and terce, before lunch and after mass. Sister Anne spells words too fast. Charlotte watches the young orphan sitting next to her draw round letters, linked together by slender strokes. In front of them, Geneviève barely raises her head from her work. Her feather squeaks. When they entered the room, she whispered to Charlotte that classes were by far her favorite part of the convent—but whenever her husband asked about her day, she told him only about prayers and meditations. Charlotte's page remains blank. To her, the words are suspended—*dévotion, Vierge, prières*—repeated so many times that they seem peeled from their meaning.

She listens to Geneviève read. Her neighbor picks up where she had left, then passes the book to the next row, to the little girl sitting on Charlotte's right. Perrine runs her finger through the paragraph. Her mouth moves fast. Charlotte feels chilled when the girl hands her the thick volume.

"Please continue," Sister Anne says.

On the paper, the letters blur. Charlotte doesn't try to focus on one sentence but impulsively skims the text, as if the overall meaning will become clear once she reaches the final point. She feels her cheeks burn like they did when she'd spend hours rehearsing by herself at home on Rue de Bourbon. Then she knew how to make things better—how to endlessly repeat the hardest parts of the piece, how to hide the labor and effort no one wants to hear in a song.

Charlotte looks up from the page. She meets Geneviève's pale blue eyes—turned around on her seat, she hides Charlotte from the sister.

Then Geneviève starts mouthing syllables, slowly, the pink of her tongue flashing between the little gap of her front teeth. Book open on the desk, Charlotte starts reading from Geneviève's mouth, unable to look away.

. . .

Charlotte discovers yet again that she isn't the only one Geneviève helps. It is just before sext when she steps outside under the faint December sky and starts walking in the garden despite the chilly wind. Between prayers, classes, and meals, there is barely any time to move around, something that her marriage and widow routines didn't accustom her to. In the coop, chicken and geese cuddle in the straw, trying to keep themselves warm. Charlotte is about to turn around when she spots Geneviève sitting on a bench with the Native girl who cried in the chapel. Geneviève is pointing out various objects and spelling them in French.

"Maybe you'd like to join us," she offers to Charlotte, who isn't sure whether she is saying that only to break the silence that fell as soon as she approached them. "We are doing a short review of this morning's class." Next to Geneviève, the young woman gets up. She barely looks at Charlotte as she heads back to the house.

"I surely didn't intend to scare her."

"Scare her! *Voyons*, there is a difference between fear and dislike."

Yesterday Charlotte asked Sister Marie-Madeleine about the enslaved African and Native girls. The nun smiled. She proudly explained that back in August, a few days after they had settled, officials had brought the pensioners, now four in total. The nun explained that once converted, they would be sent back to their communities, where they would raise their children in the Christian faith. Who knows: in the future, a few women might even stay at the convent and enter the novitiate, serve as examples to the ones who would follow. As for the day students, they returned to their masters after their two-hour lesson. "One must ensure that our people's houses do not teem with impiousness," the nun had concluded.

"I can tell you Sor'kor Sokon doesn't appreciate any of us here."

Charlotte doesn't quite grasp the girl's name. She doesn't dare ask Geneviève to repeat it. Instead, she says: "Not even you?"

"Maybe slightly more when I help her with her French."

"Don't you need books to do so?"

Geneviève waves toward the fragile fences and the dead blackberry bushes. A raccoon runs behind the log hut. "Prayers aren't the only words you can spell."

Charlotte regrets her question. She knows the sisters only teach them how to read and write so that they can focus on religious texts, be ready for the Christmas mass in twenty days. She can barely imagine what they would think of a student upending their efforts by using a frozen garden to give spelling lessons; yet part of her can't help but admire Geneviève's confidence in her own skills.

Geneviève turns to face her. Her breath steams like broth. "I wrote to Pétronille that you were here," she says. "I was happy to see you again last week, when you first came into class."

Charlotte feels confused, defenseless. She was happy too, in a sense; the thought weighs heavy. She chases it away. "How come you aren't home all day?" she asks.

"Did M. Charpillon ever question why you left France?"

"No, never."

"Well, M. Melet didn't either. But he has a way of knowing these things without asking." The cold light falls on Geneviève's eyes, where it ripples like sun on a tidal pool. "And he decided that he alone couldn't correct all of my mistakes. So when the sisters arrived, he was first to ask if they would help me."

"But you go back to him every night."

Geneviève cuts a thread coming out of her sleeve. "I wish I didn't."

Charlotte is tempted to ask about Geneviève's years in the Illinois Country, about her daughter the twins once mentioned, about Governor de Périer and M. Melet's work, all the things only Geneviève could have told her about, but Sister Cécile is calling to them from the threshold. As they walk back to the house, Charlotte sees the nun holding one of the children's hands, hushing the little girl away from one of the enslaved students—probably telling Perrine that she isn't to mingle with anyone but the white women. Geneviève doesn't say anything but shakes her head, gives Charlotte a sympathetic look. They walk back together to the house, the high, cold grass sending chills up their thighs.

. . .

It's now mid-December. In bed every night after compline, Charlotte examines her conscience. In the cloudlike atmosphere of the convent, memories of Étiennette take on a new dreamy, intangible quality, just like the wet months on *La Baleine*, the pin endlessly turning in the lock of the sailors' quarters. As Charlotte deciphers more and more words, Étiennette appears among the women of the texts she reads, dramatic stories of torn-off breasts and quiet girls, mouths full of arena sand, staring into the chocolate eyes of lions. Women Charlotte will never meet, and whose stories she uses to bury Étiennette, replace her with immovable fates of long-gone Christian girls. Already, when she kneels at night in prayer, Charlotte thinks back to the night in the warehouse as a parable she would read—herself a confused, unrooted *vagabonde* and Étiennette a wise, fierce figure rising from the linens to say no.

At the convent, her sins no longer seem irrevocable. They aren't a sentence, like her barren belly was. Here, Charlotte can decide to fight back or surrender.

Her reading skills gradually improve. It isn't thanks to the sisters, who are too busy teaching, keeping the accounts, caring for the animals, and curing the sick girls in the windowless room they use as an infirmary. Whether Charlotte likes it or not, it's mostly thanks to Geneviève, who takes their two daily breaks—after dinner and supper, when the women's bellies are full of green peas and white potatoes, catfish or salted cod on Fridays—and guides Charlotte's finger on the page, from one line to the next. Charlotte glances at her; words pour out of her mouth as if she already knew *La Règle de la Compagnie de Sainte-Ursule* by heart. At night, they part at seven, Geneviève to go home, Charlotte to say the Little Office of the Virgin, the final service of the day. Only once does Geneviève mention her daughter. She says she never would have accepted—and she pauses at the verb, as if she's used the wrong word—coming here if it weren't for Belle, who has to take care of Mélanie when Geneviève is at the convent. Then she waves it all away, pushes the open book on the table, looks into Charlotte's eyes. "I was so sorry to hear about your child," she says. Charlotte's body goes rigid. She doesn't want to believe Geneviève is being genuine. Charlotte grabs the book, flips the page, leans over it. This, she reminds herself, is why I came here.

It hasn't been hard to convince Sister Marie-Madeleine to let them use the prayer books. The young nun was too happy to see them ask for more study time; they sit in the dining room as rain digs mud streams through the garden, and Charlotte practices reading, in a muffled voice, the texts of Sainte Angèle Merici. After the talk about their children, Charlotte never asks anything else about Geneviève's routine as a married woman. Charlotte ignores her complaints about her husband. Something in her tells her that it is wrong, but her concern for Geneviève blends with a bigger fear—that the outside world, if she lets it, will invade the convent. It seems very important to keep the town, and the girl she used to be there, at a safe distance.

So when Geneviève brings up M. Melet, Charlotte barely answers, barely registers a word. Just like Charlotte builds a carefully arranged story for Étiennette, she restricts Geneviève to this one role: the older sister who learns faster than everyone else, who knows the key to prayers and litanies, who can show her how to catch up on years of impiety. They come from the same place. They traveled the same ocean. They both have sinned. Geneviève feels familiar, her presence comforting, so even when her hand meets Charlotte's on the page, Charlotte lets it rest there, ignoring the warmth that sometimes runs up her arm like tepid ants crawling from wrist to shoulder. She tells herself it's nothing. She makes the book her sole obsession, accepts Geneviève as the travel companion she once was, who could be forgiven if she tried.

• • •

Then, ten days before Christmas, Geneviève doesn't sit next to Charlotte at dinner. She doesn't seem to hear Sister Marie-Madeleine's inspirational readings and stares at her plate, hands under the table. Women plunge their forks in boiled beans and hoecakes, drink their beer in silence. When Charlotte brings a prayer book and paper, Geneviève shakes her head. "I'd rather read in the garden today, if you don't mind," she says.

Outside, the sky is crystal clear, with only two soapy clouds. Charlotte walks next to Geneviève, keeps following her when the trail disappears. Holding the book with two hands, she wishes they were inside. The garden, with its smell of stamped earth and the acrid wind blowing from the river, reminds her too much of the city—her yard from which she used to listen carefully for the sound of Louis's boots, the streets she crossed to go to Étiennette's. They reach the wood hut. From here, the windows of the house look like portholes, and for anyone standing behind, Charlotte imagines that she and Geneviève are no bigger than two silhouettes waiting in a harbor. She has never been as far from the house, as close to the forest. Geneviève lets herself fall on a pile of logs.

"We should go back," Charlotte says.

But Geneviève shakes her head and gestures for her to sit. Splinters rub against the fabric, the wood sways against her feet, and then there is Geneviève's hand, the same thin fingers that drew elegant letters, spread in front of Charlotte's eyes—the thumb's nail as dark as a beetle shell, the last two fingers, broken, hanging like petticoats on a laundry rope. There is no need to get closer; Charlotte sees how bad it is from here. But she can't help placing her own hand on the ravaged fingers, very softly, suddenly starving for a reaction—pain as a simple, more acceptable extension of touch. Geneviève doesn't flinch. Charlotte watches her tense then relax as she follows the swollen skin with the tip of her nail, brings it to her dress, letting it rest on her lap. She remembers these same hands clasped against a straw hat in September 1721, the last time Charlotte saw her in New Biloxi. Geneviève was leaving the following day for the Illinois Country. Charlotte was pregnant, she was scared, her entire body hurt. She'd just retreated to her bed when the nausea started, when the world shrank and pain swallowed everything. Charlotte hadn't wanted Geneviève to see her in this state, to notice the sour smell rising from the bucket by her mattress. It had saddened her in an unfathomable way.

Geneviève didn't make any recommendations that morning. Rather, she asked about Louis, speculated about Pétronille's life in Natchez. She talked about the colony's future, whether it was true that La Louisiane's air and food turned French vagabonds into even more mediocre individuals. Then Geneviève stood up, adjusted her straw hat. She stopped on the threshold, recommended resting as much as Charlotte could, as if it were an afterthought, as if she weren't really trying to help. After the front door closed, Charlotte remembers sinking into herself, remembers the total, absolute abandonment that took hold of her. She remembers thinking of calling for Geneviève to stay, please, just a bit longer.

Then there is nothing to think of anymore because Geneviève's lips are too close to her face, and Charlotte is leaning forward too, gently pressing against them, until it hurts.

• • •

There will never be more than this one kiss in the brutal December air, broken fingers meeting frosty hands. But it hits Charlotte harder than a slap. It means that even here, enclosed within the high walls of the temporary convent, she can fail. Charlotte knows how to read now, but she stops borrowing books. During the arithmetic lessons, she sits away from the other students so that she doesn't have to share her counting beads with anyone else—and she moves the *jetons* distractedly, wishing she could be on her own, repeating the Ave Maria she assigned herself.

In the chapel, she loses herself in the chorus. But the other women's voices don't make her feel strong, like they used to—only lonelier.

Geneviève has become smaller ever since Charlotte stopped approaching her. Her wax-colored face behind the nuns' dark veils, working a needle in the afternoon dusk; her curved waist in a blur, glanced at during terce from the other side of the chapel. Charlotte never wants to get close enough again to see the little gap between her teeth. She wants to forget how touch feels, like she did after Étiennette left, after Louis died. She has done it twice. She can do it again.

One December afternoon right before vespers, Charlotte runs into Geneviève as she comes out of the classroom. The corridor is narrow, the door heavy, Charlotte's hands holding two ink bottles. When they shatter between them, the sound is deafening. Dark liquid splashes on the ground, the walls, the bottom of their dresses. "I'll do it," Geneviève says, but Charlotte is already kneeling, reaching for the glass shards. They start cleaning in silence. Charlotte does her best to focus on her stained fingers, the black puddles, the wooden floor shining with glass in the semi-obscurity. But as Geneviève leans forward to reach for one of the broken caps, the collar of her dress loosens and Charlotte thinks she notices a bruise on the side of her neck, one that Geneviève covers as soon as she feels Charlotte's eyes on her. "I'll go fetch a broom and some rags," she says, and stands up in one quick motion. By the time Geneviève comes back, Charlotte has been joined by Sister Marie-Madeleine. "Do not worry," the nun tells Geneviève with a smile, "we are almost done here."

Over the next few days, Charlotte can't help but return to that afternoon. She forces herself to embrace the deep discomfort that seizes her whenever the image of Geneviève's neck pops in her mind. Did she really see a bruise? Geneviève retreated so quickly, Charlotte can't be sure. So she does what she has become so good at over the past few years—kill her own intuitions, diminish them so much that they shrink to nothing.

• • •

Three days before Christmas, Charlotte returns later than the other women to the dormitory, just before the bell rings for compline. Long after the day students left, she has been busy spreading garlands of mountain laurel on the altar—holly and mistletoe braided on the seats, as if the pews have grown deep green leaves. On their beds, Perrine and Marie-Annette smell each other's hands. The two orphans spent the afternoon mixing pungent herbs and charcoal to make incense. Charlotte is about to kneel next to her bed when she notices something poking out of the bedsheets. She glances at the laughing girls. But when she slides her hand under the blanket, she doesn't find bits of rose or charcoal, only a folded piece of paper. She drops it on the ground, takes her clogs off to avoid drawing attention. There are three sentences: "I can no longer go home. Help me. You'll know when."

That night, Charlotte tries to pray for Geneviève. But whenever she thinks of her, sharp images sneak up between the "never again" and "please forgive her, forgive me." Blackened fingers and a sweet-corned kiss, logs piled next to sleepy women, murmuring in the damp darkness of a warehouse. She wishes for the divine, invisible guidance she came to the convent to find—the kind she could share with the nuns, the kind that cannot be taken away.

• • •

The day before Christmas, Geneviève enters the kitchen with a child. The morning lesson has been canceled to help the two maids; Charlotte's lap is covered with pigeon feathers, damp and sticky. She stops plucking when Geneviève sits the little girl at the end of the table. Mélanie can't be older than five, but she's almost as chubby as babies before they learn how to walk. She has her mother's eyes and curls. She is biting into the prune that Sister Marie-Madeleine just handed her.

"All the way from France," the nun says. "A kind present from our sisters of Tours. Do you know where Tours is?"

The child shakes her head.

"How come we've never seen you?"

The girl answers excitedly. "I came because of—"

Geneviève cuts her off. "She'll only stay for the day."

"She wasn't here for terce." Sister Cécile closes the rag around the dried fruits. "Neither were you."

"We arrived a bit later this morning."

Charlotte glances at Geneviève when she hears the tone of her voice. Sister Cécile ignores her. The nun probes the dough resting on the windowsill. She looks at Geneviève. "The *brioche* still needs some kneading."

"Let me do it," Geneviève says. Mélanie starts to get up, but Geneviève tells her to stay put, and the little girl does. Charlotte returns to the bird. In the corner of her eye, she can see Geneviève's fingers lifting, pressing, tapping the dough. Charlotte can't watch. She thinks of the *brioche*, tomorrow soft and yet so hard. How flabby Geneviève's fingers had felt against her palm when there was nothing to shape them. She plucks faster.

"Careful."

Charlotte raises her head. Sister Marie-Madeleine is guiding the little girl away from the bubbling broth.

"*Un moment*, I'll take care of her," Geneviève says. Her hands sink into the dough again.

Charlotte drops the pigeon on the table. She gestures for the child to come closer. "No," she says, "I will."

During the next hour, Charlotte puts whatever she can into Mélanie's hands. Parsley and bear oil to sprinkle, fava beans to peel. She doesn't acknowledge Geneviève's thank-you, tries to ignore her expression—overly relieved, lips pinched, as if she is about to cry. Charlotte tells herself she would have done it for anyone. She turns to Mélanie, gives her simple tasks: more dough, knives away, no tasting. She finds herself captivated by the girl's meticulous moves, the way she silently asks for approval—the solace it is to take care of a child, even if not her own. She handles Mélanie methodically, empathetically, like you do with books and prayers.

• • •

Charlotte is summoned by the Mother Superior shortly after sext. She's spent the rest of the morning in the kitchen, looking at Geneviève as little as she could. It wasn't hard: the monthly cramps started right before dinner, making it hard to focus on anything but the boiling pain in her lower belly. When Sister Marie-Madeleine said the Superioress asked for her, Charlotte went upstairs without a word, shoulders hunched, fingers clenching her hips. But she didn't leave Mélanie without making sure that she had something to busy herself with—rancid butter as glue, enough chicken feathers to draw whatever the child would fancy. Now that Charlotte sits in front of Mother Tranchepain, the cramps recede faintly, briefly sparing her as they sometimes do whenever her mind needs to be alert. Still, she is slightly slouching, her hands resting on her stomach. She hopes the Superioress won't notice. But the Mother Superior is smiling.

"I am extremely pleased with your accomplishments." She leans forward as if about to tell her a secret, and for an instant, Charlotte forgets the pain. It seems like the Superioress might be ready to hear her out, that if Charlotte could only get a bit closer to the desk, nearer to the Christ painting on the wall, she could finally explain why she came to the convent, how hard she's tried—swear she'll never fail them again. It even seems possible that the nun would forgive her. But Mother Tranchepain sits back, her arms crossed as she speaks. "Which is why I wanted to ask for your opinion considering one of our day students' requests. Mme

Melet told me that you two have known each other for a long time. She said you'd be in the best position to answer for her abilities."

Charlotte shrinks inside. The spasms in her lower abdomen hit once more. The Mother Superior isn't interested in hearing about her. It's about Geneviève, always about her, her deep blue eyes popping out right in this tiny room, sneaking between Charlotte and Mother Tranchepain, between Charlotte and Étiennette, between Charlotte and her resolutions.

"She came to see me a few days ago," Mother Tranchepain is saying. "I have my own opinion concerning her request, but I thought I'd consult you nonetheless." The nun pauses. Charlotte gives her a small nod. "Mme Melet wishes to become a boarding student."

"Does she really?" A latent buzzing crosses Charlotte's head. She presses one of her hands behind her back, as if it could mute the pain. She hears the Mother Superior explain that, of course, she doesn't exactly imagine how Mme Melet could conjugate her role as a mother and a wife with that of a boarding student, but after all, Sainte Ursule's first disciples lived in their own houses and met only to hold services. Naturally, Mme Melet's request is unprecedented—but then what isn't on this side of the Atlantic?

Charlotte doesn't say anything. Geneviève isn't looking for God in this convent. She is looking for something else altogether. Things you can find in an icy garden, hidden behind a wood hut, when logs wobble and the ground isn't firm anymore. She cannot be trusted. Now all Charlotte wants is to curl up in bed, wait for the pain to ease. She opens her mouth. But Mother Tranchepain isn't done.

"I only question her devotion. Considering how much time she's given to new students like you, I was tempted to try and find a way to thank her for her engagement."

Charlotte feels herself blush. Her belly is cramping so regularly that she can hardly tell one throb from the next. She fiddles with her suffering, her anger. With something else too. She is unworthy of Sainte Angèle Merici's religious family. She needs to be fairer to Geneviève, recognize the good she has done. Admit that without her, she never would have known her letters and prayers by Nativity Day; that she never could have dreamed of starting her novitiate next year. It strikes her that if she truly is to become an Ursuline sister, she can't let Geneviève go; but neither can she allow her to be more present than she already is.

"I am afraid I cannot vouch for her," she says.

The Mother Superior looks surprised, then worried. "Is there anything I'm not aware of that I should know about Madame Melet?"

Charlotte shakes her head. The pain inside explodes, shatters, reaches places she didn't know existed. "There isn't," she hears herself say. "We did travel together to come here. But it was a long time ago. We were never close."

• • •

Christmas is a success at the convent. A *tourtière* is cooling down next to berry- and poultry-filled mince pies, the Yule log ready to be lit. In the chapel, the crushing vapors of incense are underlined by the minty smell of winter plants. Each woman knows the lyrics of the songs, and except for the little ones—Mélanie included—who try to keep going after the last words of the psalms, all the women sing in chorus. Charlotte sits in the first row, voiceless. She stares right in front of her at the Mother Superior, who ends her sermon about the holiness of motherhood while Father de Beaubois nods approvingly. She tries to stand straight. The cramps didn't let her sleep last night or eat this morning. They refuse to go away.

"Now is the time to welcome our sisters among us," the priest says.

There is some movement from behind. The four enslaved African and Native pupils make their way to the altar. To the satisfaction of the nuns, all the girls know their letters and prayers; they are ready to be baptized. One after the other, they stand in front of Father de Beaubois. His damp hands touch their faces. Sor'kor Sokon, the young woman with the amber eyes, dry today, goes last.

"Our Father who art in heaven, hallowed be Thy name, Thy kingdom come . . . ," starts the priest.

The Native girl doesn't look at him, nor at the Mother Superior or the small Virgin statue. Sor'kor Sokon is now to be called Isabelle. When Charlotte turns around to see what she is staring at, she sees only the whitewashed wall of the chapel. And below, in the last row, Geneviève, standing very straight. She doesn't look at Charlotte, nor at Mélanie sitting next to her. Her eyes are closed.

Father de Beaubois congratulates the Superioress and her congregation for a first few fruitful months in La Louisiane; there is a last sermon, a last song, and the service comes to an end. Starving for dinner, the women walk quickly out of the chapel. Mother Tranchepain and the priest speak in low whispers as they pass by Charlotte. Nobody shushes the little girls when one of them lets out a strident giggle. Mélanie mingles among them like children did at La Maison Saint-Louis. Charlotte drags herself behind them, trying to recognize Geneviève's silhouette among the dark dresses.

Geneviève stands next to the exit as if waiting for the ceremony to start all over. A curl falls against her temple. Charlotte doesn't get any closer. Words scare her. The cramps climb from her belly to her chest. Before she reaches the door, she pauses, considers Geneviève's interrogative face; a blinding feeling cuts through the pain. An urge to console, embrace, comfort—an urge so sudden that her mind races to catch on, to remind herself of what she did.

She'd like to say that she is only trying to save them both. She is convinced of it. She has to be.

When she stops in front of Geneviève, Charlotte shakes her head. At first Geneviève remains impassive, then she wipes her eyes with a brisk gesture of her hand. They study each other's face, two strangers who know each other too well. Then Geneviève pushes the door open, and Charlotte is left alone in the chapel—this dark, plain room which, like so many things in La Louisiane, is only a shadow of what it wants to become.

Utu'wv Ecoko'nesel

Utu'wv Ecoko'nesel wishes she didn't have to go to the white woman's house.
She takes her time as she walks down the mound, leaving the Great Village behind her. The Green Corn ceremony was just held, mulberry season is at its peak—the grass as tall as ever, grazing against the little sun tattooed on her shoulder, her bare arms and sun-cracked nipples. By the time the moon is full again, the white men will have burned the prairie so they can travel more easily across the land, their horses galloping over scorched plants and their carriages' wheels plowing the darkened soil. The grass will grow again, fast and green, and the buffalo hunt will start. Utu'wv Ecoko'nesel can't remember the time before the puffs of smoke marked the end of hot weather. She was born after the white men came. But she's convinced plants don't need French fires to grow, that they have their own way of knowing when to disappear.

Utu'wv Ecoko'nesel follows the creek. From here, she can already see the wooden building where the French store their iron weapons. She rarely comes this close to what they call Fort Rosalie, doesn't usually walk by the white men's huge houses, which have grown more and more numerous over the past five winters. In fact, they have doubled, as her older sister Lv'vlk Lac'kup often insists, her jaw suddenly visible under her round cheeks—her tattooed hands clenched around the kettle, her oldest son's bow. When Utu'wv Ecoko'nesel left the family hut earlier today, she avoided Lv'vlk Lac'kup. She knows what her sister thinks of the task she's about to perform; she doesn't need to hear the warnings again. If their aunt Vhvl' Kutnuf hadn't ordered her to go, Utu'wv Ecoko'nesel wouldn't be on her way to the French woman, with her name full of strident syllables—sounds that remind her of a poisonous plant, like the red buckeye trees' flowers, the ones that tear away at stomach skin. Maybe that could be the first thing to tell the pale woman about. Vhvl' Kutnuf decided Utu'wv Ecoko'nesel was to teach her how to fight illnesses with plants in an attempt to calm the tensions with the French.

Utu'wv Ecoko'nesel feels her entire body tense as she passes by their farms. It isn't the first time she's had to interact with white people. Her aunt made a point of teaching her a bit of French, lessons that Lv'vlk Lac'kup always refused to attend. Utu'wv Ecoko'nesel obliged Vhvl' Kutnuf but was always more interested in the other kind of knowledge her aunt agreed to share with her. Since Utu'wv Ecoko'nesel's mother traveled to the Great Beyond nine winters ago, she has been learning everything Vhvl' Kutnuf knows about flowers and seeds and the immense powers they conceal. As the niece of the Sun Woman, she first helped relieve the pain of pregnant women in the Great Village. By the time she started bleeding, she moved on to other towns, soothing babies' aching teeth in the Tioux and Flour villages. Now, at seventeen winters, she regularly tends to warriors' injuries.

She never doubted plants could heal. They'd eased her pain when nothing else would help her—not even Lv'vlk Lac'kup's embrace, her older sister rocking her in their smoky hut until the world disappeared. The plants had kept her mind busy when all Utu'wv Ecoko'nesel could think of was her mother's face, her low voice, the way she used to braid her hair and readjust her skirt, firmly and softly at once. Vhvl' Kutnuf's recipes kept Utu'wv Ecoko'nesel's hands moving. They unlocked time back when she thought the next moon would never arrive and she'd be sad forever.

Along the creek, she is walking through clouds of midges. Ferns tickle her thighs, bend under her basket. For once, it weighs like a feather; its double bottom, which other women use to hide their jewelry, carries only a few wild okra flowers, a branch of yaupon holly. She didn't know what to bring when she left. She's used to packing exactly what she needs, priding herself in guessing the exact required quantity so as not to burden herself, leaving enough room to collect whatever she'll find on her way back. But today is different. The white woman doesn't need to be healed. She wants to be taught.

At first the whole idea made Utu'wv Ecoko'nesel laugh. She saw how the French cured diseases—doctors with fake hair using needles to suck blood out of weak bodies. Heard one of them recommend resting in unspecified herbal waters to appease painful muscles; to burn a tired red eye so that the fluids release, and swear to the patient that the cornea would only be scratched. Dark-skinned people were much better surgeons, something even the French must have known, for she knew of slaves who were exploited as doctors. The rare times Vhvl' Kutnuf asked her to prepare a tincture for a white family, Utu'wv Ecoko'nesel resisted an urge to grind the bark too roughly, omit an ingredient, let flowers sink for just a bit too long. She didn't mean to hurt these settlers, but she didn't want to help them either.

She had to change her mind yesterday when Vhvl' Kutnuf sat her against the reed mats in the house of the Uv'cenv Cu'nv Uv'sel, their Great Sun. They were the only two of the Suns in the hut, the other members of the ruling family busy outside. Vhvl' Kutnuf had looked at Utu'wv Ecoko'nesel with her gray eyes like two lost river stones set in wrinkled skin, and explained that this knowledge wasn't hers to keep. That they've been trading with the white men for almost thirty winters and it would be wrong to push back when one of their women made a step toward them.

Right then Utu'wv Ecoko'nesel could hear her sister's voice in her mind—Lv'vlk Lac'kup, who grew up in a world where French people were, to most, barely more than a rumor. Utu'wv Ecoko'nesel knew exactly what she would have replied to their aunt. That they didn't owe this white woman anything, that Vhvl' Kutnuf forgot too easily the diseases the French brought, the conflicts that occurred two winters in a row back when Lv'vlk Lac'kup had just given birth to her first child. Lv'vlk Lac'kup always said Vhvl' Kutnuf had too many French friends anyway—once even a lover who gave her the son who was now their leader, the Great Sun. She repeated that there was a reason why white people were literally called *ku'yukup*, crazy men. Times had changed and French farms were everywhere now: helping them today wasn't like welcoming them as the Suns did all those winters ago, extending their hospitality to the first settlers like they had traditionally done for other foreign nations. But the French had nothing to do with the Caddo or the Chickasaw; they were different from all the other tribes they knew.

Utu'wv Ecoko'nesel agrees with her sister. She too wishes Vhvl' Kutnuf didn't have to accept all the requests brought forward by white husbands. But Utu'wv Ecoko'nesel doesn't speak her mind like Lv'vlk Lac'kup does. Their mother used to say her daughters' names could have been the other way around, that Utu'wv Ecoko'nesel looked more like the soft goose her sister was supposed to be, when Lv'vlk Lac'kup had more of the beautiful she-wolf Utu'wv Ecoko'nesel was named after. Then she would add, smiling secretly, "But a mother is rarely mistaken about these things. One day you'll realize that I was right all along."

• • •

Utu'wv Ecoko'nesel leaves the rice field behind. Dark-skinned women crouch in the watery crops, their children digging fingers into the moist soil. Flooding fields were something else most of the white men didn't know about and learned from those they brought to the Suns' land. An enslaved girl once told Utu'wv Ecoko'nesel how, along the Gambia River, her people had known how to build earth dikes, master the tides, turn the alluvial soil into rice fields for longer than she or her grandmother could remember. The white people's house towers above, wide and long. Utu'wv Ecoko'nesel despises the French for how they thanked dark-skinned people for their help—stealing them from their homeland, feeding them barely enough to survive, while having them work incessantly. She knows they inflict worse harm on them—from the hill, she once saw hounds rushing in their quarters, heard the violent sound of a whip, and never forgot the woman's cries. She searches the house for a dog, a white man. But on the porch, there is only a little girl milling wheat, holding on to the big pestle. She is too dark to be the white woman's child.

"Madame! Madame!"

The enslaved child keeps on calling for her mistress, never glancing away from Utu'wv Ecoko'nesel. A hot wind rummages through the girl's dress, flattens Utu'wv Ecoko'nesel's mulberry-bark skirt against her thighs. She feels steps echoing on the wooden floor.

"No need to scream like—"

The white woman stops when she sees her. For a brief moment, Utu'wv

Ecoko'nesel forgets her frustration. She didn't expect to know the person she is supposed to help, and yet she never could have forgotten the livid stain, even paler than the rest of her skin, that stretches on the French woman's right cheek. Utu'wv Ecoko'nesel can't exactly remember how old she was the day they met—only that her mother was gone already, that it was the first time Vhvl' Kutnuf had told her to bring an ointment to the French village. That afternoon, even if her aunt had assured her there was nothing to fear, Utu'wv Ecoko'nesel kept her distance. Two women stood on the threshold of a wooden hut, observing her. When the blond one started walking toward her, Utu'wv Ecoko'nesel wished she'd stay where she was; the other woman didn't move, the white stain glowing on her face.

She won't go anywhere today. She studies her host more closely. Her brown hair is lighter than hers—she has a round chin that softens her features. She keeps on reaching for a strand that escapes her bun even though, on the wooden deck, there is no risk it'll get caught in branches or twigs. Just like the other French girls', her body disappears under layers of clothing. If she recognizes Utu'wv Ecoko'nesel, she doesn't let it show.

"*Allons bon*, M. Ducros surely didn't tell me that you would be coming today."

The sentence comes rushing in a soft flow, much faster than when Vhvl' Kutnuf spoke French words.

"A bit slower, *s'il vous plaît*?" Utu'wv Ecoko'nesel asks.

The white woman's stain moves on her cheek when she smiles. Her dress is as blue as a parakeet's belly, with patterns that look like red beans.

"Yes. *Pardon*. Please come inside."

Utu'wv Ecoko'nesel follows. As soon as the door closes on them, the sound of the child's blows starts again. Voices and the smell of meat travel her way from the left side of the house.

"Please sit." The ground is bare, but the woman gestures at what resembles a bed. "I'll be back."

Utu'wv Ecoko'nesel finds herself alone in a room big enough for three families to live in. There are many holes in the walls to watch outside, and the door doesn't face east, toward the rising sun, but north. Everything is elevated, pots on wooden boards and fabrics on little beds spread throughout the room—nothing touches the floor, as if to save the furniture from a flood.

"I hope you enjoy tea."

The bowls are small, with a strong smell of flowers that rises in dense smoke. Here, her host asks questions even before the guests are fed and rested, something no one, be they Suns or commoners, would tolerate in the Great Village. The water burns Utu'wv Ecoko'nesel's throat.

"Your name is Utu'wv Ecoko'nesel, *n'est-ce pas?*" The French woman pronounces her name "Utu'wa Ecoko'niseli."

"You have to say: 'Oodoo'wah itchoko'nishel,'" Utu'wv Ecoko'nesel clarifies.

Pétronille says it again, but this time she gets the last three syllables wrong. Utu'wv Ecoko'nesel shrugs, then points at the blue dress: "*Et toi?*"

"Pétronille."

Utu'wv Ecoko'nesel refrains from mentioning poisonous plants and strident syllables. The white woman has a way of expressing herself and moving around that reminds her of a sun-dazed duck, something heavy and slow that would be easily killed on the Small River. Some words stick out—*merci*, *Bras Piqué*, and *plantes*. She understands she is being thanked, makes out her aunt's name in relationship to plants, but deciphering the sentences brings her no joy.

"You are Tattooed Arm's niece," Pétronille says, and Utu'wv Ecoko'nesel frowns. Her aunt is known by so many French people that they translated her name into their own language. In this woman's mouth, it feels wrong. Utu'wv Ecoko'nesel is relieved that Pétronille doesn't know the meaning of hers; even if she one day manages to say it right, the sounds will remain a mystery to her. The white woman is staring, but Utu'wv Ecoko'nesel doesn't want to satisfy her curiosity—doesn't want to explain to her what being part of the ruling family entails, that her cousin, although a frail boy, is the Sun's youngest brother, the Chosen One.

She touches her basket with her foot. "Where do we work?" she asks.

Pétronille reaches for her hair again, but her awkward gesture loosens her bun even more. "I'll show you."

When Utu'wv Ecoko'nesel follows Pétronille into the next room, the swan feathers in her hair brush against the doorframe. Lv'vlk Lac'kup warned her: French people need many houses in one.

"This is all I have for now."

The room is narrow, much more like one of the Great Village's huts, even if the walls are too white. The prairie sun filters in through only one small hole—at least here, Utu'wv Ecoko'nesel can relax. The room reminds her of home: crushed scent of button eryngo, rigid holly, soft pussytoes flowers, figworts and their nectar devoured by bees. In a basket, mulberry and peach barks are piled up. Pétronille points at a twig. "I found this yesterday."

Utu'wv Ecoko'nesel recognizes one of the most precious woods, which the French call *épine de la passion*. Her throat goes dry. She wonders what the white woman expects. She says what she thinks Pétronille wants to hear: "Good for many things. Also lost love." She turns one of the small branches in her hand. "To bring the beloved man back."

When she sees Pétronille's distraught face, she swears to herself she won't ever tease her again. The white woman's expression is familiar, reminiscent of her cousin's face when she lost her man to a hunting party. She shakes the thought away; it's impossible for her family and Pétronille to have anything in common.

She scans the table for inspiration, for the ingredients of a real remedy this time. She thinks of her aunt and blushes—Vhvl' Kutnuf despises liars.

"The snakeroot," she says, grabbing what probably looks like a big onion to Pétronille. "It sucks the venom out. And the land creepers over there, they ease childbirth pains."

It takes a moment for Pétronille to answer. Then she moves closer to the table. "How do you make it?" she asks.

Utu'wv Ecoko'nesel quickly turns back to the plant. "Water and . . . Like *thé*."

"What about this one?"

For the next hour, Utu'wv Ecoko'nesel shows Pétronille how to make a decoction of wormseed leaves. She tells herself that Vhvl' Kutnuf gave her a mission, that she won't disappoint her. Words come to her more easily. There's something reassuring about the small space filled with roots and leaves; no need to worry about how low the sun is, what she'll tell Lv'vlk Lac'kup when she heads home. The white woman doesn't ask questions. Silent, she points at this and that in her gentle way, until there is a thud.

"Who?" Utu'wv Ecoko'nesel asks, pointing toward the main room.

"What do you mean?"

When the door opens, a thick afternoon sun splashes onto the walls. For a moment, Utu'wv Ecoko'nesel can make out only a shape.

"How glad I am to find you here. I was getting worried." The voice is deep; the white man places his hand on Pétronille's shoulder. Fat cheeks, dark hair, and huge eyes that make his face seem too small.

"I was here all day. With her," Pétronille says. "This is my husband, M. Ducros." Her hands hang over the bowl, motionless. For a second, she reminds Utu'wv Ecoko'nesel of a deer stopping short in the prairie, assessing a threat, then resuming its careful stride. Pétronille grabs a rag, dries her wet fingers.

Utu'wv Ecoko'nesel stares at the white man but doesn't introduce herself. Lv'vlk Lac'kup once joked that French women wore so many layers to protect themselves from men. Now, under M. Ducros's gaze, Utu'wv Ecoko'nesel wonders whether her sister's words held more truth than she thought. Uneasy, she crosses her arms, and the man turns toward his wife, says something about slaves and tobacco, children being a distraction in the fields. He doesn't pay any attention to Utu'wv Ecoko'nesel. He leaves the room without waiting for an answer, and Utu'wv Ecoko'nesel realizes she's been holding her breath.

"I'll see you tomorrow afternoon," Pétronille whispers.

Utu'wv Ecoko'nesel would have liked to tell her to cover the mixture so that bugs don't fall in. But Pétronille barely looks up from the table when she leaves the room. Outside, the little enslaved girl keeps on milling wheat. Ahead, the wind combs through the prairie, and the sound of the pestle follows Utu'wv Ecoko'nesel long after the house has disappeared.

• • •

One of Utu'wv Ecoko'nesel's clearest memories is one winter old: the former Great Sun had just died, and she sat in his hut with her cousins and relatives. The dances and procession would soon begin; for now the old man lay on a bed, his face reddened with burned ocher, a crown of white feathers resting on his head. At his feet, his weapons, as well as all the calumets he had ever received, had been gathered—a double-barreled shotgun, a bow, a quiver full of arrows, a pistol, a tomahawk, and an endless chain of reeds, one link for each enemy killed. Sometimes one of the servants brought food to the dead man, mumbling, *Touwvtekek*—He is quite dead—before leaving with a howl that was echoed by the people in the Great Village and by all their neighbors in the prairie.

Utu'wv Ecoko'nesel sat between Vhvl' Kutnuf and the Great Sun's favorite wife. She remembers the fear sinking in her stomach when her aunt stood up, arms full of the bloody scratches she'd carved in her own skin when the sadness became intolerable. After the war chief had died, his wife had decided to follow him—strangled with a bowstring to keep him company in an afterlife full of pink fish, buffalos, and sweet water. Many servants had imitated her, just as the Great Sun's concubine, doctor, and hunter soon would. So when Vhvl' Kutnuf looked at each one of them, Utu'wv Ecoko'nesel jumped to grab her hand. Her aunt couldn't already be joining her mother in the Great Beyond. But Vhvl' Kutnuf only shook her head. She said she couldn't leave just yet, that her son, the new Great Sun, still needed her advice to reign.

"The boy is as weak as a baby opossum," Lv'vlk Lac'kup had whispered a few days after the funeral, "he doesn't stand a chance." Back then her words had already worried Utu'wv Ecoko'nesel. And now that, to Vhvl' Kutnuf's despair, the White Apple Village's leader has indeed taken power, Lv'vlk Lac'kup's clairvoyance unsettles her even more.

It wasn't the first time her sister seemed able to predict what was to come. The spring day their mother left for the Small River, Lv'vlk Lac'kup commented on the color of her cheeks and said she looked unwell. Utu'wv Ecoko'nesel had shrugged off her sister's words, returned to the skirt she was making. Their mother was strong; she was rarely, if ever, sick. She had given birth to three boys who had grown into warriors and to two daughters with wide hips and careful hands. She had stroked Lv'vlk Lac'kup's pregnant belly and said so once again, right before she headed down the mound and toward the water. "She looks healthy to me," Utu'wv Ecoko'nesel had told her sister, not knowing that she would regret those words forever.

• • •

Utu'wv Ecoko'nesel wakes up at dawn the morning after her first visit to Pétronille. Inside the hut, her sister's family is asleep. When Utu'wv Ecoko'nesel walks out, she sees her youngest nephew tossing in his sleep, pressing his hands against the woven mats that cover the walls as if he is a kitten kneading his mother's belly. His two brothers are snoring, their noses barely visible above the blankets. Utu'wv Ecoko'nesel doesn't feel ready to start her own family quite yet, even if she expects to get married in a couple more winters. Lv'vlk Lac'kup had her swear she would wait to find the right man, and she intends to keep that promise. For now she is helping her sister as much as she can, sometimes catching herself caring for her nephews as her mother did for her.

She glances beyond the square and toward one of the highest mounds, where the temple and its eagle sculptures stand—the smoke of the perpetual fire forever blowing above the town, curling gray and lazy in the rose light. Soon the Great Sun will bow in front of his eldest brother. Utu'wv Ecoko'nesel usually hears his three cries from the edge of the village as she gathers penstemon and milkweed, walking along the cornfields where commoner women harvest the crops. She enjoys the buzzing of the cicadas, the wetness of the grass under her feet, the growing warmth of the sun on her back. Whenever she raises her head, the Great Village rises toward the sky—the fields and the first wattle and daub huts, then the main square, more houses, and towering over it, on either side, the two flat-topped mounts and their buildings. Her home is easy to find: as part of the Suns, she sleeps a flight of stairs away from the leader's hut.

But this morning, Utu'wv Ecoko'nesel doesn't rush down the hill as she usually would. She wakes the fire, gathers beans to make soup, boils the water left from the last meal. She didn't have a chance to speak to her sister yesterday. The children were hungry, tired, fussing for a long time before Lv'vlk Lac'kup hushed them inside the hut, whispering, *Hvpvt petkup*, Go to bed. When they didn't, she told them the panther child story—the boys interrupting her for details about the tiger parents, the living bird costume, the horn to make them sing. After a while, their voices fell quiet, and Lv'vlk Lac'kup's man came back. With his arrival, Utu'wv Ecoko'nesel knew her last chance to talk about the day was gone; her sister always gave her husband undivided attention. Utu'wv Ecoko'nesel heard them later in the night, their reed mat shifting under their weight.

Behind her, the deerskin that closes the hut's entrance flaps in the warming air. Crickets have started singing. Lv'vlk Lac'kup's eyes are still tiny, the tattoos on her chest melting with the rash on her ribs, her skin reddened from sleeping too long on the same side. She gently touches Utu'wv Ecoko'nesel's hair, accepts the bowl handed to her. She eats in silence, then wipes her lips.

"Vhvl' Kutnuf must be proud of you," she finally says.

"I haven't seen her." Instinctively, Utu'wv Ecoko'nesel glances above them, toward the Great Sun's home perched on the mound and the hut next to it, where her aunt must still be asleep.

"She is worried," Lv'vlk Lac'kup says, moving farther from the fire to avoid the smoke. "The Sun from the White Apple Village is angry with the French." A brief cry filters through the thatched-grass roof, and Lv'vlk Lac'kup pauses to listen to her child. She then turns back to Utu'wv Ecoko'nesel. "As he should be."

Utu'wv Ecoko'nesel thinks of herself going back to Pétronille's this afternoon. She resents her sister for making it harder. "But he doesn't mind the British," she replies curtly.

She expects Lv'vlk Lac'kup to react, but her sister nods. "*Ehema'ce*— true," she says, "he doesn't." A bright green katydid jumps between them and disappears in the weeds. "Remember when Mother worried about the Choctaw attacking us?" Lv'vlk Lac'kup asks. "We didn't talk so much about the white men back then."

Utu'wv Ecoko'nesel nods even if she doesn't remember. She keeps other memories of their mother—the way her wet hands moved the earth when she did pottery, how she once cut her own hair to perfect Utu'wv Ecoko'nesel's cornhusk doll, how cold her mother-of-pearl earrings felt against her cheek when she held her close. Utu'wv Ecoko'nesel was too young to care about the tribes' dissent.

They sit in silence for a moment. Below them on the square, commoner women get ready to leave for the forest, their long braided hair swinging against their skirts, sometimes reaching all the way to their ankles. The lower clan girls will come back at sunset bruised with mulberry juice, wasps flying above the delicate fruits.

"What kind of woman is she?" Lv'vlk Lac'kup asks.

Utu'wv Ecoko'nesel doesn't need to ask whom her sister is talking about. She tries to think of a good way to describe Pétronille. "*Unckwen'ce*—quiet," she says, then adds, stroking her own cheek, "This part of her face is even whiter than the rest of her skin."

Lv'vlk Lac'kup shakes her head. "The whitest of all white people," she says. Her tone is bitter and amused. "I didn't expect anything less from our aunt."

"It's only for a little while," Utu'wv Ecoko'nesel says. On the other side of the square, two guardians of the temple carry white walnut logs up the mound, their shadows growing dark and assertive in the morning sun.

Lv'vlk Lac'kup nods. Her deep brown eyes are fixed on the flames. Then she turns toward Utu'wv Ecoko'nesel and gives a sigh that makes her look both worried and a bit sad. "That time might be even shorter than you expect," she says, and glancing at her, Utu'wv Ecoko'nesel can't help but think about everything her sister foresaw—their baby opossum of a leader; their mother lying on the river shore, her wide-open eyes staring at the sky as if scanning it for the evil that struck her, when there was nothing to see but clouds and birds.

. . .

When Utu'wv Ecoko'nesel goes back to the plantation, Pétronille isn't alone. Her son, Émile, a dark-haired boy too young to use a bow, disappears as soon as she steps in. "He's very shy," Pétronille says. "Quite unlike his sister." This morning she welcomed Utu'wv Ecoko'nesel as if she had always come here. Pétronille was already leaning over a table, cutting thyme so finely that it looked like gray-blue powder. They work in the main room today, followed around by a little girl—skin as pale as her mother's, mouth as red as a crawfish's pincers, thick eyelashes that curve up over green eyes. She keeps trying to touch Utu'wv Ecoko'nesel's hair, on tiptoe.

"Hélène! Please quit it."

The girl falls back on her shoes and pets a squirrel pulling against the tiny chain that holds back two of its paws. Its muzzle shivers and Hélène claps her hands together. As she feeds it nuts, Utu'wv Ecoko'nesel looks away. There is something disrespectful about keeping an animal inside if not to eat it. She opens her basket—if she stays too long without doing anything, she will start asking about the motionless beaver above the fireplace. She once again reminds herself that this knowledge isn't hers to keep. Pétronille stands next to the table, her bright scarlet dress disappearing behind the jugs filled with plants.

"Are you ready?" Pétronille asks.

Utu'wv Ecoko'nesel shows her how to use beard climber to fight fevers. Together, they cut a finger-long piece of the climbing plant, the thick hooked stems pricking their hands. Utu'wv Ecoko'nesel slits it, and an enslaved woman with sharp cheekbones brings boiled water to Pétronille. Behind them, Hélène mimics the squirrel's cries, laughing when the downy muzzle sniffs her. Her brother sits beside her, keeping his distance from the animal. Utu'wv Ecoko'nesel is relieved to keep her hands busy—there is no more talking today, just Pétronille imitating her, sometimes pausing to look as Utu'wv Ecoko'nesel throws plants in the bubbling water, boiling them until there is only a third left. The explanations come easily. Pétronille asks specific questions, and Utu'wv Ecoko'nesel has only to nod or shake her head. Yes, the sick one should fast before drinking it. No, the decoction shouldn't be used more than once a day.

When Utu'wv Ecoko'nesel comes home that night, Lv'vlk Lac'kup doesn't mention Pétronille. Neither does she the following day or the next. She acts as if Utu'wv Ecoko'nesel has been spending her days at the Flour and Tioux villages, helping out warriors and old women, and Utu'wv Ecoko'nesel mentally thanks Vhvl' Kutnuf, who must have talked to her sister. Lv'vlk Lac'kup might often forget her place as a woman, but she knows when to respect their aunt's decisions.

At first the questions Vhvl' Kutnuf asks Utu'wv Ecoko'nesel are about the tinctures she prepares with Pétronille. The wrinkles on her aunt's arms make her tattoos wave when she pats Utu'wv Ecoko'nesel's hand. She nods, but her eyes are on three boys fixing a pirogue, a baby blinking from its cradleboard, and her thoughts appear to be elsewhere. One day, as men bring back more and more corn in the village, she asks Utu'wv Ecoko'nesel about the French settlement and whether she senses any disquiet there. Utu'wv Ecoko'nesel thinks of the houses within the house, of Hélène's fingers poking at her hair, of the silence that falls once Pétronille starts working. Of Pétronille's man coming in today, sneaking behind her and looming over her shoulder, observing her hands until she became so acutely aware of her movements that she had to stop stirring. Utu'wv Ecoko'nesel decides this isn't the kind of unease Vhvl' Kutnuf is referring to. She says no, and for a moment, her aunt's face relaxes.

• • •

The corn harvest is well underway by the time Utu'wv Ecoko'nesel arrives at the house and doesn't find Pétronille there. She has had time to show her how to use the three-leaved climber to cure the cramping that comes with the full moon, giving Hélène some of the plant's nuts, keeping the rest for cooking; she taught her how to chew on the bark that Pétronille calls *bois d'amourette* to fight tooth pain; how to make the most of the sweet gum trees towering above her house to prepare an ointment that cures wounds and ulcers; how to boil *esquine* roots and use their water to wash the head and grow hair as long as hers. Pétronille finally got her name right—the children took to simply calling her "Oodoo'wah." They are never far: Hélène playing with a rag doll, Émile drawing at a small table. He is the only one she finds in the house on the exceptionally warm day when Pétronille isn't there to welcome her. To her question about his mother's whereabouts, he answers by pointing an ink-stained finger toward the window. "Outside," he says.

The word buzzes in Utu'wv Ecoko'nesel's mind as she retraces her steps. Sap sticks under her toes, and she kicks at little pinecones underfoot. Bees wander around her, their fuzzy bodies crawling on the flowers, petals drooping under their weight. When Utu'wv Ecoko'nesel hears dry leaves crack under her feet, she realizes that she is walking faster than usual, that the thought of Pétronille alone, outside, unsettles her. Utu'wv

Ecoko'nesel has never even seen her step onto the grass and mud of the alley that leads to her home.

Pétronille isn't hard to find. Beyond the tobacco fields, by the forest, her dress is a bright yellow that stands out against the tall bushes. Her calves resting on its sinuous roots, her fingers on the bark, she kneels by a mulberry tree, stripped bare from its fruits by now. Her hair is messy, and sweat darkens her back. Utu'wv Ecoko'nesel has never seen her like this.

Pétronille raises her head when Utu'wv Ecoko'nesel stops by her side. "Here you are," Pétronille says, and a flush of quiet rage rises in Utu'wv Ecoko'nesel's throat. Of course she is here. The question is what Pétronille is doing squatting in the weeds. Why she'd step out of her house to invade Utu'wv Ecoko'nesel's world. Then Utu'wv Ecoko'nesel spots the trail of red ants climbing on her dress, and the anger dies as quickly as it came. Pétronille is smiling, unaware of the water moccasins, black widows, and rattlesnakes that could bite her. Utu'wv Ecoko'nesel chases the insects with a clap that startles Pétronille. She can wander outside all she wants: the prairie will never have her.

"Thank you," Pétronille says, watching the remaining ants scatter. "I hadn't noticed."

How would you with those endless skirts? Utu'wv Ecoko'nesel thinks but doesn't say. Two fat lizards chase each other in the grass. Utu'wv Ecoko'nesel stands up and Pétronille does the same, shaking her dress. Utu'wv Ecoko'nesel studies the tree, scratched as if an animal sharpened its claws.

"What are you doing?" Utu'wv Ecoko'nesel asks.

"Gathering bark," Pétronille answers.

"With your hands?"

Pétronille blushes, then laughs, and the sound surprises Utu'wv Ecoko'nesel.

"You know," Pétronille says, "at home, I used to have many tools to garden." She looks around as if expecting to find them somewhere. "But I couldn't bring them with me."

"Why?"

"Because they wouldn't let me."

At their feet, termites roam across a sunken trunk. The idea of Pétronille being forced to do something is new. Utu'wv Ecoko'nesel has never seen her do anything she didn't want to—save being with her husband. The thought of the man disturbs her, and she quickly chases it away.

"Where did you live before traveling here?" she asks, and something shifts on Pétronille's face.

"Very, very far away," she says. "Across the ocean."

Utu'wv Ecoko'nesel has heard of the water that never ends, but she's never seen it for herself. She knows only the turbulent green of the rivers, the currents that carry you so fast you don't have to row or swim. She rarely considers the place where white people came from. To her, they appeared one day with their horses and diseases, their guns and slaves, and never left. "Are there many fish and game there?" she asks.

Pétronille nods. "Flowers too."

"Then why did you go?" Utu'wv Ecoko'nesel says. She didn't mean to ask the question, but now that she has, she realizes that she cares about the answer.

For a moment, it seems like Pétronille won't reply. She is playing with a short piece of bark, dirt gathered under her nails, rubbing the pulp of her fingers with the sharpest part of the wood. "I guess I didn't have much of a choice," she finally replies.

Utu'wv Ecoko'nesel frowns. She isn't sure what Lv'vlk Lac'kup would say to Pétronille. If the French didn't choose to come here, then she doesn't know what to do with the anger she feels for them—these people who live on the land of her ancestors, who decided that the prairie had a beginning and an end, that it could be divided into parts and handed over.

"Did your man mean to settle here?" she asks, and this time Pétronille's answer satisfies her.

"Yes," she says. "He did."

• • •

Over the next few days, Utu'wv Ecoko'nesel can't help but look at Pétronille differently. Their conversation by the mulberry tree lingers. There, for the first time, she taught Pétronille without a second thought, without hearing Lv'vlk Lac'kup's voice—a voice she now understands was always a bit hers too—nor questioning what she did and why she did it. She handed Pétronille the short knife she kept in her basket and showed her how to peel the bark from the tree so that the wood remained thin and smooth, layers you could cut later as easily as fresh corn bread. Knowing that Pétronille may not be responsible for her own presence here makes it slightly easier to walk to her home, sit at her table, and give her what Utu'wv Ecoko'nesel used to think should never leave the Great Village.

Utu'wv Ecoko'nesel can't extend these feelings to the other white woman whom she finds at the Ducroses' house a few days later. She isn't a complete stranger either: the first time Utu'wv Ecoko'nesel saw Pétronille, years ago, she was taking a remedy to this very same French woman. Marie, as Pétronille calls her, scolds her two daughters with a commanding voice; her abrupt gestures threaten to send to the ground the tiny gowns and breeches she brought for Pétronille's children. She acts as if Utu'wv Ecoko'nesel wasn't in the room. She cradles her baby boy, speaks in a low voice about the settlement, tensions, her husband's desire to go back to France. She says that her neighbor, a farmer, lost three more cows last week. "Natchez Indians stepped on his property and slaughtered them," she says, lowering her voice. Utu'wv Ecoko'nesel can't help but glance at her. She's heard already of French settlers complaining about their cattle being killed. But how are you supposed to guess the boundaries of their land? Does it mean that all cows on the prairie belong to only them now? "I don't think they meant any offense," Pétronille says, and Marie snorts. "Of course you'd give them the benefit of the doubt," she says, and Utu'wv Ecoko'nesel feels the awful woman's gaze on her.

She returns to the kettle of boiling water. She focuses on the sumac leaves scattered in front of her, on the children whispering at the feet of her working table—anything but these conversations that make her jaw clench. Marie's eldest is kneeling beside Émile. The two children lean over a large piece of paper, adding details to their drawing, oblivious to the charged atmosphere. Marie's daughter seems slightly younger than Émile, yet they look so much alike, so little like their mothers, that it is as if Pétronille's husband were there with them.

He comes by that afternoon, very finely dressed, as always. He doesn't greet Marie, and she ignores him too. He asks the children about the odd animal they sketched. As he tours the room, the conversation between Pétronille and Marie progressively dies. He stops once again behind Utu'wv Ecoko'nesel's stool.

She freezes. He smells like tobacco and something else, a bitter scent that tickles the back of her throat and makes her want to cough. She feels him slightly shift and her breath slows down. She realizes that in this wide-open room, her body is trying to hide her from him.

"More Spanish needle, right?" Pétronille suddenly asks, her voice louder than usual.

Utu'wv Ecoko'nesel shoots her a grateful glance. The poultice they are making requires sumac leaves exclusively. Yet Pétronille's words broke the moment and set things in motion again. The man leaves Utu'wv Ecoko'nesel's side, steps over the long sunbeams that stretch in the middle of the room, and kisses his wife on her forehead. Pétronille closes her eyes as he does.

• • •

The following day, Pétronille isn't waiting for her in the main room. For a second, Utu'wv Ecoko'nesel thinks that she'll be told to look for her outside, like she did half a moon ago. Instead, one of the house slaves welcomes her at the door. Somewhere behind her, there is shouting. Utu'wv Ecoko'nesel jumps when she makes out the voice of Pétronille's husband. She tries looking for him in the main room, but it is empty.

"Madame would like you to start without her," the young dark-skinned woman says. She has thin lips and a little scar that runs where her bonnet meets her temple. Around them, silence has fallen. The girl seems uneasy; Utu'wv Ecoko'nesel isn't sure how to behave around her either, here in this place that Utu'wv Ecoko'nesel can leave any time but not this woman who will never be allowed to. The slaves she saw in the Great Village had been enemies of her tribe; their freedom was the price to pay for fighting the Suns. But she's never heard of a war between white- and dark-skinned people. All she sees are enslaved men, women, and children exploited in the tobacco and wheat fields while the French settlers rest in their homes.

"Thank you," Utu'wv Ecoko'nesel says, and the young woman nods.

Utu'wv Ecoko'nesel sits at the table, which has been moved closer to the fireplace to keep them warm. Outside, drizzle turns the garden gray. The kitchen door has barely closed behind the girl when the voices rise again. This time Utu'wv Ecoko'nesel recognizes Pétronille's, but she is speaking too low to understand. None of my business, Utu'wv Ecoko'nesel tells herself. She stretches her right hand, which she has been holding in a fist, and grabs a stick of *bois d'amourette*. She starts peeling it, the blade running fast against the wood.

When she hears a thud on the floor in the other room, she almost hurts her thumb. Her knife freezes in midair, the stick raw and pale in her hand. She worries for Pétronille but mostly for herself. Right as she decides to leave, she hears steps, the back door slamming in the distance.

Pétronille enters the main room, her face flushed, her hair undone, but she seems unscathed. In her left hand is a small box, its wood cracked, its lock broken.

"Is everything good?" Utu'wv Ecoko'nesel asks, but Pétronille only shrugs, wipes her hand across her face. She meets Utu'wv Ecoko'nesel's eyes briefly, then lets herself fall on a chair by the fireplace. Through the window, Utu'wv Ecoko'nesel spots Pétronille's husband trudging through the dying rain, yanking the bridle of his horse, and she is relieved when he trots away. She turns to Pétronille, who didn't even glance outside at the sound of her husband's departure.

"He just threw them away," Pétronille finally says, biting her lip.

"What did he throw away?"

Pétronille looks at the broken lid, then back at the fire. Utu'wv Ecoko'nesel sits next to her. She repeats her question.

"My seeds," Pétronille answers. "The ones that were shipped from La Rochelle. He——" She shakes her head, pats her wet cheeks with her sleeve. Then her face changes, and she lets out a sad laugh. "I ordered them so long ago, I thought they would never arrive. I guess it would have been better to believe they were lost." She pauses, sets down the box at her feet.

"Why would he do that?" Utu'wv Ecoko'nesel asks.

"Why wouldn't he?"

The fire spits tiny embers that go out instantly as they touch the ground. Worse things than seeds can be lost; Utu'wv Ecoko'nesel doesn't want to spend the afternoon sitting on this chair, doesn't want to be here when Pétronille's husband comes back. She stands up, moves knives and bowls to make room for a bouquet of greenbrier. When Pétronille speaks, her eyes are still on the flames.

"If I hadn't come in on time, he would have thrown my mail in there," she says, pointing at the hearth. "My friend Geneviève just wrote to me," she adds. "Her husband passed."

Utu'wv Ecoko'nesel has no idea what Pétronille is talking about, nor does she care much. But Pétronille is joining her at the table and seems calmer, so Utu'wv Ecoko'nesel doesn't interrupt. "Geneviève is about to marry for the third time," Pétronille explains. She starts separating the leaves from the stems. As she does, she goes on and on about her friend, and Utu'wv Ecoko'nesel grasps only a few words—*malchance, pauvre femme, violent*—that give her a faint idea of how unlucky this other French woman has been. She asks about the new husband but only because Pétronille seems to be waiting for her to say something.

"He can't be worse than the previous one," Pétronille answers. She falls silent, goes back to work. Utu'wv Ecoko'nesel imitates her. She thinks of Lv'vlk Lac'kup's marriage, the ear of corn and bay leaves their mother gave her, how they pushed the mats against the hut's walls and danced until day broke. Pétronille's somber expression seems wrong until Utu'wv Ecoko'nesel remembers her husband. The atmosphere of the room is suddenly suffocating.

"Do you have any other plants from France?" she quickly asks.

At that, Pétronille gives her a small smile. "Yes," she answers. She glances outside the window. The rain has stopped, and everything outside drips. "Come, I'll show you."

The stools rattle on the wooden floor when they push them away. Pétronille opens the main door without bothering to close it behind her and leads Utu'wv Ecoko'nesel to the other side of the house, to a part of the garden that she never saw. Here, Utu'wv Ecoko'nesel breathes more freely. The late afternoon is chilly, the red earth muddy from the drizzle. On an elm branch, a woodpecker turns its head to observe them; wrens set off with alarmed cries when they come nearer. In front of them, flowers climb against the facade. From the length of the stems, you can tell that in the summer, the wall must be covered with them—layers and layers of petals, growing bigger and bigger as they stretch away from the flowers' heart. The shape isn't foreign to Utu'wv Ecoko'nesel; she faintly remembers that the species she knows might be used for dysentery. But she's never seen them that color, a greenish white infused with pink.

"At least he didn't throw my rose seeds away. I didn't know whether these flowers would grow here, but they did," she hears Pétronille say. Utu'wv Ecoko'nesel glances at her. Pétronille is staring at the wall, her arms crossed over her chest. Her eyes are swollen from crying, her hair puffy in the humid air, but she doesn't look sad anymore. "I never would have known so many flowers could heal if it weren't for you," she says.

Utu'wv Ecoko'nesel feels her cheeks blush. She doesn't want Pétronille to notice and turns to face the roses. "What are they for?" she asks.

"You won't like it," Pétronille replies. "But they aren't for anything more than their looks."

Utu'wv Ecoko'nesel takes a step closer. The smell is overwhelming, melting with that of the wet soil and wood. She reaches for the petals, and they are as soft as pussytoes. It occurs to her that it'll probably be one of the few flowers from France that she'll ever touch, and she wonders how many plants will remain unknown to her. She'll die before she is familiar with every flower, every weed, of the prairie. The thought is fleeting, inconsistent. What madwoman would regret the things she can't see? Utu'wv Ecoko'nesel digs her fingernails right below the buds, careful to avoid the thorns, and detaches one flower.

"Maybe they are for something," Utu'wv Ecoko'nesel says, "but we just don't know it yet."

• • •

Great Corn season is drawing to an end. The shortening of days always makes Utu'wv Ecoko'nesel yearn for her childhood, back when early sunsets found the entire family inside the hut, gathered around the fire by their mother, ready to listen to her stories. Now it is Lv'vlk Lac'kup who speaks, smoke passing in heavy clouds across her face, across the children's. But the stories are of a different kind. Tonight she talks about another Natchez man incarcerated simply because he used one of the

French pirogues—as if borrowing were robbing, as if the white men weren't the experts in stealing—and Utu'wv Ecoko'nesel listens, watching her nephews roll a small ball between them. As pine needles escape the deerskin and scatter on the mats, she wonders how much longer they'll be able to play.

When she asks Pétronille about the French settler who had the Natchez man thrown in jail, Pétronille blinks. "This shouldn't be," she says. She lowers her eyes. "I hadn't even heard about it," she whispers.

The following day, the sun already hangs low in the sky when Utu'wv Ecoko'nesel walks out of Pétronille's home. Crickets have grown mute; the ground is crisp with dead leaves. A cardinal spits one of its long, sad songs. She has reached the grove at the end of the fields when she hears footsteps. She stops. Behind, houses scattered across the prairie; ahead, the forest and its early night. A mosquito sinks its sting into her ankle, and Utu'wv Ecoko'nesel enters the grove, hair strands held together so as not to get tangled in the creepers. She is still far from the Great River when the sound returns. She considers making a left and running for the water in the hope that fishermen might be there, packing their nets. She starts toward the river and knows almost instantly she won't make it. The sound is back, the steps much faster and closer this time, feet not caring about the noise of dry reeds breaking, one or two wildcats jumping ahead, and parrots flying away with a bitter cry.

There is no time to flee. Pétronille's man is already there, his hand holding her wrist. In the dusk, his huge eyes seem whiter. As he leans toward her, he says something about *sauvages* girls, but the words get smashed by the cardinal's song, the rats trotting on the fallen leaves, the faraway splash of a waterbird.

Vhvl' Kutnuf once told Utu'wv Ecoko'nesel a story about a silly warrior who had gone bear hunting on his own. He used fire to get the animal out of its rotten trunk, thinking that he would be fast enough to reach for his arrow. Vhvl' Kutnuf had stood up and spread her arms wide to show how big the bear got when he jumped on the man. When Pétronille's husband pushes her on the ground, Utu'wv Ecoko'nesel doesn't resist. She knows she will lose. Instead, she focuses on her anger, as raw as the sharp reeds that sting her back, as the man weighs more and more against her belly.

Above her, smoke curls up, gray and inconsistent by the time it meets the clouds. The French have started to burn the prairie.

. . .

Utu'wv Ecoko'nesel had men before, men she carefully chose at the dances of the Great Village and drew close to her at dawn, in the dry-herb stuffed blankets of her mattress. She liked feeling their quickening breath against her neck, their hands going from her hips to her bottom. They were boys her age, most of them commoners. She never had their babies. Like all the other noble women, she would one day have to marry below her status. It didn't matter: she would give birth to children with eyes and hair as dark as walnut bark, and because they were hers, they would be part of the Suns. After her, her daughters and granddaughters would keep on extending the ruling family—sons and grandsons turned into chiefs and warriors only for a life span, their nobility doomed to die with them.

It is the first time a man—any man, not just a white man—has forced himself on her. She finds herself wondering if Pétronille's blue and red dresses help her hide wounds like the ones that cover her own skin, where the reeds cut along her spine. Utu'wv Ecoko'nesel hides her own behind her hair. She uses witch-hazel leaves to prevent them from turning yellow and purple but doesn't ask any other woman to help her spread the ointment. She won't go back to the house. She won't tell anyone about what happened in the forest, not even Vhvl' Kutnuf. Twice Utu'wv Ecoko'nesel considers opening up to Lv'vlk Lac'kup. But the thought fills her with shame—the man's act a confirmation of everything her sister ever warned her about. At night she lies between the buffalo skin and the mat, looking at the embers dying in the middle of the hut. She focuses on the breathing of her sister's family, hoping that it will chase away the memories of bulging eyes, smoky sky, and foreign hands.

When she boils climbers or prepares ointments, she thinks of Pétronille. She isn't sure if she misses her, or their quiet afternoons together, or maybe the unsuspected pleasure of seeing someone learn from her. But she's taken on a new habit. Every time the man's face pops up in her mind, she forces herself to focus on Pétronille. Convincing herself that the white woman is the one who needs comfort because she will see him moon after moon, winter after winter.

• • •

Half a moon after the night in the forest, Utu'wv Ecoko'nesel follows her sister to the Small River. Lv'vlk Lac'kup's youngest sons are three and four winters old—big enough to know the water but too small to accompany the eldest, who teaches their older brother and other young boys and girls how to swim. They've walked for a while through the pink dawn, carrying the children when the roots got too tangled. Yesterday they followed the same path. Utu'wv Ecoko'nesel didn't want to go swimming, didn't want her sister to see her damaged back. But Lv'vlk Lac'kup insisted. And by the time her sister helped her take off her tunic, Utu'wv Ecoko'nesel realized Lv'vlk Lac'kup must have known all along. She didn't say a word about the wounds. She pressed her palm against the thin scars as if to erase them. She brought Utu'wv Ecoko'nesel close to her and they stayed there, the clear and motionless river repeating their embrace.

Last night's rain dampens the earth. Utu'wv Ecoko'nesel wears her favorite tunic, the one with embroidered red threads, best suited for colder days. She holds the boys' hands tight. For once, she feels lighter. The roots pushing against the arch of her feet, the morning breeze, and the turkeys' hurried steps are familiar. Her sister walks ahead like she did when they were children—their mother always last, making sure none of her daughters and sons fell behind. On this path, Utu'wv Ecoko'nesel thinks it might be possible to forget she ever left the creek and the prairie.

Then her sister stops. From the cypress grove, they can hear voices. By the water, a plump woman, one of their people, dips her feet with her child. She shifts to face them and calls: "*Cenko'lo'lo*—greetings, Sun women!"

Lv'vlk Lac'kup only looks at her, taking off the buffalo-wool garters from her son's knees. Where the river bends, ibis probe the silt with their sharp bills. From the simple turkey feathers in her hair, Utu'wv Ecoko'nesel knows the stranger is a commoner.

"We have never seen you. From which land of ours are you?"

The woman waits to answer until Utu'wv Ecoko'nesel leaves her tunic at the feet of an elderberry tree and Lv'vlk Lac'kup steps into the cold water. The little boys gasp as it reaches their thighs.

"The White Apple Village," the woman says, "where great miseries are falling upon us."

At that, Lv'vlk Lac'kup raises her head. "Speak now," she says.

The river is up to Utu'wv Ecoko'nesel's knees. She moves forward, unties the mulberry thread that holds her hair together.

"Our Sun came back yesterday from the pale skins' fort," the woman starts. "Their new chief wants our land to build his own *habitation*."

"What did your Sun say?" Utu'wv Ecoko'nesel asks before her sister has had time to speak.

The woman splashes water over her eyes. "He said our people had been on this land for more winters than he had hair in his braid. But the man isn't like the other French people. He gives orders to our Sun as if he were one of his slaves." One of the children coughs, moves his legs faster to stay above the surface. "Where would we go?"

Utu'wv Ecoko'nesel ignores the question. She feels hot all of a sudden, despite the breeze that gives her goose bumps. Her anger grows, relieved to find something else to latch on to, something she can share with this woman and Lv'vlk Lac'kup. She can feel her sister's eyes on her, but Lv'vlk Lac'kup remains silent, lets her do the asking.

"Will your Sun give him the land?"

"*Mv'kupok no'kv*—it might happen. He asked the man to wait until we gather our crops. Soon he'll bring together the council, and they'll decide."

Lv'vlk Lac'kup's oldest son laughs as a monstrous carp passes him by. Her youngest one, shivering, plays with mother-of-pearl shells on the shore.

"Do you know when he'll go back to give his answer to the white man?" Lv'vlk Lac'kup finally asks.

"*Noco*—I don't know." The woman sighs. "Everybody talks about the terrible French chief, but I don't know what will happen." She brings the little girl close, and the child begs her to stay. "Maybe I'll see you another day."

Lv'vlk Lac'kup nods, and Utu'wv Ecoko'nesel tells her to be well.

As the woman and her daughter return to the shore, her sister gives her a knowing look.

"This is what was always meant to happen," she says, and Utu'wv Ecoko'nesel expects her to add something about revenge, about punishment, but her sister remains silent. She holds her son against her chest, his small hands resting on her nipples, and walks back toward the shore.

Utu'wv Ecoko'nesel stands alone with the stream pushing against her. Dry leaves float around her, as if indicating the way to go. In the trees, a bird's white feathers flicker. She glances at Lv'vlk Lac'kup, helping her children dress, her face empty of anger, tensed in an expression that Utu'wv Ecoko'nesel so rarely sees on her that she doesn't immediately recognize fear. She takes another step forward and plunges headfirst. The cold seizes her entire body. She feels her hair spread all around her, the silt lifting from her toes like dust in the sun. Here, there are no emotions, only deep vibrations—a branch caught in alluvium, a sardine shoal fighting the current, or maybe a brill turning its round body toward her. Utu'wv Ecoko'nesel doesn't see anything; she keeps her eyes closed, lets the tasteless water cool her down, swimming farther and farther, where the river runs too fast to be owned by anyone.

• • •

One of Utu'wv Ecoko'nesel's clearest memories is four winters old: it was a warm evening, and peaches were growing again, announcing the beginning of her favorite season. She sat in the main square, smashing clamshells the way her mother would into a powder that she mixed with fresh earth. She turned the dough into a tight knot, and her closed fist carved its shape into it—the raw smell of the creek, the bottom of the piece of pottery flattening under her wet palms. Then there was a scream. The children playing with their roe-skin ball fell quiet. The women looked up, pots of half-finished fish glue at their feet. The men stood, knives in hand, the unbreakable wood of their bows still rugged.

The sky had vanished. Or rather, it had disappeared under high gray clouds gathered so close to each other that it seemed they had been embroidered. For a moment there was no light either; then the outline of the clouds became luminous, as if golden threads were sewing them together. When the sun reached the horizon, stuck over the hills, the tiny window of sky turned red, throwing a violent glow on some of the clouds, leaving the rest of them in the darkness. What Utu'wv Ecoko'nesel remembers best is the silence, the clearly cut silhouettes against the agonizing sunset, and the freshness of the clamshell powder hardening on her hands—and, once the night fell, the eldest reading the furious sky as a sign of terrible times for their people.

• • •

When Utu'wv Ecoko'nesel reports to Vhvl' Kutnuf the words of the woman from the river shore, her aunt looks concerned. She ignores questions and hurries toward the Great Sun's home. During the next full moon, no other news from the French chief reaches the Great Village. Still, Utu'wv Ecoko'nesel can sense tension in the air. On the prairie, looking for flat wood to help her neighbor's newborn sleep, she meets a girl who whispers to her that in her village, all the women have been asked to prepare food supplies. One cold, early dusk, as Utu'wv Ecoko'nesel turns the first persimmon fruits into bread, she sees the Great Sun returning from the temple, walking on the woven mats leading to his residence. His face is tensed and sad; he looks even younger than his seventeen winters. A few nights later, the chiefs and their warriors enter his hut; none of the women Suns are called, not even Vhvl' Kutnuf, and Utu'wv Ecoko'nesel watches her aunt nervously playing around with the multiple ranks of her mother-of-pearl necklace.

People have wrapped themselves in roe skin and lit bigger fires by the time Vhvl' Kutnuf tells Utu'wv Ecoko'nesel that she is needed in the Flour Village, where one of their relatives is sick with fever. Basket in hand, Utu'wv Ecoko'nesel follows her aunt through the prairie. Her blue earrings, the ones that belonged to her mother, touch her neck with every step. Vhvl' Kutnuf progresses slowly. Her painted hand rests on Utu'wv Ecoko'nesel's shoulder. Except for a fat squirrel, they don't see anything; the animals are gone, scurrying close to the ground before the cold days settle.

"*Pe-etce*—sit down," Vhvl' Kutnuf finally says when they reach the first rocks of the Small River.

Utu'wv Ecoko'nesel feels the fresh stone skim her skirt.

"I brought you where no one can hear us," Vhvl' Kutnuf says. "Listen: there will be a war, much worse than the ones in the past."

Her aunt tried hard to protect her from the previous fights, so Utu'wv Ecoko'nesel keeps few memories of them—some people killed by a foolish white warrior's actions, and then the calumet that the French men gladly smoked. None of it happened in the Great Village. The Grigra, Jenzenaque, and White Apple villages were involved. Not hers.

"The Great Sun is very young and ignorant, and he has tried to hide from me, his mother, from us all, what his intents are."

"Will the French men be attacked?" Utu'wv Ecoko'nesel asks. The anger comes back, but sweeter this time.

Vhvl' Kutnuf doesn't seem to hear. Her eyes are full of tears. "*Kokenesv*—my son," she starts, "who would have died without my milk, who wouldn't be Sun if it weren't for me, lied to me. But finally, he spoke the truth. Here, on this very rock I brought you to." She lets her hands fall on her knees. "The French chief demands the White Apple people's land. He rose a wave of anger, and the Sun of this village convinced all our villages, convinced my son, of a horrific design."

Vhvl' Kutnuf speaks fast, clenching her jaw. She explains that the council said the French men had grown too numerous, that they became dangerous neighbors; that the Suns decided to kill them all at once; that the French chief agreed to wait until the White Apple Village crops were ready before he could have the land and build his house; that the Suns promised to bring him wheat and chickens; that on that day, they will have weapons too. She says three warriors for every one French man in each house.

"There was a time when the land we inhabited was more than a twelve-day journey from east to west, when we had five hundred Suns. Then the white men came, and we thought there was enough land for everybody and we could all live together under the same stars."

Utu'wv Ecoko'nesel shivers. She realizes her neck hurts from turning her head toward Vhvl' Kutnuf, staring at her sad face. "*Tvcukv*—I know," she says. "Why are you telling me this?"

"Because the white men are ingenious. They have more of everything than we do, and this scheme of our council will fail. Many will perish." She pauses. "Some of our women, who know French men, chose to warn the French and avoid the slaughter." Her eyes search those of Utu'wv Ecoko'nesel, who looks away at a fox rushing through the bushes. An old family debate plays in her head: Lv'vlk Lac'kup criticizing a friend for being involved in a relationship with a settler and Vhvl' Kutnuf's coming to the woman's defense. Although Utu'wv Ecoko'nesel agrees with her sister, she knows that these relationships can't be avoided—not after thirty winters spent so close to the French. "My son shouldn't have hidden the truth from me," she hears Vhvl' Kutnuf say. When Utu'wv Ecoko'nesel glances at her, her aunt's face is tensed with fury. She has never seen her like this. "Our Sun is less than a man if he lies," she spits. A bird, too big for a hawk and too small for an eagle, flies away above them. All Utu'wv Ecoko'nesel can do is nod.

When Vhvl' Kutnuf motions to stand up, Utu'wv Ecoko'nesel scoops her elbow to help her. "Go kill off the fever in the Flour Village," her aunt says, adjusting her skirt.

"I will," Utu'wv Ecoko'nesel answers simply.

Images of war follow her for as long as she walks. The sky alight with fire, warriors gathering their bows and tomahawks. Her basket seems heavy today, the forest unusually calm, almost empty of animals. When Pétronille's face flashes in her mind, Utu'wv Ecoko'nesel feels her pulse quicken.

• • •

She crosses the tobacco fields again to reach Pétronille's house. Dark-skinned people now wear thicker clothes. Some enslaved men and women look up as Utu'wv Ecoko'nesel passes by; they might have been told about the coming attack the day after tomorrow. Lv'vlk Lac'kup said they would be freed after the white men die, at least the ones who sided with them. The ones who remained with the French would be enslaved again and sold to the Chickasaw.

Utu'wv Ecoko'nesel trusts they will make the right choice. During the previous wars, most of them did. She remembers the free Black man who hid for a few years in one of their villages and fought against the Tunica, allies of the French, as bravely as if he were a Natchez warrior.

She walks faster, bare toes hugging the moist earth. She can already see the chickens pacing and smell the smoke that doesn't come out of the door but out of the roof. She made a choice where Lv'vlk Lac'kup would have told her there wasn't any to make. Utu'wv Ecoko'nesel knows she doesn't owe Pétronille anything. Yet she can't help remembering the late-summer afternoon when she found the white woman peeling mulberry bark with her bare hands, when she first heard of Pétronille's journey to the prairie. If she hadn't had to leave France, she wouldn't have two days left to live. No matter what Vhvl' Kutnuf says about the French superiority, the settlers will soon be punished, including Pétronille's husband. Now Utu'wv Ecoko'nesel can only hope he isn't home yet.

"Oodoo'wah!" Hélène runs down the porch steps to meet her. The child's face crashes against her thighs.

"Where is your *maman*?"

"*Viens*." She takes Utu'wv Ecoko'nesel's hand.

In the main room, Pétronille is busy poking a needle into a sheet much thinner than the porcupine skins Utu'wv Ecoko'nesel uses for embroidery. Pétronille looks both surprised and pleased at the sight.

"I was very much worried for you," she says. "Why didn't you come back?"

Utu'wv Ecoko'nesel doesn't pay attention to her. She looks around, scanning the room for a French hat, a man's coat. She sees only a bouquet of roses and a plate filled with apples and elderberries. In the armchair by the window, Émile reads from a thick book. He glances at her, seemingly relieved to see that it's only her, then flips a page.

Utu'wv Ecoko'nesel sits close to Pétronille. When she speaks, her voice is a whisper. "My people will fight you soon."

Pétronille stops smiling; the stain tightens on her jaw. "*Les enfants*," she says and gestures toward the door. Émile raises his head but doesn't move. Hélène grabs a cat as big as a marmot and hurries onto the porch. The squirrel is nowhere to be seen.

"My husband told me about the threats. He says they're only rumors." Pétronille pauses. "Soldiers came to Commandant Dechepare to warn him, but he called them liars and threw them in jail. My husband says it would make us seem weak to prepare for an attack that isn't likely to happen."

Utu'wv Ecoko'nesel leans back. She isn't surprised to hear that the French men are too proud to prepare for death.

"*Mais je te crois*—but I believe you," Pétronille continues. "When I gathered the creepers you showed me, I saw your soldiers—your warriors—crossing the woods, following Indian chiefs."

"I did too," Émile echoes.

Utu'wv Ecoko'nesel forgot the child was here. Pétronille tells him to check on his sister, and the boy obediently closes his book. "You told your man?" Utu'wv Ecoko'nesel asks once he's gone.

"Yes. He says it is womanly fears."

Utu'wv Ecoko'nesel looks at the room—fire licking stones in a wide hearth, a dead beaver holding still in the pale afternoon light—then back to Pétronille, her brown hair tied into a bun, her expectant leaf-green eyes. She pictures her people here, in a couple of days, and what will be left after they walk away.

"You and the children," Utu'wv Ecoko'nesel hears herself say. "After tomorrow. Wait outside, and I'll come. Don't tell your man."

"What about Mme Cléry? Her family, they—"

"You and your children, no one else," Utu'wv Ecoko'nesel says.

Pétronille nods slowly, resting her hand on Utu'wv Ecoko'nesel's as if it has nowhere else to go.

• • •

It's still dark when Utu'wv Ecoko'nesel returns to Pétronille's house, draped in bearskin. It was easy to leave the village without anybody noticing. Lv'vlk Lac'kup sat in the hut reassuring her alarmed children, and for a second Utu'wv Ecoko'nesel wished her sister had asked where she was going. But Lv'vlk Lac'kup didn't pay any attention to her. She kept on speaking to her children in a low whisper. "*Wetvwe'tes*—never," Utu'wv Ecoko'nesel heard her say when Lv'vlk Lac'kup's eldest son asked his mother if they would have to leave their home.

Outside, Vhvl' Kutnuf watched men preparing for the battle. They were adding feathers to their arrows, imitating the warriors from the White Apple Village who were arming themselves as if going on a hunt to avoid the French suspicion. They would go knock at the settlers' dwellings and trade supplies of grain and oil for French guns. They'd promise white men to bring them venison in exchange when, in truth, the hunt would happen inside the French homes.

Up until then, Utu'wv Ecoko'nesel's offer to help Pétronille remained impulsive and abstract. But passing by the warriors, she found herself looking away, trying to ignore the question that had just sneaked into her mind—was this not betrayal? Was this not involving herself in war?

She hurries across the fields. She hears Pétronille, Émile, and Hélène long before she sees them, their murmurs interrupted by the flight of an owl. They aren't waiting under the porch but beside the stables, on the other side of the enslaved's quarters. Pétronille wears a cape that falls to her feet. Hélène disappears into a beaver-skin blanket against her mother's bosom. Émile stands by them, motionless.

"I feared you would have changed your mind," Pétronille whispers, and Utu'wv Ecoko'nesel shifts on her feet, uneasy. When Pétronille kneels to grab a small trunk, Utu'wv Ecoko'nesel stops her: "Leave it here. We need to be fast."

The faint light blurs Pétronille's features. "But this?" She points at a bundle.

Utu'wv Ecoko'nesel sighs but takes it—the fabric itches her hands when she throws it against her shoulder. "We go."

Hélène fusses as they cross the fields. Pétronille too makes a lot of noise as she walks, but Utu'wv Ecoko'nesel can't make her hurry more because her dress gets tangled in the tobacco crops. They follow her, breathing out small clouds of smoke. Reeds break under their shoes. Faster, Utu'wv Ecoko'nesel wants to say. Instead, she turns around to check behind them. At dawn, a thin fog descended on the prairie. Still, it would be easy for anybody in the house to see them stamping through the crops. She doesn't want anyone to spot them—to spot her. By the time they enter the grove, Utu'wv Ecoko'nesel's muscles feel twisted into a knot.

"*Où allons-nous?* Where are we going?"

Hélène's voice is sleepy. Émile murmurs something to his sister. Pétronille doesn't answer. She looks at Utu'wv Ecoko'nesel, who forces herself to say: "To the Great River. In the forest."

A timid sun slides through the foliage, striking the dew that soaks their feet. Utu'wv Ecoko'nesel shows Pétronille how to avoid the tangled roots. She reminds herself that Pétronille didn't necessarily choose to come here. But what did Pétronille ever do for her? Utu'wv Ecoko'nesel lets her carry the child, deeply asleep from the leaves of flat wood she has her chew under her mother's worried look. Briefly, looking at Pétronille's desperate face, seeing how vulnerable she is, Utu'wv Ecoko'nesel finds it easier to tell herself that she is doing the right thing.

They make their way under heavy branches. Above them, woodpeckers angrily hit their beaks against trees. When Utu'wv Ecoko'nesel hears the warriors, she freezes. She makes Pétronille and Émile kneel behind a fallen trunk, remain silent even while a spider as big as a chicken egg crosses the boy's coat. She suddenly sees herself through the warriors' eyes—one of their girls hiding a white woman and her children on the morning of a war. She holds her breath as the men pass by, their earlobes dilated by swaying hooks. Some of them carry jars of oil and baskets of wheat, the others hold spears and light bows. Among them, she recognizes a commoner from the Great Village, a thin ax in hand. The council despises the French chief so much that none of the Suns wants to dirty their hands with his blood.

When they are gone, she realizes she is shaking. She feels Pétronille's hand on her back, turns in time to see her opening her mouth. Utu'wv Ecoko'nesel gestures for her to stay quiet, to stand up. There is no time for doubt anymore. They have made it this far; she'll lead them to the Great River. Then she'll go back where she truly belongs.

When they reach the water, Utu'wv Ecoko'nesel stops. Pétronille looks exhausted, her hair full of dead leaves, arms hanging low from carrying the child. Three ducks turn their red eyes toward them as Pétronille lays Hélène down on her dew-wet cloak, and Émile digs a stick into the dry silt. The sun ripples on the river, and Utu'wv Ecoko'nesel climbs on a rock against which the current crashes.

She doesn't hear the signal—the gunshots aimed at the French chief and his interpreter. But as the other warriors answer with their guns, sounds reach her, coming from the farms farthest away from the white men's fort, closer to them. Utu'wv Ecoko'nesel wraps her arms around her knees. The distance distorts the screaming. She pictures herself at the

Great Village, wonders what she would have heard from the main square if she had made a different choice. What if they were Pétronille's cries instead? Then the sounds are covered by the flapping wings of wood pigeons, alarmed birds rushing out of the forest—so many of them that, for a moment, the sky becomes a cloud of feathery bellies.

• • •

The houses burn around Fort Rosalie. The smell of charred flesh fills the morning air; the flames warm up the winter breeze. The prairie grass has turned red, as if strawberry season has come early. When Utu'wv Ecoko'nesel hears the white women howling in the house on the mound, she ignores the image that flashes into her mind—Pétronille, dark circles under her eyes, staring at the opposite bank while Hélène and Émile watched opossum babies slide into their mother's fuzzy pocket. Pétronille didn't cry once during the attack. She stayed silent, massaged her temples. Before she left, Utu'wv Ecoko'nesel gave her the dry buffalo meat she had with her. She said goodbye as quickly as she could.

She hurried along the Great River. She was about to enter the woods when she heard paddles slapping the water. She stopped and looked around. Trees leaned toward the fast-running river, their branches caught in the current. She hid before the French man could spot her. Looking terrified, his clothes a mess, the only white survivor she saw on her way home.

He was heading toward Pétronille and her children; he could miss them, but there were good chances he'd found them on the shore. Part of Utu'wv Ecoko'nesel would have walked back, told Pétronille about the man traveling down the river to her Great Village, the one she calls New Orleans. But the settler had already faded away; there was no time to go to Pétronille, and she wasn't sure she wanted to. She decided she'd let the white man do his part and take Pétronille home, wherever and however that may be. She'd let her be rescued by her people while she went back to hers.

By the time she reaches the Great Village, the injured warriors have been brought back. Hearing their pain, meeting Lv'vlk Lac'kup's interrogative gaze, Utu'wv Ecoko'nesel wishes she had never left, that she had spent the morning preparing the tinctures and remedies she knew would be needed. But there is no time for regret, at least not yet. In her hut, she gathers her baskets filled with herbs. She makes her way through the main square, busy with women sorting the French goods, warriors cleaning their weapons, tattooing an ax and the sign of the beaten nation on their right shoulders, needles and coal dust gathered at their feet. She goes to the other men, the ones who might die for having defended the land that took care of them. She kneels at their side, cleans their open wounds, tends to their bleeding limbs like she used to. She tries not to think of Pétronille, for whom she did everything she could but shouldn't have. She gives her plants to the people they were always meant for.

Pétronille

Fourteen months have passed since the Natchez attack, but the events of that winter morning remain as vivid to Pétronille as if they happened yesterday. After Utu'wv Ecoko'nesel left, she collapsed. She was alone with her children on the shore of the St. Louis River, almost one hundred leagues away from the capital; on the other side of the woods, battles were raging. When Émile said there was a French man on the river, she didn't immediately believe her son. Then she heard the paddles, recognized the man's voice. She was so stunned to see a survivor, not even a stranger but M. Cléry, that she couldn't move. Then she rushed to help M. Cléry hoist the pirogue onto shore—two betrayed spouses escaping together, an irony which, in other circumstances, would have amused her. She would have given everything to return to the world that had just been shattered.

He showed nothing of Baptiste's confidence on water. His gestures were so jerky that he tripped and fell on the riverbank Utu'wv Ecoko'nesel had chosen as a shelter—Utu'wv Ecoko'nesel, who disappeared so fast Pétronille wasn't sure she heard her say goodbye. Without her, Pétronille never would have reached New Orleans and Geneviève's home, where she now lives. She wouldn't be visiting M. Cléry every week, in the heavily furnished parlor of his landlady, the freezing wind teasing a dying fire, listening to the man's animated whispers. The tone of his voice, both feverish and unusually focused, erases time for Pétronille, gets her mind off all the work she did over the past year to keep the Natchez attack at bay—the bundle full of flowers she half hid in her bedroom, the horrific images that torment her, the nightmares that shake Émile and Hélène awake.

The morning of the attack, M. Cléry spoke in a distant, frenzied voice as the pirogue reluctantly detached itself from the sand and silt.

His sentences barely made any sense. "I saw them," he insisted, looking around so frantically it became contagious. He threw a paddle into Pétronille's hands as if she knew how to row, and she did her best to steer the canoe to keep it from crashing into driftwood and trees. Hélène was crying. Émile hadn't uttered a word since they'd heard the gunshots and watched birds flee. Only M. Cléry could be heard over the water flow. It took Pétronille a few minutes to understand what he was saying. That he was returning from one of his engineering trips, following one of his shortcuts home, when the triggers went off—that he'd arrived early enough to see the Natchez warriors take Mme Cléry and the children away, but too late to save them.

Pétronille can still feel the splinters of the paddle digging into her palm. She remembers the only other time she found herself traveling on the St. Louis River, almost ten years ago now, when rowers brought her to Fort Rosalie with M. Ducros—how she'd envied the control they had over the current. The day of her escape from Natchez, Pétronille's hands were moving the pirogue in the right direction. And yet she felt as powerless as ever.

. . .

Today M. Cléry's speech is perfectly coherent. He has just heard news of Governor de Périer's last attempt to destroy the Natchez, one of the many French expeditions launched over the past year. M. Cléry, who came back wounded from the first campaign, continues to live the war through these stories. The troops reached the village of their allies, the Tunicas, almost a month ago, at the end of December. They are back on the yellow rivers, the boats sliding in a storm fierce enough to carry them all the way north. They are looking for the surviving Natchez's hideout, somewhere west of the St. Louis River. At least that's what a captured ten-year-old Native boy confirmed almost two weeks ago, on January 12.

"And then?" M. Cléry asks. His copper hand lets out a knocking sound when it hits the table. "What could have possibly happened next?"

"We'll know more when the next envoy arrives."

"This envoy is an idiot! He left much too early. Why should we care to know they entered the Black River? What about the battle?"

"I thought you'd rather hear something than nothing at all," Pétronille answers, but M. Cléry ignores her. He glances outside the bull's-eye window, and his breath clouds the freezing glass. Pétronille follows his gaze. She has only a few seconds of silence before he starts fulminating again. Between Rue Royale and Rue de l'Arsenal, a young girl picks up the firewood that fell from her shoulders. If M. Cléry were to lean in—as she does and as he almost never would—he'd see a lot more: New Orleans's straight streets taking him all the way to the riverfront's levee or, on the other side, to the town's eastern gate. Windmills plowing the colorless January sky. Smoke coming out of the brickworks' chimneys. Cattle grazing in recently cleared fields, their warm tongues over cold grass. In the corridor, Mme Lemoine screams the name of her other tenant, startling M. Cléry. He barely goes out anymore.

"Don't you think this is it?" he says. "We have them."

Pétronille sighs. "We shall see," she answers. She has learned to be cautious with him. She doesn't ask anymore what he means by "it." Victory, revenge: they are the same to him. Pétronille learned of the advance of Governor de Périer's troops last week but managed to keep it from M. Cléry until now. She knew it would throw him into a frenzy, bring back his belligerent memories of his own battles against the Natchez, revive his hopes of ever seeing his wife and children again. M. Cléry learned about the affair between M. Ducros and Marie only after it was over. While he never spoke to Pétronille's husband again, he always treated Marie's eldest daughter as if she were his own. Today he worries as much about the little girl as he does about the rest of his family. But Pétronille can't talk about Marie this afternoon. There are very few days when she can.

"We shall see," she repeats, avoiding his gaze, scraping away dead skin on her thumb. "Who told you about the battle?"

M. Cléry mumbles to himself: "How many Tunica warriors sided with us, anyway?"

His right leg resumes its bounce, like Émile's when he thinks something over. In a second, M. Cléry will be rambling about her *amie sauvage*, never calling Utu'wv Ecoko'nesel by her name. He says something about massive gallows on the Place d'Armes.

"Please quit it." Her voice comes out sharper than intended, yet it seems to sober him. He knows he can't talk about executions. Last summer, a Natchez woman was captured by a tribe allied to the French and put to death in the square frame.

"Now," he says, his tone softer. "How long have you known about this?"

"A week," Pétronille answers.

He smiles. He uses two of his copper fingers to wedge his pipe in place while his other hand fumbles in his tobacco pouch. Pétronille sees him doing exactly that, back in Fort Rosalie, while Marie would serve her tea. The time when her friend was in love with M. Ducros already seemed so far gone it might never have existed. Pétronille had discussed it with Marie only twice—once after their horse ride, when her friend apologized; then a few months later, as the affair abruptly came to an end. Pétronille didn't stay angry for long; Marie's friendship meant more to her than her marriage. Both are lost.

"Impressive." He nods to himself. "But I shall know more before you do."

"Maybe," Pétronille says, although she doubts it. She asked the landlady not to mention any topics related to the war. M. Cléry, once considered a hero, has few friends left.

When she gets up to leave, his lips meet her hand. Months ago, that would have been impossible. Touch, in the months that followed her return from Natchez, became as threatening as it once was at Château-Thierry, back when forced embraces left her light-headed. She knows Émile and Hélène suffered from her lack of affection—Hélène especially. When her daughter would wake up at night, sobbing, only kisses would soothe her, convince her there wasn't any spider caught in her hair. Pétronille would pretend to look for it, like she had the morning of the attack. On the riverbank, she did find a horrific insect crawling on Hélène's skull. She called it a spider because she didn't know how else to name it. She doesn't know how to call the imaginary beasts that invade her daughter's bed in New Orleans either. But she does her best to chase them away.

She puts on her cloak. M. Cléry carefully lays out his drawing materials—his left-handed sketches have improved a lot over the past year. Pétronille hasn't made two steps toward the door when he asks: "Are M. Bienvenu's building projects moving forward?"

Geneviève's third husband was recently talking about the land he just bought near Lake Pontchartrain, yet she can barely remember a word of what he said—only his frustration with the lack of supplies. When she reached New Orleans, Pétronille couldn't believe Geneviève had turned into a wealthy woman—and yet, at the same time, she could. Her friend had told her more than once about her family, how they had died in Paris, deprived of everything; Geneviève had always known how to fend for herself and be resourceful. She welcomed Pétronille into her home six months ago. M. Bienvenu is nothing like M. Ducros, yet Pétronille still struggles with his ambitions for his *indigoterie*, one that painfully reminds her of her husband's idea of success.

"I think he is still discussing construction plans with one of his engineer friends," she offers. "The land hasn't been cleared yet."

"He should be careful. Negroes are as vicious as Indians."

Pétronille keeps her answer to herself. M. Bienvenu doesn't own slaves yet, even if she knows he one day will. She hopes that in Fort Rosalie, her husband's enslaved Africans sided with the Natchez during the war, like most did. Naturally so. Why would they have chosen the French?

"Please give my respects to Mme Bienvenu," M. Cléry says.

"I will," Pétronille answers. She won't. Geneviève would only shrug; she doesn't approve of the visits to M. Cléry: "He is keeping you from moving forward," her friend insists. Pétronille knows Geneviève is partly right. And yet she can't help but walk from Rue d'Orléans to Rue de l'Arsenal to visit him twice a week. M. Cléry brings her back to her life in Natchez, makes her hope she's only arrived too early for supper, that Marie, late as always, might just be getting ready to join them, that Utu'wv Ecoko'nesel would soon knock, and that together they'd start peeling, cutting, mixing the plants she'd have brought.

It took Pétronille so long to feel at home: until recently, Fort Rosalie and its village were all she knew of La Louisiane, her home for eight years. One of the colony's biggest settlements that came to seem so small—four hundred people, families who learned to know one another, if not in person, then at least by name. The mulberry grove by the tobacco fields, where Utu'wv Ecoko'nesel once taught her how to peel bark from the trunk. The roses that climbed under her bedroom window, white and pink bushes from which her friend picked a single flower that she took with her. The bedroom where Pétronille gave birth to her two children, now burned into the soil. When she thought of her house, she used to picture ashes, consumed logs, ruined walls. Then, as months went by, she started seeing other things. The seeds Utu'wv Ecoko'nesel once brought growing in the ravaged kitchen. The vine she planted creeping over the broken staircase and the roof structure, building a delicate ceiling of leaves. The parlor filled with tulips and musk roses, a swallow nesting where the door used to be. The unbreakable quiet that must have taken over the land now that it didn't belong to anyone anymore.

· · ·

This isn't the first campaign report Pétronille has heard since she came back. Far from it. The war is inescapable: months after the attack, it is still consuming La Louisiane, ruining the colony, throwing a last blow to the directors of the Company of the Indies. She saw it for herself in both Fort Rosalie and New Orleans: the Natchez attack spread panic among the settlers. There were not enough supplies or manpower to fight back; in December 1729, Governor de Périer hastened to dig trenches and protect the capital. In town, Pétronille heard people whisper that only the king could save the Mississippi.

She didn't want to hear more, didn't feel pleased when the backup troops disembarked. She was torn between her desire to see Marie again and her hope that Utu'vw Ecoko'nesel might have survived. To Pétronille, the war wore the face of these two women.

After she arrived in New Orleans, it took her a few weeks to understand the scope of the conflict. As she did, she grew more and more baffled by her own ignorance, by how little she had known that morning of November 28 as she ran with the children behind Utu'wv Ecoko'nesel. When they heard the gunshot, she couldn't have imagined what she later learned: that the Natchez had attacked the commandant of Fort

Rosalie the second Dechepare bent to seize the pretend gifts they had come to offer him, that warriors infiltrated each French home, killing the men and enslaving their wives and children. That before night fell that day, one hundred and thirty-eight French men, thirty-five women, and fifty-six children were dead.

Only two Frenchmen were kept alive by the Natchez. A carter from Sainte-Catherine Concession, in charge of bringing the French goods back to the Great Sun—carts that Pétronille pictures filled with Hélène's bed and toys, M. Ducros's desk, the tin box where she kept Geneviève's letters. The tailor's life was also spared. He was asked to sew new pants and shirts out of fabric seized from the storehouse, and to mend the clothes of the French who were killed, so that they fit the Natives. He used colored scraps to make them bigger, which pleased the Natchez very much. Pétronille pictures Utu'wv Ecoko'nesel's brothers wearing M. Ducros's coats. She pictures the tailor fixing the clothes of dead people and wonders how many could be saved, how many had to be thrown away.

But her ignorance felt deeper than that. The summer and fall she spent working with Utu'wv Ecoko'nesel, M. Ducros didn't bother telling her the last absurd request made by the commandant at Fort Rosalie. All of a sudden, M. Dechepare had chosen one of the Natchez villages as the ideal site for his house. He gave several hundred people two days to abandon their home. This final request ended up destroying the fragile relationship with the Natchez.

Each time Pétronille learns about a new detail—of the war, what provoked it, its aftermath—she thinks of Utu'wv Ecoko'nesel. The young woman's help grows more and more unfathomable, mysterious, precious.

Why and how, Pétronille sometimes wonders, am I even alive?

• • •

The day after she visits M. Cléry, she finds herself unable to get up for supper. She knows she is expected, that M. Bienvenu is coming back from Lake Pontchartrain tonight, that Belle has been busy cooking all day. She knows Geneviève is exhausted enough by her pregnancy, the second in a not even three-year-old marriage, that Pétronille shouldn't be add-ing to her difficulties. Not the way to give back to her friend everything she owes her.

But Pétronille has no control over the harrowing images that have overwhelmed her since the war. When she moved into the Rue d'Orléans mansion, she didn't think they'd follow her into the room Geneviève had prepared for her. Bedridden for hours in a row, Pétronille understood her mistake.

She imagines M. Ducros wandering through their house the morn-ing of her escape. Her husband asking for his horse to be saddled. Step-ping outside to face three warriors. Or sometimes Natchez men entering the house before he had time to rush out. Whatever followed—how many strokes it took to finish him. One, three, six. Less than half a league from there, Marie, dressing her two girls, blowing her baby boy's nose. The noise she heard or didn't hear. Which child cried first and how hard Ma-rie fought back. In the home of her new employer, somewhere close to the fort, Renée boiling water, then hiding where she could. The images always morph. They take over her surroundings.

How do you wake up from a nightmare if you aren't asleep?

Late afternoon now. She lies in bed, petrified, waiting for the next scream. But the children downstairs don't cry out of fear. They are only playing, her boy and her girl, in the nursery. She repeats it to herself. She feels for the nightstand, her hand meeting a cup of tea, now tepid, that someone must have brought. A bouquet of lavender hangs upside down by the bed canopy. She is in her bedroom, in this house Geneviève inherited from her second husband, the man her friend rarely even men-tions. Here is Émile again, his voice as high-pitched as Mélanie's—the two eldest teaming up to torment Hélène, Belle telling them to be quiet or they'll wake up Geneviève's baby—ten-month-old Louise, the chubby little girl who is probably asleep, curled up in her crib. No one is coming for them. They are all safe.

"Pétronille?" Geneviève doesn't wait for her reply to open the door. "We are expecting you."

Her friend comes into focus—the yelling recedes. Geneviève's belly is huge, the baby due next month. Geneviève's body, in comparison, seems dangerously slim. Her cheeks have grown hollow: when she smiles, the gap between her teeth seems wider. Her face has hardened, matured, but her eyes are as pale and piercing as ever. She has just turned thirty-three.

"I can't," Pétronille says.

"Yes, you can."

Geneviève moves toward the bed but doesn't sit. One of her hands rests above her belly button. The other presses against her lower back. "You visited him again," she says.

Keep on talking to me, Pétronille thinks. Around her, the room comes back to real life. The earthenware vase Émile broke. The intricate shadow of the embroidered curtain on the red carpet. The bundle filled with Natchez plants, flowers she looked at yesterday and was relieved to find, if dry, still beautiful.

Geneviève sighs. "If only you were seducing him," she says. When Pétronille does not answer, she asks, "Do you hear me?"

"I'm not."

"I know." Geneviève pauses. "Please do not marry him."

"I'm not trying to seduce him," she says.

"What does seduction have to do with marriage?"

Pétronille can't explain the pull she feels toward M. Cléry. It has nothing to do with love. When she is with Marie's husband, she feels understood—fortunate too. The images that haunt her will never be as vivid as his memories. Utu'wv Ecoko'nesel didn't spare only her life and her children's: she brought them to safety before they could witness horrors that neither Pétronille nor Hélène and Émile could have forgotten. M. Cléry wasn't as lucky. For once, in his landlady's parlor, Pétronille is the one bringing consolation.

The only time she tried to explain this to Geneviève, the words came out so wrong she had to stop. Her friend remained silent for a long time. Then she asked: "You know you don't have to punish yourself for anything, right?"

Geneviève points at the door. Her hand looks swollen, her ring carving into the flesh of her finger. "I don't think M. Bienvenu would be happy to hear you won't join us tonight."

This is Geneviève's first reason for why she should leave her room. They both know it carries little weight. M. Bienvenu does whatever

Geneviève wants him to do—one of the few reasons she married him, as she often swears. "A much kinder Pierre," Geneviève said the day she told Pétronille that M. Bienvenu bore the same birth name as the two previous men she had married. As for the death of her second husband, M. Melet, Pétronille learned nothing more than what Geneviève wrote in the letter that reached Pétronille in her Natchez home. Fallen down the stairs, an accident. Her friend couldn't be questioned further on that matter. "You already know everything there is to know," she'd say, an answer that never satisfied Pétronille. She told herself she'd ask once again after the baby was born—now wasn't the right moment.

She tries straightening up her foot, but the sheets are too taut. Geneviève goes directly to her second plea. "Your children are asking for you."

Pétronille feels her throat tense, readying for tears. She feels ashamed of her weakness yet powerless. "I'm so sorry."

"No," Geneviève says. She frowns, moves one of her hands to the bed's footboard. Last spring, Dr. Le Cau didn't hide his concerns when she became pregnant again so quickly after giving birth to Louise. "You aren't. Otherwise you'd be standing up."

"You should sit."

"Not until you're up."

Pétronille doesn't say anything. Her body feels immense, unmovable.

Her friend stares at her. The hand on her belly shakes slightly. "What would your Indian friend say?"

This is Geneviève's last card, one she rarely uses. The first time she came to visit in New Orleans, in December 1729, Pétronille couldn't stop talking about Utu'wv Ecoko'nesel. She was staying at the Hôtel-Dieu then, where she was urgently sent the day the St. Louis River vomited their pirogue into the city. The fat, buoyant surgeon who took care of her was right across the hallway. Geneviève shushed her. That same morning, three enslaved escapees had arrived in the capital and described what they'd seen at the destroyed settlement—the heads of French officers lined up alongside the French settlers' scalps, houses burning from the fort to Sainte-Catherine Creek. No one would have tolerated Pétronille calling a Natchez woman a hero. "Forget her," Geneviève said that day.

Pétronille would never be able to. She doesn't speak her name anymore, except to take Utu'wv Ecoko'nesel's defense in front of M. Cléry.

Pétronille pushes the sheets away from her. Her hands feel smaller, clumsier than usual. When she stands up, she is careful not to catch her reflection in the mirror. More than a year after the attack, she hasn't gotten used to her hair, how drastically white it's turned. Geneviève assured her it was in vogue, that she wouldn't need to use powder anymore—as if either of them cared about fashion.

Geneviève lets herself fall on the mattress. She sighs, shakes her head, laughs. "Let's save these sorts of challenges for when the baby is born," she says. A flash of fear strikes her face, gone as quickly as it appeared. She attempts a smile.

"Take my hand," Pétronille says.

• • •

Pétronille didn't spend more than a week at the Hôtel-Dieu in the early days of December 1729. Her memories of her stay at New Orleans's hospital are hazy. Hélène's and Émile's warm bodies against hers. The fireplace always lit, the surgeon coming into the room once a day to check on them. Dr. Lancert had traveled from Paris a few months earlier and seemed unimpressed with the chaos that reigned in the colony. She appreciated him: he never came too close, listened carefully to the one or two plant remedies she dared to mention. She couldn't figure out whether the man's interest was genuine. She didn't care. Sometimes he played with the children. He always let Geneviève stay longer than permitted.

It was during one of these visits that he announced the Ursuline sisters had kindly offered to welcome Pétronille and the children at the convent. Pétronille always knew she wouldn't stay at the Hôtel-Dieu forever. Nor did she want to: the hospital's sick ward nearby reminded her too much of La Salpêtrière. Geneviève was sitting by the bed when Surgeon Lancert brought the news. She fidgeted with her ring, the tiny blue one. She waited for him to leave before she spoke. "You'll get to see Charlotte then," she said, but when Pétronille asked about Charlotte, Geneviève remained evasive: "She is still a boarding student at the Ursulines'. She sings in the choir, helps raise orphans, seems more devout than ever." Charlotte had decided not to become a nun, but when Pétronille asked about the convent, Geneviève only shrugged. "It could be a good shelter for you, at least temporarily," she said.

And it was. Last year Charlotte did everything she could to help Pétronille feel at home. Winter lingered, and the Ursuline sisters could talk about nothing but the building they'd soon move into, its thick walls that would keep the cold out, its second infirmary, a room for the sister in charge of the linen, a bigger classroom, and a separate refectory for the orphans and students now so much more numerous. A cloister's vault, even, with painted arches full of clouds, leaves, and angels. The new convent was only a dream in the first months of 1730. Charlotte wasn't much into talking—neither about the Ursuline sisters' permanent home nor about what Pétronille went through. She had a mattress placed next to hers, to be close to Pétronille and the children if one of them were to wake up from their nightly terrors. She taught Émile how to perfect his calligraphy skills and enrolled Hélène in the choir. One cold March morning, after lauds, she found Pétronille in the yard, her lips and hands gone dry with cold, a chamber pot at her feet. Piss had frozen overnight at the bottom of it. In the refectory, she watched as Charlotte held it close to the fireplace, breathed the harsh smell of warmed urine. She stayed inside when her friend went back out to clean the bucket for her.

She remembers Charlotte's shock at the end of the spring when she said she and the children would be moving in with Geneviève. Charlotte's face grew pale. She struggled with the sealing-wax sticks in her hands. She was then twenty-two, she was being given more and more responsibilities at the convent, but at that very moment, she looked like the girl Pétronille once knew in Lorient. "Aren't you happy here?" she asked. "I am," Pétronille answered, but her mind was elsewhere. The army had just brought back the French wives from Natchez, the women who had been captured after the attack; they were being sent to the Ursuline convent for shelter. Pétronille was in both shock and despair that Marie wasn't among them. She thought of her friend's unfair sentencing in Paris, of her dreadful journey to La Louisiane—of this new person Marie had managed to become, the life she had built despite everything she had endured. And yet she was not among the survivors. "I'm certain Geneviève will take good care of you," Pétronille heard Charlotte say. "Much better than I would."

• • •

The first few days of February, Pétronille wakes up rested. She won't let M. Cléry take that feeling away from her, she won't go visit him this week. She reminds Hélène to be careful with the ivory comb, but the five-year-old girl doesn't listen, keeps on playing at the dressing table. Émile is drawing by the window. Outside, Mélanie cares for the baby birds, born too early, that fell from the cherry tree. At almost nine, Geneviève's eldest daughter is a lot taller and bigger than Émile—but even if she were half his size, Mélanie would lead him wherever she wanted to. Émile's pencil skids on the page. Pétronille picks at his hair, as dark as M. Ducros's.

After the attack, in the forest, the children kept on asking about their father. At first she remained elusive. There was no right way to tell them the truth. "He is gone," Pétronille finally said. When Hélène started to cry, her brother held her in his arms for a long time. The image of her children comforting each other often visits Pétronille, bringing back the same interrogation—should she have alerted her husband? But then she had, even before Utu'wv Ecoko'nesel returned to warn her: M. Ducros wouldn't believe her. Something in her knew Utu'wv Ecoko'nesel wouldn't have saved him too, although Pétronille couldn't have said why. All she knew was that she could have either stayed with her husband and died, or followed her friend and saved herself and her children. One day they will understand the choice she made. Émile rolls his shoulders to shake her hand away. "Please," he says.

He is very much like her in nature, so predictable that Pétronille is often torn between compassion and annoyance. Looking at her son now, in deep concentration, she sees herself trying to grow a new rose from a cutting and snapping at the first person interrupting her. It's easier to tell Émile to be kinder than to say it to herself.

In the garden, Mélanie stands up, glances toward the windows of the first floor. Then she starts running toward the house, leaving the birds and nest behind.

"What is the matter with her?" Émile asks.

Pétronille hadn't noticed he'd stopped drawing. "I don't know," she answers. "I'll go see."

She hurries downstairs, her reflection consecutively caught in the two round mirrors hanging in the hallway. Belle, the enslaved woman who has had no choice but to stay with Geneviève through widowhood and remarriage, blocks the view of the salon. Her salt-and-pepper hair pokes out from her bonnet, unusual for a woman always perfectly put together. Her small mouth is tense, her eyes squinting, her round chin held high.

Geneviève is unconscious: she lies on the green sofa, her disproportionate body sinking into the feather cushions.

"She started complaining about her belly," Belle explains. She doesn't turn toward Pétronille, her hand resolutely planted on the corner cabinet. She rarely speaks to her, seems to distrust everyone, though Geneviève a little bit less, perhaps because Geneviève once insisted that M. Melet mustn't buy Belle without her son, Alexandre, and her husband, Constantin. It was early on in their marriage, Geneviève told Pétronille, and he had listened to her and kept the family together. Belle was with Geneviève when M. Melet turned against her. She helped raise her children at the same time as she raised Alexandre, whom Pétronille once overheard her call Latorin. When Pétronille expressed her surprise, Belle raised her eyebrows and said it was his real name. She reluctantly told Pétronille hers: Iyawa.

Pétronille kneels by Geneviève, whose breath is steady. She pictures the bundle of plants in her room—tries to remember whether she brought back three-leaved climber, button eryngo, or figworts from Fort Rosalie. She might have or might not have. It doesn't matter: even if she had all the ingredients, she wouldn't be able to come up with the right recipe. She was never a Natchez woman, nor a doctor. "I'll go fetch Dr. Le Cau," she says.

Constantin hurries the coach through the town. At the corner between Rue d'Orléans and Rue Royale, the horses almost run into two men trying to get a broken weaving loom out of their workshop. Pétronille hears Constantin mumble to himself in a language as foreign to her as the Natchez's, then he screams, "Go!" and the horses are trotting again, people's faces flashing, broken teeth and muddy wigs, sagging breeches and tired leather. As they approach the Place d'Armes, the crowd's volume intensifies. Despite her urgency, Pétronille sits back away from the carriage window. Loud noises bother her in a way they never used to.

The horses halt. It isn't mass day, but the Place d'Armes bustles with people. Two dozen soldiers, going back and forth between the harbor and the barracks, their quarters' gate open after two months. Pétronille can't believe the army is back already: after the victories of February and March 1730, Governor de Périer's and General Le Sueur's troops held celebrations of all sorts, and news of their return preceded them. There are too few soldiers walking up and down the gangway, alligator weed sprouting under the city's main levee. She leans forward. Only two ships at anchorage, a galley and an oar boat, slightly bigger than models from this corner of the square. Men—maybe not the entire army but undeniably one of its detachments—pushing cannonballs, rolling powder barrels, carrying muskets and pickaxes back into the warehouses. Men who would know what happened on the Black River, deeper in the bayou. Pétronille doesn't want to hear what they would have to say. Last spring the triumphant soldiers did not carry only good news.

After the attack, Pétronille soon understood that she would never see her husband again—in Natchez, unlike women and children, men hadn't been spared. But in the early months of 1730, she hoped with M. Cléry that Marie would one day appear with her baby and little girls. So whenever Pétronille would pass by the harbor, her first months in New Orleans, she'd picture Marie there among the filthy soldiers in fatigues, buying corn bread from street vendors. Her friend would be making fun of the drunk officers, her baby boy asleep against her chest, the girls playing at her feet.

After Le Sueur's troops and their Choctaw allies brought back the French wives, M. Cléry kept on complaining that the governor was more interested in retrieving the enslaved Africans than in reuniting families. Geneviève explained M. de Périer's decision easily: the wives and children were the future of La Louisiane, but there would be no future without a present. People to clear lands, harvest fields, trim woods, build watercraft, maintain levees.

M. Cléry still swears that not all the women have been saved from the Natchez. Pétronille knows neither Marie nor her daughters and son will ever come back.

The carriage turns on Rue Saint-Pierre, and the military disappears. The cold filters through the soles of her shoes. She'll learn news about the war soon enough. But no one would answer the only question she has left—she isn't allowed to pronounce the name of the one woman she holds out hope to see again.

"Almost there," she hears Constantin say as the doctor's house comes into view.

Dr. Le Cau looks nothing like the enthusiastic surgeon who took care of her at the Hôtel-Dieu: he is narrow, expressionless, reserved. In Geneviève's bedroom, he listens to M. Bienvenu say that she fell asleep an hour ago, asks Belle to wait outside. Thrown off guard, Belle suggests the doctor might use her help. But he only glances at her and says, "I'll be fine, thank you." The door closes with a thud behind Belle, and Pétronille turns to the doctor. He is barely touching Geneviève, as if a look could suffice to know what a woman needs. "Rest," he whispers to M. Bienvenu, "until she is due to give birth." M. Bienvenu stares with him, as if he too is focusing hard to read Geneviève's face, his thin lips an elegant line below his red mustache. "The baby might come early," Dr. Le Cau says. He explains that it is often the case with successive pregnancies like Geneviève's, much too close to one another, especially at her age. He says so looking not at M. Bienvenu but at Geneviève, as if she were the only one responsible. From the corner of the bedroom where she sits, Pétronille hopes her friend is not faking sleep, that she cannot hear any of this conversation.

"But there is hope," Dr. Le Cau concludes.

M. Bienvenu's shoulders sink. Something shifts inside Pétronille. She wouldn't have made it to La Louisiane if it weren't for Geneviève, whose death used to be unthinkable.

When Pétronille exits the bedroom, she can hardly breathe. The corridor feels overly furnished, the rugs too thick, the air damp. She makes her way to the back door, stumbles into the garden. The tears wash over her so forcefully that there isn't room for anything else. She lets herself fall on the bench, her eyes slowly adjusting to the darkness, the sobs rippling like hot flashes through her chest. She can't remember when she last surrendered so fully, can't be sure for whom or what she is crying anymore. She doesn't know how much time passes before she becomes aware of the night breeze soothing her aching throat. She moves her shoes in the grass; white pansies glow pale at her feet. Above her, there are more stars than sky.

"What did the doctor say?"

The voice startles Pétronille. Belle's lantern sends shadows on her cheeks. She must have gone to the well; the bucket she drops on the ground is full. She cautiously sits at the other end of the bench, placing the light between them.

"He was very worried," Pétronille tells her, aware of Belle studying her face.

"You are too."

Pétronille doesn't contradict her. Belle has never said more than five words to her. The woman seems different, and Pétronille realizes she has never seen Belle's features reveal any emotions, except when she is around Constantin and Alexandre. Belle is frowning, fingering two fresh stains on her apron. Her eyes are on her dress when she says, "She spoke about you often, you know." She raises her head. "Back when she was married to the madman."

"M. Melet?" Pétronille asks, even if she knows it's the answer.

"She said you were one of her only friends."

"I wasn't the only one. She used to be close to Charlotte as well."

Belle shrugs. "The woman at the convent? I never met her." She shifts on the bench and considers Pétronille. Somewhere in the garden, a night bird gently cries. "Madame Geneviève is stronger than you think." Pétronille's cheeks are rigid with dried tears, and she brings her shawl closer to her shoulders. When Belle resumes speaking, her voice is slow and careful. "I was there the night it happened. About to go to sleep when I heard him. Yelling, like he always did. I waited by the staircase, just below them." Belle gazes back at the dark garden. She shakes her head. "He was so drunk he didn't see me from the top of the stairs. But she did."

Pétronille wants to ask what happened next, but she knows better than to speak. She leans toward Belle, whose voice is even lower.

"He could barely stand straight, and she was right behind him. He started going down the stairs and stumbled. She reached out her hand. I think she meant to catch him." Belle's eyes are back on the lawn. "Then she saw me as I was just standing there. I looked back. But when he fell, she didn't move at all."

Geneviève is suddenly some stranger. Cold at first, Pétronille then imagines herself in a world where Utu'wv Ecoko'nesel wouldn't have been there to protect her family. The kind of violence she might have been capable of to shield Émile and Hélène from danger. She can't guess what she would have done and finds she is grateful not to know. Belle grabs the bucket and the lantern. Then she turns to Pétronille, her chin cupped in a warm glow. Her smile is gone.

"Sometimes I wonder," she says, and pauses. She glances at the flowers, then strengthens her grip on the bucket handle, stares at Pétronille. "I don't know who would be looking out for me if I needed it."

She walks to the house without turning back, stepping into the puddles of light the candle throws at her feet.

• • •

Pétronille would still be mulling over Belle's words, trying to understand the pang of guilt she felt after the woman left, to reconcile the Geneviève she knows with the person Belle described, if not the news she learns the following morning.

The Natchez people have been captured, and it's all anyone can talk about. The small detachment spotted yesterday left the bayou before the other ships; they went down the Black River, the Red River, then the St. Louis River, and, lighter, traveled fast. These two boats are the first of many: soon the entire victorious army will be back, and with them, almost four hundred enslaved Natchez men and women. Three hundred and eighty-seven. The number spirals in Pétronille's head.

Trapped, sinking at the bottom of her mind, numbers turning into people, people into women into girls into Utu'wv Ecoko'nesel.

Now it's Tuesday, the day she takes Hélène and Émile to Charlotte at the convent for their catechism. In the carriage, Hélène keeps on pulling on her brother's breeches. "Mother," Émile whines, but Pétronille barely hears him. Her own children, sitting just in front of her, seem far away. She's felt restless and removed since this morning. Almost four hundred people. Through the window, a limping boy passes by the length of the carriage, carrying a basket of live crawfish. Pétronille is relieved she has somewhere to go. She wouldn't have left Geneviève alone, but her friend looked better today, and anyway, M. Bienvenu is at her side every moment.

Outside the convent, enslaved Africans break another arpent of cypress swamp. For whom, Pétronille isn't sure. The hope of exporting tons of tobacco vanished when Fort Rosalie collapsed, although some optimists argue the production could be transferred to Pointe Coupée. Even so: she can't remember the name of the last boat that brought in settlers. These days, ships sailing away are more likely to be carrying disillusioned workers back to France than unloading new ones.

The Ursuline grounds smell like rising flour, long-burned incense, and freshly cut grass. Sister Marie-Madeleine welcomes Pétronille and the children with one of her exaggerated smiles, her smallpox scars deepening. As always, the nun's desire to help is so urgent it becomes aggressive. When Pétronille arrived at the convent, Sister Marie-Madeleine had to temper an eagerness to comfort her. The nun could never quite admit that nothing would ever fix Pétronille—neither she, nor God, nor the Virgin.

Charlotte waits for them on the threshold of the classroom. Her face has thinned with the years, her round mouth now just the right size to fill the dimple of her muscular, freckled cheeks. She gestures at Pétronille and the children to come in, barely acknowledges Sister Marie-Madeleine. For months, Pétronille has known the story well, after Charlotte confided in her at the end of a lesson: when Charlotte officially became leader of the choir and started teaching the young recruits their letters, Sister Marie-Madeleine hadn't approved, arguing that a boarding student shouldn't have so much responsibility. But more girls kept approaching the Ursuline sisters, novices and students the nuns had sworn to educate. The Mother Superior was too worried by the everlasting construction of their new convent to care about the sister's complaints. Charlotte liked to repeat Mother Tranchepain's final words to Sister Marie-Madeleine: "This is La Louisiane, get over it. We need women like her."

Charlotte closes the door, and the nun with her frozen smile disappears. "Sister Marie-Madeleine will never change," she says and throws Pétronille a knowing look.

The room is empty, the furniture sparse. Pétronille sits by the window, where she usually waits while the children study. In the parlor next door, a girl laughs; then everything turns quiet. Émile pulls one of the commode's drawers open to retrieve a book, and the tired wood growls; the February light draws a triangle on the beige stone between Charlotte's chair and Pétronille's.

"Not this one," Charlotte tells Hélène, busy tickling her palm with a dark-blue feather. "Take one of the goose quills." Then she turns to Pétronille, who knows exactly what Charlotte will say, because each of her weekly visits starts with the same question—three words that Charlotte shyly pronounced for the first time last July, with a false assurance again in August, then repeatedly during the fall and winter. "How is Geneviève?" she asks.

Hélène pushes an inkpot on the table. "Better," the girl answers.

Charlotte's hands drop on her knees. "Better?" she repeats.

"Hélène means rested," Pétronille says. Émile glances at his sister. He grabs her hand and drags her back to their table.

Charlotte follows them with her eyes, her lips pinched. "Rested has nothing to do with *better*," she says.

"She was simply tired these past few days."

"Pétronille, you don't know how to lie."

Pétronille crosses her legs, then unfolds them. She knows Geneviève hasn't told the whole truth about the few weeks she spent at the convent four years ago. She talked about it only once at the Hôtel-Dieu. Back then Geneviève spoke of a kiss, and Pétronille thought of her friend's lover in Paris, of the many stories Geneviève had told her about Amélie on *La Baleine*. Pétronille was happy for her and Charlotte, as brief as that moment was. She didn't feel surprised by Charlotte's behavior; she had noticed how close she was to Étiennette but hadn't ever thought much of it—at Château-Thierry, Pétronille once stumbled upon two maids kissing, the women not even bothering to hide from her, probably convinced that this odd child didn't understand what she was seeing anyway. But when Pétronille asked about the outcome at the Ursulines', Geneviève looked away, then switched topics. Pétronille didn't insist. At the convent, questioning Charlotte proved even more difficult; the mere mention of Geneviève's name seemed to upset her so much that Pétronille quickly gave up. Last summer, when Charlotte started asking about Geneviève, Pétronille was taken aback. She chose her words carefully; she was aware the answers weighed heavily. "Hélène is right," Pétronille says, "she is better. Much better than last Sunday."

"Did the surgeon come?"

"Yes. She will rest until the baby is due."

Charlotte brings a hand to her temple, scratches something Pétronille can't see. She seems about to say something but clears her throat. "Children, we should start," she calls.

"Please do not worry about her," Pétronille says.

Charlotte throws her a look so raw that Pétronille feels her cheeks burn. "I'll try not to."

The lesson lasts for an hour, until the bell rings for vespers. Émile is so absorbed in his copying exercise that he doesn't notice his sister putting the ink away. Charlotte's voice hasn't flinched once during class. It is softer when she says goodbye to Pétronille at the door of the convent, the wind rushing between them, the children jumping in the puddles by the gate.

"Would you send for me if anything happens?" Charlotte asks.

Pétronille tells her she'd be the first to know. On the way back, she tries remembering whether Charlotte has always been like that, changing and unpredictable, then remembers her mood swings on *La Baleine*—the red-haired child sulking in the hold who was also the courageous girl who saved them all. Through the window, a pastel, foggy dusk falls on the city. Pétronille wonders whom Charlotte wants to become.

At home, M. Bienvenu is reclining in the bergère by the staircase.

She is surprised to see him here: this morning he had to lie down because of a recurring stomach pain. He told her not to say a word about it to Geneviève, and although she found him worryingly pale, she nodded. Yet he stands up when she enters, waits for Belle to take her cloak from her, to lead the children to the kitchen and wash their ink-stained fingers.

"Someone came for you today," he says. "Your friend. M. Cléry."

His cheeks are flushed, his hands crossed behind his back. He starts pacing the room. His anger is extremely transparent, Geneviève used to repeat when Pétronille moved in with them; the sentence sounded like a compliment. "It is nothing like M. Melet. His rage doesn't stay, it doesn't boil," she used to marvel. "It is here, and then it is gone."

M. Bienvenu stops at the foot of the staircase. "He came in screaming," he says, "howling about his wife, speaking in horrendous terms of everything she escaped, of the rape and murder and God knows what else."

Pétronille brings her palm to her forehead. She feels a pulse, slight but insistent. "Marie escaped?" she asks. She corrects herself, tries to resist and beat down the part of her that wants to believe what she hears. She tells herself what she already knows. The French women came back almost a year ago, but not Marie. Pétronille sees the lonely galley in the harbor last week, the detachment unloading its hull; she pictures M. Cléry learning about those freshly arrived troops, his rekindled hope—how he would have rushed down Rue de l'Arsenal, asked the soldiers if anyone had seen his wife and children. And then the new number—the one she can't talk about with anyone—looms back. Three hundred and eighty-seven Natchez people. She wonders how far despair can lead.

"The hell I know her Christian name! This madman is delusional. He came rushing in, unannounced, yelling . . ." M. Bienvenu kicks something—a fallen screw, a child's toy. "I won't tolerate that kind of behavior in my house." He lowers his voice, as if he hadn't been shouting a moment before. He suddenly seems incredibly worried. "Don't you think Mme Bienvenu is struggling enough? Do we need to upset her with this insanity?"

"I apologize," Pétronille whispers.

M. Bienvenu sinks back onto the chair. Night fills the only window of the hallway. Upstairs, Louise howls, and hurried steps pound above their heads. M. Bienvenu glances at the ceiling, then back at her.

"Inform M. Cléry that he's no longer welcome here," he says.

"I will."

He nods. He no longer seems angry. Just weary. He starts up the stairs. "You know," he says, "I don't think he is doing you any good either."

• • •

This is the last time I'll see him, Pétronille tells herself, at least until Geneviève's baby is born. She would never allow M. Cléry to come back to the Bienvenus'. He didn't belong to this house—the past shouldn't. Geneviève's home was where Pétronille tried to get better. For the first time, it occurs to her how happy she might be if she were to move into a new place—one that never saw her suffer and struggle, where everything would still be possible.

She heads to M. Cléry on foot the day after his unannounced visit. Despite the weather, she didn't want to ask anything from the Bienvenus' household today, not even a carriage; but the icy wind crushed her face as soon as she stepped outside, pulling her skin as if to crack it. She didn't tell Geneviève where she was going. Right before Pétronille left, Geneviève was sitting in her bed, drafting a letter. They laughed when Pétronille asked if she was really using her huge belly as a writing desk. "I'm enjoying it while I can," Geneviève joked, patting the mount of blankets, but fatigue tainted her voice.

On Rue de l'Arsenal, the door opens before Pétronille has had time to knock. Mme Lemoine is as wide as the doorframe. The heat of the house seems to radiate from her body. "Who designed this town? Who? The wind with these straight streets . . . Look at your face! Full of snot!"

Pétronille closes the door behind her. On the wall, the portrait of a melancholic man hangs, crooked. The cold sticks to her back like a damp chemise. "Is M. Cléry in?"

"He is," Mme Lemoine breathes, "and he is not alone."

Pétronille frowns. M. Cléry is always alone. Her breath quickens. "Who is with him?" she asks.

Mme Lemoine shrugs. "Some soldier," she says, and Pétronille's muscles loosen, hope and disappointment overwhelming her in one thick jolt. Mme Lemoine gestures toward the stairs. "Not the most respectful kind of military, if you ask me."

Pétronille recognizes M. Cléry's laugh, a contagious neighing sound, long before she's reached the small salon where she usually meets him. In the smoky room, both men fall completely silent. The table is a mess of dishes—a collapsed *tourte*, chicken soaked in jelly. Except for the bull's-eye window, the linen curtains have been shut; it might as well be midnight. Even sitting, the soldier is tall, his shirt loose over his bony torso, his spoon filled with soup dropping on the tablecloth. M. Cléry holds a glass of wine between them, as if to raise a toast; at the sight of her, his smile expands.

"How wonderful!" he says. "No, not wonderful. Perfect. This is even better than if I'd found you at M. Bienvenu's yesterday." His voice is excited, tendons visible in his neck. Pétronille sits in the chair M. Cléry pulls out for her. "You never mentioned M. Bienvenu was so ill-tempered."

"He isn't," Pétronille replies. "And you should know better than coming to—"

"Mme Ducros," M. Cléry says, turning to the soldier, "is the dear friend I was just telling you about."

"Madame," the man says. His features are gathered in a tight knot in the middle of his face. He sips from his glass. His eyes don't leave Pétronille as he swallows.

"And this is Private Blanchet," M. Cléry says. He pauses, as if the name should ring a bell to Pétronille. The candle flickers under his breath. He smells like mashed potatoes and liquor. "He saw Marie," M. Cléry says. "He saw her. I know what you're thinking, but listen to him. Tell her," he calls to Private Blanchet.

"She was one of the French women whom Tattooed Arm kept close to her until the end." The soldier stops. "Does she know who Tattooed Arm is?"

"Do you—" M. Cléry starts.

"Yes," Pétronille says sharply. Utu'wv Ecoko'nesel's aunt, she thinks, yet keeps her mouth shut. The pipe smoke burns her nostrils.

"She is the female Great Sun," Private Blanchet explains.

"I said I knew her."

The man glances at her. He seems surprised—worried, almost. "Personally?" he asks. Then he helps himself to more wine, as nonchalant as ever. The bottle almost knocks his glass over.

"No," she answers.

His face relaxes. "Well, it seems like she didn't let go of all the French women who served her last April. She kept the canniest with her."

"Marie," M. Cléry says.

"Petite, determined, fair hair."

"Marie," M. Cléry repeats. He looks at Pétronille. He must not like her expression because he instantly spins around toward the soldier. "She needs more context, tell her about the expedition."

"Of course," Private Blanchet says. "We started our ascent up the Black River mid-January and, a few days later, stumbled upon two parties of Natchez Indians. We swiftly took the lives of two *sauvages*, a man and a woman." Pétronille shudders. She forces herself to listen to the story of the final battle: how the French army traveled the rain-filled bayous to the Natchez fort, how they established camp behind a mount so close to Fort Valeur they could hear the musketry of the enemy, how they threw grenades when the Natchez refused to release the enslaved Africans, how they kept on fighting despite the hard rains that turned gunpowder into mush. The trenches that were dug until, after four days of battle, peace was finally concluded with the young Great Sun.

As the man speaks, Pétronille studies him. He reminds her of the many dirt-poor, alcohol-filled boys who used to roam around Fort Rosalie. Nothing to lose, ready to do anything to become the somebody La Louisiane was supposed to turn them into. Then her gaze drifts to M. Cléry. His pupils are dilated; he nods energetically at everything Private Blanchet says, as if he too had been there on the battlefield. "The chief of the Flour Village escaped with his people," Private Blanchet concludes, "but we are still bringing home most of these Indians."

"Tell her how you saw—"

"No," Pétronille says, her voice loud and clear. "I didn't come to hear about the war." She deeply inhales. Speaking feels incredibly hard. "She is gone," she says to M. Cléry.

He stares at her, his eyes as empty as a fish's. His lips are half opened; his copper hand dips in meat juice. He seems so pathetic that she wonders if he might cry. She thinks of Utu'wv Ecoko'nesel, the last she saw of her, standing alone on the riverbank, ferns brushing against her bare calves. "She is gone," she repeats, and realizes she is talking about both Utu'wv Ecoko'nesel and Marie.

Noises sneak into the silence that falls between them. The landlady moving pots downstairs, the wheels of a lonely carriage braving the winter. The glass of Private Blanchet hitting the wood.

"The troops should be back by the end of the week," he says. His voice is slightly frantic. He doesn't motion toward the carafe to pour himself more wine.

M. Cléry ignores him. He searches Pétronille's face and then turns to Private Blanchet. "I think you should go," he says.

The soldier protests, but without much conviction. He whispers something into M. Cléry's ear, reaches for his coat and a worn-out hat, and staggers to the door. M. Cléry doesn't turn away from the bull's-eye when the door shuts.

He turns to Pétronille. "You too," he says.

• • •

Five days later, the wind blows high. Pétronille blinks at the winter sun in between the fast-moving clouds. She looks down at Mélanie and Hélène, playing by the pond for the first time since Christmas. The water quivers: it looks like raindrops, but it's only insects jumping on the surface. Hélène kneels in the grass and silt, Mélanie patiently—for now—watching over her.

Under the same sun and clouds, a few blocks from here, the returning army celebrates its victory at Fort Valeur. Three hundred and eighty-seven Natchez women, children, and warriors will soon disembark. They have been waiting all morning, since the galleys started filling the harbor. When Belle came back from the Saint-Jean Bayou, she said she had never seen the market so empty—even the freshly brought vegetables from the German coast went ignored by the distracted inhabitants. "Everyone is waiting on the square," Belle concluded, shaking her head, looking disgusted.

Mélanie sits next to Pétronille, hands her a blue flower that opens like a mouth. "Hélène wants to know what this one is, and also what you call those," Mélanie says, dropping a handful of large pink-red petals on the bench. "They were already in the grass. She is very protective of her plants." The girl laughs—just like Geneviève, lips slightly curled up, showing the pink of her gum. "I'm lucky she even let me bring them to you."

The flower is a pansy. Pétronille doesn't know to which species the petals belong. Recently, she surprised herself with a renewed interest in plants. She even started replacing some of the dried flowers and herbs that fill her Natchez bundle with fresh ones. Pétronille brings one of the reddish petals closer to her eyes. "If it were summer, I would have said hibiscus," she ventures, cautious.

"Mme Ducros, there is someone for you," Belle calls, standing at the threshold.

"I'll be right here," Pétronille answers. She always expects M. Cléry, although she knows he won't come visit any time soon. After she found him with the soldier, she didn't hear from him until she received a note in which he apologized for the scene with Private Blanchet and said he'd like to be left alone for a while. He said he knew she would understand. She hands the pansy back to Mélanie. In the grass, a dead fly clasps its legs in a dramatic embrace. "Watch over Hélène," she says, but Mélanie is already walking back to the arbor.

Inside, one of the youngest recruits of the Ursuline sisters waits by the staircase, arms crossed against her dark dress. She is holding a letter in her hand. "From Mme Charpillon," she says.

The sealing wax bled in two neat streams. Pétronille points at Geneviève's name on the folded paper. "I'll give it to her."

She finds Geneviève's door cracked open. This morning her friend looked like she was doing better. All she could talk about was the latest news from France, how a royal decree had just formalized the retrocession of the Company of the Indies's land to the king of France. After years of struggle, La Louisiane had finally crushed the Company's dreams: the colony would never become the prosperous, thriving business they had hoped for. The news seemed to alarm Geneviève. "This land is doomed, if even its former directors relinquish their concessions," she insisted. It felt good to see her friend angry, passionate, her voice her own again.

Now Geneviève sits in an armchair by the window. Her eyes follow Hélène and Mélanie walking to the bench, Hélène's hand closed in a fist. "I think they caught a newt."

"This came in for you," Pétronille says, handing her the letter. Geneviève considers her own name, and Pétronille wonders how long it will take her to recognize the huge loops of the "B" and "G" that characterize Charlotte's writing. There are other questions Pétronille asks herself about the letter, but she doesn't say anything. The sun hits the window unevenly so that she can see part of her reflection floating on the lawn, the two girls walking through it as if she were a ghost. "Hélène would never carry anything so slimy in her hands," Pétronille observes in time to see the wet-looking salamander escape her daughter's grip.

"You never know," Geneviève says, still looking at the paper.

"Charlotte seemed worried about you," Pétronille says.

"Did she really?" There is bitterness in Geneviève's voice. The winter light flattens her features, turns the shadows under her eyes gray.

"I'm afraid Hélène mentioned Dr. Le Cau's visit when we last went to the Ursulines'," Pétronille says.

Geneviève drops the letter on her lap. She looks at Hélène and Mélanie, now cross-legged in a puddle of sun, so close to the window that their voices buzz behind the glass. "Will you be going?" she asks Pétronille.

"To the convent?"

"No, to the harbor."

The number, three hundred and eighty-seven, pulses in her head. Pétronille has been asking herself the same question since Belle came back from the market. Outside, Hélène yells, "Don't!" at Mélanie, who stops short, a torn pansy in her hand. "You should pick as few flowers as possible," Hélène says, speaking so loudly that Pétronille can make out most of her words. She easily guesses the other half of the sentence, because she is the one who once whispered it to Hélène. They had been outside with Utu'wv Ecoko'nesel, kneeling in the avenue of orange trees leading to the house, looking for milkweed and flat wood. "You should pick as few as possible, and only if you intend to do something meaningful with them," Pétronille said when Hélène returned with a huge bouquet of iris and snapdragons. Later, the little girl asked which of the things she did were meaningful and which weren't. "That's for you to decide," Pétronille told her.

"Will you?" Geneviève asks again. Outside, Mélanie has stepped away from the flower bed. The girls cross the lawn empty-handed.

"What if Utu'wv Ecoko'nesel is there?" Pétronille says.

"Then you'll know," she answers.

"I don't want to know."

Geneviève uses her toes to bring a footrest closer to her armchair, her jaw tightening as she does. "I heard that two hundred Natchez people escaped with the Flour Village chief."

"I know. And if I don't go, I can imagine that she is among them."

Geneviève nods. She readjusts her robe, and her belly button shows under the fabric of her chemise. Protuberant, taut, like something about to break. "You know, it took Utu'wv Ecoko'nesel courage to help you."

Pétronille freezes. It's the first time Geneviève pronounces Utu'wv Ecoko'nesel's name. She gets it right. At the Hôtel-Dieu, Pétronille said it once or twice, then was silenced. Geneviève brought up Utu'wv Ecoko'nesel only as her last resort to get Pétronille out of bed, but otherwise, she'd avoid that part of Pétronille's story. Rather, she'd ask about the days that preceded the attack, about the commandant of Fort Rosalie, whom she called a "magnificent idiot," or she'd wonder about the specifics of the skirmishes of 1722 and 1723, the ones Pétronille once confided in her, the summer day of their reunion in Natchez. Her questions remained factual, precise. But Geneviève never acknowledged that Utu'wv Ecoko'nesel's memory should survive the role she once played in Fort Rosalie.

Pétronille stands up. She thinks of the Place d'Armes, the galleys, everyone gathered there. She wonders whether the Natchez people have started disembarking yet. Hélène's and Mélanie's quick steps pound up the staircase. "I'll be back before supper," Pétronille says.

Geneviève smiles. "When did you last see me eating in the dining room anyway?"

. . .

Boats sway in the harbor, their masts like harpoons pointed at the sky, the clouds moving past behind them, whole and dense. Pétronille leans close to the carriage window. For the first hour, the scene looks eerily familiar: soldiers hurrying from the water to the barracks, fleur-de-lis drooping on sloppy uniforms, men singing between clenched teeth—troops everywhere, like the ones she witnessed three weeks ago on her way to fetch the doctor. Except that this time the soldiers are ten times more numerous, twice as joyful. There is a victory to celebrate, and their cheerfulness, the eau-de-vie they gulp down, the pistols they fire, remind Pétronille of being nine in Château-Thierry, stuck in the dining room with her mother's merry guests—the same feeling of being so removed from the scene around her that the two things couldn't possibly belong to the same world.

"Is everything all right, ma'am?" Constantin asks from the driver's seat.

Pétronille watches an unruly cannon roll down the gangway, threaten to crush a fat sergeant, collapse in the mud with a splashing noise. Men laugh, then resume unloading. She keeps on watching—powder falls from the bulls' horns used as containers; women call for help with casks of marsh peas and salted meat; by the levee, soldiers pile axes and muskets. The galleys seem to grow with each weapon and ammunition vomited ashore, as if the ships' hulls were magical, growing, expanding, big enough to carry a war on water.

When the first Natchez people appear on the deck of *L'Aigle*, Pétronille opens the door of the berlin. Her ankle feels fragile on the carriage step. She leans against the wheels, her cloak growing wet as it absorbs the debris of the axles.

Men exit first. Warriors, the paint on their faces gone dry and crumbling at any touch. Red and blue loincloths hugging their crotches. A few feathers, holding so precariously in their beads that the wind will soon carry them away to where they came from. The feathers would be easy to readjust, but the men's hands are tied. The warriors walk between rows of soldiers toward the city jail. Pétronille leans harder against the axles, and the wood sinks into her shoulder blades.

When the first girls arrive, Pétronille looks away, up at the vaporous clouds. She forces herself to lower her gaze. Passersby and soldiers have come to a halt. The seemingly endless file of Natchez women is the only movement in the harbor. One of the youngest girls' hands are free, and she reaches for her mother's mulberry-bark skirt. The way the woman's thighs push against the fabric twists Pétronille's chest. She always marveled at Utu'wv Ecoko'nesel's clothes—the wood, once a tree, turning tender when it met her skin. She scans the women's faces, tilts her head when she misses one. A tattooed breast or a vermilion snake on a fleshy arm, a chestnut-haired girl with dried blood on her forehead, a suckling baby staring into the void. Pétronille wants to look away so badly, to tell herself later that she might have missed Utu'wv Ecoko'nesel. The gangway is brought to the second galley, and another rank of women conceals the first from Pétronille's sight. A dark-bearded captain yells to hurry up, quick now.

Pétronille watches until the sun goes down, until the harbor and the Place d'Armes empty and all there is to hear is a roaring sound sneaking out of the army barracks—then the voices of two soldiers, closer, brushing against Constantin, the younger man complaining that the jail is too small, that most of the women will have to be sent to the slave quarters of the king's plantation. "Another good reason," his companion says, "to promptly ship and sell them in Saint-Domingue."

"Ma'am?" In front of the carriage, Constantin warms his hands under the mares' nostrils. His lips are dry from the cold. "Should we go home?"

"Yes," Pétronille answers.

She briefly wonders what Constantin thinks of her, a French woman who made a point of attending this morbid show. She does not know if he has heard what she went through in Natchez. She now wishes for only one thing: go home and see Geneviève, tell her that she stayed until it was all over. Utu'wv Ecoko'nesel wasn't there, she'll say.

She knows it doesn't mean she couldn't have missed her—Utu'wv Ecoko'nesel could have been standing too close to another woman, her round face hidden by another. She could have died during the siege or on the trip, or sought refuge with an allied tribe somewhere far away, as many others did. Pétronille will never learn what happened to her friend. She will have to live with that.

When they return, the children are nowhere to be seen or heard. Belle comes out of Geneviève's room, hot water trembling in a small cauldron. She frowns when she sees her husband rubbing his freezing hands—Constantin gives her a quick nod, then walks down the corridor. When Pétronille asks about Geneviève, Belle shakes her head. The steam rising from the pot clouds her features. "Contractions," she says.

"Has labor started?" Pétronille asks.

"The doctor came by and said no," Belle answers. "I say soon. She needs us," she adds, hurrying toward the kitchen.

Blood runs painfully into Pétronille's frozen fingers. In the sitting room, she catches a glance of M. Bienvenu drinking a glass of brandy, his back turned to her. The house feels as foreign as it did the first time she stepped in it—a warm day seven months ago, Geneviève telling her that she was home now.

Pétronille makes her way to her friend's bedroom, and the smell reaches her before she's pushed the door. Iron and sweat, something that lingers on your tongue. Then comes the noise. Hoarse, air scraping a throat. Her friend's body on the bed like a wounded animal's.

Pétronille sits by her. She could be thinking of Lorient, she could be watching a reflection of themselves almost eleven years ago—Geneviève leaning over her lying in bed, waiting for her own child to go. Of Geneviève telling her that nothing lasts forever, not even the pain she felt. Pétronille could be remembering these words, how relevant and yet unspeakable they feel today.

Instead, she thinks of Utu'wv Ecoko'nesel. A glorious mild afternoon in Natchez, the end of summer finally reaching the perfect balance between light and breeze; no one dead yet, the settlement resting in its precarious peace—unfair but existent. In front of her, Utu'wv Ecoko'nesel leans over the table, the streak tattooed across her nose creased with concentration, her mother-of-pearl earrings softly oscillating—her yellow eyes so focused on her gestures that Pétronille doesn't dare interrupt her. Utu'wv Ecoko'nesel is showing her a very simple recipe today, one meant to relieve labor pain. A small remedy that doesn't pretend to save anyone. Only to try, when and if you can.

"I'll be back," Pétronille says. She takes Geneviève's hand and holds it firmly in hers. "I have something that might help you."

Geneviève

It is already late when Geneviève comes back from the plantation. Lake Pont-
chartrain is only a couple of leagues away from New Orleans, but in this
heat, the journey seemed endless. When her carriage enters the city, its
streets are finally cooling down. Soldiers from the nearby barracks whisper to kohl-eyed women.

Her goal for this trip was a failure. She had worked hard to arrange
a meeting with M. Rachard, one of the most important indigo producers
of Saint-Domingue. She gave him a tour of the *indigoterie* she inherited
from her third husband two years ago, showed her guest the steeper filled
with decomposing branches, the sediment drying in wooden trays. She
explained that her indigo was of the best quality; even the Spaniards acknowledged that. She offered him twenty percent of her best batches:
since he was producing four crops a year against her three, it would be
only fair for her to take the same percentage off his sales when she would
still wait to harvest. She assured him it would be a win-win situation:
they could share a percentage of profits to keep the production steady.
Better be allies than rivals.

Instead, M. Rachard promised he would write to her soon, a mysterious parting shot that left her reeling. His reaction worries her. When she
welcomed him earlier in the afternoon, the man's smile reminded her of
a horse eating out of her flat hand—something awkward, surprisingly
soft, vaguely threatening. By the time he told her he had something
else in mind, Geneviève didn't think of a downy muzzle but of apples
smashed in an eager jaw. She spent the journey back fighting off images
of M. Melet, how he'd succeeded in hiding who he really was until they
left the Illinois Country together.

M. Bienvenu had been nothing like him: stubborn as a child but incredibly kind and considerate. After the hellish months with M. Melet, this had come as a surprise; she no longer had to fear the sound of a man's boots, no longer had to lock Mélanie's door at night. With a new husband, no one would lay hands on her home. So when M. Bienvenu, who had come to La Louisiane to start his own *indigoterie*, proposed, she said yes.

He was convinced that this new industry would save the colony—yet he never lived to see his plantation grow, to work with the manager who would live in the big house M. Bienvenu wanted to build by the fields. Geneviève had known all along that it was a waste of money, but M. Bienvenu insisted it was for show, to impress the slaves he was hoping to buy soon to clear the land. "They need to be reminded of their position," he started saying in June 1731, when a group of Africans led by Samba Bambara, an enslaved interpreter, was accused of conspiring against the French. On a summer day, M. Bienvenu came back shaking from the Place d'Armes, repeating over and over that, according to the Supreme Council of La Louisiane, the members of the conspiracy had plotted to murder all whites from Pointe Coupée to La Balize.

That summer Geneviève hadn't paid much attention to the trial. She couldn't afford to, a few months after Elisabeth's difficult birth. Back then she could rely completely on Belle to help with the children—something, she realizes today, she shouldn't have taken for granted. The only time she mentioned the plot, Belle chuckled. "My people are called Yoruba," she said. It wasn't the first time Geneviève heard about her home—about the birds drying their wings in mangroves, the Ifá priests' divination boards, and the August dances performed in honor of a certain Oshun. Geneviève could never understand Belle's religion, her supreme god named Olorun, the orisha spirits; yet over the course of the years, she learned to turn a blind eye to whatever prayer took place in the slaves' lodging. She only forbade Belle to share her beliefs with the children. "I don't know what you're talking about," Belle concluded regarding the supposed rebellion. "I'm no Bambara. I cannot speak for them."

Back then Geneviève assumed all the enslaved Africans came from one single country. It was before M. Bienvenu argued that the Bambara people had planned on enslaving any other Black person who didn't belong to their nation after they took control of the colony. Or at least that's what the governor said.

Geneviève never meant to have anything to do with her husband's plantation, yet she couldn't live without an income; she was terrified at the idea of ever being as destitute as she had been as a child. When Dr. Le Cau announced M. Bienvenu's kidneys were to blame, as her husband's health rapidly declined, she started writing down everything he managed to tell her about the production of indigo. Later, she asked New Orleans gentlemen who had never put their hands in a steeper, who only knew of this novel industry in theory, and listened as they described fermentation, oxidation, and sedimentation, pausing each time they used a fancy word to see if she was paying attention. She was. For the first time in her life, she was in a position to make decisions, decisions that depended solely on her.

She finally understood what she had been too poor to realize after Pierre's death in the Illinois Country and too shocked to grasp after M. Melet's funeral. She understood why widows should be feared. They were free women.

She remembers the manager's surprise the day she came back to the plantation for the first time on her own, when she asked him to gather in front of the main house the fifteen enslaved Africans M. Bienvenu had bought. Hérin twitched, opened his mouth, and walked away. A moment later, she watched the men and women sit on the turned-over earth, children fall on laps, shushed by a hand on their shoulders. Under the winter light, Geneviève described to them how to ferment indigo leaves, how to siphon the dark liquid into the beater, how to stir for hours so the air would fasten the process. How to leave it there and wait for the indigo to slowly rest at the bottom of the lower vat. She showed them the plants and the seeds; she pointed at the large warehouses.

They listened, they watched. But she also remembers the grins that morning. It took her days to understand, in the middle of a conversation with Belle, that her husband and the gentlemen in New Orleans who had described the process of cultivating indigo had failed to mention that white settlers had learned these methods from Black people. "My mother was a dyer," Belle told her, "and I used to be one too." Geneviève felt herself blush. She had been describing to an assembly of enslaved African men and women a process they had invented: she felt so ashamed that she didn't return to the plantation for weeks. When she asked Belle why she'd never mentioned her profession before, Belle took her time to reply. "Because you rarely ever ask."

This evening, as the carriage arrives, Belle meets her outside, the lantern light glowing on her high cheekbones, the gray dress falling perfectly on her narrow hips. Constantin takes the horses' bridles, whispers in the animals' ears as he leads them to the stable. Belle grabs the trunk in one swift move. Geneviève hopes she never left the children's side, that Alexandre is doing better. She used to trust her without a second thought, but ever since Belle's fifteen-year-old son fell sick a few weeks ago, she has been spending more and more time with him, less and less with Mélanie and her siblings. Geneviève knows she herself should be more present, but she doesn't have any other option for now.

"The children thought you'd come back yesterday," Belle says.

The hall is barely lit, and Geneviève trips over fallen breeches— something else Belle hasn't taken care of. At the plantation, Geneviève always avoids thinking of her five children. Hérin holds her in enough disdain as his mistress. No need to remind him that she is also a mother.

"I thought so too. Is Alexandre doing better?"

Belle shrugs. She barely ever pronounces her son's and husband's French first names; she finds them meaningless, maintains that they'll never compete with those they received at birth. The only time Geneviève asked her about her Christian name, Belle let out a bitter laugh. If she had to renounce who she used to be, she might as well choose a name as flattering as her real one.

"The fever rose again this afternoon," she answers.

This isn't the first time they are having this conversation. When Geneviève went to see Alexandre shortly after he fell sick, he had nothing of the alert and smiling boy she often saw in the stable with his father. His forehead was humid to the touch, little veins ran under his closed eyes; there was a jar full of water by his mat. Every day at dawn, Belle walks to the river to fill it—Geneviève doesn't know why. When she offered to fetch the surgeon, Belle refused. She said he wouldn't be able to heal her son's body and spirit.

"Maybe Mme Lancert would have something else to suggest," Geneviève tries now, hoping that Belle would more easily place her trust in Pétronille than in Dr. Le Cau.

Belle straightens her back. "I took good care of your children while you weren't here, if this is what you want to know," she says.

Geneviève takes a deep breath. Belle is right—of course that has been on her mind. But she also knows the plantation manager would never let a slave speak to him like this: it is one of the reasons why she would never send Belle, despite her skills as a dyer, to Lake Pontchartrain. Last month Hérin let the hounds loose on Jasmin without consulting her first. The old man was captured a week later, but his foot was badly hurt. Hérin ignored Jasmin's insistence that, according to the Code Noir, he shouldn't receive more than twenty-five blows for running away. "I told him that according to this damn Code Noir, he should've gotten a fleur-de-lis and lost his two ears," Hérin told Geneviève. "And brag to all potential buyers that he's a runaway?" Geneviève asked. Because he didn't answer, she added: "While you're at it, why don't you have him judged in New Orleans and pay for the wood they'll use to make him speak?" Money, devaluation, potential loss of his slaves: these are Geneviève's only arguments to keep Hérin from punishing them too harshly. Six months ago, when she decided to increase their daily ration, she didn't tell him she wanted them to be healthier. He would have neither understood nor obeyed. She said she wanted to increase productivity—that, he could hear.

Still, she has won a few battles with him. When she allowed Éléonore to marry James Mingo, a British free Black man who arrived last winter from Carolina, there was nothing Hérin could do. This morning Éléonore's fiancé paid her the first ten percent of his bride's price. When Geneviève told Hérin the couple's children would be born free, she thought he would have a stroke.

But once she's returned to New Orleans, she can't be sure her orders are respected—that he lets the enslaved Africans sing in the fields, that he is giving them more than the regular one and a half pounds of corn, that he replaced tainted lard with proper meat. All she can do is try and ensure that in her own home, things are handled differently.

"I won't be leaving for at least a few weeks," she tells Belle now.

Belle nods, carries the light trunk upstairs. Geneviève lifts the basket full of mulberry leaves that she gathered in Lake Pontchartrain. The house is uncannily quiet when the children are asleep. No Céleste crying over nothing, licking the dry mucus above her mouth; no Elisabeth pulling the security strips Geneviève sewed on Laurent's gowns to keep him from stumbling after the two-year-old brought back more bruises than flowers from the garden.

On her late husband's will, her only son's name appeared first. Geneviève remembers looking at the then baby, silently thanking him. She wouldn't have to fight for her rights to inherit her husband's property like she would have had to after M. Melet died, if she hadn't remarried. No one would try to steal anything away from her this time. Laurent was the man of the family; he would spare her another husband.

After M. Bienvenu's death, she had considered her pact with La Salpêtrière's Superioress fulfilled. She had given five children to the colony. She was done paying for her freedom from La Grande Force.

Three years ago, she wrote to Mlle Pancatelin. Geneviève was pregnant with Elisabeth, terrified she might die. Now she no longer remembers what she said to her. But it doesn't matter. The sealed letter itself told the most important message: Geneviève had survived, and she wanted the director of La Salpêtrière to know this. Eight months later, she received a reply. The handwriting was firm and round. It was signed Mlle Bailly, Superioress. The woman, this stranger, regretted Mlle Pancatelin's abrupt passing, after fifty-six years of loyal service, on October 26, 1725.

October 26, 1725. The Illinois Country, her first Pierre still alive, three-year-old Mélanie struck with a bad fever, and an injured horse to put down. What was Geneviève doing when Mlle Pancatelin breathed her last breath? Where was Madame d'Argenson, and did she cry when she learned of her sister's death?

It's all gone now. The director had been the only person left to whom Geneviève owed anything. Mlle Pancatelin dead, their deal done, she would ignore her second husband's colleague, the governor's officials. She would ignore their complaints that she traveled to Lake Pontchartrain too often for a decent mother—ignore their offers to "help" with her possessions and manage Laurent's belongings until he was old enough.

In fifteen years, her hair would be too gray, her skin too wrinkled, to attract any suitors. In fifteen years, she might not be here anymore.

Geneviève tiptoes across the silver-lined carpets in her house, one of New Orleans's rare brick homes. After M. Melet passed, she had the wallpapers changed, new paneling installed. She never wanted to touch the walls where she was thrown at or bled against. When M. Bienvenu decided that their bedroom would be upstairs, Geneviève was relieved she'd never have to sleep in the room she once shared with her second husband. At the dark doorway, she drops the basket at her feet, rummages through her purse for the key to the tiny room. Behind her, she hears Belle's quick steps on the stairs, her voice telling her that Mme Lancert stopped by.

"Pétronille? What did she say?"

"To me, nothing. She'll tell you about it at tomorrow's supper."

Geneviève waits to hear Belle close the door of the lodging, by the kitchens, to push the key into the lock. The room used to be M. Bienvenu's cellar. Her third husband liked few things more than wine. He'd paid to have bottles imported from France long before he was sure his plantation business would be profitable, even though the construction of his *indigoterie* was taking much longer than expected. The day before he passed, in November 1732, he had asked her to fetch a bottle of Bordeaux, one covered so thickly in dust that it made her cough. He was barely able to sit upright by then. Although Geneviève had grown used to her husband's stomachaches, she hadn't foreseen that they'd kill him before he turned thirty-eight.

She was four months into her fifth pregnancy at that point, thirty-four years old and exhausted. At the funeral, she leaned hard against Pétronille's arm. She doesn't remember much of that afternoon. Her friend's citrusy smell, the world clotted in black through her veil, and, sheepishly standing by the cemetery gate, Charlotte, her convent petticoats perfectly suited for the occasion.

They said only a few words to each other that day, nothing memorable. Before that, Geneviève hadn't heard from Charlotte since the letter she'd received from her, back when she was pregnant with Elisabeth in 1731. It was Pétronille, then living with them, who brought her the note. There had been a second one when Geneviève found herself pregnant with Laurent, a letter she kept to herself—by then Pétronille had long since moved out of the Rue d'Orléans mansion and married the surgeon. Geneviève knew Charlotte was still teaching at the convent. She used to wonder why Charlotte never chose to become a nun. Her letters, although indirectly, brought her an answer. In them, Charlotte was concerned with only one question—whether Geneviève was healthy and safe.

At first the question angered Geneviève. Then she started to see something else in the letters—guilt, shame, remorse that, she hoped, kept Charlotte from taking the veil all those years ago. Geneviève might not know exactly what happened in the Superioress's office on that winter morning, but she perfectly recalls Charlotte's silence and distance during her final weeks at the convent, back when Geneviève needed her the most. Charlotte had shown none of the kindness and forgiveness that the Ursuline sisters were said to value most.

The cellar is a narrow room. The silkworms arrived from France three days ago, a sealed mahogany box full of eggs, rounder, darker, than lavender seeds. Geneviève opens it, notices tiny black circles on the fattened eggs. They like the darkness, the humid air; tomorrow or the day after tomorrow, hungry caterpillars will appear. Although Geneviève ordered the silkworms months ago, the children know nothing about them, nor are they allowed in the cellar. Last week Mélanie asked why. "This is the place I use to go back to where I am from," Geneviève answered. Laurent waited for his sisters' reaction, then burst into laughter; Louise and Elisabeth stayed silent, their yellow and brown gazes lingering on her. Mélanie is the only one who inherited her blue eyes.

She puts the box back in place. It's always cool in here, almost as cool as it was at the farm in Provence, where the thick walls kept the summer out. Geneviève places the basket full of white mulberry leaves on the floor, next to the bouquet of red ones. One more handful of plants—the sweet white kind—and she'll be ready to start her experiments.

* * *

On July 1, the usual guests gather at Geneviève's for the supper she hosts every Wednesday. She keeps M. Bienvenu's tradition alive with these weekly meals; after the mourning period, when she resumed her invitations, she found she was mostly pleased to welcome those people into her home again, to ease back into the routine her late husband had crafted. Also, she had missed having the latest news of the colony brought to her own table.

Tonight Surgeon Lancert and Reverend Father de Ville insist they were disappointed to see last week's meal canceled; Pétronille hasn't said anything the whole supper, but Geneviève doubts it is because of the missed rendezvous. She spent the past few days thinking about M. Rachard and what to add to her offer—something not too important to her that would make all the difference to him. She didn't have time to visit her friend. There had been the children too, flaunting their songs, eel games, and new breeches, following her to the cellar door, hoping to see what hid there—the hatched eggs, dark silkworms so tiny that Geneviève could barely tell them apart without M. Bienvenu's magnifying glass.

Unless it is the governor's latest decision that upsets Pétronille. Bienville, forgiven by the Crown and appointed head of La Louisiane for the fourth time, was launching yet another expedition against the Chickasaw. The Natchez attack marked only the beginning of the campaigns: wars were as violent as ever, the French army in peril. Geneviève heard that her neighbor doubted so much his own return that he freed his slave before joining the troops, granting the eleven-year-old girl freedom in recognition for her services. Such a decision would be enough to start a storm at her weekly suppers—Pétronille would applaud it.

Geneviève has tried to catch her friend's attention ever since the main course was served, but as always, Pétronille's husband gesticulates in front of her, and Geneviève has a hard time meeting her eyes. People say that Surgeon Lancert is as voracious with his patients at the hospital as he is with his food and words; though she knows Pétronille trusts him, Geneviève prays that if she gets sick, she'll never end up under his watch. She'd much rather have Pétronille take care of her. Ever since she went back to her plants and flowers, her mysterious but effective remedies have prompted some women to nickname her *la sorcière*—an easy stretch for people who aren't used to her birthmark and white hair.

Surgeon Lancert knew better than this twaddle about witchcraft.

Pétronille had met him at the Hôtel-Dieu in December 1729, after escaping from Fort Rosalie. He was a buoyant man who seemed to calm down around Pétronille. It took him almost two years to propose to her. When she accepted in 1731, the summer that followed the Natchez's final defeat, Geneviève couldn't hide her surprise. Pétronille just shrugged. "Aren't you the one who told me that marriage was an agreement?"

Pétronille said the surgeon was the only person even remotely interested in the medicinal virtues of this country's forests, rivers, and prairies—the only man who'd allow her to wander at the edge of town, accompanied by a small army of servants and soldiers, so that she could gather the ingredients for her remedies. Sometimes he'd call her at the hospital and ask her to come give him an opinion regarding a patient. Pétronille always went. "This knowledge is not mine to keep," she once explained to Geneviève, who, knowing Pétronille was thinking of her lost Native friend, simply nodded. Pétronille told her that each time she arrived in the sick ward, her husband would yell at everyone around him to be quiet so they could hear her.

At first Geneviève couldn't quite understand how two people so different could get along so well. Surgeon Lancert was impatient, spoke too loudly, wore all his expressions on his face. "He talks enough for two," Pétronille finally explained to her, "so at least with him, I don't have to pretend to be someone I'm not."

Geneviève knew remarrying had been impossible for Pétronille as long as her mad friend M. Cléry was around. But he resolved to head back to Paris in the spring of 1731, shortly after the victorious French army had returned to New Orleans with the surviving Natchez people. Geneviève's memories of that winter are blurry. She gave birth to Elisabeth shortly after the Natchez captives were locked in the capital's jail. Her third daughter was born almost silent; she slept against the wet nurse's chest instead of searching for her nipples. Throughout the first few months of Elisabeth's life, Pétronille fed her tinctures of fennel and herbs that Geneviève didn't recognize; her friend never stopped believing that the baby would grow stronger.

"You can't imagine the *sauvages*' response when he threw his wig on the ground," Lieutenant Magnole is saying, grabbing his glass of wine.

"What did he do this for again?" Reverend Father de Ville asks. Geneviève can't stand the priest. It takes him twice as long as anyone else to understand the simplest facts: it's a miracle he survived so long in La Louisiane. Surgeon Lancert leans toward the reverend, probably out of pity. "The Indians," he explains, "had just argued that it'd be easier to scalp the secretary and his family and take their goods than to engage in any sort of trade with them."

"So he took off his wig and said, 'If you want my hair, well, here it is!'" the lieutenant cries.

People laugh. Pierre, the first one Geneviève married, would have been revolted to hear someone talk about Natives that way. It upsets Pétronille too—she's pushed away her untouched strawberries, brought her chair against the wall, and now plays with a meringue that crumbles on her dress. Surviving a war made her eccentricities more acceptable. Geneviève rarely hears anything mean about her friend's occasional absentmindedness or too honest answers.

"What did the Indians do?" Surgeon Lancert asks.

"Of course, they were convinced that the wig was inhabited by some spirit. They offered him a fair amount of furs if only he would take the demonic hair back."

The melons have been carved out clean and the wine bottles emptied. If no one says anything for another thirty seconds, she can direct the men to the smoking room and the ladies to the salon. The lieutenant's wife, with her upside-down smile, will throw herself into a critique of every piece of furniture, and Geneviève will finally get to talk to Pétronille.

"So," the reverend says, breaking the silence and further delaying the closure of the meal, "I heard you recently met with quite an important man."

Geneviève forces herself to smile. She recites who M. Rachard is and what he does. She doesn't say she needs to turn this rival into a partner if she wants to ensure the stability of the exports; the reverend wouldn't understand anything about the subtleties of growing and trading indigo.

He turns toward Surgeon Lancert. "But *Docteur*, isn't he the man you met at the governor's last week?"

Geneviève keeps her emotion in. The surgeon briefly glances at him. "Right," he says, then hastily turns back to Captain Foyer.

"In any case. A very ambitious man," the reverend comments.

"That I know already."

Reverend Father de Ville leans toward her as if he didn't hear what she just said: "I've been told he has enough money to buy the city's plantations. I don't know about his relationship with the governor, but he seemed to be rather engaged in his conversation with M. Beauregard when I saw him."

"Beaulieu."

"*Exactement*. M. Beaulieu."

The reverend keeps on talking, but Geneviève isn't listening anymore. The name chilled her. Just like her second husband, M. Beaulieu had turned out to be very different from the Canadian who once stood in her parlor and playfully asked Mélanie about Illinois artifacts. Geneviève likes M. Beaulieu as little as he does her. When his friend M. Melet passed away, he hadn't hesitated to imply that he believed her a murderer and, later, after the death of M. Bienvenu, to let her know what he thought of the fact that, in burying her third husband, she had become yet wealthier.

He knows her weaknesses. Last year, when she ran into him at the reception of a friend of the intendant, he immediately asked about her son. Geneviève had mentioned Laurent's health issues only in passing—had been careful not to describe the terrible coughing fits that sometimes turned the child's face blue. Yet M. Beaulieu mentioned a widow he knew, what a pleasure it had been to the governor's administration to help the poor lady manage her properties. He had managed to stay on the Supreme Council when M. Bienville resumed his function as governor. With M. Rachard, he might have seen another way to take away from Geneviève everything she has.

Surgeon Lancert will know more. Napkins are folded, chairs pushed, and the men head toward the smoking room without interrupting their conversation. Geneviève is about to call to the doctor when she feels a hand on her forearm. Pétronille's hair is coiffed in a precarious bun. A white strand falls on her birthmark. "So this is the reason."

"What do you mean?"

"Why you didn't take me with you to Pontchartrain as you said you would."

Two weeks ago, Pétronille had mentioned needing some plants there and asked if she could accompany Geneviève. Then Geneviève had learned that M. Rachard would be in town. She had been so busy arranging his visit that she had forgotten all about the invitation. "I'm sorry," she says. "Next time you'll join me."

"Next time you'll go to meet with this Rachard man again."

Geneviève knows what Pétronille thinks of plantation owners in Saint-Domingue. They own Natchez people, the ones who were sold on the island a few months after being captured and jailed in New Orleans.

"Didn't you hear what the reverend said?" Geneviève asks.

"Since when do you listen to the reverend?"

"M. Beaulieu has already befriended M. Rachard."

Pétronille remains silent. She has never been interested in politics. Since the Natchez attack, she says they only lead to war, to slaughter. Geneviève lowers her voice, even if they are the only ones left at the table. "I need to conclude this deal."

Pétronille looks around, gestures toward the richly decorated dining room. "Do you?"

Her friend knows perfectly well why she is trying so hard to find an arrangement with him. She can't afford another husband. She has managed to escape the misery of poverty that killed her family in Paris, that terrified her for years, that incessantly struck the colony: she has seen for herself how easily one's luck can turn on this side of the Atlantic, especially when people like Beaulieu are involved. She has no time for these petty arguments.

"Just talk to your husband for me. He seems likely to meet him again."

Pétronille raises her eyebrows. "Thank goodness you do not speak to Belle like this," she says, walking away. "Or at least I hope you don't."

• • •

The following morning, Geneviève regrets her harshness with Pétronille; she promises herself she'll go see her before long and apologize.

In the garden, the children play the ribbon game, a semicircle of young faces turned toward Louise, who tells the story of a spiderweb so big it caught birds.

In the letter Geneviève finally receives from M. Rachard, he doesn't tell any stories. He writes that he thought for a long time about her offer but can't accept. He doesn't apologize. He adds that he will be staying on the continent for another month, until August. He says he has another idea that will get everyone to agree.

• • •

Two things bring Geneviève back to Provence: lavender and silkworms. She wishes she could forget the fire that destroyed her parents' farm, the animal smell of burning silk, and keep only the memory of summers in La Bastide-des-Jourdans, the ripe ears of corn that burned your skin if you ran too fast. The beating her brothers took when they stole two silkworms to have them race each other. How her older sister wrapped herself in mimosa and called herself a queen, ordering the younger ones to reel her cocoons. Geneviève left southern France twenty-five years ago.

Once, in New Orleans, she had lavender seeds shipped from France. It was right after M. Melet passed away, this vicious husband whom she could never bring herself to call Pierre. Fallen down the stairs; an accident. There had been rumors. Stories of hands pushing hard against a male coat, of dry, very blue eyes staring as the skull hit the bottom step.

People didn't know a thing about her marriage. They had no idea how she felt the first time her second husband turned on her—how she had merely been showing interest in the stable's layout when he said it was none of her business, and couldn't she just shut up for once? The following day, when Mélanie touched the bruise on her hand, Geneviève told her there had been a sudden draft and the main door had closed on her.

She often wondered why he had chosen her as his wife. It took her months to understand his decision—the reason was so obvious she had rejected it for a long time. Her husband was animated by a violence that obeyed its own logic, stupid in its simplicity. In Prairie du Rocher, M. Melet had seen there was still something to break in her and had proposed.

That very last night, she had come home as late as she could from the Ursuline convent. She had been standing two steps above him. She had been desperate. She had noticed, that morning, the way the rug slid on one of the steps. She had tripped herself but noted it only to avoid, to fix, before five-year-old Mélanie could fall. When her eyes met Belle's that evening, right before M. Melet took the one step that would cause his fatal fall, she pictured the newest bruise growing on her own temple, how it would look by the following day. She saw all the wounds that were to come.

After the funeral, her mind kept on bringing her back to the accident—the very second when she should have reached for her husband's shoulders and kept him from stumbling forward. The moment when she should have taken the bourbon bottle away from him, called for help. But then there were so many things he shouldn't have done to her. "Don't let him haunt you," Belle told her as she helped her into her mourning dress.

The seeds from France arrived a few days later. The Rue d'Orléans mansion was eerily quiet. No more careful listening before pushing doors open; no more quick retreating into Mélanie's bedroom. For the first time, Geneviève wandered through the house freely. She unpacked the seeds in the salon, marveled at the idea that maybe they came from the very lavender fields behind her family silk farm, the ones that dyed the hills violet. She planted them herself in the black earth of New Orleans, but they never sprouted—killed by the moist air of La Louisiane. When M. Bienvenu asked if she intended to fill the hole in the flower bed, she told him no, that something was already there.

She didn't consider silkworms until she was a widow again. In the north, she hadn't dreamed of Provence: there, little reminded her of the place where she was born. But she was thinking about southern France more and more by the time she came back to Lower Louisiane—as Mélanie became obsessed with fig season and brought back insect bites as big as the ones Geneviève used to scratch in La Bastide-des-Jourdans. It was strange, this longing for a bygone era. But these memories had the quality of childhood—of lost, happy times. Provence was an escape from her wounds for the year and a half she was M. Melet's wife.

During the infinite amount of time their marriage lasted, she often regretted running to him at the Illinois Country governor's house. But even then Geneviève had known this journey, like the one from Paris to New Biloxi, would come with a cost. She just hadn't known at the time how heavy it would be.

She prided herself on only two things with M. Melet. She hadn't given him any children. And she had made sure he never raised a hand to anyone but her.

By the time she started thinking of raising silkworms, both he and the next Pierre were gone. But M. Bienvenu was the one who left her with more. The plantation east from Lake Pontchartrain, and three daughters and one son, babies that filled her with dread and love every time her belly swelled. She liked to believe her body had waited for her to settle in order to give her children. It had taken her a long time to find her home—too long. She was thirty-one for Louise, thirty-three for Elisabeth, thirty-four for Laurent, thirty-five for Céleste. Her pregnancies grew dangerous a month before Elisabeth was born. Barely a year later, she thought her son would kill her, then, finally, that her death would be her younger daughter's deed. Had she realized in time, she wouldn't have kept this last child; aborting had crossed her mind too when she expected her son, yet then her fear was still tamed by hope, by an irrational confidence in the future, by her longing to know those children. With each new baby, the doctor ordered longer rests. Afternoons dreaming about blue-tainted water and buried men, fat-lipped infants brought and taken away, nipples squeezed and left alone, until she resolved to hire a wet nurse—and always, in the back of Geneviève's mind, the battle between her and the unborn baby because they couldn't both survive now that she was thirtysomething, like the doctor said.

But the man knew nothing about the child she had decided not to have in Paris, about what she had survived on her way to La Louisiane, what she had gone through in the Illinois Country and New Orleans. Geneviève proved him wrong every single time.

• • •

Experiment 1, a week after hatching: she gets to the wine cellar early, before the children's chamber pots are emptied, before Constantin feeds the horses. Belle must already be preparing one of her spicy soups; the smell sneaks inside the tiny room. Geneviève closes the window to keep the wind where it belongs. She opens the mahogany box; on the table, she places four leaves of white mulberry, four of red mulberry. She doesn't forget to leave space between the two sets, as if one were France and the other La Louisiane—she remembers that silkworms, just like she does, have preferences. Then she lets the French caterpillars crawl free. Watches their short black hair roll above their flawless skin as they pull themselves toward the leaves. They don't care one way or the other: they eat equally of the leaves gathered from white and red mulberry trees. Now she adds, in the middle, a sweet white mulberry leaf. She watches them rush toward it, linger between the plants' veins, suck the syrupy sap she will never taste.

• • •

July 10. Geneviève watches M. Rachard as he leans toward the huge clock towering in the salon. Her rival is very young. This is the first thing that struck Geneviève at the plantation, when she found him entertaining children with tales of oysters clenching at the branches of island shrubs. When he glanced at her, she understood why his audience listened so intently—expressive eyes that seem to fall on his temples, and dimples to hold them back. She thought of M. Melet, who brought her back to New Orleans, who thought the Ursuline convent would wash away her sins. Back then too, danger had a pretty face.

"He who marries a beauty, marries trouble," Belle once told her as she cleaned her wounded forehead, the second time M. Melet lashed out at her. "A proverb from my home. If it's true for husbands, then it must be for their wives too."

Geneviève wipes her temples with a handkerchief. M. Rachard now moves to the stuffed bird hanging from a silk thread above the compass rose. In the next room, Louise tells some story to Elisabeth, about a frog jumping high enough to feed itself clouds. Geneviève can't hear Belle's voice anymore—she probably slipped back downstairs to see her son.

When Geneviève found Louise and Elisabeth alone in the kitchen yesterday, she told Belle this had to stop. Belle listened. But when Geneviève was finished speaking, she replied that the girls weren't in more danger than Alexandre, and when Geneviève tried to challenge that, Belle shook her head. "My son needs me." Geneviève swallowed her anger, left the kitchen. In the other room, Louise screams.

M. Rachard gestures toward the bird. "Which species does it belong to?" he asks.

His question takes her aback. The dead bird, like Mélanie's timid watercolors and the engravings M. Bienvenu traveled with, has become invisible to her. "I believe it's a kingfisher. My second husband insisted we take it with us when we returned from the Illinois Country."

"This is a rather odd, cumbersome item to carry on a pirogue."

She wishes he would get to the point. She was ready to negotiate as soon as she welcomed him. Now she feels herself dropping her guard. In the hallway, Belle screams for Laurent to stop, but the end of her sentence is drowned out by cries. At least she is back with them. Geneviève clears her throat.

"My first husband, M. Pierre Durand, came to hold for truth a number of Illinois beliefs," she says. She makes an effort, points at the beak turned toward the door. "See, this bird is well known for always flying against the wind. The Indian chief my husband befriended told him that even in death, the bird's spirit would stay in flight."

"Do you believe that?"

"As a matter of fact, it moves with the wind every day. Today it faces north, tomorrow it might look through the window."

The children have stopped yelling. Geneviève smiles as best she can—she'll go to them right after this. Constantin enters as he always does, pushing the door open with a soft knock of the elbow. He leaves the tray on the lower table and glances at M. Rachard as if he were a new addition to the salon furniture.

"Do you have other items that remind you of your late husbands?"

"You have seen them all. This house was M. Pierre Melet's. The plantation I inherited from M. Pierre Bienvenu. Sometimes I tell myself that with another husband, I might have had enough Pierres to build a castle."

He doesn't laugh at her joke, one that usually amuses gentlemen. Uneasy, she focuses on the jasmine flower lying on the porcelain.

"Madame, I've come here to ask you if you'd like to marry me." He looks at her. "I'm well aware that my birth name isn't Pierre, but I was hoping you'd make an exception."

She grows cold. No more percentages. So many indigo barrels that they'd need more ships; but also: M. Rachard, a plantation owner who'd mistreat slaves, who might even decide to open another *indigoterie* under the boiling Mexican sun. Herself, confined at home with the children, banished from business matters; her silkworms, taken away. She sees M. Rachard's fingers reaching under her corset to stroke or strike, this man turning into another monster she never suspected. And then the terror, not theirs, not his, solely hers—her already tired body challenged by another abortion, or bloodless weeks turning into bloodless months, Dr. Le Cau ordering longer and longer rests, the fear of never waking up. Everything she had accomplished since she left La Grande Force, only to succumb to a banal death.

"I'm afraid I can't accept." She spoke fast when she wanted to sound steady.

His cup hits the saucer. "Madame, enable me to ensure that you fully understand what your answer entails."

Geneviève thinks of M. Melet. Younger than she was, so gentle the first time she had supper with him in their new home. She was aware that she couldn't be that lucky, to find a man kind enough to save her from losing Mélanie, marry her, and move them into this mansion. She was so nervous she fidgeted with the pear on her plate all through the meal. Beaulieu too was there that night. By the end of the evening, the fruit was bruised.

"Please give me some time to consider your generous offer," she says.

"I'm leaving for Pointe Coupée the day after tomorrow, then will travel to Mobile. I'll be back by the end of the month. Mid-August at the latest." He smiles. "Hopefully, by then, I will have heard from you."

• • •

Experiment 2, two weeks after hatching: she brings in another box, less fancy this time. She decides that the mahogany box is the home of the deprived, the silkworms that will eat only ordinary leaves. The others, the ones that gather on the sweet white plants, live under the coal-dark walnut wood. She comes in more regularly to feed them, and the children grow more and more curious—the night of M. Rachard's visit, she finds Mélanie in front of the door, peering through the lock. She doesn't tell her about the caterpillars or their different leaves; she doesn't explain that she wants to see the quality of the silk each will produce. She suddenly doubts she'll be able to follow through with her experiments, or that silkworms were ever meant to grow and thrive in La Louisiane.

• • •

Beaulieu's letter, the one Geneviève receives five days after M. Rachard's proposal, goes like this:

Madame,

I was delighted to hear from Surgeon Lancert that you are well and healthy. I encountered him yesterday evening at the banquet organized to celebrate Captain Poiret's arrival. As you are undoubtedly aware, subtlety and diplomacy are unfortunately not among the qualities one might expect to find in doctors. I feel obliged, as your late husband's friend and conseiller, to give my opinion on one of the matters the doctor mentioned in passing. When inquiring about Monsieur Rachard, he explained that you were taking time to consider his marriage proposal, something which, I have to admit, came as a surprise to me. I thought a woman like you would have immediately seen the countless advantages of such a union.

I do admire how diligently you have been leading the affairs of your household considering the tragic events that have struck you repeatedly over the past few years. However, I believe to be voicing the concerns of many when expressing my worries regarding your present situation—as the sole guardian of both an important industry and a large family.

I, of course, inquired about your children and was terribly sorry to hear that your son's condition seems to be worsening. I find myself wondering what an ignorant slave like the woman who is, from my understanding, watching over your children, could do to alleviate his pain, and raise him and his siblings in the Christian faith.

Children are precious, fragile beings. One must do everything in one's power to protect them, especially in these beautiful but perilous regions of the French kingdom.

I trust, Madame, that you will place your family's interests before anything else.

What stays with Geneviève once she is done reading: no more hope that her son could provide a guardrail to keep the governor's officials away from her and her family. Beaulieu's vague threats that she knows could one day become real. The treacherous and too familiar feeling of having to fight off uncontrollable forces, much more powerful than when Laure tried to claim custody of Mélanie—not one but five children to lose now. Two-year-old Laurent: still amusing himself with the rattle-shaped knob of the carriage door, dropping it to cough, ignorant of the horses that might soon be coming out that way.

The letter has been on her nightstand for three days. Three days of warm, savage rain that she spent in her bedroom listening to her daughters and her son running downstairs, exhausting themselves in the house. She went into the cellar only once. The silkworms feel fragile, irrelevant. Their cocoons, a prison.

It's July 17 and she still hasn't visited Pétronille, though she said she would, though her friend's husband could know more about M. Rachard's plan and connections—give her something, anything, she could use to fight back.

Geneviève opens another inkpot. She has spent hours drafting notes to potential new captains who could carry her barrels of indigo to trade. The owner of *L'Espérance* is getting so old that the last time she saw him, he could barely stand on his bad leg. She can almost hear Beaulieu— M. Rachard would have fresh boats to offer her, with young, experienced crews. Her account book lies open on the writing desk, by the bronze statue—*The Rape of Proserpina*: a woman trying to escape a bearded, demented-looking man. Geneviève pores over the numbers again, calculating and recalculating the costs of the next crop export.

"Madame Geneviève?"

Belle cracks the door open. Alexandre has been doing slightly better since Belle had a healer and her brother, some kind of spiritual guide, come over yesterday. They work as a cook and a butler in the biggest house of Rue Saint-Pierre. Belle didn't say anything else about them when she asked Geneviève's permission; Alexandre is eating again, and the chills have stopped. Now Geneviève feels ashamed for ever questioning Belle's sense of priority. But she is exhausted, she isn't thinking straight. She can't handle it all. She lets her feather sink in the ink. "What is it?"

"Someone for you."

"Tell them to come back."

"It's me."

When Geneviève recognizes Charlotte's voice, her breath turns shallow. It cannot be her former friend standing on her doorstep. The Ursuline convent is close enough to Geneviève's home, yet years away. "Come in," she says.

When Charlotte does, Geneviève can't hide her surprise. She hasn't seen her in anything but her convent clothes since their days in New Biloxi—a lace cap and a baby-blue dress, still modest but nonetheless unsuitable for a boarding student at the Ursuline house. Charlotte stands straight, her arms dropped by her sides, her hands rigid, and her face serious. Geneviève is about to ask about her clothing, about the Ursuline sisters, but Charlotte beats her to it: "Would you let me tutor your children?" Her voice is precise, each syllable tended to. When Geneviève doesn't answer, Charlotte timidly goes on: "Last Tuesday, at the convent, Pétronille said you were desperate for help at home."

Geneviève turns to the window. She isn't sure where the anger comes from, but it is sudden and fierce. She'd like to believe that it is about Rachard and Beaulieu. Easier that than acknowledging it comes from the past, from a note left on Charlotte's bed at the convent a very long time ago. She looks at Charlotte. Her presence here today has nothing to do with the conversation the two of them had in the graveyard on the day of M. Bienvenu's funeral. It has nothing to do with the letters Charlotte sent when Geneviève was pregnant. In the notes, by the cemetery gate, she didn't ask for forgiveness.

"I only mean to help," Charlotte says.

"You only mean to help." Geneviève feels an itch in her wrist. She wants Charlotte to say it again.

"I do," Charlotte repeats. "If you'd have me." She is still leaning against the door.

Geneviève gestures for her to have a seat. "I can't believe the Superioress let you go."

"You speak of that place as if it were a prison," Charlotte answers, her voice empty of reproach. She pauses. "I told Mother Tranchepain I had done my time with them. I didn't need to say more. She said she'd always known I wouldn't stay forever, that otherwise I would have done my novitiate by now. I assured her there was more than one sister who'd be happy to teach, which happens to be true." Charlotte looks at her hands, then gives Geneviève an impossible smile, one that reminds her that this woman, once a girl, fought pirates. "Would you happen to miss my black dresses?"

"No," she answers. "They made you look sick."

"They make everyone look sick."

Especially me, Geneviève thinks, but you didn't care about that back then. "Was tutoring my children Pétronille's idea?" she asks instead.

"No, mine," Charlotte says. "I had been thinking about it for months when she told me about your situation." She pivots on the stool, and her knee brushes against Geneviève's. Genevieve shifts hers away. "Listen, I could help them with their letters and prayers, but I could also watch over the younger ones." Charlotte pauses. "At night as well. I know some of them are still babies."

Geneviève leans back in her chair, passes her hand over her forehead. She can't deny that she needs Charlotte's help—can hardly ignore the relief she feels pulsing through her chest, the warm current springing from her belly to her throat. "For that, you would have to live with us," Geneviève says.

Charlotte seems confident when Geneviève would have expected to see her weaken. "I would. Unless you don't want me to."

"When could you start?"

"According to the rumors, there is a lot of work to do here," she says with a smile. "But not anything that might resist the instruction of a former Ursuline."

Geneviève is about to answer when she hears noises outside. Military fifes and drums, screaming on Rue d'Orléans, and the faint melody of a song she can't quite make out. She glances at Charlotte, who stares back, seemingly more interested in her than in the street's racket. Geneviève is suddenly conscious of her own stained gown, her tired face. She gets up to open the window. Behind her, she hears Charlotte saying: "I doubt any of them will have time to miss me now."

Geneviève leans against the railing. Charlotte joins her there, her body a solid presence by her side. Outside, the mud left by the rainstorm is everywhere. Children are running ahead; the song has become clearer. It's a hymn, sung high and loud, by eleven Ursuline sisters now visible in their dark dresses. Lazy, unthreatening clouds dot the sky. They walk behind a heavy canopy, crushed with the reserved sacrament, and then come a few other nuns, mouths quickly modeling the song lyrics. Women keep on joining the procession—Native girls and plantation mistresses, enslaved African women and armorers' wives. The nuns are already taking their song to the next street.

"The convent on Rue de Chartres," Charlotte says. "It is finally ready. They have been waiting for this moment for seven years."

• • •

Experiment 3, three weeks after hatching: Geneviève has called La Louisiane her home for thirteen years, so in fairness, she decides to give silkworms that hatched in the colony a chance too. She arranged to have them shipped from the newly reconquered Natchez land. When they arrive, it's dinnertime, but she still rushes to the cellar, almost runs into Charlotte, who is carrying her baggage to the garret. Since their conversation yesterday, they kept it to practical matters—sleeping arrangements, lesson schedule, children's needs. Geneviève both wants and doesn't want to find herself alone again with Charlotte. When Charlotte asks what is inside the box, Geneviève shakes her head and answers, "Nothing."

The local silkworms are fat, several weeks old already. They look like a bunch of chubby puppies cuddled against each other. Geneviève places them on the table; they are neither slow nor sleepy. Here: they can't stop moving—silent, obstinate, with splinters of wood stuck under their multiple feet. Geneviève cuts pieces of leaves that she scatters in the box. She is leaning above the table when she hears the children clapping, then Charlotte's voice rising on its own. Geneviève tries focusing on the caterpillars, but the lyrics escalate so quickly that she can't help picturing herself running down a steep slope, carried away too fast to think, reaching its bottom not out of breath but full of it.

Charlotte starts a new song. Geneviève listens; as she does, she drops a little branch of mulberry tree on the table. The music sneaks into the cellar. She keeps on listening, watching—how quiet the silkworms turn when there is wood to climb, when there are sweet leaves at the end.

• • •

Pétronille's home is as far as possible from the hospital where her husband works—an irony that Surgeon Lancert has no shame summarizing in so many words at the Wednesday suppers: I do not wish to live so close to the place where people come to die. The house gives out on the river, a pleasant view in the winter, a nightmare most of the year, with clouds of mosquitoes as early as April. By July, the world there smells like it does when you are pregnant. She takes her fan out as soon as she exits her carriage, shakes it in the semidarkness of Pétronille's working room. Sweat drips in the beige mixture her friend is leaning over. Pétronille slits another lemon open, squeezes it, stirs. "This isn't right," she says.

Pétronille explains what she's working on, but Geneviève isn't paying attention. Outside, the strange rumbling sound that washed over town last night is back. It comes from the sea. This morning Geneviève had to console a sobbing Elisabeth, terrified by the noise. She heard Belle talk about an avenging spirit with her husband; on Rue Sainte-Anne, two stable boys were pointing at the sky. Rumors have swirled that another great storm is coming. But Pétronille doesn't react to the sound, too absorbed by her description of whatever she's making—iron rust, herbs, lemon—a paste meant to cure scurvy, which she learned from one of the enslaved African doctors after much insistence on her part. The rumble has already died. When Émile pops his head through the door, Pétronille barely glances at him. "No," she says, and the boy disappears without a word.

"I am heading to Pontchartrain in ten days. I thought you might be interested."

Pétronille continues stirring. "Is that why you came?"

"Partly," Geneviève answers. "I meant to thank you for talking to Charlotte." Watching Charlotte soothe Céleste to sleep yesterday evening, Geneviève was struck all at once by the loneliness, the burden of every single responsibility she took upon herself since M. Bienvenu's death. She closed the door on her daughter and Charlotte. Pétronille smiles at the mention of Charlotte but doesn't look up from the bowl. "I also wanted to ask about M. Rachard," Geneviève says.

Pétronille's smile drops. "When will you be leaving for Pontchartrain?" she asks.

"August fourteenth."

The date daunts her. By then she will need to have answered M. Rachard's proposal. She will soon be counting how many days passed since her last period, might have lost all her possessions—either to a new husband or to the governor's administration. She explains it all to Pétronille. Her friend pulls a chair in front of her and rests her lemonade on the corner of the table. "Would it be all that bad if you received some help from the governor?"

Geneviève bites her lip—Pétronille has never been a businesswoman. "You know that they aren't trying to help me."

"Well, assist you. You'll have enough to keep yourself busy."

Her friend helped arrange for silkworms to be shipped from Natchez. She's the only person Geneviève has told about the silk, the only one who knows what it means to experiment with something precious and risk being disappointed. "I should hand over to them the decisions of what and when to sell?" Geneviève asks. "The right to give me a tiny annuity and move us out of the house?"

"Who said anything about that?"

"I'm sorry." Geneviève's glass is empty. She drinks out of Pétronille's. "But I'm afraid I'm too tired to start all over again."

Far behind them, the sound rises again, rolling up the quiet river all the way to New Orleans. It's unnerving, but Pétronille still doesn't seem to notice it. She rocks on her chair, and it takes Geneviève a few swings back and forth to notice that they match the echo that seems to rise from the sea.

"I understand," Pétronille finally says. "But sometimes you aren't the one to decide."

• • •

Four days later, Geneviève tends to the silkworms late into the evening. She told Pétronille there was something she'd like her to see, and her friend dropped by earlier today. Pétronille followed Geneviève down the hallway, stopped by the salon to say hello to Charlotte, who was surrounded by Mélanie drawing a series of "L," Louise and Elisabeth making a mess of a watercolor. As Geneviève opened the door of the cellar, she listened to the two of them chatting, laughing. Then Pétronille was back at her side, stepping into the tiny room with her. Pétronille leaned over the caterpillars, asked about the different kinds of mulberry leaves; she listened carefully as Geneviève described the silkworms' four stages of development. "You're the only person whom I have taken here," Geneviève said as she locked the door behind them. Her friend squeezed her hand. "I know," she answered.

The house is now perfectly silent. Geneviève leans over the mahogany box, rag in hand. Wetness seizes her below when she thinks of her dream last night, how she felt cold air rushing through lifted sheets, how her mind jumped to memories of her husbands, their faces, indistinct, blending into one man. But then it was Charlotte she found lying next to her. In the dream, Geneviève leaned toward Charlotte, stopping short when their noses touched. The lips that found hers were soft; their kisses, hungry—long hair getting in her mouth, tickling her cheeks. Charlotte had firm, high breasts that hadn't known any pregnancies. She was so slender that her heart beat closer to the palm. She wasn't shy.

The dream wouldn't leave Geneviève. It softened the edges of her resentment, gave a voice to a deeper part of herself; she couldn't help revisiting it. It had been two years since she had held anyone in that way—almost fifteen since she'd shared a bed with a woman she desired. Each time she thought back to the dream, she waited for new details to appear, though she knew that she wouldn't discover anything new—if so, it would be the deliberate fruit of her own imagination.

Geneviève drops the rag. She listens. She thought she heard Charlotte's steps in the hallway. Instead, the rumbling sound again, faint but persistent, gone by the time she starts to worry. She focuses on the task at hand. She is done cleaning the mold that appeared on the wood. Silkworms like cleanness: rot could kill them all. They are a lot bigger, far from the black dots they were almost a month ago. They have just molted again, and she picks off the bits of old skin, her fingers meeting the silk thread that the caterpillars used to anchor themselves on leaves, twig, wood. They aren't picky: they can make a home of nothing.

She grabs a candle, closes the door behind her, climbs the stairs. She should be considering what she'll write to M. Rachard, start drafting a letter, open the accounts book again in case she missed something. But she continues down the hallway, doesn't stop when she passes Mélanie's and Louise's bedrooms. All doors are closed. She becomes aware of her heartbeat as she realizes where she is going, up, all the way to the garret, the candle flame moving under her chin.

Pétronille is only partly right, she thinks. She might not be able to decide what Rachard or Beaulieu will do to her, but she can decide what happens inside her home.

Her blood pulses hard in her ears; her knock at Charlotte's door is assertive. She lets herself in. On the bed, Charlotte raises from her pillow. Geneviève feels her gaze on her, but the room is too dark to see her features.

"I didn't expect you to come here," Charlotte says, breaking the silence.

"Me either." Geneviève looks at her for a moment in the candlelight. She doesn't know what to say next.

"I guess you should snuff the candle," Charlotte finally suggests. "In case someone sees the light."

"Any other rule I should be aware of?"

"No knocking?"

Geneviève sits on the bed.

Charlotte's eyes search hers. She adds, "Do not marry a fourth man?"

Geneviève blows out the candle. For a minute, Charlotte's face is a lighter shape in the blackness. "I don't know what to do," Geneviève admits.

"Neither do I. You haven't told me anything."

"You're right, I haven't." Charlotte moves to the side, and Geneviève lies cautiously next to her. She sees herself in her dream, resting her head against Charlotte's bony shoulder.

She isn't sure what Charlotte knows of the whole Rachard business, so she doesn't omit anything. As she speaks, her shoulders relax; she's turned to her side to face Charlotte. She says that Charlotte's tutoring the children helps but that it doesn't solve everything. She explains she can either accept M. Rachard's proposal now or wait for Beaulieu to use him as a pawn to take everything away from her. "It's the opportunity he has been waiting for."

Charlotte leans farther back on the pillow. "Remember when we left La Salpêtrière?" she asks. "It was a choice, but it wasn't. We could either rot there or hope for the best here." Geneviève watches Charlotte's belly swell slightly with each breath. "Maybe that's what it's all about here," Charlotte says. "Choosing between plague and cholera."

"Is M. Rachard plague?"

"I would have said cholera."

They laugh. Geneviève readjusts the pillow she was leaning against, lets her cheek rest against her hand. She never realized Charlotte's freckles reached all the way to her upper back. In the moonlight, she sees them cascading over the nape of her neck. It moves her in a way she can't quite explain.

"What made you decide to come see me?" she asks.

Charlotte's arm goes rigid against hers. "I owed you," she answers. "This isn't the first time I've come to your house." She reaches for the candle, scrapes the bubbles of wax off. "I came by a month after you left the convent." Shortly after Christmas 1727, M. Melet hit Geneviève so hard the cut in her lip took a week to heal. She had been utterly alone then. She doesn't remember anyone visiting. M. Melet would spend days at the council, trying to figure out what little could be saved from the colony. At home, Geneviève too wondered about rescue—how to save herself and Mélanie from him. Charlotte's nails dig into the wax. "I couldn't bring myself to knock at the door," she says. "So I stayed outside. But I couldn't bear either the idea of never knowing what would happen to you."

Geneviève considers their hands, moonlight blue in the dark. She sees herself again that winter at the Ursuline house, back when she hoped to become a boarding student. She had been so scared that her fear had, she could see it now, impeded her thinking. Otherwise, how could she explain that, were she to stay with the nuns, she had planned on sneaking Mélanie inside the convent, just like she'd introduced her to the kitchens in the Illinois Country, hiding her in the log hut that had already seen some of her secrets? It didn't make any sense. Little did at the time. She turns to Charlotte. "The Mother Superior never would have let a mother, a wife, become a boarding student," she says. "You couldn't have done anything anyway."

"I could have." She lets go of the candle, stares at Geneviève. "I never pleaded for you."

The words ring in Geneviève's ears. Echo again and again. There is a dull anger but no surprise: just a confirmation of what, she realizes, she has known all along—something did go astray in Mother Tranchepain's office that day before Christmas. She searches Charlotte's face, looking for something that would turn her into the stranger she should be now.

"You'll never hate me as much as I hated myself back then," Charlotte says. "And ever since, for making that decision."

Geneviève waits for the resentment to spike, like it did last week when Charlotte first asked whether she could tutor the children. But this time the words feel irrelevant. Geneviève left the convent almost seven years ago. She can barely recognize the two girls kissing behind the log hut, broken fingers reaching above their dark dresses. Those women are like strangers, strangers making decisions and mistakes—decisions and mistakes that needed to be made, without which they wouldn't be lying in this garret room today. You can only afford so much grief in La Louisiane: that much Geneviève has learned by now.

"I'm sorry," says Charlotte, her voice low.

Geneviève nods. Some animal runs on the roof, and they fall silent for a while. Geneviève reaches for Charlotte's hand, touches her cheek. When she kisses her, Charlotte's mouth feels round against hers, one of her nails a bit too long on her thigh. Charlotte moves cautiously; when she apologizes, Geneviève shakes her head. "Don't," she says. As her hand goes up Charlotte's leg, her breath comes out sharp and raw. Geneviève brings her mouth back to hers, kisses her neck and belly where she knows it never tickles, all the way down, where there is only room for the two of them. Rachard, Beaulicu, the nuns: all gone. Charlotte's freckles drown in her flushed cheeks, her legs tensed, her face pressed against the pillow; Geneviève knows the exact moment when she comes.

She holds her tight afterward, and they stay like this for a while, legs intertwined, listening to each other's breath, to the crickets' thick song rising from the garden. The room feels different to Geneviève, as if she's never been here; she is acutely aware of her own body, of Charlotte's, both foreign and familiar against her. When Charlotte's fingers start trailing her side, Geneviève freezes, afraid that the moment will shatter if she moves. But Charlotte isn't going anywhere. She is only moving closer, her hair flashing red in a moonbeam and then turning dark again, her sharp hip bone meeting the tender flesh of Geneviève's belly. She shudders when Charlotte's hand touches her between the thighs. She focuses on the warmth building there. She stares at her half-opened, expectant lips and sees Charlotte leaning toward her in the convent's icy garden; lying in the bed of her New Biloxi house; in the wet hull of *La Baleine*, hunched under the blanket Geneviève handed her after the pirate attack. Sitting in a dusty barn lost in the French countryside, wishing Geneviève could be gone, that she could stay. The two of them crossing La Salpêtrière's main yard under a blazing sun, climbing onto the carts that would soon take them away from everything they knew. She sees the women they both used to be, disappearing, becoming other.

· · ·

Experiment 4, four weeks after hatching: the French silkworms are translucent. Replete. They have stopped eating. They lie in the boxes, sparing their energy, waiting for what will inexorably happen next—for the silk to form, for the spinning to start.

. . .

When the hurricane finally hits, Geneviève has gathered her five children and Charlotte in her bedroom. In the candlelight, all their eyes dim. Charlotte holds Elisabeth under one arm and Céleste under the other. Outside, gusts of wind whistle against the bricks, so violently that the sound reminds Geneviève of two rocks rubbed against each other to light a fire. The rumbling of the sea is gone: all day long, the wind has grown stronger. Little by little, streets emptied, windows lit up; the children stopped playing. Geneviève repeats to them what she has heard, that it will be over soon, that it could never be as bad as the last decade's storm, the one that destroyed the young town's huts and almost all its flotilla, the boats carrying their loads of supplies sunk to the bottom of the river. But she wasn't here for that one—and Charlotte won't talk about it. All Geneviève can do is soothe herself and the children with reassuring words.

Now comes the rain. Geneviève has never heard or seen anything like it. It slams the roof like a hand slaps a face, as if there weren't any drops. Through the windows, there is nothing to be seen anymore; the neighboring buildings disappear behind a liquid gray wall. Geneviève looks at Charlotte and knows what she is thinking: they are back on *La Baleine;* the house has turned into a tiny *flûte* lost in deep green waves.

"We need to bring everyone upstairs," Charlotte says.

"But surely the rain cannot get in through—"

"Trust me, it will."

Geneviève nods. She thinks of the people in the shacks of the Lake Pontchartrain plantation up north. "Hurry," she says.

Charlotte stands up. Céleste starts howling, and Geneviève brings her close, tucks her under a fox fur. Laurent stumbles toward Mélanie and hides his face under his oldest sister's round arm. Then there is a freezing gust, and everything goes dark. Elisabeth screams. It takes a second for Geneviève to realize that the gale rushed down the fireplace, extinguishing the candles. That the furniture they put against the windows will never last against this wind and water.

"*Maman*," Louise says, but nothing more.

Charlotte is already back, followed by Belle and her family. Constantin sits by the door, Belle whispers soft words in her language. Against the bed, Alexandre holds his hands like his mother, one palm hugging a closed fist, as if he carries something secret and magical. Geneviève gestures toward the furs and bedsheets. Soon everybody is wrapped in blankets, in small, safe-looking cocoons.

That's when she remembers her silkworms. In the late-afternoon rush, when it became clear that the storm was coming, she found herself so busy giving orders to seal the windows and doors that she forgot about them; she hadn't realized until now that the first floor could be entirely flooded. She quickly readjusts Céleste against her, and the baby lets out a kitten scream.

"Please look after them," she tells Charlotte. She hands her Céleste. "I will be back shortly."

"Where are you going?"

"I will be back shortly," Geneviève repeats loud enough over the crackling rain. She leans to readjust the furs on Louise's and Elisabeth's laps. In the storm, M. Rachard's proposal seems petty. Her silkworms indispensable, the one business actually in progress that might save her, if she can save them.

"I can go, tell me where."

She turns toward Constantin. His thick arms are crossed against his chest, his hair disheveled. Belle has reached for his hand and is shaking her head, gesturing for him to come back next to her and Alexandre.

Geneviève offers Constantin a grateful smile. "You stay here. Make sure the windows remain tightly shut."

There are a few more protests, somebody sobs. Charlotte's hand escapes the children's fingers to find hers, then lets go. In the distance, muted by rain and wind, a horse screams. Geneviève feels for the little key in her purse and leaves the room.

It takes her eyes a few seconds to adjust to the darkness of the windowless corridor. Around her, the house cracks and whines; it seems as flimsy as a child's toy, as if air and water could blow away bricks and tiles. She walks toward the stairs, her fingers on the wall, but she can't be sure what is shaking, the wood or her hands.

When she reaches the staircase, she understands Charlotte has been right to tell her to gather everybody in her bedroom. The floor has turned darker, and the carpets shimmer in foot-high water, their silver lining shining like coral under the sea. In the salon, the door has blown open. At the end of its silk thread, the stuffed kingfisher twirls madly. Geneviève gathers her petticoats and continues down the stairs, steps turning more and more spongy as she progresses, until she reaches the hall and her ankles sink into the rain.

She hurries toward the kitchen, but her waterlogged dress slows her down. Even louder than the gale, she can hear her heart hitting against her temples, the beats moving down her neck, her wrists. Then she is in front of the cellar, turning the key in the lock, feeling the water swirl as she forces the door open. Half of the beehive compartments have already sunk in. She tries to steady her hands and grabs the two boxes as gently as she can, feeling the silkworms slide against the wood inside. She places them on mulberry leaves in a basket and hurries back toward the open door.

When she reaches her bedroom, she doesn't tell anybody what she saw downstairs. She doesn't answer Charlotte's inquiring looks, Belle's questions, or the children's screams.

Instead, she sits on the floor, waves for them to come closer. Faces lean next to her cheeks, arms fold above her shoulders, tiny hands fiddle with her wet gown. Charlotte's knee is against hers. Geneviève opens the box. As the storm rocks the house, they watch the grown caterpillars crawl on the leaves, their transparent yellowish skin glowing in the early night.

• • •

People were right: the hurricane wasn't as bad as the one of September 1722. They say this storm lasted only a day and a half, when the previous one struck the town for three full days. To Geneviève, it seems disastrous enough. On her way to visit the new Ursuline convent, Charlotte heard of floating bodies and dead cattle all the way up to Lake Maurepas. Belle burst into tears when a girl came to tell her that Yaba, the healer who cured Alexandre, had perished in the storm. The huts by the river where she and the other enslaved Africans lived were too fragile to resist a storm of such magnitude.

Pétronille is safe, but the roof of her home was blown off. She seems unnervingly calm when Geneviève comes by. For a moment she can imagine her friend in Natchez after the attack: how she must have looked when she placed her children on the pirogue that M. Cléry guided to New Orleans. Pétronille shrugs. She says that it isn't the first storm, and it won't be the last—she adds that her damaged house might convince her husband to move to another neighborhood. As long as she can bring her children and her herbariums, she can go anywhere. Out Pétronille's windows, the harbor overflows with wrecked boats. *Le Neptune,* used as a gunpowder supply ship, is entirely destroyed, its contents turning the river black.

Pelicans have fallen over the ruined town. They consider the chaos with their placid, patient eyes. They are organized; they swim and fly in flock, break the surface with one exact dive, opening their beaks wide as if they could breathe underwater, as if they belonged as much there as in the air. They are looking for something to eat and, from what Geneviève can tell, finding plenty.

The children are forbidden to go out on the flooded streets. Inside Geneviève's home, the rooms are all the same shade, a washed-out gray. But all of this is little compared to the news that she learns a week after the storm, when a pathetic Hérin appears in front of her, stuttering that there won't be any more crops. That the slaves took refuge in the main house, sturdy enough to endure the bad weather; he insists that only one man and a child were wounded. There is nothing left of the warehouses and indigo fields.

Geneviève immediately sends Constantin to the plantation. As she suspected, Hérin hadn't told her the full story. Several enslaved people are missing, and Geneviève demands they continue the search.

It's August 14, the date by which she should have given her answer to M. Rachard. She doesn't write to him straightaway. She wants the news to reach him first—that there is no more rival plantation, that she's just another widow in her mid-thirties with five young children and a broken house, in a land too wild to be tamed.

She tries her best to fix the mansion: for a week she has the water drained, the holes filled, the wallpaper ripped. In the end, she doesn't even have time to write to M. Rachard. He does first. In his letter, he says he was devastated to hear about the tragedy, explains that he will have to postpone his previous offer—she notices he doesn't mention anymore the words "wedding" and "proposal"—to take care of his own plantation, which has been hit, although not as badly as hers, by the hurricane. She doubts this is the truth; it seems unlikely that the storm could have spiraled all the way from the continent to the islands. But it doesn't matter. What is left of the Rue d'Orléans house is hers. Her five children, Charlotte, and Belle are by her side. None of this matters to M. Rachard and the government's officials. To them, she has again become invisible, free.

. . .

Experiment 5, six weeks after hatching: there is no more experiment room, so she visits an empty shelf in the food pantry several times per day. By now the mulberry branches are plumbed with thick white cocoons—she can't tell if they remind her more of snow or spiderwebs. This is what the men ignore; this is what keeps her from dwelling on everything she's lost. She hears the children play in the ravaged garden. There are no more holes in the flower bed where she once planted the lavender seeds. Charlotte scolds Elisabeth for eating dirt. Earlier, Geneviève invited her to come to the food pantry, but Charlotte gestured toward the children. "You go," she said, "I'll come another time," and Geneviève knew Charlotte understood that, despite her invitation, Geneviève would rather be alone today.

She pours warm water in a cup. Then, very carefully, she unties one of the cocoons made by the French silkworms. She dips it like sugar in hot tea. She watches as the glue dissolves, the threads released as the thin mixture holding them melts away. Somewhere in the house, Laurent calls Mélanie. Geneviève takes a small brush, not unlike the one she uses for her hair, and passes it around the cocoon. The first layer of threads falls—a coarse, ill-looking entanglement.

This is her favorite part. The silkworms can do so much better than that, and she is about to find out. She rolls the cocoon in her palm, looking for the entry point, her nail scratching the surface. She knows that silk only looks fragile, that it is in fact much more difficult to break than it seems.

So when she finds the beginning of the thread, Geneviève pulls hard, her way.

• • •

Some women grow old, some don't. Those who remain have learned not to think about France, which, in their memory, has turned either grander or grimier—in any case, a tale they keep to themselves. They'd rather look at the bats spiraling out of the attic, listen to the voices rising from the newly built nearby cabaret, watch their grandchildren making wigs out of Spanish moss. The women wouldn't dare interrupt them. They pat their runny eyes with hands that would be paler had they stayed in Paris. When the first granddaughter finally offers to bring them milk or cider, they don't mention that it would upset their stomach, but rather pretend they aren't thirsty and say, "Why don't you sit for a bit?"

The grandchildren squirm in their chairs at first, yet no one ever leaves. They've heard these stories before, but the knowing, the mild frustration it brings, is part of the pleasure that draws them in. The women speak of journeys so perilous that some grandsons are left fidgeting with the tiny medal that burns cold against their chest, wondering how they are even alive. Stories of people who passed away, those they were taught to care about, those they weren't. Once and only once, one of the women says, "We live in a cemetery," and her daughter, passing by the yard on her way to the kitchen, tells her to hush, quit with your nonsense already.

The grandchildren are told about a land that—as the women enjoy saying every time the nearing storm aches their bones—was once dangerous, a prison of trees, a maze of marshes, an ocean of mud. They swear the horizon is wider in La Louisiane, and a few even admit that they didn't first feel at home in the colony. Most lie.

The grandchildren are told about girls barely older than them, who left their city never to return. The women describe the people they learned to love, a husband or a neighbor, and those who departed, making them feel that they would now have to start all over again; they talk about the men and women they betrayed, failed, or hurt; the compassion and the cruelty they were capable of, the destruction they caused; but, no matter what they think once they finally fall silent, this list is never complete.

Later, while some grandchildren will walk the women to their bedrooms, others will step outside, look up at the sky, soon to become a battered sea—swallows flying low, pelicans already in shelter before their feast. The wind will already buzz with alarmed mosquitoes, and the next gale will force the children's eyes shut. In the dark, they'll suddenly remember the odd sounds that often trouble their sleep at night and how, the more they think of them, the less they resemble anything they know. They'll think: Has anything really changed, and will it ever?

AUTHOR'S NOTE

This book is a work of fiction, as any historical novel must be. However, in search of authenticity, it is also deeply researched, and I have attempted to stay true to what is known about the period and these women's collective story. This novel never could have existed if it weren't for the wisdom of many experts, many books that became my companions as I traveled back in time and space to eighteenth-century Louisiana and created characters to explore that particular world. Most information about French Louisiana in the early 1700s is found in the accounts and memoirs of French settlers such as Antoine-Simon Le Page du Pratz (*Histoire de la Louisiane*), Jean-François-Benjamin Dumont de Montigny (*The Memoirs of Lieutenant Du-mont, 1715–1747: A Sojourner in the French Atlantic*), Marc-Antoine Caillot (*A Company Man: The Remarkable French-Atlantic Voyage of a Clerk for the Company of the Indies*), and Lamothe Cadillac and Pierre Liette (*The Western Country in the 17th Century: The Memoirs of Lamothe Cadillac and Pierre Liette*).

For the first part of the book, I visited La Salpêtrière in Paris, today one of France's largest hospitals, where the building of La Grande Force still stands. If a plaque celebrates the *filles du roi*, French women sponsored by the king and sent to Canada in the late 1600s, the fates of the women who traveled on boats such as *La Baleine*, *La Mutine*, or *Les Deux Frères* remain unsung. One of the first ships to bring women to La Louisiane, in 1704, was called *Le Pélican*. The pelican is a symbol of Louisiana, hence its nickname the "Pelican State." These birds are gregarious: they hunt, migrate, and nest in groups.

During my research at the archives of L'Assistance Publique Hôpitaux de Paris (APHP), I encountered key works on La Salpêtrière and Paris such as Jean-Pierre Carrez's *Femmes opprimées à la Salpêtrière de Paris : 1656–1791*, Louis Bouchet's *La Salpêtrière : son histoire de 1656 à 1790, ses origines et son fonctionnement au XVIIIème siècle*, Germain Brice's *Nouvelle description de la ville de Paris, et de tout ce qu'elle contient de plus remarquable*, or Michel Fleury's and Jean Tulard's *L'Almanach de Paris des origines à 1788*. Contrary to what appears in this novel, the Cour Lassay didn't receive its name until 1756. Scarlett Beauvalet-Boutouyrie's *Être veuve sous l'Ancien Régime* and Emmanuelle Berthiaud's "Le vécu de la grossesse aux XVIIIème et XIXème siècles en France," published in *Histoire, médecine et santé*, were crucial sources to help me write about widowhood and pregnancy in eighteenth-century French society. For fictional purposes, Marguerite Pancatelin spends fifty-six years serving La Salpêtrière instead of fifty-four.

Marthe's recipes in chapter 7 originate from *Les secrets du Grand Albert : comprenant les influences des astres, les vertus magiques des végétaux, minéraux et animaux*.

Utu'wv Ecoko'nesel's remedies in chapter 10 derive from Le Page du Pratz's descriptions of Natchez recipes, the Native American Ethnobotany Database, Lyda Averill Paz Taylor's *Plants Used as Curatives by Certain Southeastern Tribes* and John R. Swanton's *Religious Beliefs and Medical Practices of the Creek Indians*.

To balance clarity with authenticity, I chose to refer to the French settlement by the Natchez villages as "Natchez" rather than "the Natchez" or "the Natchez trading post," as settlers called it back then. Similarly, Pétronille and Utu'wv Ecoko'nesel speak to each other in French in the novel when, in truth, the settlers and the Natchez (as well as many Native American tribes at the time) used the Mobilian Jargon to communicate.

One French league equals about four kilometers (or three miles).

ACKNOWLEDGMENTS

I'm grateful for all the help and support given by the late Randall Ladnier, descendant of one of the women who made the journey across the Atlantic Ocean on *La Baleine*. Everything started with the email I sent him in the fall of 2016; his book *The Brides of La Baleine* was my very first encounter with the extraordinary stories of these women.

In 2017, thanks to Oregon State University's President's Commission on the Status of Women Scholarship, I was able to travel to New Orleans, where I visited the archives of the Historic New Orleans Collection, Tulane University Archives & Special Collections, as well as the Ursuline Convent. Sister Marie-Madeleine Hachard's *Relation du voyage des dames religieuses ursulines de Rouen à La Nouvelle-Orléans* and Emily Clark's *Masterless Mistresses: The New Orleans Ursulines and the Development of a New World Society, 1727–1834*, proved indispensable for chapter 9.

All my gratitude goes to Hutke Fields, principal chief at Natchez Nation. I can't thank him enough for his time and guidance during our two-year-long correspondence, for recommending Natchez resources, including Natchez Indigital and the Natchez dictionary available on www .natcheznation.com; for advising me on the Natchez characters' names; and for his thorough feedback on my novel. Just as he stressed during one of our conversations, the Natchez people kept up their resistance against the settlers for years after 1731, finding shelter and support with allied tribes in and throughout the southeast, where their descendants live today.

I thank Dr. Gilles Havard, historian, professor at the EHESS in Paris, and author of *The Great Sun and Death, Anthropology of the Natchez Coup of 1729*. His revision and guidance helped strengthen the chapters featuring Natchez characters.

Many thanks to Dr. Ibrahima Seck from the Whitney Plantation Museum, who kindly shared with me his book, *Bouki fait Gombo: A History of the Slave Community of Habitation Haydel (Whitney Plantation) Louisiana 1750–1860*, and recommended Toyin Falola and Matt D. Childs's *The Yoruba Diaspora in the Atlantic World*. Oyeronke Olajubu's *Women in the Yoruba Religious Sphere* and Gwendolyn Midlo Hall's Louisiana Slave Database were also instrumental in writing the characters of Iyawa (Belle), Latorin (Alexandre), and Obe (Constantin). My deep gratitude goes to Dr. Jacob Kẹhinde Olupọna, professor of African religious traditions at Harvard University, who agreed to read excerpts of this novel, and to Dr. Stefania Capone, thesis advisor at the CNRS and author of *Les Yoruba du Nouveau Monde*, who provided me with essential information regarding the Yoruba culture and religion.

I thank Ariel A. Vincent for their careful read and thorough feedback.

I'm grateful to the Fondation Belem and Lieutenant Gabriel Maumené, who gave me a private tour of *Le Belem*, France's last three-masted barque, when it dropped anchor in Le Havre. He patiently explained to me the capstan, sextant, shrouds, and more, and gave precious feedback on some of the marine terms used in this book. Many thanks to Léa Surrel and Éric Rieth from the Musée national de la Marine, for guiding me through the archives and teaching me everything I know about eighteenth-century *flûtes*. *La Baleine* wouldn't have come to life if it weren't for all their support.

Joan DeJean's *Mutinous Women: How French Convicts Became Founding Mothers of the Gulf Coast* provided me with crucial information and details as I went through the final rounds of revision at the end of 2022. Thanks to her book, I was able to reimagine Marie Cléry's backstory—inspired by that of Marie Baron, who was truly arrested on false charges for stealing a ribbon in Paris. I'm very grateful to Joan for taking the time to read my novel and for giving me her perspective on the many French women who were sent to the Mississippi in the early 1700s.

In the spring of 2019, La Fondation des Treilles gave me the time and space I needed to revise one of this novel's many drafts; these two peaceful weeks of writing on their gorgeous property in southern France were bliss. In the summer of 2022, I was lucky enough to be one of the residents at the Vil•la Joana in Barcelona, which gave me a chance to finish the French draft of this novel.

I'm forever grateful to my American editor, Millicent Bennett, and my British editor, Frances Edwards, as well as to everyone at HarperCollins and Headline, for their stunning feedback, their daring vision, and their unwavering support.

My deepest gratitude also goes to my French editors, Raphaëlle Liebaert and Léa Marty, and everyone at Stock, for their immediate trust, their thoughtful insight, and their guidance as the story of this book reinvented itself in French.

I have no words for my agent, the amazing Sandra Pareja, who believed in this novel when I was about to give up. I thank her for the thousands of hours spent with me in muddy 1720s La Louisiane, for feedback so spot-on it made me want to rewrite these chapters for the fifteenth time, for her contagious enthusiasm that made this book travel around the world.

Thank you to all the foreign editors for joining us on this adventure with joy and excitement.

All my gratitude goes to the very first readers of this novel. To Sam, who had me live what I needed in order to write it—whose rigorous, kind suggestions benefited more than one draft of this novel. To Mackenzie and Sarah, without whom *Pelican Girls* wouldn't have existed. To Suzanne, who eagerly read each of the new chapters in 2020, who gave me enough strength to reimagine my fourth draft.

To my English-speaking friends who were my proofreading heroes and so much more: Megan, Gabriel, Mark, Andy, Morgane, Armelle, Cate, Isabelle, Al, Peter, Steven.

To my French friends who read parts of this novel in two languages: May, Anoushka, Martin, Pierre-Yves, Karine.

To all my friends and family who never ceased to encourage me, who kept asking me for eight years straight when my novel would be out: Cécilia, Élise, Astrid, Julie, Antoine, Thara, Yazid, Camille, Hélo,

Louis, Alexandre, Marina, Ignacio, Pierre, August, Morgan, and many more.

To my fellow writers in Corvallis, Oregon, my literary family on the other side of the ocean.

To my mentor and creative writing professor Kevin Moffett, without whom I wouldn't have discovered that writing can be taught and learned.

To my professors from Oregon State University's writing program in fiction, whose words of advice follow me every time I start a new page: Nick Dybek, Susan Jackson Rodgers, Marjorie Sandor, and Keith Scribner.

My most heartfelt thanks go to my mother, my father, and my brother—I couldn't have written this book if it weren't for all their support, feedback, and love.

ABOUT THE AUTHOR

JULIA MALYE is the author of three novels published in France and works as a translator for Les Belles Lettres publishing house. At the age of twenty-one, she moved to the United States to study the craft of fiction and graduated from Oregon State University's MFA program in 2017. Since 2015, she's taught creative writing to hundreds of students, both in the United States at Oregon State University, and in France at La Sorbonne Nouvelle and Sciences Po Paris. *Pelican Girls* is being translated in twenty-five languages.